Blood and Bone

Blood and Bone

William Lashner

HARPER LUXE

An Imprint of HarperCollins*Publishers*

BLOOD AND BONE. Copyright © 2009 by William Lashner. All rights reserved. Printed in the United States of America. No part of this book may be used or reproduced in any manner whatsoever without written permission except in the case of brief quotations embodied in critical articles and reviews. For information address HarperCollins Publishers, 10 East 53rd Street, New York, NY 10022.

HarperCollins books may be purchased for educational, business, or sales promotional use. For information please write: Special Markets Department, HarperCollins Publishers, 10 East 53rd Street, New York, NY 10022.

FIRST HARPERLUXE EDITION

HarperLuxe™ is a trademark of HarperCollins Publishers

Library of Congress Cataloging-in-Publication Data is available upon request.

ISBN: 978-0-06-171982-0

09 10 11 12 13 ID/RRD 10 9 8 7 6 5 4 3 2 1

To my dad,
who is with me every day

Why might not that be the skull of a lawyer?
Where be his quiddits now, his quillets, his cases,
his tenures, and his tricks?

—HAMLET, *in the graveyard, act 5, scene 1*

Blood and Bone

Chapter 1

1994

Kyle, all of twelve years old, hated the suit.

He hated everything else about this day, too—his Uncle Max's voice droning on from the driver's seat of the battered black pickup, the bright sun shining into his eyes, the way the truck was filled with smoke from his mother's cigarette, the expectant dread that twisted his stomach. But most of all he hated the suit.

His mother had bought it for him just yesterday, snatched it off the rack at some discount warehouse and held it up for him, limp and gray, as if it were some dead animal she had shot and dragged home. "For tomorrow," she said with that same detached smile she had been wearing ever since he came home from school, backpack still on his shoulder, and she told him the news.

"I don't want to wear a suit," he said.

"I bought it big," she said, ignoring his declaration, "so you could have it for next year, too."

And now there it was, wrapped around his body like a fist, his first suit. It didn't fit right; the pants were too long, the shoulders too narrow, the tie choked him. He wondered how anyone could wear such an uncomfortable thing every day. Especially the tie. His father always had one slung around his neck whenever he came for a visit. Navy blue suit, dark thin tie, yellowtoothed smile and shock of white hair. "Hello, boyo," he'd say whenever he saw Kyle, giving his hair a quick tousle.

"I never liked the son of a bitch," said Uncle Max. Uncle Max was Kyle's mother's older brother. He had come out from the city for the funeral, which was a treat in itself. Not.

"Stop it, Max," said Kyle's mother.

"I'm just saying."

"You've been saying for twelve years."

"And I've been right all along, haven't I?" Uncle Max wiped his mouth with the back of his hand. "Where was he anyway when he got it?"

"New Jersey."

"What, he had someone stashed there, too?"

"Quiet."

"Yeah, yeah. Okay. But we're better off without him, all of us. What did Laszlo say it was?"

"Heart."

"Figures. Is he saving us a place or something?"

Kyle's mother didn't answer. She just inhaled from her cigarette and leaned her head against the window.

"Let me guess. You wasn't even invited."

"Laszlo suggested that it might be best if we didn't come."

"Well, then," said Uncle Max, "this might be more fun than I thought."

Kyle, wedged in the front seat between his uncle and his mother, craned his neck and shaded his eyes as he peered through the windshield. In the sky a dark cloud kept pace with the car. Kyle was missing school today, which was good, but he had a game that afternoon, and he'd probably have to miss that, too, which sucked. And then he hadn't cried yet, which only confirmed what he had always believed, that there was something seriously wrong with him. His mother hadn't cried either, as far as he could tell. She had her strange smile, like in that painting of that Mona lady, and she was smoking, nonstop, which was a sign of something, but Kyle had seen no tears from her. And Uncle Max certainly didn't seem so cut up about the whole thing. So maybe it wasn't such a deal after all. Except in the soft, untrammeled depths of his heart, he knew that it was, knew that it was bigger than everything and that he should be bawling his eyes out and that there was something seriously wrong with him because he wasn't.

The neat little houses passing by gave way to a low stone wall. Beyond the wall were gravestones and small marble crypts like out of *Scooby-Doo*. The quick change in scenery jolted Kyle back to the unpleasant task at hand. He stuck his thumb into his collar at the front of his neck and yanked it down. It didn't help.

Uncle Max turned the truck into the cemetery. There was a chapel off to the right, like one of the crypts, only large enough to inter an army of ghouls.

"Showtime," said Uncle Max as he pulled into one of the remaining spots in the parking lot and killed the engine.

A thin crowd of mourners milled somberly at the entrance as the three approached. They walked side by side by side—Uncle Max, thick-shouldered and in a loud sport coat; Kyle's mother, tall and drawn in a long black dress; and Kyle, in his ill-fitting gray suit. A few faces turned toward them, and the crowd suddenly stilled, as if they were a trio of gunfighters walking down a dusty street in a black-and-white western on TV. Kyle hesitated for a moment, but his mother raised her chin and kept on walking as though she hadn't noticed the stares. Kyle hitched his pants and caught up.

On the wall of the chapel, behind a sheet of glass and pressed into a black background, was a series of white plastic letters.

FUNERAL OF LIAM BYRNE

10:30

MAY GOD GRANT PEACE UNTO HIS SOUL

"Fat chance of that," said Uncle Max under his breath as he held open the heavy metal door.

Kyle stepped through the doorway into the cool, dark interior. The chapel was built of stone, with rows of dark wooden pews, most already filled. Sunlight slipped through a stained-glass image of sunlight slipping through clouds. A line of people snaked through the middle aisle toward a heavy table in front. Faces from the pews turned to look at the three of them, a few did double takes. Kyle's mother stepped confidently forward and sat in one of the rear pews. Kyle slid in next to her. Uncle Max dropped down heavily beside him.

"Everyone is looking at us funny," said Kyle.

"Let 'em, the sons of bitches," said Uncle Max loudly.

Someone shushed him. Uncle Max made a face.

"You should go on up and touch the urn," said Kyle's mother to Kyle.

"Why isn't there a coffin?"

"I guess he wanted to be cremated."

"So that's all that's left?"

"Go on up."

"I don't want to."

"You need to say good-bye."

"What about you?"

"I said good-bye already. Go on."

There was more behind the request than mere politeness; it was like she knew everything—how he felt now, scared and yet cold and distant from all this, and how the future would play out for him because of it. His mother was never one to be lightly ignored, so Kyle rose slowly from his seat, climbed past Uncle Max, and sheepishly made his way to the back of the line.

It moved slowly, in fits and starts. People fell in behind Kyle, talking in hushed voices, important-looking people who had taken time out of their important days to honor what was left in the urn. Kyle stared at a man in a dark suit standing by the table. His shoulders were broad, his hands clasped before him. Kyle wondered if he was Secret Service or something because of the way he stood, but why would the Secret Service be in this crappy little chapel? The woman in front of Kyle stepped to the left, and suddenly there it was.

Two huge bouquets of flowers surrounding a funeral urn, shiny and blue, its body covered in grasping green vines and tiny white flowers. The urn was shaped like a squat man about the size of a football, flaring wide in his shoulders with just a tiny head. When Kyle saw it there, he stepped back involuntarily, bumping into the man behind him.

The man gently pushed him forward. "Go ahead, son," he said.

Kyle hesitated for a moment. He liked the warmth of the man's hands on his shoulders, the reassuring sound of his voice. "Son," he had called him. Yeah, right. Kyle took a step forward, reached out to touch the urn as his mother had instructed, when he was blocked by a large hand sticking out of a dark-suited arm.

"No touching," said the man standing guard.

"My mom told me I should—"

"There's no touching."

"But," said Kyle, ". . . but it's—"

"Keep moving," said the man, as if he were a cop at an accident. *Keep moving, nothing to see here. Just some useless ashes in a stinking pot.* The man directed Kyle to the left, where the line bent toward a row of people sitting in the front pew. Kyle stared at the man for a moment, looking for the earpiece he knew from television that all Secret Service agents wore. Not there, he wouldn't go to jail if he ignored him, but it didn't seem like the smartest idea just then, so he nodded and turned away.

Those in the line were giving their condolences, one by one, to the faces in the front pew, taking the proffered hands between their own and offering tender words of commiseration. *I'm so sorry for your loss. We will all miss him. He was a terrific lawyer and a better person. So, so sorry.* It made Kyle sad and angry both, all these people offering their condolences. Who were those getting comforted? Why weren't they comforting him?

He didn't want to be here anymore. On the far wall was a door, and he thought of escaping through it, out of the chapel, into the sunlight. Maybe if he started running now and kept on going, he could get to the police field in time for the game. Would they let him pitch in the suit? He was about to head right for the door when he noticed the red emergency-exit bar signaling an alarm if it was opened. He felt trapped, like a gray-suited badger in a cage, as he was pushed forward with the line.

A small, hunched man with slicked-back black hair and lidded eyes was standing at the head of the pew. He tilted his head at Kyle and attempted something like a kind smile. The man reached out a hand and took Kyle's in his own, forcing an awkward shake. "Thank you for coming," he said quietly.

"Sure," said Kyle.

"And what would be your name, young man?"

"Kyle," said Kyle, and suddenly the man's kind smile became a little less kind. Still gripping Kyle's hand, he turned his hunched back as best he could and craned his neck to peer behind him. Craned his neck until he spotted Kyle's mother. Then he gestured to the man in the dark suit standing by the urn.

As the man started over, the hunched little man gripped Kyle's hand even tighter and said in a soft, insistent voice, "You should go now, Kyle. The nice man over there will help you find your way out."

"Who is this, Laszlo?" said a woman seated next to him, an older woman with large dark glasses and styled black hair. She spoke in some sort of accent. Like Pepé Le Pew.

"It's just a boy," said Laszlo.

"Give your hand to me, young man," she said. Laszlo reluctantly let go of Kyle's hand, and the woman took hold of it in one gentle hand as she patted it with the other. Her lips were bright red and puffy; she smelled of some ferocious perfume that was vaguely familiar. "Thank you so for coming today," she said. "Did you perhaps know my husband?"

"Who is your husband?" said Kyle.

"How darling," she said. "He does not know. My husband was Liam Byrne. It is his funeral service today."

"Let the boy move on," said Laszlo.

"He came to pay his respects," said the woman. "He is a sweet-looking boy. Tell me, young man, did you know my husband?"

"Sort of," said Kyle. "He was my father."

It was her lips that he noticed most of all, the way the bright red slabs of flesh tensed and froze at his words before opening up in soft sympathy. He couldn't take his eyes off them; they seemed unaccountably beautiful. He stared at the woman's lips even as she lifted her hand and placed it on Kyle's cheek.

"So you are the one," she said. "My poor boy."

Her hand felt warm as it lay against his flesh, and strangely consoling. He leaned his head into it, as if this were the touch of sympathy he had been waiting for since he heard the news.

"My poor, poor boy."

Her flesh was so warm and comforting that it took him a moment to recognize the growing locus of pain beneath her touch for what it was. The old bat was pinching his cheek. And as she did, her lovely red lips tightened and twitched.

"You shouldn't have to suffer through this."

The pinching grew harder and the pain so severe he tried to step away, but her grip on his skin was excruciatingly tight and he was unable to pull free.

"A boy like you has no place here," she said. "You can only pollute the remembrances. Laszlo, take this boy away, now, before this sad day becomes too painful for him to bear."

Outside the chapel Uncle Max and the man called Laszlo were arguing loudly, or at least Uncle Max was arguing loudly, while Kyle's mother leaned on the rear end of a parked car and smoked. There was a certain unsurprised quality to her smile now, as if this argument was exactly what she had expected when she showed up at the funeral and sent her only begotten son to the front of the chapel to touch the urn containing his father's ashes.

"What are you going to do to take care of this family?" said Uncle Max. "We need this settled here and now."

"This isn't the place to have this discussion," said Laszlo.

"Why the hell not? This looks like a perfect place to me. Let's bring out that Mrs. Byrne and all hash it out together. Why the hell shouldn't his son have a right to sit in at his own father's funeral? Who the hell are you and her to tell him that he can't?"

"Can we talk about this later?"

"Hell no, we'll talk about it now, you son of a bitch. And if need be, we'll get our own damn lawyers."

"I'm sure that won't be necessary."

"Why is it that when a lawyer says getting another lawyer involved isn't necessary, it always turns out to be necessary as hell?"

While the two men argued, Kyle squatted in the sunlight and rubbed a stick along the parking lot, leaving trails of bark atop the asphalt. His cheek ached, as if the witch with the puffy red lips had thrown a fastball at his face. But even worse was the sight of all those important people giving their condolences to her. Why weren't they giving their condolences to him? *I'm so sorry for your loss. Your father was a fine, fine man. Please know we're all thinking of you.* He wanted condolences. Where were his condolences? He guessed they were lost, along with his tears.

Liam Byrne had never been a huge physical presence in Kyle's life. Kyle couldn't remember anymore the time when his father had lived with them, he only knew of it from his mother's say-so. What Kyle remembered was his father's "Hello, boyo," when he would show up at the house every other month or so, to be served drinks and dinner by his mother, or maybe very occasionally at the field behind the police station to watch Kyle pitch. Kyle assumed his father called him "boyo" because he couldn't remember his real name. His father had always been more a ghost in Kyle's life than anything else, so it seemed almost natural that he had become the real thing. The only difference for Kyle was that from here on in, when he looked at the stands from the Little League mound, he wouldn't be disappointed over and again.

Still, he knew in his heart there should be something more than this emptiness: no tears, no condolences, just a bruised cheek and a sordid argument in a hot parking lot. He thought of going back inside and telling everyone who he was, going pew to pew asking for condolences. *He was my father,* he'd say. And then they'd all start in. *We're so sorry. You must be such a brave boy. If there is anything we can do.* Maybe he should just go in and touch the urn like he had tried to do before, maybe that would break the dam and let everything flow. Except the Secret Service man was still there to stop him.

Kyle stood up, tossed the stick away, went over to his mother. "How come they won't let us back inside?" he said.

"It's complicated."

"His wife talks funny. Is she French?"

"Yes."

"Is that why he wouldn't leave her?"

Kyle's mother let out a bark of a laugh.

"They didn't let me touch it," he said.

"Excuse me?"

"The urn."

"That's too bad, Kyle."

"Who gets it after this is over?"

"I suppose they'll bury it."

"Why don't we get it?"

"Would you really want it?"

"No, not really," he said, but it was a lie.

Kyle was not one of those kids who needed the latest of everything. He hadn't begged his mom for a super-powered aluminum baseball bat or a Wilson 2000 baseball glove, hadn't whined for the Nintendo Super NES when his Sega system became outdated. But suddenly, more than anything he had ever wanted in his entire life, he wanted that urn.

He started walking toward the chapel door as Uncle Max continued his argument.

"We just want to know how you're going to step up and satisfy his obligations," Uncle Max said, his face red, spittle flying. "Tell us that we'll get what's fair. Let's hear it, come on."

At the entrance Kyle stood for a moment rubbing his cheek. Then he opened one of the doors and slipped inside.

When the door closed behind him, Uncle Max's bray disappeared, replaced instead by the soft and insistent voice of a priest, talking from the altar. Kyle didn't look at the priest or the heads that swiveled to take in his presence, or even the Secret Service man, who noticed him enter and started walking toward him from the front of the chapel. All he saw was the urn, flowery and stout, like a jolly little man, waiting to be touched, held, waiting to be lovingly embraced.

And then time slowed down into discrete and perfectly understandable moments.

This was how it felt sometimes on the mound before a crucial pitch, or just before a play in football as he dropped into his stance in the backfield and the quarterback began to bark the signals. Things slowed down. And the action, when it came, seemed to happen unhurriedly and step by step, with the simple geometry of a pool game, even as it happened haphazardly and all at once in real time.

The Secret Service man in the dark suit came up the aisle, slowly, jerkily, like in an old movie. Kyle charged right at him, threw out a straight arm, bounced off toward the front of the chapel. He sprinted up the aisle, snatched the urn, popped a spin move before dashing to the side door. His left hip slammed into the latch bar.

In the chapel's parking lot, when the alarm went off, Laszlo started searching around even as Uncle Max continued with his rant. "You look at me when I'm talking," said Uncle Max, jabbing his finger right into Laszlo's face. Kyle's mom, still leaning against the car, turned her head to see what was happening. And then she started laughing, a light, sardonic laugh. She laughed as she spotted her son, Kyle Byrne, suit jacket flapping behind him, tearing off like a flushed fox into the depths of the cemetery, the flowered urn tucked into the crook of his arm like an oversize green football.

Years later, when questions about his father's death rose like a cobra from its basket, when he found himself caught within a story of low violence and high aspirations, of family pathologies and political ambition and murder, in that time of mystery and blood, Kyle Byrne would think back on that sprint through the graveyard as the purest moment in his sad, misspent life.

He hadn't gotten far, actually. After a few seconds of glorious freedom, alone with just his father by his side, his foot had caught the top of a gravestone he was trying to hurdle, sending him sprawling and the urn flying through the air. The urn landed with a thunk and a crack, loosing a fine cascade of ash and bleached bits of bone into the air.

When the wiry gravedigger in overalls found him, Kyle was sitting on the ground, desperately trying to stuff what was left of his father back into the broken urn.

"What have we here?" said the gravedigger, calmly leaning on his shovel.

"It's my daddy," said Kyle.

"I'm sorry to hear that."

"He was a lawyer."

"Even so."

"They burned him."

"Yes."

"I need to get him back in the pot."

The man smiled kindly. "No you don't, son. I'll be glad to take care of it."

"But it's my daddy."

"Don't you worry, little man. No matter what happens to his remains, he'll still be with you."

"My daddy? How?"

"That's just the way of it with sons and their fathers. He'll be living on in your blood and bone. For better or for worse, he'll always be there." The man lowered himself on one knee. "Let me help you."

"No thank you," said Kyle, as the pounding footfalls and the shouts of indignation came from the direction of the chapel. "I think I need to do this myself."

In the truck, on the way out of the cemetery, Uncle Max was complaining loudly about that rat Laszlo Toth while Kyle's mom stared out the window, smoking. Kyle sat between them, his hand in one of his jacket pockets, feeling strangely happy.

He had liked the way the gravedigger had knelt to help him. It was the nicest thing that had happened to him all day. Maybe he would grow up to be a gravedigger, it seemed just then to be the noblest of professions, a helper of children and burier of griefs. He looked down at what was left of his suit. The knees on both of his pant legs were torn and marked by blood, and one elbow of the jacket was in tatters. The suit was ruined. That, at least, had turned out well.

With all that had happened, he felt relieved and almost normal. It was true that he still hadn't cried for his dead father, he thought as the fingers in his pocket sifted through a handful of fine gray powder, but he had bled for him, and that had to mean something, didn't it?

Didn't it?

Chapter 2

NOW

The name was Robert, not Bobby or little Bobby or Bobby dear. Robert. How many times had he told her? And still, with her it was always the diminutive. *Bobby, I have something I need from you. Bobby, can you do this one important errand? I knew I could count on you, Bobby.* In court, or in his pleadings, or atop his letterhead, he went by the name of Robert, Robert Spangler. It was a name of respectability, of sobriety and accomplishment. He was Robert, always, except when she needed something from him, one of her favors. Then, with her chin raised and her little sneer, she would call him Bobby, because she knew exactly how it made him feel.

"Bobby dear," she had said just that afternoon, "do you still have your gun?"

Maybe he should just turn around, forget about her little task. That would show her, that would put her in a pickle. Who else could do for her the things that he could do for her? But he wouldn't turn around, he knew that and he knew she knew that, for they both knew she held out for him the one thing he yearned for most. And even though he had begun to suspect he would never get it from her, still the scantest possibility was enough to ensure that Robert would always do her bidding. It had been that way from the beginning between the two of them.

But he was Robert, damn it, Robert Spangler, Esquire, and he had a job to do. The job was distasteful—it left an acid taste in his mouth, there was no way around that—but it was not outside his range. In fact, in the way it made him irreplaceable to her, he almost longed for the bright, bitter taste of acid, the taste of his devotion. Let her have her Thomases and Williams, her Stephans at the charity balls, her precious Francis. When it came time to take that final step, where others would falter, she always came to him. And he wouldn't disappoint. And maybe with this one, this final one, she'd finally have to admit the truth, that he was the only one she could rely on, that he was the only one truly worthy of her love.

The building was now on his right, an old stone town house, a number of brass plaques bolted beside the heavy wooden door announcing the various businesses housed inside. He looked up at the dark building. The only windows lighted were at the corner of the second floor.

There was a parking spot directly in front of the building, but he passed it by, went a block farther, turned south on Fifteenth Street. He circled around and found an open meter about half a block away. After parking, he took his briefcase out of the car and quietly closed the door. It was too late for the meter to matter. He backed away a couple of steps, looked at the car in the spot. As ordinary as a rental car could look. He pressed the button on the key fob to lock it and headed north.

Before he reached Locust, he turned into a small alley behind the building. Amid the garbage cans and black bags filled with trash was a door. When this house had been a grand residence, this was the servants' entrance. Fitting, he thought as he put down the heavy briefcase for a moment. She always seemed to make sure he entered through the servants' entrance. Out of one jacket pocket, he pulled a pair of pale rubber gloves, which he yanked on and tightened with a *thwack*. From the other pocket, he pulled out a key.

She was a marvel, with a snap of her perfectly manicured fingers she could get anything. Even a key. He imagined the blue of her eyes for a moment, the coolness of her touch, and then wrenched himself out of his reverie. There was a procedure to follow in matters like this, a process that could go horribly wrong if you lost your concentration and missed a step. Later he would think of her, the way she insinuated herself into every part of his life, the way she played with his weaknesses like a cat worrying a ball of yarn. Now there was just the job.

He slipped the key into the lock, gave it a turn, pushed the door open with his shoulder. He grabbed his briefcase, stepped inside, closed the door tight behind him without locking it. Slowly he made his way through the pitch-black hallway.

He had memorized the layout from the hand-drawn map she had handed him along with the key. There was a storage room on the right, though he couldn't see it, and boxes piled on the left. Through a door he passed into the ornate lobby, gently illuminated by the streetlight filtering through the gauze-covered windows. A desk for the receptionist, a conference room off to the side, an elevator. He skipped the elevator and took the steps that circled the shaft, climbing as silently as the old wooden staircase would allow.

On the second floor, the staircase opened directly onto an outer office, dimly lit, with a number of secretarial desks and doors leading to four offices, only one of which, the corner office, was occupied. There was a copy machine on one wall, a teetering stack of white boxes on another. The phones on each of the secretarial desks showed a single line in use. He could hear one side of a conversation.

"I just have something to finish up here. . . . No, I won't be long. . . . Don't be foolish."

Robert took off his gloves, put them in his pocket, and waited for the phone conversation to end. He could simply have rung the bell at the front door and allowed himself to be buzzed in, he could have taken the elevator and had his meeting without the skulking about. But then he might have been spotted in the street. And he wouldn't have had the joy of walking silently toward the lit office, standing in utter stillness, seeing the startled expression on Laszlo Toth's greedy little face when Toth looked up from his desk and saw the dark and upright figure of Robert Spangler looming ominously in his doorway.

"Oh, it's only you," said Laszlo Toth after he had regained his composure. He was a small wizened figure, humpbacked and gnarly, with a burst of wild gray hair. Three fingers on his left hand were set in a cast. "I figured you'd be the one she sent." Was that a note of derision in his voice, or was Robert just imagining it? "How did you get in?"

"Through the door," said Robert. He kept his voice soft and even, his legal voice.

"It wasn't locked?" said Toth. "I thought I locked it."

"Close the blinds, Laszlo."

"Don't worry, no one—"

"Close the blinds," said Robert, and Toth, noticing the sudden edge in Robert's voice, bowed his head slightly before pushing himself out of his chair and pulling the blinds on all three of his windows. With the wooden slats now closed, Robert entered the office and sat in one of the client chairs facing Toth's big mahogany desk.

"I'm glad you came so quickly," said Laszlo Toth. His voice was surprisingly sonorous for someone his size, trained by decades in the municipal courts of Philadelphia. "I hope it wasn't inconvenient for her, but once I found the file, I was sure it was something she would want to get her hands on immediately."

"You were right about that," said Robert.

"She needn't have bothered sending the family lawyer, though. I was willing to take it directly over to her. I told her that."

"This is better for all concerned. She is, of course, very grateful for your tact. She is curious, however, about where you found the file."

"In a box."

Robert tilted his head, offered a bland smile that made it very clear he needed more.

"The firm is winding down," said Laszlo. "It's now only me and two young associates running around and cashing their paychecks without enough to do. I tried to keep it going for as long as I could, but Byrne & Toth has run its course. Sad, but there it is. Since Byrne's time we've had files in storage at a warehouse. I decided to stop paying the monthly fees. They can destroy the files for you at these places, but I thought we ought to see what was there before we put them to the flame. Maybe send them off to whatever clients still might want them. So when the boxes came, we went through them."

"We?"

"Me, I mean," he said quickly. "Just me."

"We're talking about the boxes piled in the outer office."

"That's right."

"Quite a job to do all by yourself."

"The associates are too young to have any idea of what is junk and what might be valuable. So it has been left to me to go through the boxes one by one."

"And?"

"And then there it was. Quite a surprise. I didn't remember it—it was Byrne's case, his chicken scrawl was all over the file—but as I went through it, things became clear."

"I'm sure they did."

"Shocking, actually. I can imagine the anguish it caused her, knowing it was in Byrne's possession all those years. He wasn't the most discreet soul. And you know what they say about the authentic Irish recipe for lamb stew. Step one: Steal a lamb. But right away, as soon as I understood what it was, I knew that she'd want to get her hands on it."

"And she is grateful, Laszlo. Very grateful. How old are you?"

"Too old."

"You look tired."

"Keeping the office open as long as I have has been a strain. Byrne always said he wanted to die in court, but I was never so dedicated. When the end comes, I'd like to be on a beach somewhere."

"And you have a place in mind."

"We've always liked the Outer Banks. It's quite beautiful down there."

"Expensive."

"I don't need much. Just a little cottage with a view of the sea."

"A little cottage. How sweet. And then you found the file. Convenient."

"What are you insinuating?"

"Do you have it here?"

"Yes, of course I do."

"Let me see it."

Laszlo bit his lip for a moment, as if he were considering whether to call or to raise in a poker game. The little eyes burned bright for a moment and then dulled. Call. He opened a desk drawer and took out an old green file folder. He put it on the desktop, looked at it for a moment, pushed it over to Robert as if pushing in his chips.

Robert took the file, opened it, paged through it quickly. It had copies of the settlement agreement, a copy of the signed and notarized statement, copies of letters from and to Liam Byrne. He had seen it before, years before, and didn't need to go through the whole thing again to know it contained all the proof he would ever need that his efforts with her were in vain, that the die had been cast against him long before he was old enough to even care. Actions didn't count; it was only a matter of blood. The impossibility of his situation shot a dose of anger into his voice.

"Where's the rest of it?" said Robert.

"That's it, that's all of it. I swear. Everything I found. I'm trying to help here."

"And you think Byrne put it in storage long ago and forgot about it?"

"Obviously."

"Where else might he have left a copy?"

"I don't know. I've been through everything in the office and in storage, and I found nothing."

"There must be someplace else. Think."

"I'm thinking."

"What happened to your hand?"

"An accident."

"You'll have another if you don't think harder."

"Byrne did have an old file cabinet. We bought a number of them when we first set up the office. He claimed one as his own, put all kinds of personal stuff in it, but that disappeared long ago."

"Disappeared?"

"Just before he died, he moved it out of here. A heavy metal behemoth, like the others in the storage room. I came in one day and it was missing. He called later and told me he'd taken it home. He was living on Panama Street then. His wife still lives there."

"See what you can come up with when you think hard, Laszlo? Did he have any children?"

"No, they couldn't. Cissy Byrne was . . . Oh, wait, there was one. A son. Illegitimate."

"The boy at the funeral."

"That's right. Were you there?"

"What's his name, this boy?"

"Kyle. The woman gave him his father's last name even though they weren't married. An impudent act, which fit her personality. Kyle Byrne. It's a shame about him."

"How so?"

"Talented kid, but things never worked out. He dropped out of college, has gone from job to job. Last I heard, he was bartending at some dive and living off friends."

"What dive?"

"Don't know."

"Where?"

"Here. Philadelphia. Near South Street."

"Okay. Now, Laszlo, answer me as truthfully as you are able. And I don't expect much. Did you make any copies of this file after you found it?"

"No."

"Are you sure?"

"Yes, yes, of course I'm sure. What are you implying?"

"What I am implying," said Robert, "is that you are a stinking Hungarian blackmailer who might not be satisfied with one dip from the bucket."

"Don't say that. Please don't say that. Is that what she thinks?"

"No," he said. "She considers you a loyal friend who is looking out for the best interests of her family."

"And she's right. She is. You should be ashamed of yourself, thinking the worst of everyone."

"Not everyone." Robert closed the file and lifted his briefcase onto the desk. He opened it so that the top lid stayed upright as a barrier, blocking Toth from seeing what was inside. Toth shifted to his right and tried to peer around the open lid.

"Uh-uh," said Robert, wagging a finger.

Toth sat back in his chair and waited.

Robert reached into the case, took out a thick bundle of bills bound with a rubber band, smacked the bundle onto the desktop. He thought for a moment and smacked another right on top of the first.

Laszlo stared at the stack of money, rubbing his lips with the good fingers in his left hand.

"I figure that should do it," said Robert.

As he gazed at the money, Laszlo's demeanor changed. All his careful obfuscation of motive seemed to pass away as if the money itself had chased it, like the sun chasing the clouds. He turned his gaze to Robert and let the slightest smile twist his lips. "For the roof, maybe," he said.

Robert stared back, shook his head sadly, reached into the briefcase. With his left hand, he took out two more bundles. He tossed them onto the table toward the others. As Laszlo Toth's eyes tracked the cash, Robert took an automatic pistol out of the briefcase with his right hand and placed it on his lap.

"And now we have a living room," said Laszlo.

Robert took out three bundles and lobbed them at Toth. "Here are the kitchen and two bedrooms," he said.

"We'll need a porch—and a view."

"You already have more than you need."

"But the view is the most expensive part."

"Why don't I just give you everything in the case?"

"I would think that should do it, Bobby," said Laszlo Toth.

Robert stared for a moment before he spun the briefcase around, so that it faced Laszlo with the top still raised. Laszlo's eyes lit as he reached both hands into the case.

Robert pointed the gun directly at the raised lid.

"Don't call me Bobby," he said.

And then he fired.

Later, after he had undone his cuff links and pushed up his sleeves and slipped his rubber gloves back on, as he moved about the office searching and obscuring, setting the scene, as he danced around the dead body of Laszlo Toth, the taste of acid in Robert Spangler's mouth was so strong and bitter he could feel it rotting his teeth. She had done it to him again. He didn't need that file to prove the impossibility of his ever gaining what he most desired from her; his life was proof enough. Every step toward her took him further and further from what he had sought to become. He had dreams, hopes, he had fervent plans for his future. But she had made of him an errand boy, a thug, a murderer. And all he ever wanted from her was her love. Was that too much to ask?

Evidently.

Chapter 3

Kyle Byrne spied his father watching him play in the seventh inning, which was a little disconcerting considering that his father had been dead for fourteen years.

It was on the diamond at the Palumbo Recreation Center at Tenth and Fitzwater, during a lethargic Monday-night beer-league-softball battle between Dirty Frank's and Bubba's Bar and Grill. The field was scabrous, the fence surrounding the lot was close and high, the bleachers were dotted with family and friends getting a start on the evening imbibitions. Kyle, Bubba's shortstop, was sitting on the bench, having a few swigs of his own from a can of Rolling Rock as Bubba Jr. looked on disapprovingly.

"What's the rush?" said Junior. "I need you sober."

"Dude."

"Don't dude me, dude. I been duded enough by you to last me through the rest of the decade. What I need from you is to close my bar tonight."

"Junior, I'm finding your lack of faith in me frankly dispiriting. I said I'll be there."

"You said the same thing last Monday."

"But you should have seen her. I mean, my God. And she had these little puppy-dog eyes."

"Puppy-dog eyes?"

"You know, the ones that are just saying, 'Pet me, pet me.' How could I resist that?"

Bubba Jr. tried to stare Kyle down.

" 'Pet me,' " said Kyle in his little-dog voice.

"You seeing that puppy again?"

"If I can find her number. It's in some pocket or other, I don't know."

"But you do know you're going to see me again. Think about that next time you're deciding who to screw."

Bubba Jr. was about as un-Bubba-like as anyone could be. The bar was named after his father, who at six-two, 240, and with a laugh like a trombone, had been Bubba to his bones. A heart attack at forty-eight passed the bar and the name to his small and wiry son.

"I need to be able to rely on my people," said Junior, "or I'll find people I can rely on."

"Aw, Junior, this is sad. You should hear yourself talk, ranting on about your people. Reading all those business books is rotting your mind. When did you start going all CEO on us, dude?"

"In January, when my father died and left me the stinking bar. By nine-thirty, all right?"

"You don't need me till ten."

"Nine-thirty."

"It's under control," said Kyle, before downing the rest of his beer. "I love you, dude. I do. Not as much as I loved your father, but then he never read a business book in his life. You know I'm there for you, Junior. Stop worrying."

"Okay, fine, I'll stop worrying. Now, grab a bat. You're on deck, and we need some runs."

"You think I'll get my ups?"

Junior looked through the cage at Old Tommy Trapp, gray, grizzled, toothless as a whelp, awkwardly taking his stance at the plate.

"Pitch it in, you pussy," screeched Old Tommy.

"Like my daddy always told me," said Junior, "miracles happen."

Kyle stood, grabbed a bright red bat from behind the backstop, and started swirling it one-handed about his head as he surveyed the field.

Bubba's was trailing Dirty Frank's, which was a crime, really, because Dirty Frank's was just about the worst team in the league and Bubba's had the league's best player, who was Kyle himself. Bubba Sr. had spotted Kyle playing on that same field in a fast-pitch league a few years before. Bubba's needed a shortstop, Kyle needed an occasional bartending gig to supplement his lack of income, a deal was struck. It had worked out great at the start, but Junior had been taking it all a bit too seriously. To Kyle it had started feeling like a job, and really, who the hell needed that, right?

"They put in a new center fielder," said Kyle to his pal Skitch, who was leaning against the backstop. "And he's playing in. Can he go back?"

"Who, Duckie?" said Skitch. "Like a gazelle." Skitch pushed his squat upper body away from the fence and spit a glob of sunflower seeds onto one of his cleats. "An overweight gazelle, with two bad knees and a hippo on its back."

Skitch was about Kyle's age, but a foot shorter and built like a fire hydrant. He played catcher because he ran like a fire hydrant, too. But he also pissed like a hydrant from all the Bubba's beer he drank, which made him a valuable member of the team, at least to Bubba Jr.

"We're going out to McGillin's after," said Skitch.

"That dump?"

"You coming?"

"I have the bar tonight."

"When?"

"Ten."

"Hell, we'll be passed out by nine. You won't miss a thing. I got some friends coming in from Atlantic City you should meet. Friends of the female persuasion."

"Persuasion? That mean they're not sure?"

"Oh, they're sure. Let me tell you something, Kyle, they're too damn sure for me to handle by my lonesome. That's why I need you on my wing."

"How many?"

"Three."

"Who's handling the third?"

"Old Tommy's coming."

Kyle looked at the geezer at the plate, so skinny it was like the bat was swinging him. "Give me something to hit, you pussy-assed fraud," shouted Old Tommy at the pitcher in a voice as ragged as his cleats.

"Okay," said Kyle, who was partial to Old Tommy primarily because he never said a kind or thoughtful word. "But I can't stay long, I need to be at the bar by nine-thirty."

"I thought you said ten."

"Junior's nervous."

"Worst thing ever happened to him was inheriting that bar."

A splash of sound signaled that Old Tommy had slapped a ground ball through the second baseman's legs. Cheers and claps, catcalls. "You dogs suck pig tits," shouted Old Tommy from first. "My mother plays better than you, and she's been dead four decades now." Two on, two outs, seventh and final inning, Bubba's down by three.

"Get on base and I'll pick up the winning knock," said Skitch.

"Last thing you knocked was that Sheryl from Folcroft," said Kyle as he stepped past Skitch and around the backstop, taking his place at the plate.

The outfielders backed up when he entered the cage. The left fielder was playing in Saskatchewan. It would be easy enough to dump a line-drive single in front of him, but that would leave them still two runs down, depending on Skitch to win the game, and the one thing Skitch wasn't was dependable. The right fielder was also playing away, scratching his back on the fence on Fitzwater Street. But the short fielder was playing in and the center fielder had retreated only a few steps. The left fielder was waving him back, but the center fielder was blithely ignoring him.

Sweet.

Kyle kicked his right foot into the dirt, placed his left foot toward the pitcher, stretched his bat high into the air before letting it gently fall into position at his rear shoulder. Here, at the plate, waiting on a pitch, here, in the middle of this moment, was the one safe place left in his life. Everyone had always told him how good he was at this—from Little League and Legion ball through high school, even at that college before his grades took him down—how he had a future at this, even if there was no one around to tell him how to reach it. And though things hadn't worked out, and he wasn't taking his stance in a major-league ballpark but instead waiting on a high-arc piece of crap in a beer-league-softball game, he still felt perfectly at home at home plate.

The pitcher's arm whirled, and the ball flew into the sky, and Kyle could see its seams spinning, could almost count them as the ball fell toward the outside of the plate, just what he was waiting for. Keeping his hands close to his body, he took his step. And he saw the ball shooting out to deep right center field, the angles the fielders took as the ball soared over their heads, saw it all even before he twisted his rear foot and shifted his hips, even before the red bat whipped around and connected, even before the sweet *thwump* flowed through his body easy and smooth.

Then he was off and running, toward first base—not sprinting hard, he didn't need to be—just chugging-chugging away, watching the center fielder back up and spin awkwardly and trip over himself as he scrambled for the ball. The right fielder charged over, but the angles weren't right. The ball skidded past him off the dirt and toward the fence. Kyle was following it all, the ball, the fielders, the angles that showed the ball rolling free and out of reach as he made the turn at first.

That was when he saw him.

A bob of gray hair, yes, that for sure. And a dark suit, a quick step, a knowing wink in the crouch of the posture. Maybe Kyle imagined the rest, but it all added up to only one thing.

Hello, boyo.

For years after his father's death, there was a part of Kyle that couldn't accept the truth of it. Even though he and his father had never been close, and even though he still had a small cardboard box filled with his father's ashes stashed in the glove compartment of his car, he long treasured the hidden hope that they would still have a tearful reunion. As a boy, whenever in crowds or walking down the streets of the city, he found himself searching for his father. And on the ball fields of his youth, he caught himself checking the stands as involuntarily as a tic, to see if maybe, just maybe, Dad had come to watch him play. Part of Kyle secretly believed that his father had run away, was hiding for some good reason, was waiting for the right moment to come back into Kyle's life. How many times had his heart leaped at the sight of a shock of white hair, how many times had the vision sent him running, only to see that the man was not his father at all, just some old guy shuffling along?

It had lain dormant for a while now, this secret and forlorn hope, he hadn't had a sighting in years. But suddenly here, on this pathetic little field, as he rounded first and headed for second and tracked the ball on its path deep into right center field, beyond the fence on Fitzwater Street, he spied the bob of gray hair, and, just that fast, something broke free in his heart.

He stopped in his tracks. And stared at the gray-headed figure. And the question came out in a breathless gasp, as desperate as the ache that suddenly ripped through his body.

"Daddy?"

Chapter 4

O h, my God, it was the funniest damn thing I ever saw," said Skitch at McGillin's Olde Ale House, the oldest continuously operating bar in Philadelphia and damn proud of it. Skitch was sitting at one of the long, narrow tables, with a red face and a pitcher of McGillin's house lager in his fist. "Down by three, two on, and my man Kyle like Casey himself at the bat."

"Who's Casey?" said one of the women from Jersey.

"Wasn't he the governor?" said another.

"Does he play baseball, too?"

"And then, bam, Kyle hits that ball an absolute ton," said Skitch. "A ton. And everyone, I mean everyone, starts howling and whooping. One run scores, Tommy, running like a sore-footed woodchuck, scores. And here comes Kyle, the tying run himself, motoring around first, heading for second, and then, and then . . ."

There were six of them huddled together at the table, Skitch and Kyle and Old Tommy Trapp along with the three women in from Jersey. Skitch had his arm around the neck of one of the women. The second was leaning as far from Old Tommy as she was able, as if Tommy were made of some overripe Limburger cheese. Kyle was dutifully ignoring the third, who sat across from him and whose name was Betsy and who was breathtakingly beautiful and seemed to know it at the start of the evening but wasn't so sure anymore.

"Then what?" said Betsy, looking at Kyle with a narrowed eye.

"Then he just stopped," said Skitch. "But not on a base or anything. He just stopped, staring out into the outfield, toward Fitzwater Street. You should have seen Junior's face when the second baseman tagged Kyle out while Kyle was just standing there. That was it—game, set, and match, and me on deck with a bat in my hands and nothing to do with it."

"As usual," said Kyle before finishing off his beer and slamming the mug back onto the table. Skitch lifted the pitcher and slopped what was left into Kyle's mug.

"I don't understand," said Betsy.

"What's to understand?" said Old Tommy. "The kid's dumb as a tick. Were you smoking that wacky weed again, you freak? I told you about that stuff."

"Yes, you did," said Kyle.

"So was you?"

"No."

"Well, there's your problem right there," said Tommy. "You got too many damn edges." He turned to the woman next to him. "You got nice tits on you there."

"Thank you," she said as she leaned farther away.

"They real?"

She turned to her friends. "Can we go now? Please."

"But why did he stop running?" said the woman with Skitch.

"Tell her, Kyle," said Skitch.

Kyle turned to Betsy. "You have something there on your mouth. No, above. Yeah, right there. That's it."

"He thought he saw his dad," said Skitch.

"Really?" said the woman with Skitch's arm still around her neck. "That's so sweet."

"Yeah, it is sweet," said Skitch. "Except his dad's been dead for fifteen years."

"Fourteen," said Kyle.

"But who's counting?" said Skitch. "Bro, Junior near split a gut."

"He was so angry," said Old Tommy, "you could have strummed 'Oh! Susanna' on the veins popping from his neck."

"Let him find another shortstop," said Kyle. "I'm sick of carrying that team anyway."

"Did you really think it was your father?" said Skitch's friend.

"I guess. I mean, it sort of looked like him. Same hair, you know that kind of moppy gray thing?"

"I still don't understand," said Betsy.

"There's a lot she doesn't understand, isn't there?" said Kyle. He stood up without looking at Betsy and grabbed the pitcher. "I'll get us a refill."

As he was heading toward the tap, he heard Skitch say, "Did I tell you about the funerals? You got to hear about Kyle and the funerals."

Kyle was at the bar, waiting on a fresh pitcher of the lager, when Skitch slipped beside him.

"You okay, bro?" said Skitch.

"Yeah, sure." He looked over at the table. Old Tommy was laughing at something, his head thrown back, his toothless mouth agape. He looked like a grizzled old rooster laughing there. "What's the name of that girl, the good-looking one, sitting next to me?"

"You mean the one you've been negging all night."

"You think I'm overdoing it?"

"She's almost in tears. Her name's Betsy. And let me tell you, if I wasn't hitting the other one, I'd hit that. Are you okay?"

"Sure, why not?"

"You don't mind me telling the story, do you?"

"You know me, Skitch, I love being the butt of your jokes. It beats being your butt, that's for sure."

"It seemed funny to me, but here you are acting all hurt and bothered."

"I guess I'm just feeling a little emotionally vulnerable tonight."

"Really?"

"No, not really. Don't worry about me, dude, it was nothing. A momentary lapse into pathetic adolescent angst. And you know what that means?"

"What?"

Kyle affected a bluff Russian accent. "Tonight we drink like fools."

"But we are fools."

"Perfect. You think she likes me?"

"Who, the babe? Well, she's a little prim, not your typical fare. And you have been insulting her all night."

"There's that, true. But I still bet I'll be making out with her before the night is over."

"Yeah," said Skitch, looking back at the table. "I bet you will, too."

Later, in the dark corner of the bar, Kyle found himself softly cupping the curve of her blouse as he rubbed her teeth with his tongue. She tasted fresh, like he imagined daisies would taste with their linen-white petals and pollen-filled centers. Her hair was blond and aromatic, her jaw trembled innocently as her lips pressed against his, her teeth were smooth, her breast was pert and responsive. And there was a moment, as he kissed her, pulled away to gaze into her dewy blue eyes, then kissed her again, a sublime moment when he felt fully calm and at peace. The bar fell away shard by shard until the surroundings turned dark and starry and they were in a universe of two and there was nothing he wanted more, nothing at all, than to lose himself in this woman's arms. And he felt safe and calm, and he began to believe that maybe, yes, maybe this was the answer that had kept escaping him all these years, an answer so elusive he didn't even know the question.

His answer pushed away and stared at him for an instant as her lovely nose wrinkled sweetly, and then she sneezed.

"I have to go," she said.

"Don't leave. I have a secret to tell you."

"What?"

"Patience. It's still early."

"Not anymore."

"What time is it?"

"Eleven-thirty."

"See, early? Why don't you stay a bit? We can go to my place. Talk about English. You teach English, right? I'm all for English. I even speak it."

"I thought you said you were staying with a friend?"

"Well, her place, then."

"Her place?"

"See, how cute is that, you going all jealous on me. But don't worry about Kat. I've known her forever. She's like a sister. Come on."

"I can't."

He followed her gaze and saw her friends standing by the door with coats on, staring daggers at the two of them. Skitch was at a table talking to two sinister characters wearing baseball caps with flat brims and pretty much sharing a single eyebrow between them. Old Tommy Trapp was nowhere to be seen.

"This was nice," she said.

"Yeah, it was. So nice."

"Here." She pulled out a pen, grabbed a napkin, wrote a number, and pressed it into his hand. "Call me."

"I will."

She leaned forward, kissed him on the lips, slipped a bit of tongue in for good measure, and then stood. "Do," she said.

He watched her as she walked toward her friends. Her legs were well shaped, her hair was shiny, she had nice posture. And she was a teacher, which he liked. It was substantial and noble, and maybe she could get all stern and cross at him when he screwed up his homework. He imagined the smart slash of a ruler on his flesh when he ended a sentence with a preposition, and then he looked at the number in his hand. Maybe he actually would call her. Betty. Or Berty. No, something like that, but with an *s*. Esther? Yeah, that was it, Esther.

Funny, she didn't look Jewish.

Skitch's head swiveled as Esther walked out, and then he waved Kyle over to join him and his two companions, but Kyle shook him off. Skitch had a steady job with Comcast, putting in cable, and a lucrative side business putting in all sorts of rogue connections, but he still was always up to his chin in some shady scheme or other, and these two goons were most likely his newest partners. Kyle had so far successfully withstood Skitch's entreaties to join in any of his nefarious business deals. The lure was easy money, and that was pretty much the only kind of money that Kyle liked, but Skitch seemed to be hustling pretty hard without getting very far. The whole point of Kyle's life was to avoid hard work, and just because the hard work was probably illegal didn't make it any more palatable.

So instead Kyle stood up, adjusted his pants a bit, and headed over the bar to grab a quick draft for the road. Just one more. There was something nagging at him that he couldn't quite figure out, but one more beer and the nagging would stop and that would suit him just fine.

He elbowed his way into an empty spot, ordered a glass of lager, blew at the head when it came, and downed a spurt. He hadn't eaten yet. He didn't have much cash left, but McGillin's had a decent burger for not much money and a hot turkey sandwich with masheds and gravy that was more than decent. He leaned on the bar, considered the possibilities as he took another drink, and then, through the windows facing Drury Street, he saw it again, the mop of gray hair bouncing along.

His emotions teetered for a moment before slipping into anger. He was being followed. Some old guy was following him. First the ball field, now this bar. Following him like a taunt. He swallowed what was left of the beer, slammed it on the bar, took out a few bills from his wallet to leave with the empty glass, and headed toward the exit.

"Kyle, yo, over here," yelled out Skitch, but Kyle ignored him and barged through the door.

He looked right, looked left, saw a figure walking down the dimly illuminated street and turning onto Juniper. Kyle hop-stepped cautiously toward Juniper, turned the corner like a spy, and saw the man heading north, toward City Hall. City Hall, where his father had plied his trade in the city's courts. He wiped his mouth with the back of his hand and then followed, quickly, hustling to get close, to get a view. His sneakers smacked against the cement as he got closer.

The man stopped, turned around. Kyle pulled up short as the man eyed him.

He was nobody, nothing, just a man walking down the street, forty-some years old with a dark shirt and a head of prematurely gray hair. The man cocked his head and then turned around and kept going.

And Kyle felt stuck there, right there, on the sidewalk, as if the rubber of his soles had melted onto the cement. He needed somebody to pry him loose, and he thought of Kat.

Chapter 5

As he walked east down Lombard, he saw her sitting on the steps of her apartment building, a converted brick town house just past Seventh Street. She was thin and tall, with lustrous black hair, tied back into a ponytail, wearing short shorts that showed off her long, athletic legs and a T-shirt two sizes too small. Had she been anyone else, Kyle would have been smitten on sight and fallen right into pickup mode. But she wasn't someone else; she was Kat.

They had been friends for as long as Kyle could remember, growing up in the same working-class neighborhood outside Philadelphia. Kat was the brain with attitude and looks, Kyle was the superstar athlete. They had been friends too long to date, but even as they went out with other people, they were a unit, far closer to each other than to their ostensible partners. For a long time it had been assumed that Kat was secretly in love with Kyle, the big man on his high-school campus. Now it was assumed that Kyle was secretly in love with Kat, the rising legal eagle with the fat bank account and the glittering future. In truth, there was nothing secret about what they felt for each other and love was but a pallid word to describe it.

As he approached, she smiled wearily.

"You waiting up to tuck me in?" said Kyle, who'd been crashing at Kat's place almost every night now, since Kyle was currently between places and had been since his childhood home had been seized by the bank a number of weeks back.

"I tried calling," she said.

"I think I left my phone somewhere."

She pulled his phone out of her pocket and tossed it at him.

"Thanks," he said. He flipped it open to check his messages.

"It helps if you charge it," she said.

He closed the phone, jammed it in his pocket, sat down beside her on the stoop. "So why are you still up?"

"I was waiting for you. Is everything all right?"

He looked at her, saw the unwelcome maternal concern in her eyes, turned away. "Word travels, I guess."

"A bit, yeah. And it got me a bit worried. There's a lot going on in your life right now."

"Is that the way it seems to you? Because to me it seems like there's nothing going on at all."

"So really, how are you doing?"

"Just dandy. And yourself?"

"Fine, sweetie, but then I'm not the one still seeing my dead father in the outfield."

"You don't have to. Yours is alive."

"You sound like you resent it."

"Sure. I resent everyone who's not orphaned. The resentment is about the only thing I have left in the world—that and my car. And it doesn't cost fifty a pop to fill up my resentment."

"You're a strapping twenty-six, hardly the image of the poor orphan boy."

"But still, when you call me an orphan, you want to hold me in your arms and mother me, right?"

She reached a hand to his face, rubbed his cheek forcefully with her thumb, examined the smear of red there. "Looks like somebody beat me to it."

"One of Skitch's friends," he said, unembarrassed.

"What happened to her?"

"She had to go back to New Jersey."

"Ahh, a Jersey girl. And a friend of Skitch, so you know she's a class act all the way."

"She was nice. A teacher, I think."

"You going to see her again?"

"Maybe, if I can remember her name."

"But that's why you drink, right? To forget."

"I only had a few." He sat, thinking for a moment. "And maybe a few after that."

"It hadn't happened in a while, had it?" she said.

"No, and then tonight I saw him twice."

"Twice?"

"Again outside McGillin's. I saw him, and I chased him down, and it was just some guy."

"It's always just some guy."

"I know."

"What are you hoping for when you chase these ghosts?"

"I don't know. He was my dad. Maybe he can teach me the one thing I need to know."

"What's that?"

"If I knew, I wouldn't need him."

"Kyle, sweetheart, don't be such a lummox."

"How's your dad doing?"

"He's fine."

"You see him a lot, right?"

"Once or twice a week."

"What do you talk about?"

"You're pathetic."

"I know, but humor me."

"We talk about stupid stuff. His kidneys. His golf scores. My sister's husband."

"Sounds nice."

"It's not like he's relaying the meaning of life to me."

"But you see, maybe he is. You're just not listening carefully enough."

"You know my dad—he's more concerned with the meaning of his phone bill than the meaning of life." She roughened her voice into a strong Korean accent. "'What is this charge here? I don't understand. Fees on top of fees. And don't get me started on damn cable bill.'"

"Sounds lovely," said Kyle. "So why were you calling?"

"To relay a message."

"Oh, yeah? From who?"

"Bubba Jr. Were you supposed to be at the bar tonight?"

Kyle let his head drop between his shoulders. "Crap," he said, in a calm, unconcerned voice. "I knew I was forgetting something. Maybe I should stroll on over there."

"Don't bother," she said. "I think he fired you."

"Fired me? He can't fire me. I'm his shortstop."

"Not anymore, honey," she said. "Not anymore."

Chapter 6

Bubba's Bar and Grill, just a few blocks away from Kat's place, was a neighborhood joint in Queens Village, a corner tap on an obscure little corner that drew a clientele from a radius of four blocks or so. It was already late, close to closing time, and all that was left were the usual suspects who were always left at closing time. Junior was behind the bar, leaning on his elbows listening to Old Tommy Trapp rail on against something. Junior glanced up when Kyle entered the bar. His eyes glowed red for a second, and then he turned back to Tommy.

Kyle took a seat at the far end of the bar and waited. And waited. Junior was ignoring him, which was Junior's right, considering how Kyle had screwed up. But what with meeting Skitch for drinks, and then getting all twisted up with that Jewish girl from Jersey, and then seeing his father for a second time in one night on the street, what with all of it, Junior had slipped from a priority to a nagging detail that he couldn't quite remember. And long ago Kyle had decided that nagging details he couldn't quite remember were best left ignored.

But now he had to make amends. Junior was playing it cool, but later he would be apoplectic, no doubt, his dark face darkening and spittle flying as he hurled invective upon Kyle's broad shoulders. Then he'd sputter a bit and slow down, looking for Kyle to say something in his own defense. Should Kyle act all contrite, like what he'd done was the worst possible thing in the world? Or should he toss it off like it was no big deal, dude, but things got in the way, and tell Junior to stop sweating the small stuff? That's the way he really felt, but he figured contrition was the way to go. As he sat at the bar, he put on the face of a penitent.

At one point, when Junior went into the back room for something, Old Tommy looked over and gaped his toothless smile. "You're dumber than a dingo," he said, "and that's pretty damn dumb."

"I know," said Kyle.

"You get any at least?"

"A little."

"What the hell does that mean? You get laid, yes or no?"

"No."

"Dumber than a blue-balled dingo," said Old Tommy, shaking his head.

Finally Junior came out of the back room, wiped the bar a bit, and slowly made his way down to Kyle.

"I'm so sorry, dude," said Kyle, his head hanging at an appropriately contrite angle. "No excuses, I just screwed up."

"My daughter had a dance recital tonight," said Junior with a scary calm. No loud words, no spittle. "I had to leave the party after it to cover for you. My daughter said, 'Do you have to go, Daddy?'"

"That's bad."

"It was like being in the middle of a country-and-western song."

"Welcome to my life."

"I hate country-and-western songs."

"Want me to close tonight?"

"No, Kyle."

"How can I make it up?"

"You can't."

"Kat says you fired me."

"I think you just fired yourself."

"Dude."

"This isn't easy for me," said Junior.

"From this side of the bar, it looks pretty damn easy."

"Well, maybe it's easier for me than it is for you. But this has been a long time coming."

"Junior, we're friends."

"I know we are, but that has nothing to do with the bar. I need someone I can rely on here, someone who will show when he says he'll show. To get someone like that, I need to guarantee hours, and the hours I'm going to guarantee him are yours."

"Well, maybe until you find someone . . ."

"I have someone lined up already."

"Already?"

"She's starting tomorrow."

"Tomorrow? That's cold. It's like you were just waiting for me to screw up."

"If I was, I didn't have to wait long. You know why my father hired you, Kyle?"

"Because I can hit."

"No. Well, not only that. It's because he cared about you."

"I loved your father."

"I know you did, and he felt the same way about you. He didn't mind that the bar always needed cleaning the mornings after you worked. He didn't mind that you were overly generous with the bar's liquor. He didn't mind that the till was never right, because he knew there was usually more in it than what was supposed to be there."

"I would never steal from this place."

"He knew that, Kyle. He explained to me that the reason there was too much cash in the till was that you cared so little about money you would sweep half your tips in with the rest of it."

"I'll keep better track if that's what you want. And I'll spend more time cleaning."

"He hired you because he wanted to help you. And then after your mother died, that cemented it. He decided he would do everything he could for you."

"He was a good man."

"Yes he was, but maybe he was wrong. Maybe letting you slide in the job, come in when you wanted, do a lousy job, maybe that wasn't helping you at all."

"No, it was. He was right."

"You're too old for this, Kyle. Sloughing off work, stopping between first and second because you think you see your long-dead dad, taking pride in your irresponsibility. It's enough already. All these years after my father first took you in, you're still lost."

"When did you become so damn grounded?"

"When my daughter was born. When I bought a house and got a mortgage wrapped around my throat. When my father died and left me the bar."

"It's a pity, dude."

"No, it's life. And I'm sorry, but this is the way it is."

"Look, Junior, I'm working through things."

"Then do it, and do it quickly. Come back after, and we'll talk."

"But I need the job, I need the money. I got nothing coming in without this."

Junior looked at him for a moment and then went to the cash register. He pressed a button, the drawer popped open, he started counting out some bills. When he was done, he closed the drawer, walked over to Kyle, slapped the stack of bills on the bar.

"What's that?" said Kyle.

"All those tips you didn't collect. My father kept track, and after he died, so did I."

"I don't understand."

"Just take it."

"I'm not a charity case."

"It's your money, Kyle. We were just holding it, waiting until you needed it."

"What about interest?"

"Take the damn money."

Kyle hesitated a moment and then stood. He grabbed the stack of bills and, without counting it, stuffed it into his pocket.

"Stay in touch," said Junior.

"Sure."

"By the way, someone was in here earlier looking for you."

"Me?"

"Yeah, you. A guy named O'Malley. He said if he didn't see you here, he'd probably catch up with you at the funeral."

"Funeral? What funeral?"

"A guy died name of Toth, he said. Something about him being your father's partner."

"Laszlo Toth?"

"That's it."

"Dead?"

"Yeah. Shot through the heart in his office. A robbery."

"Wow."

"Didn't you read about it in the paper?"

"I haven't looked at anything all weekend except the Cartoon Channel."

"Your future is so bright. This O'Malley said the funeral's tomorrow and that he'd see you there. I'll tell you, this whole thing makes me glad my dad fitted that shotgun underneath the cash register. Someone comes in here looking for an easy mark, they'll be pulling shot out of the corpse for a week."

But Kyle wasn't listening anymore to Bubba Jr. He was thinking about Laszlo Toth and his getting shot in the heart and about the funeral on Tuesday, and while he was thinking of it all he was smiling.

Chapter 7

N ice day for a funeral," said Detective Ramirez.

"For the corpse especially," said Detective Henderson.

"Sounds like you're looking forward to it, old man."

"Oh, I am, believe me," said Henderson. "One day life is nothing but worries, next day all those worries are gone, like a flock of finches flitting into the sky."

"A flock of flitting finches?"

"Didn't know I was a poet, did you?"

"Is that what you are?" said Detective Ramirez. "Because I've been wondering."

They were a team, a single unit, Detectives Henderson and Ramirez. It didn't matter that Henderson was tired and old, a burnout waiting for his full pension to vest so he could sit in his lawn chair and watch his tomatoes grow. Or that Ramirez was young and ambitious and disappointed in drawing Henderson as a partner after her meteoric rise to the Homicide Division. It didn't matter that they came from different generations, listened to different music, viewed the world from entirely different perspectives. It didn't matter whether they had gotten drunk together, because they hadn't, or whether they liked each other, because they didn't, or whether they respected each other, because they both expected they never would. It only mattered that they were partners.

"Widow looks cut up about it all," said Ramirez.

"She didn't seem as upset when we questioned her right after, did she?" said Detective Henderson.

"You think she's faking?"

"Putting on a show. But then that's only natural, foul play or no. What were they married, forty-five years? After all that time, love has degenerated into habit, and mostly the only thing that still glows bright is the hate."

"How long you been married, Henderson?"

"Not quite that long, but we sure as hell are getting there."

They were standing a bit back from the proceedings, dark glasses guarding their watchful eyes. The sun was bright, the sky lightly dotted with clouds, the air springtime fresh. It was a respectable crowd, not as large as some but enough of a turnout to know that the deceased, one Laszlo Toth, a victim of murder by gunshot, was a living, breathing person before he was a corpse. Beneath a blue canopy, sitting in the middle of a row of folding chairs set next to the freshly dug grave, the widow sobbed uncontrollably as the priest carried on about souls and forgiveness and eternity. Two old women were on either side of her. One, with dark hair and dark glasses and bright, overlipsticked lips, offered comfort as she patted the grieving widow's hair. The other sat withered and twitching from palsy in a wheelchair but remained an imperious presence nonetheless. A factotum in a navy-blue suit stood behind the wheelchair, apparently ready to answer any whim as the woman gripped her black purse tightly and scanned the crowd.

"Look at the women sitting on either side of the wife," said Detective Henderson. "It seems a little strange, them sitting there like that."

"Why?"

"You'd think it would be the daughter comforting the mother, but she's been shunted off to the side. These other two women have the place of honor. It might be interesting to know who they are. Any idea?"

"No."

"Then maybe you should find out," he said.

Detective Ramirez bristled. She never liked being given orders, and she especially didn't like being given orders by a burnt piece of toast like Henderson. "This is a waste," she said, turning her head away from the proceedings and scanning the empty landscape. "We should be on the street trying to catch the merchandise being moved."

"We'll have plenty of time for that," said Henderson. "And I've already given Robbery a heads-up on the missing items. But for now why don't you find out who those old ladies might be."

"You want me to go up and ask them?"

"People at a funeral love to talk. The only place better for learning who screwed whom is at a wedding. Just find someone who can't wait to spill and you'll get it all. Go on, now, before they start throwing dirt in that hole."

Ramirez gave him a hard, canine look, like she was about to bark him up a tree, before thinking better of it and heading off to find someone talkative to talk to.

Ramirez didn't want to spend her morning at a cemetery. She figured she had it figured, the whole murder-robbery of Laszlo Toth. A rear door accidentally left unlocked, a lawyer working late, an opportunity for mayhem. And the crime scene backed up her view.

The wallet emptied, the victim's prized Raymond Weil watch missing, files scattered, drawers rifled, a clutch of flat-screen computer monitors gone. Ramirez assumed that the killer would have taken the copy machine if he could have lifted it. To Ramirez's way of thinking, getting a line on the gun and searching for the fenced screens or the watch, keeping constant lookout for the credit card to be used was the way to go, and they could do all that while working the other open files piling up on their desks. Scoping out the dead guy's funeral was simply a lazy man's way to pleasantly pass the time as he waited for retirement.

Henderson was lazy, he'd admit it, and he did like cemeteries, admired their peacefulness and fine greenery. And Henderson agreed with Ramirez that their being at the funeral was probably a waste of time. But something about the crime scene didn't sit right in his stomach, and he wasn't willing to let any opportunity to figure it out slip away.

The murder and looting of the legal office was a bit too careful for a kid coming off the street with a gun in his belt and a habit to feed. In random robberies with drugs as the motive, the destruction often had a frenzied quality to it; the damage wrought here seemed controlled by comparison. And no one in the building could account for the door's being unlocked, which made it seem that instead of its being a burglary, the killer might have been invited in by the dead lawyer. Maybe the lawyer was staying late just for the meeting. The victim's wife said the broken fingers were the result of an accident, but Toth could have been threatened before he was killed. And what about the cuff link they found beneath Toth's desk? The widow didn't recognize it. What kind of drug-addled killer wore cuff links?

But more than anything, Henderson couldn't understand the peculiar pressure that was being placed on him to solve this thing quickly. The captain had called him in, told him the commissioner was getting heat from the mayor to climb on top of the Toth murder as soon as possible. Which meant the mayor was getting heat himself. That was a lot of pressure for a dead seventy-year-old lawyer facing financial troubles, all of which set Detective Henderson to wondering if there might not be more to this than Ramirez figured.

"I found an old man with Italian hands who couldn't wait to tell me everything," said Ramirez when she returned.

"Italian hands?"

"They were roamin'."

Henderson chuckled.

"The woman on the right is a Mrs. Byrne. Her husband was Toth's partner."

"He died, what, fourteen years ago?"

"That's right. Apparently the partners weren't getting along at the end."

"You don't say."

"Fighting about money."

"They were lawyers. Of course they were fighting about money. That's what being a lawyer is all about."

"But there is something else. Byrne was supposed to have been quite the ladies' man."

"Maybe he stepped out with the Widow Toth, is that the word?" Henderson gave the widow a new and more interested look. Her sagging jowls, her arthritic hands. She might have been something at some time, but it was hard to still see it. "How'd Byrne die?"

"The man I was talking to didn't know."

"We're going to have to find out, I suppose."

"And the woman on the other side in the wheelchair? Get this, she is a Mrs. Truscott."

"Truscott?"

"That's right."

"As in Senator Truscott?"

"The mother. Apparently an old friend of the family and client of the dead man."

"Suddenly we know who's pressuring the mayor."

"Good. Now that that's all settled, can we leave and do some real work?"

"Not until we do a drill."

"Drill?"

"Take a look around and tell me, who doesn't belong?"

"I don't do drills. What is this, band practice? And don't tell me you're expecting the killer to show up at his victim's funeral. The captain won't want to hear we wasted the whole morning on that old saw."

"Old saw, huh? How long you been in Homicide?"

"Long enough to know a waste of time when I'm in the middle of it."

"Let me tell you, lady. Old saws still cut."

"Okay, to humor you, and so we can get the hell out of here. Let's start with who does belong. I see the daughter, who we spoke to already, sitting down beside that Mrs. Byrne."

"Okay."

"Her husband's the thin guy standing behind her. The grandkids are standing with him."

"Fine."

"I see the two lawyers we questioned that were working at the firm. One has a woman with him, nice-looking, with expensive hair, wife or girlfriend probably, it doesn't really matter. They're standing there behind the family watching their future being buried."

"Good."

"And then a whole mess of old men and women saying good-bye. Friends from the old neighborhood, I would expect. And from the profession."

"Nothing makes an old man feel better than someone else dying before him."

"You sure do like funerals, don't you, Henderson?"

"And nothing's more deadly than an old friend, settling scores before the reaper reaps."

"You speaking from experience?"

"We'll check the condolence book they all signed, find the names of these old friends with scores to settle. But now look again. Who doesn't belong?"

Ramirez scanned the entire scene. The priest, the crowd of old and young, the gravediggers off to the side, waiting to close up the hole. There were some other people milling in the distance, visiting the dear departed at other graves. Nothing stood out. Except maybe . . .

"Who's that?" she said. "Standing back a bit, in the gray suit?"

"Don't know," said Henderson, the twist of a smile bending the corner of his sour mouth.

The man in the gray suit stood with his hands in his pockets, situated on a little rise behind the main mass of mourners. He was tall and broad-shouldered, his hair was unkempt, his beard casually unshaven, his loose tie stylishly askew, his stance a leisurely *contrapposto*. His eyes were guarded by a pair of Ray-Bans, and he sported a strange, crooked smile, as if he were watching an amusing lounge act.

"He's big, isn't he?" said Henderson.

"Yes, he is."

"And quite good-looking."

"I hadn't noticed."

"Oh, no? Now, is that any way to start a partnership, lying at the outset? Someone that good-looking, everybody notices. But see how he's standing close enough to keep his eye on the proceedings, yet not so close that anyone would start talking to him."

"Maybe he's just shy."

"He doesn't look shy," said Henderson.

"Well, this is a sad situation," said Detective Ramirez. "Poor boy is at a funeral, trying to hide his sorrow, and no one is making an effort to give him some of the human contact he clearly craves. I think I ought to head on over and offer the man my condolences."

"You want me to tag along?"

Ramirez took another look at the man, pulled off her sunglasses, and tossed her hair. "No thanks. I think I can handle this cutie-pie all by my lonesome."

Chapter 8

If Kyle Byrne collected comic books, Laszlo Toth's funeral would have been Detective Comics number 27, the first appearance of the Batman. If Kyle Byrne collected baseball cards, it would have been a 1909 Honus Wagner tobacco special. But Kyle Byrne didn't collect comic books, or baseball cards or stamps or coins or blown-glass figurines. What he collected were funerals. Of a certain type.

Every day, after stumbling out of Kat's spare bedroom at about noon or so, scratching his stomach, emptying his bladder, and scrounging for loose Doritos scattered around the empty beer bottles or the bong on the living-room coffee table, he gathered up the pieces of the newspaper, turned swiftly to the obituaries, and hunkered down for some serious study. He was scanning for old men, born between 1935 and 1950, men in the legal profession who had practiced in Philadelphia. Then he checked their fields of expertise. He didn't want dour corporate types, in-house hacks, he didn't want government bureaucrats, didn't want the bankruptcy or patent-law specialists with their cramped codes and closed fraternities. But if the dead old man had practiced criminal or personal-injury law, or even some insurance defense, then he might take a second look. And if he had an Irish surname or grew up in North Philly or graduated from Temple Law, then Kyle would rip out the obituary, circle the time and date listed for the funeral proceedings, and fill in another line on his very open schedule.

He owned one suit. Gray and single-breasted, the lapels quite narrow. He wore it only to the funerals. It hung all alone in the closet of the spare bedroom. Open the door of the closet and there it was, his gray two-piece, solitary and limp, waiting for adventure like the Batsuit. Add to it a white shirt, a narrow black tie, a black belt, argyle socks, black shoes. And then, as safely anonymous as any superhero in his mask and cape, he'd head off to the funeral parlor or the cemetery chapel or the grave site that was listed in the obituary. Off to stand apart and breathe in the air of bereavement, take in the expressions of brave grief, watch the condolences pool together into a sea of sorrow and loss.

For a son, every funeral before his father's death is a rehearsal and every funeral thereafter is a memorial. As Kyle Byrne stood among the mourners in his gray suit and watched body after body of old dead lawyers being lowered into the ground, lawyers whom in all likelihood his father had known, he felt as if he were standing in for his father. When he signed the condolence books, he always signed his father's name, not his own, and felt a strange exultation. His mother was dead, his past was obliterated, his present was bleak and his future was deeply in doubt, but in these moments he felt a connection to his father that induced in him an undeniable joy.

Sure, it was a little morbid, but hell, everybody needs a hobby.

That was why Toth's funeral was so special. There was no wondering if his father had really known this dear departed, Toth was his partner. And it was Laszlo Toth who had expelled Kyle from his father's own funeral, instigating the events that Kyle seemed to replay in his heart during every funeral thereafter and that remained, puzzlingly, the proudest moment in his life. Of all the funerals he had attended, or would attend in the future, the sad little affair at the grave site of Laszlo Toth would be, for Kyle Byrne, the large-size 1979 *Empire Strikes Back* Boba Fett action figure of funerals, which is to say pretty much the ultimate.

The tears came unbidden, but not unexpectedly. It was why he had worn sunglasses. In a way, as he watched the priest deliver his eulogy over the casket and as he watched the grieving Mrs. Toth be comforted by his father's widow—a woman who still had never acknowledged Kyle's existence except when she had pinched his face fourteen years ago—in that special moment he felt closer to his father than he ever had in his entire life. As he lifted his head and surveyed the burial fields, through teary eyes he thought he spotted a mop of gray hair in the distance, and the mirage, instead of feeling like a sick joke of some sad sort, seemed perfectly natural.

"Nice day for a funeral," said a voice from beside him.

So lost was he in the distant vision and the swell of his emotions, Kyle hadn't noticed the woman who had sidled up to him. Slowly he turned his head toward her, but even then he couldn't quite focus on who she was and the words she had spoken.

"Huh?" he said.

"The day," she said. "It's nice. That's all."

"Yeah, I suppose you could say so."

She was pretty, actually, young and solid, with tawny skin, high cheekbones, and lovely brown eyes. And he liked her lips, full but not too thick. He wondered what they would taste like. And just that quick, the swell of emotions he had been feeling about his dead father were replaced with the swell of something more pressing. It might seem perverse, but Kyle had learned from his funeral hobby that nothing stirred a whole bouquet of hungers more than a hole in the ground.

"Were you crying?" she said.

"Uh, no," he said, lifting his glasses with one hand and wiping his eyes with the back of the other. "Allergies."

"It's okay to cry, it's a funeral. I'm sorry for your loss."

"Loss? What loss is that?"

"The deceased. Mr. Toth. I can see that you were close."

"We weren't, actually."

"So you're not a relative?"

"Not even distantly."

"A friend?"

"Not exactly."

"A friend of a friend?"

"You couldn't really say that either."

"So what are you doing here, just enjoying the day?"

"Yes, actually. You're right, it is a lovely day. And who doesn't enjoy a good funeral?"

"Is that what this is?"

"Well, I have to admit I've seen better. This one's a little sparse on the attendance, and the words of remembrance are a tad generic, but the communal atmosphere has a certain piquant poignancy. I'd give it a solid six."

"You sound like an expert."

"Funerals are sort of a hobby of mine."

"You should get together with my partner," she said. "He loves funerals, too. Can't get enough of them. Between you and me, I think he's looking forward to his own."

"Partner? What, like a life partner?"

"Thank heavens, no."

"So you're single?"

"Yes."

"That's such a coincidence," said Kyle with a big old smile, "because so am I."

"Are you hitting on me? At a funeral?"

"Of course not. I am shocked and appalled at the implication. In fact, I think you and I need to have a rather stern talk about your perverse sense of funeral decorum. Perhaps over a drink."

She fought not to laugh and failed.

"My name's Kyle."

"Lucia," she said. "Lucia Ramirez. It's nice to meet you, Kyle."

"If you want to know the truth, this Mr. Toth isn't actually a total stranger."

"Really?" she said.

"Fourteen years ago he kicked me out of my father's funeral."

"Fourteen years ago?"

"To the month, in fact. Not that I hold a grudge."

"And that's why you're here on this fine day? Because you don't hold a grudge?"

"That's right."

"Fourteen years ago." She tapped her chin. "Isn't that when Mr. Toth's partner died?"

He looked at her again. He had thought she'd just wandered over, but there was a degree of purpose in her stance, in the way she was staring at him now.

"How did you know that?" he said.

"Was Mr. Toth's partner your father?" she said.

"Just so happens yes."

"So that's your mother sitting beside the widow?"

"No."

"But that's—"

"Yes."

"Ahh, I see."

"Do you?" He looked at her, caught the intensity of her gaze. "What do you see, exactly?"

"How did your father die, do you know?"

"Heart attack, or so I've been told."

"Told by whom?"

"Well, by Mr. Toth."

"Did you ever get any documentation?"

"Why would I?"

"Just wondering. You have the time?"

Kyle reflexively checked his watch. It was an old gold thing with a square face and an expandable metal band. "One-twenty," he said.

"Nice watch. What is it, a Raymond Weil?"

He looked at it again. "No. It's a Longines. It belonged to my mother. Who are you anyway?"

"When was the last time you saw this Mr. Toth?"

"A while ago, I don't remember. Hey, what's going on here? I thought we were mindlessly flirting."

"Where were you on Friday night? I'm talking late, now. About midnight."

"That's the night Mr. Toth was killed, right?"

"That's right," she said.

He looked at her a bit more, and then it came to him, wholly and with utter clarity, the way the most obvious things come to you when you finally grasp hold. This wasn't just a cute girl flirting as she passed the time at some boring old funeral. This was a cop, admittedly a fine-looking cop, but a cop nonetheless, a cop investigating the murder of Laszlo Toth. And Kyle Byrne realized with a shock that he had suddenly become a suspect.

How cool was that?

Chapter 9

Robert Spangler was listening to a priest drone on at the funeral of Laszlo Toth when he spotted the two police officers scanning the crowd. They were in plain clothes, but still, the moment he saw them, he knew, what with their law-enforcement stances—like prison guards on the walk—their sunglasses, their chins. Not to mention their races. The old black man and young Latino woman stood out like messengers from another planet in the sea of white Hungarian trash.

Robert had never before had the opportunity to attend the funeral of someone he'd actually killed, though he'd sat through the funeral and memorial service of Liam Byrne, whom he had tried to kill but who had died before Robert could get a second chance at him. That funeral was an odd experience, especially after it had been disrupted by Byrne's illegitimate son, who snatched the urn full of the old man's ashes and darted crazily into the depths of the cemetery. But this funeral was stranger still for Robert, an opportunity only a rare few ever had the temerity to experience. What did it feel like to stand by the open grave of a man whom you had murdered in the coldest of blood?

He took a moment to gauge his emotions, and this is what he felt: disgrace and exultation and boredom all at once. Disgrace at the humiliation that he accepted from her at every turn. In her eyes he was no better than a pet—worse, actually, because her cat was treated with far more respect than was he. Exultation at the act itself, not the killing per se but the execution of it, clean and hard. He had taken his time, he had set the scene, he had laid traps to cover his tracks. Except for a missing cuff link, everything had gone perfectly. It was a lucky thing he didn't have a taste for the work, because he was damn good at it. And finally boredom, yes, boredom, because, frankly, funerals were boring as hell.

But now, with the cops barging in on the graveside service, he felt something else, too. A shot of fear. Interesting. And strangest of all, he discovered that he liked it.

They were talking, the two of them, off to the side. She had left for a bit to question one of the old-timers who had shown up, and now she was back with her partner, surveying the crowd. For a moment her gaze fell upon Robert like the beam of a klieg light, and even as he maintained his stolid demeanor and stance, he felt something rise within him. A thrill, like being on a roller coaster, the moment at the crest of the initial rise when nothing but the fall is before you. And then her gaze passed on and the thrill disappeared.

He kept watching her as she scanned the crowd. After a moment more with her partner, she headed off, toward a man in a gray suit standing on a small hill beyond the coffin. He studied the man for a moment. There was something familiar about him. And then Robert recognized him. So captivated was he by the ebb and flow of his own emotions that he had turned sloppy and hadn't seen him clearly, but now he did.

It was the boy who had run off with the ashes, the son of Liam Byrne.

He'd been looking for this Kyle Byrne ever since Laszlo Toth had told him about the missing file cabinet. He needed to learn if this Kyle knew anything about where it might be and what might be inside, but the son had been hard to trace. The only pictures he had were of a younger, thinner figure, a teen, actually, still in high school, photos from the sports pages of the *Philadelphia Inquirer.* The address that was listed on the Internet was no longer valid; the son had moved out of the house just a few weeks before. A neighbor seemed to remember that this Kyle worked at a place called Bubba's. He had found the bar and waited there for way too long—there was only so much piss-gut beer he could drink—but the kid had never shown, so Robert had delivered his message to the scrawny black bartender and then left. He had planned to visit the bar after the funeral to sniff out what he could, but he no longer needed to.

Instead of Robert's having to search for the boy, the message had borne fruit and the boy had come to him.

Robert watched as the cop sidled up to this Kyle Byrne and started talking. The boy seemed to be lost, and it took him a moment to realize that someone had spoken, but the two eventually settled into conversation. Robert could imagine what was being said, the cop asking the kid questions about a murder. But wait a second, it didn't seem like an intense interview. It actually looked like she was flirting. And son of a bitch, it looked like he was flirting back. At a funeral, no less. He had to admire that. He'd have to be more careful with this Byrne boy than he'd thought. He watched as they chatted amiably, and then the conversation took an obvious turn.

She was turning cop on him, and he was getting defensive. Interesting. Whatever was going on between them had turned into an interrogation. Could the son of Liam Byrne be a suspect in the murder of Byrne's former partner? Why not? The more the merrier. Robert was only disappointed that he hadn't seen the possibility sooner. It would have been nice to add a piece of evidence to the crime scene implicating the boy. Maybe he'd still have his chance.

It lasted a moment more, the conversation, and then the cop slipped away to head back to her partner. They'd talk about the kid, they'd keep an eye on him, which meant Robert couldn't go right over. He'd have to wait.

His moment came after the priest had finished his monotonous oration, after a few prayers from the little pamphlet had been read, after the coffin had been lowered and dirt had been spilled onto its dark wooden surface with the pattering thud of finality. The three women from the front row had been helped into their respective limousines, the crowd was shaking heads and shaking hands and dispersing toward the cars parked tightly on the road that wound around the gravestones.

Robert spied Kyle Byrne walking alone with his head down toward an old red sports car parked well away from the others.

"Mr. Byrne?" said Robert as he came up from behind. "Mr. Kyle Byrne?"

The kid stopped and turned around and gave Robert a careful look before saying, "Yes."

"Liam Byrne's son?"

"That's right."

"I knew your father," said Robert. He stifled his smile as he saw the son's eyes widen with curiosity. He had wondered what to offer as bait, and suddenly he knew. "Your father was a fine man."

"Was he?"

"Well, sometimes he was. And sometimes not so. If you're interested in the details, maybe we should talk," said Robert, fishing a card from his pocket, offering it to Byrne. "I think we can help each other."

Byrne took the card, glanced at it. "How can you help me . . . Mr. O'Malley?"

"I know things about your father."

"Things? What kinds of things?"

"Things about his life, his frailties, his death."

"His death?"

"Things that might surprise you," said Robert. "Secrets. What child doesn't want to probe the secrets of his father? But maybe I'm wrong. Maybe you have no interest at all in your father's past. And if so, good for you. Only the foolish look back. Forward, forward is all. I'm sorry to disturb you."

"No, no, wait," said Byrne as Robert started to turn away. "We can talk. Why don't we talk now?"

"They've just buried your father's partner," said Robert. "This is an inappropriate venue for our discussion, don't you agree? Call me, and we'll meet someplace seemly."

"I don't understand."

"Call me."

"Wait, don't leave."

"Soon," said Robert as he backed away.

"Mr. O'Malley?"

"Yes?"

"You said we can help each other. How can I help you?"

Robert stopped, stared for a bit, and then walked up to Byrne so his softest voice could be heard. "I am looking for something. I was a client of your father's, and I gave him certain information that he put in a file. A legal file. With my name upon its label. I would like that information back. Do you have any idea where the file might be?"

"No. None."

"That's too bad," said Robert as he backed away and then turned again to leave.

"But we should talk."

"Find me my file and we will."

"I don't even know where to look."

"Think," said Robert over his shoulder. "Think hard, and then give me a call."

Chapter 10

The Olde Pig Snout Tavern in South Philly was as close to a real home as Kyle had anymore, if home was wherever family could be found. Kyle's father and mother both were dead, he had no siblings, and the only grandparent he ever knew was his mother's disapproving mother, who was now long gone. He was closer to Kat than to anyone else on the planet, but as far as blood went, Kyle had only one family member left, and he could invariably be found drinking away his disability check at the Olde Pig Snout.

"Well, lookie who the hell it is," said Uncle Max as Kyle stepped into the bar. "Yo, Fred, you know my nephew Kyle?"

"Sure," said Fred, the tall, lugubrious man who forever stood behind the bar of the Olde Pig Snout. "How you doing there, Kyle?"

"Good," said Kyle.

"That's good," said Fred. "That's real good. You still playing ball?"

"I was. For Bubba's."

"Good. Are they doing any good?"

"No."

"Good. Anything I can get you?"

"A beer is good."

"On my tab," said Max.

"Good," said Fred.

Conversation was always scintillating at the Olde Pig Snout, a simple corner joint that never seemed to change. The prevailing color was nicotine brown, the hamburgers were always overcooked, the television was always on, the Phillies were always losing. Over the years the clientele had shifted from all white to a mixture of white and black and Vietnamese, a veritable Rainbow Coalition, but this was no great circle of man holding hands and singing "Kumbaya." Because they were at the Olde Pig Snout, and that brought everyone down to the same low level, drinking for the same sad reasons, eating the same overcooked hamburgers. But that night Kyle wasn't there for the burgers.

Ever since the funeral that afternoon, and the conversations with that cop Ramirez and the strange Mr. O'Malley, Kyle had been plagued by questions. Why was Laszlo Toth murdered? Why were questions being asked about Liam Byrne's death? Was there a link between the two? What surprising things about his father's life and death could this O'Malley character really tell him? And what was in that file that O'Malley was seeking so keenly?

They were all mysteries most likely better left shrugged off and forgotten. And who was better at shrugging off questions than Kyle Byrne? Kyle didn't want to steer his life, he wanted to bob in the currents, take in the scenery as he floated here and there. Any idiot could dress to impress, work his ass off, kiss butt and climb that solid and respectable ladder of success, but only a few had the temerity to slack off as baldly as Kyle. He would always sooner spend the afternoon blowing dope and obliterating aliens on the Xbox than pounding the streets in search of the truth.

But there was another Kyle, secret and hidden. This was the Kyle who had run off with the urn holding his father's ashes. This was the Kyle who scanned the obituaries each day and trucked out to cemeteries north and west and south to pay his father's respects. And while all his slacker instincts screamed at him to leave this thing alone, the hole left by his father's death seemed to draw forth an undeniable initiative that annoyed the hell out of him. If the questions were about anyone other than his father, he'd spend the day on Halo, no doubt about it. But they were about his father. And the only person he could talk to who might have a sense of what he'd be getting himself into was his Uncle Max.

"So, to what do I owe the honor of your presence in this crappy little joint?" said Max when the beers had been served and uncle and nephew had repaired to an empty booth by the bathroom door, from which the delicate scent of urine cake seeped into the air about them.

"I just thought I'd stop in to say hello."

Max looked at him for a long moment. "How much you need?"

"Nothing," said Kyle. "For now at least. I actually fell into a small wad, so I'm a bit flush."

"What did you do, rob a bank?"

"Not that flush. How's the back?"

"Who's asking, you or the insurance company?"

"Me."

"Then it sucks. It hurts like a nagging wife kicking a boot into my spine every single day."

"And if it was the insurance company asking?"

"We wouldn't be having this conversation, because I can't no more get out of bed. So what's really going on? What can I do you for?"

Kyle spun his beer slowly. "Remember Laszlo Toth?"

"Your dad's partner. The one that was killed the other night."

"I went to the funeral today."

"It's a shame," said Max. "I mean, it's a shame to waste a nice day like today on that Hungarian piece of crap."

"Maybe, but some weird things happened at the funeral." Kyle leaned forward and in a quiet voice told his uncle about the strange conversations he'd had, first with the cute cop and then with that O'Malley character. Max listened with pursed lips and squinted eyes, like he was visiting the proctologist.

"That's a hell of a funeral," said Max when Kyle finished the story. "So what are you going to do about it?"

"I don't know."

"How cute was the cop?"

"Really cute."

"Still. You know, cops are tricky. Maybe you should let the whole thing die down a bit before you start slamming her with your pecker."

"But it's like all these mysteries have been tossed in my face, and I'm not sure I can let them go. I got to tell you, Max, my head is spinning."

"When that happens, there's only one thing to do," said Max. "Yo, Freddie, two more. And since he's struck it rich, put this round on the kid's tab."

When the beers came, Kyle took a swallow and then, without looking at his uncle, said, "Tell me about my father."

"What's there to tell? Truthfully, I didn't know him much, but even so, I never liked the son of a bitch."

"Why not?"

"Look, all I cared about was my sister, and then you. And this guy, he knocks her up but doesn't marry her, doesn't end up living with her, doesn't spend any time with her or the kid but instead keeps on living with his little French number. In my book a son of a bitch does that to my sister. . . . well, I'm not going to like him."

"Fair enough. What about my mom?"

"Paula? She was dazzled by him. He had big words, big ideas, big emotions, big ambitions, and he was able to con her into thinking she could come along for the ride. She fell in love and never stopped loving. Even after the son of a bitch left her for the last time, she kept missing him."

"You mean left her by dying."

"Yeah, that's what I mean."

"I miss him, too," said Kyle.

"I know you do," said Uncle Max. "And that's another of the things he done that pisses me off."

"Sometimes I wonder how different everything would have been if he hadn't died, you know?"

"All that wondering, it gives you gas, Kyle. It's better to not think about it."

"Maybe, but I can't help feeling that my father's death is at the root of what my life has become. By finding out what happened to him, I can maybe find out what the hell happened to me."

"What the hell's so wrong with you? You're doing okay, aren't you?"

"Look at me, Uncle Max, and tell me I'm doing okay."

Max looked Kyle in the eyes for a moment before his gaze slipped to the right.

"See?" said Kyle.

"Do you really think what happened to Toth had something to do with your father?"

"I don't know."

"It doesn't make any sense that it would."

"You're probably right."

"I mean, he ain't been around for fourteen years."

"I know."

"My guess is there's nothing to it."

"You're probably right."

"So it's best to forget about it."

"I guess so."

"But you're not going to."

"I don't know."

Max pursed his lips and rubbed his bulbous nose, and it looked for a moment like he was really thinking things through, which was strange, because Max never thought things through. Thinking, he always said, only served to stir up the blood. But Max thought it through for a while before lifting his beer to his lips, draining it, and slamming the bottle back onto the table.

"Maybe you got to do what you got to do," he said finally.

"Really?"

"Yeah. Maybe you ought to find out what the hell is going on. Maybe you owe it to your mother. And yourself."

"Why?"

"I don't know, who the hell knows? Did I ever tell you I saw that girl Tricia again?"

"Tricia? Wasn't she the—"

"Yeah."

"The one who blew you off when you were in Vietnam?"

"Yeah, that's her. Tricia, right. So last year I scored some tickets to the ball game, in one of them fancy lounges, and as I'm walking to my seat, I see her. Tricia."

"How'd she look?"

"Pretty good. She always looked pretty good. She didn't look great, mind you—we're all getting older now, and so none of us look all that great, me included— but still she looked . . . pretty damn good."

"It must have been hard."

"You'd think, right? I mean, I got to tell you, that broad she messed me up but good. Enough tears to baptize the whole fricking neighborhood. I mean, I was a mess when I first came back, and that was like the final push. And everything what happened to me along the way after that, I couldn't help thinking it would have been different I was still with Tricia. But then I saw her. And she recognized me, too, so we stopped and chatted."

"And she looked good."

"Yeah, but not that good. And the guy she married, he's a schlub. And she was talking about her kids like they was the most fascinating things in the world. And she was dressed like she was going to church. I mean, it's a ball game. And the schlub, he's dressed, too, like it was her that set out his clothes. And you want to know something, Kyle? After I saw her, and we had our nice little talk, and I said good-bye, and I walked along to my seat, I got to tell you, despite my aching back I had a hop in my step."

"She must not have looked that good."

"No, I'm telling you, she looked good, not great. I mean, compared to the porn, she looked like a fifty-four-year-old in turquoise slacks, but it wasn't that. It was like I had dodged something."

"Okay, Tricia."

"Look, I don't know what I'm saying, but what I'm saying is, sometimes it can do you good to find out the truth."

"Like about my dad."

"To put the legends to rest."

"Okay."

"But where would you even start? What questions would you ask, and who would you be asking?"

"I don't know. I guess I'll start by grabbing hold of that file for that O'Malley fellow and seeing what he has to say."

"Sounds screwy."

"Yes, it does."

"But what could it hurt, right?"

"Okay," said Kyle. "Maybe I'll do it."

"Good."

"Yeah, good." Kyle paused, took a sip, looked at his Uncle Max. Kyle had always felt a little sorry for him, living alone in his mom's old house, drinking his nights away at the Olde Pig Snout, but Kyle wouldn't feel sorry for him anymore. Uncle Max was living the life he chose, which was more than Kyle could say about himself.

Uncle Max caught Kyle staring. "What?" he said.

"Turquoise slacks?"

A slight chuckle. "Yeah."

"Man, oh, man," said Kyle, "that Tricia, she must have looked like shit."

Chapter 11

Liam Byrne had been many things: faithless lover, indifferent father, but more than anything he had been a devoted and passionate lawyer. And the holy of holies within the temple of Liam Byrne was always the office.

Kyle Byrne had often passed the stone town house with the sign bolted to the wall, and his heart had always skipped a beat at seeing his father's name still outlined in raised brass letters on the Byrne & Toth sign. But for all the times he had passed the building, he hadn't once stepped inside. His father had never invited him in while he was alive, and Kyle had never mustered the courage to enter after his father had died. Maybe it was the apprehension of running into the ferocious Laszlo Toth that had kept him at bay. If so, at least that fear had been buried.

So now, instead of staring up at the second-floor windows and wondering what strange and mystical clues to the truth about Liam Byrne lay inside, he moseyed up the stairs, rubbing his finger across his father's name as he passed the sign. A quick yank to open the door, and in he stepped onto sacred ground.

The woman sitting behind the desk of the ground-floor lobby gave him a who-the-hell-are-you look that was so fetching it almost made Kyle forget why he was there.

"Can I help you?" she said.

"Maybe you can," said Kyle, glancing around the fancy room. There were prints of birds on the walls, there was a wood-paneled elevator at the far end with an ornate wooden staircase wrapping around it. Kyle was wearing his usual outfit—cargo shorts, high-top black sneakers, and a ringer T-shirt—and where he usually felt at home in his clothes, here, in his father's territory with its ornate furnishings and its air of officialism, he felt strangely underdressed. He turned his attention back to the woman, who was actually quite beautiful, with short dark hair, big brown eyes, lashes. Suddenly unsure of what he was doing there, he fell into his most comfortable pattern.

"Who do you think are more inherently honest," he said as he leaned an arm on her desk and played out his lines, "men or women?"

"Excuse me?"

"I was having this bet with a friend, and I said women are more inherently honest."

"That's what you said?"

"I'm the trusting sort."

"Well, however much you bet," she said, "it was too much. But if you want me to hold the stakes . . ."

He laughed.

"Is that why you came in?" she said. "To settle a bet?"

"You have something there." He touched his own face as he leaned toward her. "Right there on your cheek. Yeah, that's it. Good. No, I need to see someone from that law firm upstairs."

"Byrne & Toth?"

"That's the one."

"I'm sorry, but the law firm of Byrne & Toth is closed for the time being."

"Vacation?"

"It's a little more serious, I'm afraid. I'm sorry to have to tell you the news, but Mr. Toth passed away."

"Really? How?"

She looked at him with sincere brown eyes. "Heart attack," she said.

"Maybe I am going to lose that bet," said Kyle. "How many lawyers are left working there?"

"Two, but I have strict instructions that there are to be no visitors."

"Why don't you give them a call? My last name is Byrne, as in Liam Byrne, though I'm the son, not the father, seeing as my father is dead. Tell them that the son of Liam Byrne is here to speak with them. That should pique their interest."

A short, sharp-faced man with a barrel chest and small, shiny black shoes came down the stairs to meet him. Kyle had seen him at the Toth funeral, standing behind the grieving widow, looking like a self-important bulldog.

"Hello?" said the man, eyeing Kyle's T-shirt and shorts as if they were an insult. "Mr. Byrne? My name's Ben Malcolm. Can I help you?" It was not a welcoming salutation, *Hello, nice to see you,* more an accusation, *Hello, what the hell are you doing here?* It's always gratifying to get off on the right foot. Kyle instinctively did the calculation. In a fair fight, he could take the man easily, but there was something in this Malcolm's eyes that told him it wouldn't be a fair fight.

"I think I saw you at Mr. Toth's funeral," said Kyle. "You were there with a very attractive woman, if I recall."

"My wife."

"Ahh, good for you. Well done," said Kyle, even as he noticed the receptionist's pretty mouth tighten. "I was hoping you could help me. I have some family matters to clear up, and I need to look through my father's old files to get a grip on things."

Malcolm stared at Kyle like he had two heads. "Your father was Liam Byrne?"

"He was."

"And you want to look through his old files?"

"Exactly," said Kyle.

"To get a grip on things."

"Your English is very good. The lessons must be working. I've got some time now, so I figured you wouldn't mind if I went up and sort of poked around."

"I'm sorry," said Malcolm without sounding very sorry, "but no, you can't poke around. I wasn't here when your father passed away, but I'm sure everything of a personal nature went right to Mrs. Byrne upon your father's death. Is that your mother?"

"Ahh, not exactly."

"Still, maybe you can get what you're looking for from her. But we can't just let you paw through our files. There is confidential matter in each and every one of them. It would be totally improper."

"I don't mean to tell anybody about anything. I just want to look."

"It doesn't matter what you intend, don't you see? What you're asking is impossible. Is there anything specific you're looking for?"

Kyle thought for a moment. The O'Malley file was what he was after, the key to unlock O'Malley's information about his father, but there was something dishonest in Malcolm's gaze, like he was pretending not to care what Kyle was doing there when in fact he cared very much.

"No, nothing specific."

"Then there's nothing we can do for you. After Mr. Toth's death, the firm can't really continue as it is currently constituted. I've already begun a new job and am just helping to close this office down. Any active cases will be given back to the clients, anything inactive will be destroyed."

"Destroyed? Before I can look at them?"

"That's right."

"But there might be something personal in the files that would mean a great deal to me. Emotionally, I mean."

"I'm sure there isn't."

"Can't I just look around? I'm trying to get a better sense of my dad. I didn't know him very well."

"All childhoods are tragic in their way, Mr. Byrne."

"Is there any other—"

"No," said Malcolm, cutting him off. "There is no other option. I'm sorry. Thank you for coming. And thank you for leaving, too."

Kyle tensed his neck for a moment, preparing to get physical, and then he noticed the woman behind the desk, watching the whole thing quite closely, more interested than a disinterested observer. Was there something going on between the two? Kyle wouldn't put it past a pug like Malcolm. So if he decked the little bastard, the receptionist would call the cops, the cops would shove him into handcuffs, and that would be the end of any chance of finding the O'Malley file. On the other hand, it would feel damn good, which was almost reason enough to just haul off and do it.

But he didn't do it. He didn't hit the stonewalling Malcolm in the face or barge right past the lawyer on the way up the stairs or even hold his ground and refuse to move until some accommodation was made. Instead Kyle shrugged, said, "Yeah, okay, whatever," and left, retreated, just walked away.

Walking away had always been his trademark move whenever he faced an obstacle that couldn't be breached. Walk away, find a bar, pound a beer, move on. And it had worked for him in the past, hadn't it? So that was it. The first step was barred, Kyle's old instincts kicked in, and just that quick his little detective play was over. Time to give Skitch a call and get hammered.

And in the lobby the lawyer Malcolm watched with the slightest of smiles as Kyle's demeanor collapsed into weakness and he retreated without a fuss. After Kyle had left, Malcolm gave instructions to the girl at the desk, whom he absolutely was screwing on the side. Then he went upstairs to the offices of Byrne & Toth and placed a call.

Chapter 12

Robert Spangler sat low in his car in the alleyway just south of Locust Street. He had parked within a wide shadow falling upon the cobbled street, so the interior of his car was quite dark. The spot was a bit far from the door he was watching, but this way a glance down the street from that same door would catch the car, yes, but nothing of the man inside, sitting low and waiting. In the shadows. Sometimes it seemed that within every individual moment of his life lay the ghost of the whole.

The call had come sooner than he'd expected. "Bobby dear," she had said over the phone, in a voice that wrapped around his gut like an anaconda, "I thought you said there wouldn't be any problems."

Robert had closed his eyes and felt her disappointment wash over him like a wave of cold seawater. The sensation had become so familiar throughout the course of his life that it was almost comforting, an assurance that the immutable laws of the universe remained safely intact. "What kind of problems?"

"It's the son of that lawyer, the one you took care of so long ago."

"Byrne? Okay. What about him?"

"He's been asking questions. I never liked school much, Bobby, did you know that? All those questions just served to infuriate me. I only wanted answers."

"Where were these questions asked?"

"At the legal offices where you had your meeting with our friend a few nights ago. The son was turned away, thankfully."

"Better had he been let inside."

"Really? Why is that, dear?"

"Because I purposely made contact with the boy and mentioned the O'Malley file. He's simply looking for it as I intended him to."

"But, Bobby dear, why ever in the world would you do something so stupid?"

"Our friend indicated that the lawyer Byrne might have taken some files out of the office before he died. I was concerned the boy might know where they were, so I set him on the trail. But his showing up at the office means he doesn't know anything more than we do."

"Don't get too clever, Bobby. It doesn't suit you."

"My guess is he's given up already. But even if he tries to break in, he'll find nothing and slink off. Either way he won't cause a problem."

"Make sure that he doesn't," she said. "Make sure that he disappears. And don't be afraid of giving him a nudge. This is no time for gentleness." The click of her hanging up on him was like the disapproving cluck of her tongue. No matter how many times he heard it, it never failed to bite.

And it was that bite that chased him here in the middle of the night, here in the shadows, outside the rear door of the building that housed the offices of Byrne & Toth where just a few days before he had killed a man and tasted anew the sweet acid of his obeisance toward her, waiting now for the son of Liam Byrne.

Robert had been impressed by the Byrne boy's size—he was a big, handsome kid with broad shoulders—and admired the way he flirted with the pretty cop, but close up there had been something wet in the eyes and soft in the mouth. Realistically, they didn't have much to fear from such weakness, but it was hard to make her appreciate that. She never understood people, only the geometry of things. The boy was loose, he was a threat, and so she would have her Bobby deal with him. Just a nudge, she had said, a nudge to make him disappear, and Robert knew very well what she meant by that. And even if she didn't expect him to go so far, a nudge might only serve to waken him. And if he did awaken, it would have to end in the same way.

But Robert didn't want to go through it again, didn't want that taste in his mouth anymore. He had thought it through and come up with an idea that might just satisfy them both. Which was why he was here, sitting in the shadows, hoping the boy fell into his little trap.

Wait, there, by the door, what was that? A pair of silhouettes, a flash of something, and then a beam wavering as it directed itself up and down and over and around until it focused on the doorknob and the lock above it.

Robert had to say this for the boy, he had more initiative than Robert had given him credit for. And he hadn't made Robert wait long.

Chapter 13

Skitch was drunk. You could tell by the way he laughed when one of his lock-picking tools fell to the cement in front of the door.

And when Kyle tipped the flashlight down, bent over to help the search for the missing implement, and banged his head into Skitch's—resounding like two coconuts smashing one against the other—you could figure that Kyle was a little drunk, too.

"Ow, bro."

"Dude," said Kyle.

"Just hold the light steady."

"I'm trying. What's taking so long?"

"This lock is just kinda tricky."

"I guess they're all tricky after six beers."

"No, bro, the beer helps. It sensitizes the fingers. What time is it anyway?"

"Two."

"Still early. You want to hit a club after this?"

"Whatever."

"Okay, got it. Now just hold the light steady and stop breathing."

"Breathing?"

"You're breathing too loud. I need to hear the clicks."

"The clicks of the wheels turning in your head?"

"The pins, bro. Now, shut up and hold your breath."

Skitch was squatting on his haunches. His eyes were scrunched closed as he manipulated the picks carefully in the lock of the rear door of the stone building that housed the offices of Byrne & Toth. This wasn't the most brilliant idea, Kyle knew, breaking into a crime scene in which a murder had occurred only a few nights before, especially with the way that cop had questioned Kyle at Laszlo Toth's funeral. But when he told Skitch how that little creep Malcolm with the hot wife had barred him from Kyle's own father's office, Skitch had turned righteously indignant, and no one did righteous indignation better than Skitch. "Bastards," he'd shouted, loud enough to draw stares from all over the bowling alley where they were drinking. And even though Kyle was ready to let the whole thing disappear, after a long bout of fortification with liquid courage and urging by Skitch, he found himself at the rear door of the office building, holding the flashlight as Skitch worked the picks.

You would think it was a fool's errand, waiting on someone like Skitch, drunk no less, to open a locked door, but Skitch had some surprising skills. He could play the "Too Fat Polka" on the accordion. He could wipe out DiNardo's on all-you-can-eat crab night. He had once downed a pack of Mentos and half a quart of Diet Coke at the same time, the calamitous results of which showed up on YouTube and went viral. And—twist, click—he could pick a lock like nobody's business.

"My uncle taught me well," said Skitch.

"What was he, a locksmith?"

"Hell no," said Skitch, still squatting as he slowly pushed the door open. "He's doing time now in West Virginia."

"Isn't family a wonderful thing?" said Kyle. "Are we really going to do this?"

"Hell yes," said Skitch. "This is your father's office. We're not going to let that bastard keep you out."

Kyle stood on the outside of the now-open door, peering through the doorway, wondering at what kinds of feral creatures from his past might lurk there. With a push from Skitch, he stumbled through the doorway. Inside, he took a deep breath, tried to sense his father's ancient mélange of aromas, smelled only dust and cleaning fluid. Skitch, still squatting, waddled in after him and closed the door.

"Keep the flashlight off for now," said Skitch. "Nothing looks more suspicious than the beam of a flashlight waving around. You said second floor, right?"

"There are stairs next to the elevator. I think the lobby's this— Ow! Fricking box."

"Go slow, bro. Be one with the hall and feel your way."

"One with the hall," said Kyle. "I am the hall. Okay, follow me."

Kyle put his arms in front of him and slowly felt his way along the corridor, moving as quietly as possible. Behind him, Skitch sounded like a drunken mariachi band, banging here, cursing there, tripping his way forward.

The faintest hint of light slipped around the thin edges of a doorframe just ahead of Kyle. He reached out until he felt the wood, lowered his hand to the knob, opened the door, and stepped into the front lobby, where he had been so rudely rebuffed the morning before. Light brushed faintly through the gauze-covered windows, illuminating the space enough so that Kyle could get his bearings. The door there, the reception desk there, the elevator and stairs there.

"Up this way," said Kyle, heading past the gleam from the ornate elevator door and toward the stairs.

Slowly he creaked up the staircase, rising higher toward his father's old office. And as he did, he began to feel anxious and deprived, as though he were trespassing on his father's oh-so-important life. He felt like an afterthought, like a mistake. It was as if with each rising step the years were peeling away. Until finally, almost at the top of the steps, when he had devolved into the twelve-year-old he had been at his father's funeral, he stopped, dead.

"Whoa," said Skitch. "What's going on?"

"I don't know," said Kyle. "I feel weird."

"Just don't hurl on the floor, bro. Bad form."

Skitch climbed past him up the stairs, turned the corner into the office, and flicked on the light switch. A painful brightness poured down the stairs.

"What the hell are you doing?" said Kyle.

"I'm trying to see."

"We're breaking in, you idiot."

"No, we've broken in, and we've entered. Those were the crimes. Now we're just here. If the lights are on, it looks like we're working late. If the lights are off, we'll be banging into things like the blind Barko sisters."

"The blind Barko sisters?"

"Don't ask, but trust me when I tell you they are loads of fun. Are you coming up?"

Kyle took a deep breath and then climbed the rest of the stairs, until he was there, in his father's old law office, the suite of Byrne & Toth. Not much to see, actually, and quite the disappointment. He didn't know exactly what he'd expected, something closer to Kat's opulent offices, maybe, someplace where it made sense for Liam Byrne to want to spend his life rather than with his son. But it wasn't luxurious or grand, it didn't echo with great import. It was just a shabby set of offices with old furniture and dingy walls. A pile of white boxes with the name of a document-storage company leaned against one of the walls.

"This is where that old Toth guy got it, right?" said Skitch.

"That's right," said Kyle. "In one of these offices."

"Yowza."

"Probably that one over there," said Kyle. "My mother mentioned once that my dad had the corner office. She worked here as a secretary until they hooked up. Then, after my father died, Toth took it over until . . ."

"Yeah, okay. Bang-bang. Now what?"

"Now I guess we look around," said Kyle. "We're looking for an old file, the O'Malley file."

"What's in it?"

"I don't know, but this O'Malley guy is looking for it, and he promised if he got it, he had something to tell me about my father. Why don't you check the boxes, and I'll go through the offices checking out the desks and file cabinets."

While Skitch rummaged through the boxes as noiselessly as a raccoon in a metal trash can, Kyle went office to office, opening small file cabinets, desk drawers, seeking something, anything, bearing the name O'Malley. Nothing. But with each drawer he looked in, each file name he skimmed past, he felt a strange deflation. As if some vault within him were being emptied out. This sad, dust-ridden office was so different from what he had imagined for so long, it was as if whole swaths of his childhood landscape were being altered.

He stepped into the corner office, Toth's office, and stood there for a moment, trying to imagine what it might have been like fourteen years ago when his father had held court in that same space. He closed his eyes, spun around slowly, tried to feel his father's presence. The white hair, the rough voice, the cigarette smoke and spicy cologne that always enveloped him like a fog. Dad, where are you, Dad?

"I finished with the boxes," said Skitch from the doorway to the office, "and look what I found."

Kyle snapped open his eyes, saw Skitch holding a file. "O'Malley?"

"Nah. Sorrentino."

"Sorrentino?"

"Anthony Sorrentino. 'Tiny Tony' Sorrentino? Bookmaker extraordinaire. Half the city has placed bets with Tiny Tony, me included. Every time the Eagles lose, he buys another Buick. And this, this here is his last will and testament."

"So?"

"So it's interesting, is all. The last will and testament of Tiny Tony Sorrentino. Probably leaves a load to Kotite. And look, in the file with the will is a bunch of betting slips. Old stuff."

"Let me see." Kyle took hold of the file, looked through it. The will was dated just months before his father died, and it had his father's signature on it, along with the John Hancock of this Anthony Sorrentino. The betting slips were also old, old enough to be anyone's. So who was betting? His father? Toth? Did that have anything to do with what had happened to Toth? Or his father?

"Anything else with Sorrentino's name on it?"

"No, but the will was in the middle of a batch of files about some company."

"What was the name?"

"Double Eye, I think it was. Double Eye Investments."

"Keep that file for me," said Kyle. "You find anything else?"

"There's a storage room around the corner with some old metal file cabinets. I looked through what I could. No O'Malley."

"What do you mean you looked through what you could?"

"There was one file cabinet, and then a gap with some boxes, and then a couple more. From the case numbers on the drawers, it looks like one cabinet is missing."

"Okay, I'll be there in a sec. Let me finish looking through here first."

Kyle did a quick search of Toth's office, the drawers, the low wooden file cabinets. He glanced out the window, and a flash of dim light caught his gaze. But when he realized it was just a gleam of a streetlight on a metal sign, he was strangely disappointed. What had he expected to see on the Locust Street sidewalk, a mop of gray hair?

In the storage room, it was the old file cabinets that drew Kyle's interest. They were metal and brown, with fake wood grain, and seemed designed solely to hold documents of great import. He walked up to one. The lock in the upper right corner was sticking out, with a key inside. He opened a drawer filled with old, tightly packed files. He thumbed through them rapidly. No O'Malley. He closed the drawer and stepped back and stared.

"See," said Skitch, pointing to a gap.

"Yeah, I see," said Kyle. "So one is missing."

Kyle thought for a moment. Where would his father have put a file cabinet? He was trying to think it through when he heard something faint, and then not so faint.

The push of a door opening, the patter of shoes across the floor below. Kyle quickly turned to Skitch. Skitch stared back, his eyes widening.

"I guess turning on the lights wasn't the best idea," said Skitch softly, even as a shout rose like an explosion up the twisting stairs.

"Police."

Chapter 14

Detectives Henderson and Ramirez stood side by side in front of the wide one-way mirror that allowed a clear view inside the green interrogation room. Kyle Byrne slumped in a chair across a table, facing them without being able to see them. The partners stood quietly for a moment, observing two very different scenes.

Ramirez saw a man fighting to control his fear, someone aware that he was being stared at and trying a little too hard not to look concerned, a clever liar trying to fake his way out of a bad situation. But to Henderson, Kyle Byrne seemed neither nervous nor scared. He didn't look like someone who was racked with doubt after having been arrested for burglary and while being held at the Roundhouse on suspicion of murder. He just looked bored.

"Doesn't seem too worried, does he?" said Henderson, pulling at the gray hairs growing out of his ear.

"He's trying very hard not to."

The man in the interrogation room stretched in his chair, yawned, lolled his head across the back of the chair.

"And doing a damn good job of it," said Henderson.

Byrne had given himself up as the uniforms climbed the stairs with guns drawn. His hands were raised, he was smiling weakly, he said, "Don't shoot. My name's Kyle Byrne. I'm not trespassing. This is my father's office." He was alone, the cops said, and they found nothing on him other than a wallet, which confirmed his identity, and a flashlight. No gun, no contraband, no lock-picking tools, nothing but a few bucks and some loose change. He was so amiable and so nonthreatening that the uniforms had only cuffed him in strict compliance with procedure.

"I would have thought you'd be more excited, Henderson, seeing all your old saws come to fruition. First he attends the funeral of the victim, next he returns to the scene of the crime."

"That makes him guilty of stupidity, not much more."

"It's a start," said Ramirez. "I thought you said old saws still cut?"

"I did, but then again, sometimes old saws are too rusty to be of much use. Has he asked for a lawyer?"

"Not yet."

"He call anyone?"

"No."

"Who notified us?"

"Anonymous call from a pay phone."

"Pay phone, huh? Those things still around?"

"Apparently."

"What did he say he was doing in there?"

"Visiting his father's old office before they shut it down. Looking for something to remember his father by. A keepsake or such. Sounds a bit demented if you ask me."

"You get along with your father, Ramirez?"

"I did, at least when he wasn't drinking. He died when I was in high school."

"How did it make you feel?"

"It hurt, and then I got over it."

"And now you don't feel abandoned, betrayed, bitter?"

"I feel nothing," she said. "Let me do him alone. We started building a rapport at the funeral—until he figured I was a cop. Give me half an hour and I'll push him into coming clean."

"That's the problem with your technique right there. Rapport is fine, but pushing's good for giving birth and not much else. Does he know we can't hold him for the burglary?"

"Not yet, and I don't want to tell him before we have to."

"I'm not surprised the landlord won't press charges. He's had enough bad publicity over the murder, and he's going to have to rent the place soon. But what was Mrs. Toth's excuse?"

"She said she felt sorry for him," said Ramirez. "Said her husband was such a skinflint he refused to give the kid a break even though he'd promised to financially support the mother."

"I guess she got over her fit of weeping at the funeral."

"Maybe we can change her mind by telling her the boy is a suspect in her husband's murder."

"Is that what he is?"

"What do you think?" said Ramirez.

Henderson looked at Kyle as he sat slumped in a strange quiescence. There was something lost and yet full of serene acceptance in his expression, as if he had no idea of what was going on and found the situation both familiar and comforting.

"I think he's a confused kid who misses his dad," said Henderson.

"You've gotten soft over the years."

"Maybe I have. But before you finger a man for murder, you ought at least to have some reasonable motive."

"Like the widow said, this Toth had promised to make payments from the law firm to the kid and his mother after the father's death, then reneged. Maybe it was revenge. Or maybe he just broke in for that keepsake he was looking for and found the victim in the office working late and panicked."

"And he looks like the panicky type to you."

"No need to get wise. We still haven't gotten a straight answer about how this Liam Byrne died. Maybe Toth was somehow involved, maybe the Byrne boy found out how, maybe he decided on a little payback."

"Why now?"

"Why not? And if he did do the shooting, it could certainly explain why he was in the office last night. If he lost something accidentally during the shooting, something that could connect him to the murder, he'd have to come back to find it. Like that cuff link we found under Toth's desk."

Henderson eyed Byrne's ragged T-shirt. "He look like a cuff-link kind of guy to you?"

"He was wearing a suit at the funeral."

"What kind of shirt?"

Ramirez thought for a moment and then frowned. "Button-down oxford."

"Good for you," said Henderson. "You might make a detective yet."

"Screw off, old man. Whether you like it or not, I'm here already. And what the hell did you mean about a problem with my interrogation technique? My interrogation technique is spot-on, it's legendary, it's why the brass put me here."

"To learn, maybe. You can't go in trying to bully a suspect, unless you want him to close like a clam. You have to care about him as a human being."

She snorted. "I can pretend to care with the best of them."

"No, see, that's just it. It's not a parlor trick, not a technique. You have to really care."

"They're scumbags."

"Most of them, yeah, but before they became scumbags, they were somebody's little boy, somebody's best friend. That's all still somewhere inside. This kid has been missing his father since he was twelve. That did something to him, and he's just looking for someone to tell it to. But he's not going to tell it unless he believes you care."

"Oh, I care, all right."

"About him? As a human being? Because what happened in that office wasn't just about a victim. You ever shoot that gun of yours, Ramirez? You ever kill anyone?"

"Not yet."

"You sound like you're looking forward to it."

"I'm ready to do what I need to do."

"I don't think anyone's ever ready for that."

"What's the point, old man?"

"Whoever pulled the trigger in that office, he didn't just kill Toth, he killed a part of himself, too. You can't forget that. The killer needs to pay a price, but he's hurting about what he did. You want answers, you got to be able to weep for them both."

"I do my weeping at the movies," said Ramirez. "Can I get on with it?"

Henderson stared at her for a long moment, wondering when the newbies got so young, thinking for the hundredth time about retirement, and then said, "Knock yourself out."

Chapter 15

Ramirez sat down across from Kyle Byrne. His eyes were sleepy. He smiled at her, like she was merely paying him a friendly visit.

"Well, now," he said. "This is quite a coincidence. Here I was, thinking about you, and bam, just like that you show up."

"Thinking about me?" said Ramirez.

"Yeah, sure. Ramirez, right?"

"That's right."

"I'm sorry, I forgot your first name."

"Detective."

"Wow, your mother must have been psychic or something. But I was thinking about your smile."

"My smile?"

"And the way things ended a little awkward between us last time. When I got pulled in here, I was hoping that you'd show up so I could apologize for being kind of short with you at the end of our conversation. It was just the questions you were asking, like I was a murder suspect or something, and it all being done at a cemetery, somehow it seemed a little too strange."

"And it's not too strange now, you and me across a table in an interrogation room at police headquarters."

Kyle Byrne sat up a bit, looked around. "Is that what this is? I thought it was just a waiting room, though I did wonder about the mirror over there. And why there were no vending machines. I didn't have any breakfast and could sure go for a sack of Doritos right about now."

She stared at him for a moment, was taken in somewhat by his smile. He was a charmer, the cocky bastard. Time to get a little hard, to wipe the smirk off his face.

"How did you get into Byrne & Toth's building this morning, Mr. Byrne?" she said.

"Call me Kyle."

"Just answer the question."

"Through the back door."

"The landlord assures us that the door was locked. He checked it himself. He's been understandably careful since the murder."

"I guess he wasn't careful enough."

"Do you have any experience picking locks?"

"You mean, like, with a paper clip?"

"Or lock-picking tools."

"No, but I always wanted to learn. That and nunchucks. I always wanted to learn that nunchuck thing, too. Whap-whap-whap. Do they teach you guys that?"

"There were scratch marks around the metal of the lock, as if it had been picked, sloppily. As if it had been picked by someone who'd been drinking. Do you know how the marks got there?"

"Maybe a drunk trying to stick in a key."

"Were you drinking last night?"

"What was it, a Wednesday night?"

"Yes."

"Then I probably was. But really, all I did was open the door."

"And waltzed in."

"Something like that, yeah. Do you dance, Detective? Because sometimes they have some pretty good bands at the North Star up on Poplar, and I was wondering if maybe you'd—"

"Is that how you slipped in the time before, through that same door?"

"What time before?"

"Friday night."

"Friday night? Isn't that when Mr. Toth was killed?"

"That's right. If you come clean now, I can make things easier for you. I'll put in a word with the D.A."

"And what word would that be? Doritos? Because that's the only thing I would want right now from a D.A. Until Mr. Toth's funeral, I hadn't been anywhere near him since right after my father died. And you want to know why?"

"Sure," she said, leaning forward.

"Because he scared the crap out of me. That old man was like the ogre in my dreams. When other kids were certain that furry green monsters were hiding in their closets, I was certain it was Laszlo Toth."

"And that's why you killed him?"

Kyle laughed. "No, that's why I stayed the hell away from him. But if I'm your best suspect, then I guess you're not having much luck with your investigation."

Ramirez stared at Kyle Byrne for a moment, caught the glitter of a smile in his eyes, then looked down at the file. Truth was, they weren't having much luck. They hadn't yet found the missing watch or computer screens, hadn't yet found the murder weapon or anything else that might help.

"Do you own a tuxedo, Mr. Byrne?"

"Why? Are you inviting me to some Policeman's Benevolent ball? If so, I could rent."

"Do you have any shirts with French cuffs?"

"No, but I have a dickey."

"A what?"

"You know, one of those turtleneck collars that go under a shirt."

She stared at him for a moment more and then turned to the mirror. She couldn't peer through it, but she didn't have to see Henderson's face to know he was laughing. She would have bet that old bastard had a whole drawerful of dickeys. Care, he had said, about the person. And against all odds, she did sort of like this kid. She glanced again at the mirror and then stood and pulled her chair around until she was sitting catty-corner to Byrne.

"It's Father's Day this weekend," she said.

"Is it?"

"Do you get lonely every year on Father's Day, Kyle?"

"Not really. I celebrate in the usual way, I suppose. I throw a ball to myself in the yard, tousle my hair a bit, play a game of Stratego with myself. And then, when I misbehave, I tell myself I've been bad and send myself to bed without dinner. It's all warm and fuzzy."

"Tell me about your dad."

"What's there to tell? I was his bastard son. He pretty much ignored me when he was alive. And then he died."

"How?"

"Heart attack."

"Where?"

"Jersey, I think."

"Did you blame Toth for what happened to him?"

"No, why would I? Did he have anything to do with it?"

"I'm asking you."

"And I'm asking you. Do you have any information linking Laszlo Toth to my father's death?"

"No."

"My dad was old already when he met my mom. It was bound to happen sooner or later. It just happened sooner, is all."

"So what were you doing in that office last night?"

"Looking for him, I suppose."

"Kyle?" Her hand slipped atop his. The gesture was calculated, she meant to show her concern as this Byrne tried to open up. But funny, it didn't feel calculated. It felt good, real.

"I don't know how to explain it," said Kyle. "How's your dad doing?"

"He's dead."

"So you understand."

"No, not really."

"Yes you do, you just don't want to admit it. I didn't get a chance to work out everything I needed to work out between him and me."

"Work out what?"

"I don't know. The father-son thing. The what's-going-on-in-the-world thing. The meaning-of-life thing. Isn't that what fathers tell you? I've always felt as if part of my answer is missing and everything else is just frozen while I search for it. I hoped I might find some answers in that office."

"Were they there?"

"No." He reached up and scratched his cheek. "You have something there. A little something—no, not there." He reached up, brushed her cheek with his thumb, rubbed his thumb clean with his other fingers. "There."

"Is it gone?"

"Yeah. The whole time you were asking all those questions, it was bothering me. Like a car crash, it was hard to take my eyes off it."

She was still feeling the rub of his thumb on her cheek when the interrogation door opened and Henderson came in, accompanied by a beautiful Korean woman in a business suit. Ramirez yanked her hand from atop Kyle's, yanked it away almost guiltily, as the woman in the suit tossed a card onto the table.

"Detective Ramirez, my name is Shin," said the woman, "Katie Shin, from the law firm of Talbott, Kittredge and Chase. I'll be representing Mr. Byrne."

"Yo, Kat, what's happening?" said Kyle.

"Shut up," said Shin.

"Okay."

"My understanding is that Mr. Byrne was found within his father's old office and that neither the landlord nor the tenant's widow, who is now holder of the lease, is pressing charges. Is that correct?"

"Possibly."

"Then why is Mr. Byrne still being held?"

"We were just talking, Kat, no biggie," said Kyle.

"What did I say?"

Kyle zipped up his lips.

"The talking has ended, right now," said Shin. "There will be no more talking. Are you charging him with anything, Detective?"

"Not at the moment," said Ramirez.

"And is he free to leave?"

"He's always been free to leave."

"Good, then we'll both say good-bye."

"Breakfast at Snow White?" said Kyle.

"If you want," said Kat.

Kyle stood up, leaned toward Ramirez. "It was really a pleasure talking to you, Detective. You have your own father thing to work out, I can tell. We don't have to do the dancing if that makes you feel awkward. Not everyone is comfortable with their body. Maybe we can just have a drink and talk. If you want to write down your number, I could give you a call."

"I'm not that thirsty," said Ramirez. "Keep out of trouble."

"That's my life's goal."

"No, I'm serious," said Ramirez. "And don't leave town, please."

"Don't you worry, Detective. Now that I know I'm a suspect in a real live actual murder case, I'm going to watch my every little step. But if you want to keep your eye on me, that's fine. That's more than fine."

"Kyle," said Katie Shin. "Are you actually flirting with the detective who locked you in this room in abject violation of your rights?"

"Well, yes," said Kyle. "Why? Is that wrong?"

"I'm so sorry, Detective," said the lawyer. "I'm sure he didn't mean to offend."

"No offense taken," said Ramirez.

"Come on, Kyle," said the lawyer, "let's get the hell out of here."

Ramirez stood as Kyle Byrne and his cheeky lawyer headed out of the room. Henderson had watched the whole thing with evident amusement.

"You sure broke him into little pieces," said Henderson when Byrne and his lawyer had left and the door was closed behind them. "But putting your hand on his, that was good. Just think how far you would have gotten if you meant it."

"He's lying about how he got into that office," said Ramirez.

"Of course he's lying."

"And how did this Katie Shin even know he was here?"

"Talbott, Kittredge and Chase. A bit high-toned for an unemployed slacker accused of burglary."

Ramirez picked up the card. " 'Katie Shin,' " she read. " 'Tax department.' "

Henderson laughed. "A friend."

"Or a girlfriend."

"Maybe, but a friend who was called by someone other than our boy. Which means Kyle Byrne wasn't alone in that office. Somebody picked the lock for him. Maybe the other guy was waiting outside after he opened the door. Maybe he was inside and our uniforms missed him. Or maybe it was Katie Shin herself. But it doesn't matter, the kid won't talk to us anymore."

"Oh, he'll talk," said Ramirez. "He can't wait to talk."

"You going to do some dancing?"

"Maybe. If only to piss off the lawyer girlfriend. But he didn't have anything to do with the killing, did he?"

"No."

"So we're back to my drug-addict-and-open-door theory," said Ramirez.

"That's a little simplistic, don't you think? Falling back on Occam's razor."

"Say what?"

"Where'd you get your diploma, Ramirez, Wal-Mart? Occam's razor is a philosophical principle which holds that, all things being equal, the simplest solution tends to be the correct one."

"Oh, yeah? Sounds good to me. What precinct does this Occam work, and does he need a partner? Because he sounds like someone I might actually be able to learn something from."

Chapter 16

Across the street from the Snow White Diner, on the corner of Second and Market, another old restaurant had been tarted up into a swinging nightspot called The Continental, bringing in hip urban sophisticates and high-living suburbanites. But Snow White remained what it had been for decades, a greasy little greasy spoon with coral vinyl upholstery and spinning stools at the counter. Rumor had it Ben Franklin ate scrapple there. The way Kyle figured, compared with the stylishly coiffed, high-heeled nightspot across the street, Snow White was like a decrepit old aunt with a bent back and support hose, snapping her gum as she rubbed her sore feet.

Which sort of described the joint's waitresses.

"Here you are, hon," said one of those waitresses, sliding a plate in front of Kyle piled with eggs, over easy, hold the wiggle, home fries, grilled sausage, rye toast. She put a toasted English muffin in front of Kat. "More coffee, dears?"

"Sure," said Kat.

"She'll have it shaken, not stirred," said Kyle with a sly smile.

The waitress looked at Kyle for a moment with one eye closed and then made her slow, arthritic way back to the counter.

"Don't deny it," said Kyle as he tucked into his breakfast. "You are so Bond. 'Shin, Katie Shin.' That cop's expression was perfect, the way her jaw dropped as you said it. 'Shin, Katie Shin.'"

"I don't have much time," said Kat, grabbing for a jelly packet from the dispenser. "I'm meeting a client this morning."

"But it's Saturday."

"The capitalist engine never sleeps."

"I thought we could do the hang today, take a run, maybe catch a movie on cable."

"Don't complain about my job too much. It pays for the apartment and the cable."

"Skitch could get you your cable for free."

"No thanks, I'll keep the job. And it puts me in a position to yank your butt out of a sling whenever I need to, like this morning."

"Yeah, well, thank you for that." Kyle looked up from his eggs, grinned. "Just when I was about to score."

"Was she rough on you?"

"She tried to be."

"Did you pull your routine on her?"

"I told her she had nice eyes, if that's what you mean."

"How big an idiot are you?"

"But she does."

"She hauls you into an interrogation room for questioning about a murder and you think you're playing tonsil hockey at a pickup bar."

"I don't know, there's something about a girl with a gun."

"You're into muzzles, go gay, it's safer."

"How'd you even know I was there?" said Kyle.

"Skitch. What the hell were you doing teaming up with that moron to break into your dad's old office anyway?"

"It seemed like a good idea at the time."

"There's your mistake right there. Anything hatched with Skitch around is not a good idea. Skitch is a good-idea-free zone."

"Skitch is all right."

"He's not a bad guy, he can't help himself. But really, right now, with the cops looking hard at you in relation to a murder, he's not who you want to be hanging with. Besides, I think he's into something he shouldn't be. After he woke me up with news of your arrest, he started talking about this deal he's working on and offered me an equity position."

"Equity?"

"And he was talking a bit fast, like he was a little more desperate than he wanted to let on."

"Don't give him anything."

"Don't worry, I'm not. It was just . . . uncomfortable."

"I'll tell him to back off."

"Good. Are you coming Sunday?"

"Nah."

"Please. My dad would love to see you." She paused, looked down at her coffee. "And my mother wants you to come, too."

"Liar."

"No, really. She's making her famous jangeo-gui just for you."

"For me?"

"Well, maybe not just for you."

"What is it?"

"Broiled eel."

"You're cute, but I'm going to pass. You know how I get at these Father's Day things, seeing as I don't really have one. And your mom will always hate me for that time I got you suspended in middle school."

"That was ages ago. She's over it."

"No she's not. Your mom holds grudges like banks hold cash."

"True."

"It's actually one of her best features. Instead I think I'll just ingest something really bad for me, watch the ball game on TV, and pass out clutching the remote."

"You are such a model for the young people of our city. And you're also going to ignore my legal advice, I assume, when I tell you no more breaking into offices, no more flirting with cops."

"But you saw her."

"I don't care."

"And I think she likes me. You want some sausage?"

"Just what I need, sausage breath when in an hour I'll be huddling with the CFO of a Fortune 500 company with offshore-tax issues."

"Shin, Katie Shin."

"It's time for you to stop the joking, Kyle, stop screwing up, stop playing at detective. You're in the middle of a murder investigation. This is turning serious."

Kyle glanced down at his plate, shoveled some egg and potato onto his toast, took a bite.

"No answer?" said Kat. "You're not going to tell me to go to hell?"

"Go to hell."

"Feel good?"

"Yes, actually," said Kyle. "And screw yourself. That felt good, too."

"But you're not going to stop."

"Doesn't it seem strange that this pretty cop keeps asking me how my father died and I don't have any real answers? Maybe I should find out what I can before it's too late?"

"Too late for what?"

"For the answers to still be there. Laszlo Toth is already dead. Who else is going to disappear before I learn the truth?"

"Your father died from a heart attack. They cremated his body. You still have some of the ashes in that bubble-gum box you've been holding since you were twelve."

"Don't you think I should get to the bottom of the whole thing right now?"

"I think you've reached it, baby." Pause. "So what are you going to do?"

"There was a file cabinet missing from my dad's office. I think my dad might have taken it before he died and a file might be in it that has some answers. I'm going to find it."

"Any idea where it might be?"

"Yeah, one. But checking it out would be like marching naked into the den of Godzilla. Frankly, I don't have the guts for it."

"So what are you going to do?"

"I'm sending in Skitch."

Chapter 17

Laszlo Toth might have been the ogre in Kyle Byrne's closet, but he was only the second-most ferocious of Kyle's demons. Number one lived in a house on Panama Street.

Kyle sat in his battered red sports car on Panama, tapping his fingers nervously on the steering wheel. He was parked well away from the house, but even so, being this close terrified the hell out of him. He was overwhelmed with the fear that a harpy with huge breasts and saber claws would fly out of that house, pull him from that car by his cheek, tear into his flesh with serrated teeth and bloodstained lips. "A boy like you," the creature would screech in her bizarre French accent, "has no place here."

As soon as he saw Skitch walk nonchalantly out of the house of horrors and saunter toward the car,

Kyle turned the key and ignited the engine. As soon as Skitch opened the passenger door, Kyle shifted into gear. Before Skitch could even close the door behind him, Kyle popped the clutch, sending the car bucking away and slamming Skitch's head into the headrest. The balding tires squealed like two frightened cats.

"Yo, what's the rush?" shouted Skitch.

"I had to get the hell away from there before she came out and ate my liver."

"Who, the sweet old French lady?"

"Don't even try. I could feel the evil emanating from that house. It was like the Eye of Mordor was staring at me."

"Old Tommy is right. You are such a pussy."

"I don't deny it."

"And you got her all wrong. Cissy's a doll."

"Cissy?"

"She even made me tea."

"Cissy?"

"Chamomile."

"Boiled newt brains, most likely."

"And there were sugar cookies."

"Sugar cookies? Dude, listen to yourself. You've been lured to the dark side by sugar cookies. Next thing you know, your skin will decay and you'll be breathing out of a black mask."

"I had a Darth Vader mask for Halloween once. I spent the whole night saying 'Luke, you have my candy.' I was so annoying they gave me double just to get rid of me. You know she's married."

"To my dad."

"No, she remarried. Her husband was there, too. Sid. Nice guy."

"I don't believe any of this."

"No, he was. He had big brown shoes and was wearing a cardigan. She seemed—and I know you don't want to hear this—she seemed okay."

"Shut up."

"I actually liked her. And let me tell you, if she was twenty years younger, I'd do her."

"Please, shut up, before I puke in my bucket seat. What did you find out?"

"It's not there."

"How do you know?"

"Because she told me."

"And you believed her?"

"Cissy wouldn't lie."

"Did you look around, search the basement or something?"

"I was too busy eating cookies. They were soft, just like I like them, and big as grapefruit."

"Dude."

"I love cookies. *Cooookies.* But I believed her. I gave her the whole O'Malley speech, like you told me to, and—get this—I wasn't the first O'Malley to knock at the door. There was another O'Malley before me, looking for the same damn file cabinet."

"Son of a bitch beat me to it. When?"

"Before the funeral."

"So the real O'Malley came to me after he couldn't find his precious file here. Okay, now I see. Maybe it's not there after all. You get anything else?"

"Well, she remembered something she hadn't told the real O'Malley. She said her husband did have a business relationship with someone outside of his legal office. It wasn't law, it was real estate. She said if the file cabinet wasn't in the law office, she thought maybe it could be with the partner."

"Who the hell was that?"

"Guess."

Chapter 18

Kyle's car was an old red Datsun 280ZX, with a ripped leather interior, an engine spewing oil smoke, and brakes that wailed like the lamentations of barbarian women. Kyle's head brushed the car's roof, one shoulder of his T-shirt rubbed against the door, the other banged into Skitch, and the oil smoke that leaked into the interior made him slightly ill. Not much to brag about, but Kyle's car was the last thing of value he still owned in this world, and he loved it. He had no job, no girl, no real money, no place of his own, no plans for the future, but by golly by gee he had that car, and in a way it was almost enough.

"How much farther?" said Kyle as he and Skitch headed into the heart of South Philly.

"Just a few blocks," said Skitch. "So will you talk to Kat for me?"

"No."

"This thing we got is going to go gangbusters, and I thought with all the money she's pulling in from that law firm, she might want to get in on the ground floor."

"She's not interested," said Kyle. "And you need to stop asking her."

"All I'm saying," said Skitch, "is it's a great opportunity."

"Dude, get it through your lead-plated skull, she's not interested. Kat's never going to be interested in any of your slimy little get-rich-quick schemes."

"That's harsh, bro."

"But true."

"Maybe, but at least I'm in there pitching. It's easy enough to sit back and smile and let the world collapse around you. When do you ever take a chance on anything?"

"I take my chances, but I'm never going to be like you, dude, chasing money like a greyhound chasing that fake rabbit."

"But you're not chasing anything, except your father's ghost, and that's just sad. I'm only trying to get a step up here. I won't be slaving for Comcast the rest of my life, that's for sure. And it's a legit thing, almost. Talk to her, please?"

"No."

"Bro."

"She's not a frigging bank."

"I guess not for the general public."

"What the hell does that mean?"

"It's not like you don't use her as your own personal ATM."

"Screw off."

"I only mean—"

"I know what the hell you mean," said Kyle as something flitted red in front of his eyes and the world slowed down into discrete moments. Without moving a muscle, he felt Skitch's thick neck being throttled in his own tensed hands, saw Skitch's beady eyes bulge and his tongue stretch out of his gaping mouth like a poodle's.

But even as he imagined the sweet pleasure of the throttling, Kyle felt a wave of shame wash through him, not just because he was about to choke his friend to near asphyxiation but because he knew that Skitch was absolutely right. He was using Kat as a bank, and even though his relationship with Kat had roots deeper than Skitch could fathom, the truth of it still made Kyle feel small and angry. There was a moment when Kyle almost lost control, but he regained it again and let the conflicting emotions wash over him and through him, and then he calmed the storm with his all-purpose verbal shrug.

"Whatever," said Kyle.

"Okay, yeah, forget I even said it," said Skitch. "There it is, over there."

On the left they passed a small, squalid storefront with a couple of poorly dressed men sitting on the sidewalk on lawn chairs. The men were squinty and overweight, the chairs seemed to gasp under their bulk, and they were situated on either side of the open front door, like the lions at the New York Public Library. A couple of squinty, overweight lions with arms like legs. Painted roughly on the plate-glass window were the words TINY TONY'S TICKET BROKERAGE, with rough approximations of the emblems of Philadelphia's four professional sporting teams underneath. The Phillies' logo was the psychedelic maroon *P* abandoned by the team during Kyle's childhood.

"A friendly-looking crew," said Kyle.

"Are you sure you want to do this?" said Skitch. "I mean, Tony's outfit, they generally put the little guys out front. How are you going to get past those bulls?"

"Hopefully, that file you found in my dad's office will be the ticket. I still don't know how you squeezed yourself behind those boxes in the storage room before the cops came in."

"It wasn't easy, trust me. I still have an old subpoena up my ass. Maybe you shouldn't go in alone. Maybe you ought to have someone on your wing."

"You volunteering?"

"I was thinking you might want to give Bubba Jr. a call."

"I'll park around the corner," said Kyle. "Wait for me."

After Kyle parked, he slipped out of the car and stretched, the file Skitch had taken from the offices of Byrne & Toth in his right hand. He gave the contents a quick look, the last will and testament of Anthony Sorrentino and a pile of betting slips. Satisfied, he tapped the file on the hood of the car and made his way around the corner.

"Can I help youse?" said one of the big, squinty men in front of Tiny Tony's Ticket Brokerage.

"Maybe you can," said Kyle. "Is Mr. Sorrentino in by any chance?"

"You looking to buy some tickets?"

"No."

"You looking to sell some tickets?"

"Not that either."

"Then, mister, believe me when I tell you, you is very much in the wrong place."

"Nah, I think this is right. Do you know where Mr. Sorrentino might be?"

"Pawtucket," said the second man. "Or maybe Piscataway. I get them two confused."

"Anybody send you?" said the first.

"Nobody sent me."

"Then why are you here?"

"I have something from my father for Mr. Sorrentino."

"Yeah? Why don't you give it here, and I'll make sure it's delivered."

"I need to give it to Mr. Sorrentino personally. Just tell him that Liam Byrne's son is here."

"I never hearda this Liam Byrne, and I already told you he ain't in."

"He's in Cleveland," said the second man. "Or maybe Cincinnati. I get them two confused also."

"You seem to be confused a lot," said Kyle.

"Well, life's like that, innit? We find ourselves in situations all the time, without knowing how we got there in the first place or what we should do. Look at yourself, for instance."

"Why don't I just go inside and see if Mr. Sorrentino's there?" said Kyle.

"Why don't we just pound on your head until your ears bleed?" said the first man.

"Why don't you try?" said Kyle.

"Wrong answer," said the man as he shook his head with a resigned sadness. Slowly he rose from out of the lawn chair and stood in front of the door, his arms crossed. "This is a private business, and we don't do business with somebody nobody sent."

Kyle looked at the two overweight men, one still seated, one standing but not braced against anything, checked the angles and made the calculation, and then said, "I'm going inside."

"Hey, Vern," the standing man called into the open door, "we got a hard case out here wants to see Tiny."

There was a scrape and a rumble from inside, and then Vern appeared in the front door. As broad as a four-by-four on steroids and wearing a purple velvet sweat suit. Vern loomed over the standing man as he peered out of eyes squashed narrow by the folds of fat in his face.

"What the hell do you want?" said Vern.

"Mr. Sorrentino. I have something he'll want to see."

"Oh, yeah, what the hell's that?"

Kyle thought it through. He could back away like he'd backed away from that lawyer Malcolm at his father's office. He could keep bantering with these behemoths, hoping somehow he'd pull an open sesame. Or he could force his way in, past the two cement lions and through

Vern, into the office to find Tiny Tony Sorrentino, who Kyle had the sneaking suspicion wouldn't be any tinier than either of the three goons arrayed before him. Leaving was smart, bantering was useless, rushing these three was clearly a foul mistake. But he hadn't liked the way he'd felt when he let Malcolm push him around. And he was still pissed at the truths Skitch had hurled at him in the car. And the whole scene was getting tiresome enough to engender in Kyle the overwhelming urge to throw a punch.

"What I have here," said Kyle, taking a step back and waving the file even as he knew with perfect certainty the effect his words would have, "is Anthony Sorrentino's last will and testament."

There was a flash of incomprehension on the mugs of these lugs. Then the first man uncrossed his arms. The second man began to stand from his chair. Vern pushed the first man to the left as he moved his right arm to reach for something behind him.

And as Kyle saw them making their moves, the world slowed, and the angles came clear, and he was back on the gridiron with a football in his arm and a goal line in the distance. Quick as that, he raised a straight arm and made his cut.

The first man, briefly off balance from Vern's shove, took a hard shot to the solar plexus and tripped over the second man's chair, collapsing two squinty, overweight men and one lawn chair into a scene of horror as flabby arms flailed and nylon snapped.

And Vern, even as he reached behind with his right hand to grapple for something stuck in his belt, was sent reeling backward by a sharp shoulder slamming into his chest. One of Vern's arms wheeled as he tried to regain his balance, but a forearm shiver to the jaw sent him spinning atop a round table, which shattered under his substantial weight. And before he knew it, his arm, still behind his back, was pinned by a shoe, and a bare knee pressed like an iron bar upon his throat, and Kyle Byrne stared down at him with something dark and empty in his eyes.

"My, my, my," came a soft, gravelly voice from the edge of the room. "What have we here?"

The sound pulled Kyle off the football field and back to the present, where he was stooped over a red-faced fat man, his knee pushing hard upon the fallen man's thick neck. In a now-open doorway at the far end of the dusty outer office stood an ancient man, very small with an ashen face and a loose black suit draped over his emaciated frame.

The old man didn't look near death so much as like death itself. And in his tiny fist was an oversize pistol pointed straight at Kyle's heart.

Chapter 19

"Who the hell are you?" rasped the small man with the big gun. His voice seemed to bubble up from a deep well of death.

"Kyle Byrne."

"Byrne, huh? Byrne?"

"Liam Byrne's son."

"Of course you are. It's amazing how his name is suddenly on the tip of everyone's tongue. And why are you sitting on Vern?"

"He was rude."

"That's what I pay him for, though I can see now that I pay him too much. What do you want, Byrne?"

"To talk to you. I have a file of my father's I want to give you."

"A file of your father's? To give to me? How marvelous. With the untimely death of Laszlo Toth, I was just thinking about such a file. And now it's as if his ghost has led you straight to me. Be a good boy, Liam Byrne's son, and get the hell off of Vern's chest before he defecates in his pants and stinks up the office for a week."

Kyle lifted his knee from Vern's neck and his foot from Vern's arm and then stood. Vern jerked to a sitting position and rubbed his neck while staring insolently at Kyle.

"Want us to haul him away, boss?" said one of the men from outside.

"A little late, isn't it? Since he's already past the two of you."

"It's just he was quicker than—"

"It don't take much. No, leave him be. If this is Liam Byrne's son, he is always welcome here. Why don't you and Frank stuff another cannoli in your gullets while this boy and I talk about old times. But first, each of you, you need to apologize to our guest."

"But, boss, we was just—"

"He is the son of Liam Byrne. He deserves respect."

"We didn't know—"

"Apologize," screamed the little man, his face reddening, the gun shaking with anger as spittle flew in deranged arcs from his suddenly foaming mouth. Peeling paint flaked off the walls at the sound.

Vern scrambled to his feet, and the three huge men started mumbling apologies like schoolkids caught slipping frogs down the backs of little girls' blouses, complete with slouched postures and toes kicking into the ground. *We didn't mean nothing. Sorry about that. We didn't know.*

"Okay, enough of your sniveling," said Tiny Tony, shutting off the embarrassing display. "You three make me sick. Come along, young Byrne, and we'll take a look at that file."

Tiny Tony stuck his gun into one of the side pockets of his jacket and ushered Kyle into the inner office, before closing the door behind Kyle and leaving him alone for a moment. While the storefront was shabby and the outer office a bare, dusty wreck of a space, the inner office was as lushly overdecorated as the bar of an Italian bordello. An obscenely red couch, an easy chair covered with a golden throw, velvet wallpaper, a marble fireplace, above which hung a huge painting of a woman lying on a divan wearing a fortune-teller's turban, and nothing else. Kyle was still eyeing the painted woman's fantabulous breasts when the door opened and Tiny Tony Sorrentino reentered the room.

"Nice painting," said Kyle.

Tiny Tony turned and stared at it for a moment. "My first wife," he said. "Eleanor. Her breasts were marvelous, but she turned out to be as vicious as a polecat. My second wife was even worse. But we're not here to discuss my catastrophic family life. Sit, sit." He gestured Kyle toward the easy chair and then moved behind an ornate mahogany desk, picked a box off the desktop and flipped open its lid. "Cigarette?"

"No thank you," said Kyle, sitting.

"A man of good habits, then, unlike your father," said Tiny Tony as he pulled a cigarette from the box, tapped it on the desktop, lit it with a crystal lighter the size of a grapefruit. "All my habits are bad, which is why I'm still alive. No one cared enough to kill me, seeing as I was doing such a good job killing myself."

Just then the phone on the desk rang. It was a big black phone, with a heavy handset that lay in a cradle. Tiny Tony put the huge handset to his ear, listened. "Six and a half, five and a half," he said. "How many? Done." He scratched something on a small pad, hung up the phone. For a moment, as a waft of smoke rose from the half-hidden face, he stared at Kyle with eyes burning bright and angry. "I didn't know Liam had any children," he said finally.

"He wasn't married to my mother."

"And that makes you . . ."

"Yes, it does."

"Ahh, I see. But still you were close."

"Not really."

"Yet here you are, like a responsible young son. And you have for me a file."

"I was going through some of my father's old things in his office," said Kyle, raising the file in his hand, "and I found this."

"And the lawyers there, they let you rifle through the files?"

"Well, they didn't quite let me."

"Ahh, a scoundrel. You are indeed Liam Byrne's son."

The phone rang again. Tiny Tony stared at Kyle for a moment as if Kyle were responsible for the ring itself, and then picked up the phone, listened. "Three to one against. Even money the sap doesn't last six. Done."

Tiny scribbled a few more lines on his pad, scratched his nose with a thumb, snuffed out the cigarette, took another from the box, flicked the crystal grapefruit to life, inhaled, exhaled. "Okay," he said, "enough with the suspense."

A greedy little hand reached up from the desk, and its fingers snapped.

"Before I hand the file over," said Kyle, "I have a question."

"A question, hey?" The old man reached into a pocket, pulled out the gun. He slapped it on the desktop, gave it a spin until the barrel pointed at Kyle. "Okay, shoot."

"Double Eye investments."

"You get right to the meat of it, don't you?"

"Who are the two eyes?"

"Double Eye, the Italian and the Irishman. Your dad and I were partners of a sort."

"What sort?"

"Quiet partners. Your dad did all the investing, kept all the papers, made all the filings."

"What did you do?"

"I paid."

"So Double Eye was a way to launder your gambling earnings."

"Clever, aren't you? You know, in this part of town clever usually gets you dead. Let's cut to it, shall we? What is it you're after?"

"I'm looking for a file cabinet of my father's. It is big and heavy and brown, with fake wood grain painted on the metal. I wondered if you might have it along with the partnership records."

"You're looking for a file cabinet of your father's."

"Yes."

"And so you've come to me."

"Yes."

"And that is why you beat the hell out of my men."

"Yes."

"If the cigarettes hadn't taken all my wind, I would be laughing now."

"I'm glad I can be such a source of humor."

"Oh, you are, young Byrne, you are. Your father and I were partners, yes. But things don't always work out the way we would want them to. Have you noticed that most stories end either with a marriage or with death? This story didn't end with a marriage."

"I'm not sure I understand."

"You will, in time. Now, let me have the damn file." Tiny Tony snapped his fingers and then snapped them again.

Kyle looked at the old man's hand, once more outstretched, and the barrel of the gun, still pointing in his direction. He stood, put the file in the old man's hand, sat down again. He watched as Tiny Tony pushed a pair of glasses onto his nose, lifted his chin, and paged through the file quickly.

"What the hell is this?" said Tiny Tony.

"Your last will and testament."

"I can see that. But why the hell would I want this?"

"I thought you might need it in case—"

"In case?" He threw the file atop his desk. "Since your father made this for me, I've had three more. Each new will revokes the last. This is useless to me."

"What about the betting slips?"

"As valuable as yesterday's lottery tickets. If this is all you're bringing to the table, what the hell good is this to me?"

The phone rang. Tony answered, listened. "He's going off at seven to two. You won't make me send Vern this time, right? Okay. Done." He slammed down the phone and made a jot on his pad even as he gave Kyle another accusatory stare.

"You don't care about the file cabinet, do you?" said the old man. "This is something else. The bastard son on a quest to learn the truth about his long-dead father. And you think I have it, or at least some of it. And you may be right."

"How did my father die?"

"I heard it was his heart."

"Were those his slips?"

"No. Your father didn't gamble. At least not on football or the horses. Toth was the bettor. After your father died, Toth took over some of the matters your father was working on for me. And over the years he discovered a predilection for wagering."

"Was he any good?"

"Terrible." Another waft of smoke, a wave of the cigarette. "They're all terrible. That's how I can afford the wives." He looked up to the painting with the breasts. "Eleanor is dead, roaring at the devil in hell, I suppose, but I'm still supporting all the rest. Thanks to fools like that wily Hungarian, I'm on my fourth. In fact, Toth owed me two arms and a leg before his death, which meant he was screwing me more thoroughly than my current wife. But he said he had a way to pay me off, which was good, since Frank had already broken three of his fingers."

"Ouch."

"It happens. Laszlo said he found something, something of your father's that was going to get him off my hook and out of his stinking law office for good. A file that he said had vast worth. He called it the O'Malley file."

Kyle nodded, as if it all made perfect sense, which it actually was starting to. He didn't understand everything yet, but suddenly he knew that O'Malley's name wasn't O'Malley and that as soon as he got out of here, he was giving that fake O'Malley a call.

"I was hoping it was this file that you were bringing to me," said Tiny Tony.

Kyle thought a moment. "If there was a file of great worth, why would I be bringing it to you?"

"You don't know?"

"No."

The phone rang, Tiny Tony answered it. "Even. How much? Done." He hung up, scribbled in his book, flashed another accusatory stare at Kyle.

"Why do you keep looking at me like that?" said Kyle.

Sorrentino stared a bit more and considered the question. "It's just that I see him in you. There's something in your face, in the way you hold yourself. It's uncanny the way the dead continue to haunt us. The son of Liam Byrne," he said, shaking his head. "Funny thing is, all this time I didn't know the son of a bitch had any kids."

The phone rang. Tiny Tony stared at Kyle from behind the desk as it rang again and then again. Finally he answered the phone. "Hold on," he said into the handset, and then put his palm over the mouthpiece. "Listen, Kyle, I need to take this in private, you understand."

"Sure," said Kyle, rising.

"We'll meet again, I promise you, and I'll answer all your questions then. Meanwhile, I'll do what I can to try to find that file cabinet you're so interested in. There are some possibilities I need to check out."

"I'd appreciate that. Thank you."

"We're going to get along famously," said Tiny Tony Sorrentino. "Just like your father and me. I can tell. We're going to do business together. I am certain. Write down your phone number, and I'll give you a call."

Kyle leaned over the desk and scribbled his cell number on a proffered piece of paper and then, to be safe, Kat's number, too. "If you can't get me on the cell, the second's where I'm staying now. I'll be waiting."

Tony watched him as he headed for the door to the outer office.

"Kyle, can I give you some advice? As a dear friend of your father's? I don't think it wise for you to go out the front door. You humiliated my men, which was quite impressive but isn't calculated to make lasting friendships. Perhaps it would be better if you avoid all three by going out the rear. There is a door to the alley behind that curtain that would be safer."

"Thanks," said Kyle.

"It's nothing. We are almost family, you and I. Now go, and be well, and I'll be in touch."

Kyle nodded at the old man, stepped toward the curtain and pushed it aside, revealing two doors, one open, leading down a set of stairs to a basement, and the second closed, leading, Kyle assumed, to the alley. As he opened the second door, he could hear the old man behind him barking into the phone, "Willis. Seven to five. Done."

Kyle looked around, stepped past a few scattered trash cans into an empty passageway leading to the alley. When he reached the alley, he turned to the right, only to see Vern, in his purple velvet sweat suit. Vern was standing in front of him, holding a baseball bat in one hand, pounding it into the palm of his other.

Pound. Pound. Pound.

Chapter 20

Henderson and Ramirez were at a crime scene when they got the call from the hospital. The crime scene was sordid and familiar and tragic: a little girl on a stoop, a shooting a block away, a stray bullet finding a stray target. For Ramirez this was new and wrenching; for Henderson its very commonness was one of the things shoving him toward retirement. There had been a plague of such killings in the city the past couple of years, as if the cruel calculations of nation-states had descended upon the streets.

The scene had been taped closed, the blood spatters had been marked, but in a crime like this the victim had nothing to do with the solution, so the blood didn't matter. While the uniforms were going door-to-door asking about the shooting, well down the street from the bloodstains Henderson and Ramirez were standing behind the rough line defined by little number placards, each denoting a found cartridge, and trying to figure out where the shots had been headed so they could maybe figure out who was being targeted so they could maybe figure out who was doing the shooting and why.

"Two witnesses said the shooter was in a car," said Ramirez, "black or blue, late-model sedan or small import, muffler busted or the music pumping."

"The specificity of the description is devastating," said Henderson.

"If the car was here and the shooter was sticking his automatic out the window, then the shots were in this direction."

"Aiming at one of those houses?"

"Or someone walking along the street."

"Anyone see anyone walking?" said Henderson.

"Just a lot of running. After."

"Nothing you wouldn't expect. Any names?"

"No."

"Descriptions?"

"Nothing specific."

"Black or white," said Henderson. "Six feet tall or under five foot. Over forty or just a kid."

"Something like that."

"I am so weary."

"You giving up already, old man?"

"You know what I'm going to get when I retire?"

"What's that?"

"A puppy. Something to lap at my face and soothe the nerves. Something to run on up and jump at my chest when I call. I can close my eyes and see it."

"A Labrador?"

"Nah, a mutt. Something dumb and happy. Just like I want to be. But to answer your question, no, I'm not giving up. Can't give up, not with a girl dead and a killer on the loose. But a crime like this is beyond us. It will get solved only if one of these neighbors talks. Except they're afraid to talk, because the shooter will come back and we can't protect them. And we can't even pretend that by solving this we can stop the next one, because it's a plague that can't be solved case by case. Something bigger than us has to step in, but they won't, because it's only a little girl who's lying there. So what we really are, you and me, is a salve to the conscience of the city, to make everyone feel like something is being done when nothing is being done."

"You make me want to cry," she said.

"You ever hear of Sisyphus?"

"What is that, an STD?"

"Yeah, something like that."

His phone rang. He stepped away from Ramirez when he answered it, holding the little piece of metal in his huge, latex-covered hands. Henderson had already locked down his emotions, so the words from the uniform, who happened to be in the hospital when the beating victim was brought in, didn't register as anything other than another sad fact on an already dismal day. He thanked the uniform and snapped his phone shut.

"Now, that's peculiar," said Henderson.

"What?"

"You know that kid you were questioning on the Toth murder, the one that broke into his father's old office?"

"Byrne. Yeah?"

"He just got brought into the emergency room at Methodist, beat all to hell."

"What is that about?" said Ramirez.

"Don't know for sure, but my guess is he wasn't minding his own business. Before they discharge him, maybe you ought to find out who he pissed off."

"After we finish here."

"That won't be for a while," said Henderson, looking beyond the placards to the row of houses on the other side of the street. "Lot of stories I got to hear, and then I need to talk again to the girl's family."

"They don't know anything but the grief."

"Maybe, but still, that's what I need to do. Go on over to Methodist and find out what you can about what that boy is up to. And while you're there, see if you can convince him to mind his own damn business."

Chapter 21

Detective Ramirez felt a slight but undeniable thrill as she was let into the working space of the Methodist Hospital emergency room, and it worried her. She hadn't made her fabulous climb up the police department's ladder of success by letting her emotions get in her way. In every post she'd been assigned, from her first beat on up, she had been the hard one, *la reina del hielo*. It hadn't made her many friends, but she wasn't looking for friends, she was looking to rise, and Lord knows she had risen. Like a rocket ship. And the key had always been the ability to keep her emotions in check. Let burnouts like Henderson weep over the blood and the futility—she had more important things to do. Like rise and rise some more.

But there was something about the big, goofy Byrne kid, the way he smiled so easily, the way he seemed to take nothing all that seriously, especially not her. He was as unrilable as he was unreliable, and both traits appealed to her in a perverse sort of way. And she did have to admit that he was easy on the eyes. Given how things had fallen apart with thin and grim Henry, letting herself feel something for someone like Kyle Byrne would have been sort of nice.

Except for the fact that he was neck-deep in one of their murder investigations.

She stopped outside the curtain wrapped around his assigned bed and took a deep breath before pushing the curtain aside. The bed was empty. She took the pulse of her disappointment, very much as the nurses would take the pulse of the patients surrounding her. It was steady and strong and worrisome, along with a fear that maybe something more serious than a mugging had happened to him. Get it together, girl, she told herself.

She heard a shuffling behind her. She turned, and there he was, struggling across the floor like an old man with a bent and crooked posture, taking baby steps as he dragged along his IV.

"My, how you've aged," she said as he stepped slowly past her and then carefully, and with an old man's grunt, lifted himself gently into the hospital bed. "I haven't seen such a pathetic display since my grandfather had his prostate removed."

"How's he doing?"

"Dead."

"That's too bad. I'm sure he was quite the lively dancer."

"What happened?" she said.

"Well, you see, there was this truck."

"A truck. And did this truck have a name?"

"Vern."

"Well, for a truck this Vern is quite the pro. A concussion, a couple of broken ribs, a bruised kidney, and according to your chart you are pissing blood, which is a lovely image, let me tell you. But your face, which actually could have used the work, is virtually untouched, except for a small mouse under your eye."

"Is it cute?"

"Your face?"

"The mouse."

She stepped toward the bed, leaned forward. She was filled with a strange worry that was almost maternal. She couldn't help herself from reaching and tenderly brushing the swelling under his eye. The skin of his face felt soft and hot, electric—

—but to Kyle the back of her hand felt cool and soothing, until she pressed down hard and he felt a squirt of pain.

"Call it Darryl," said Kyle, jerking his head away and feeling his cracked ribs shiver within his chest. He grunted and gritted his teeth until the pain turned into a dull ache. "I used to have a pet mouse named Darryl."

"What happened to him?"

"My mom buried him in the backyard of my house, next to Swimmy the fish."

"You want to tell me what happened?"

"I think the cat broke its neck."

"I mean to you."

"Not really."

"Why not, baby?"

He smiled and it hurt, but he couldn't help himself. "Baby?"

"Yeah, baby," she said, leaning forward now, staring right at him so that Kyle could see the golden flecks in her pretty brown eyes. "That's what I say when I see fear leaking out of some poor kid's eyes. And right now you are such a baby."

"Then that's your answer right there," said Kyle, turning his head aside, and it was. He wasn't going to tell her what happened, because he was afraid, afraid if he started blabbing those comical goons would come back and finish the job.

The moment he had spied Vern with that baseball bat, he sensed how much trouble he was in. He spun around to run, but as he turned, one of the two squinty guys from the front, standing behind him all the time, threw a steel garbage can at Kyle's feet. The can flipped his legs into the air and sent him sprawling to the ground, where the other fat man from the front stomped hard on his chest.

Kyle instinctively curled up like a pill bug as the kicks came from all sides, slamming into his chest and back and legs. He closed his eyes and loosened his muscles and waited it out. It was like being on the bottom of a rugby scrum, it hurt like hell, and he could tell there was damage being done, but still there was no out but patience. If they were going to kill him, there was nothing he could do about it, but he didn't think they were going to kill him, or he'd already be dead. They were just pissed off about what he had done to them at the front of the store and were getting in their licks. Fair enough, he thought, until the blows stopped and the sandpaper voice of Tiny Tony Sorrentino sounded in his ear.

"I didn't know Liam Byrne, that son of a bitch, had a son of his own. I didn't know who the hell to take it out on. But now I do, so I'm taking it out on you."

A kick thudded against his side, and Kyle's back clenched involuntarily, opening up his chest for another blow, which landed with a pain-racked thud just above his groin.

"You want to know the truth, you little shit? I hate taking bets. And I had enough saved up to retire fat and happy in Waikiki. So why am I still answering the phone, scribbling down orders from fools with a sports jones? Because your father screwed me up the ass so hard it's still whistling 'Dixie.' And then he died, and poor me, I had no one to take it out on. Until you walked into my joint, and now I'm taking it out on you. And let me tell you, I see your face again before you make it up to me, you better have on a pair of boots, you understand?"

"Boots?" gasped out Kyle.

"So you don't mess up your Sunday shoes when digging your grave," said Vern.

"And I will see you again, count on it," said Tiny Tony Sorrentino. "But you find me that file and maybe our next meeting will be a little more pleasant. Maybe you'll be my partner, just like your old man. And maybe you'll even survive it better than he did."

And then a final kick to the back of his head that almost put Kyle to sleep and left him imagining strange gray-headed figures peering at him from the far end of the alley.

So yeah, he was scared, and he had a right to be scared. But telling this cop about Tiny Tony Sorrentino wasn't going to make him any less scared. She'd make an appearance at Tony's shop, she'd get all up in Tony's grill, and the questions would give the whole thing away. And quick as that, Big Vern would show up with more emphatic orders than to administer a simple beating.

"You're not going to tell me?" said Detective Ramirez.

"There's nothing to tell," said Kyle. "I was hit by a truck. I didn't get the license plate. That's all I know."

"A truck named Vern."

"There you go."

"Did the guy in the red 280ZX who dropped you off at Emergency have anything to do with it?"

"No."

"Did you know that three of Laszlo Toth's fingers were broken a week or so before his murder? The coroner said the break was clean. It's as if they were snapped by the same kind of pro that put you in here. Any connection?"

"What I hear, that was done by a truck named Frankie."

"And you're not going to tell me anything about it."

"Nothing to tell."

"You're not playing detective, are you?"

"Now, why would I do that?"

"To clear your name, to solve Toth's murder, to find out what really happened to your father."

"I know what happened."

"Do you?"

"I told you already."

"Yeah, but you didn't sound sure. And maybe now you think one death might have something to do with the other."

"What could one have to do with the other?" said Kyle, though he'd been thinking exactly as she surmised, and that this pretty cop had pulled it out of the air was damn impressive. Was she just sharp as hell, which he sort of liked, or did she know something he didn't?

Detective Ramirez took hold of a chair and pulled it close to the bed before sitting down. She put on her face that firm yet concerned look that Kyle had seen too many times lately, on Bubba when Kyle showed up late at the bar, on Kat when she dragged him out of the interrogation room, even on Skitch in the car in front of Sorrentino's place. He was getting sick of that look; he'd rather face Vern again.

"Please don't," he said.

"Don't what?"

"Don't start lecturing me on what I need to do to get my life together. I've had enough of that lately."

"What is going on with you?"

"I don't know. I'm just going on, is all."

"You know, I heard about the funerals."

"What?" Pause. "Where?"

"Kyle, we found you trespassing in what had been the scene of a murder a few nights before. You are a person of interest in a homicide investigation. We were in the process of interrogating you before your tax-lawyer friend pulled you out. You didn't think we were going to ask around?"

"I guess I didn't think about it."

"We're detectives. We ask questions. While fake detectives like you are getting the hell beat out of them, real detectives are asking questions. Like, what is that all about, you going to the funerals of dead lawyers?"

"Not all dead lawyers. They have to have maybe known my dad."

"And that qualifies them because . . ."

"Because I go and pay my father's respects. It's a family thing. I sign his name in the book, I sit there and think about him and the way things might have worked out if he hadn't died on me. And sometimes I feel his presence, like he's watching over me."

"Sounds like church."

"Call it what you want to."

"So that's why you were at Laszlo Toth's funeral, to get in touch with your father's spirit?"

"That's right."

"Did it work?"

"Sure. He sends his regards."

"Does he ever actually say something?"

"No."

"The strong, silent type, is that it?"

"Now you're just cracking wise." Kyle struggled to sit up, but he got dizzy, and pain pushed him back into the bed. "I don't care what you think, I can feel him."

"Okay, baby. I believe you."

"Well, don't worry. Whatever I thought I was doing, I was being an idiot. But it's over."

"Really?"

"Yeah, I'm through," he said, and it was the truth. He was afraid of what could happen to him, afraid of what he'd find out about his father, afraid suddenly of the O'Malley file and everything it might contain. Tiny Tony Sorrentino had made it clear what would happen if that little thug saw his face again—Kyle was going to make sure it didn't happen. Uncle Max was wrong, putting the legends to rest could hurt, and the effort had left Kyle pissing blood. One more call, one more meeting, just to tie up one more loose end, and then he was through. "I don't have to be run over by a truck twice to learn my lessons."

"What are you going to do now?"

"I don't know. Sleep, drink, heal, take a trip. Maybe Arizona."

"I have relatives in Arizona. They hate it."

"But it's a dry hate."

"So you're going to run."

"Running's good. Running works. It always has at least."

"You don't seem the running type, but maybe I misjudged you. Can I just tell you one more thing?"

"Sure."

She leaned forward until her lips were right at his ear. He could smell her scent, spicy and sweet, could feel her hair tickling his cheek and the gentle press of her breath on his skin. Even with the steady throb of the pain, he felt himself stir from her proximity.

"I don't trust a word you say, baby," she said softly, her lips almost brushing his ear. "Deep down, in your heart, I don't think you're a runner at all. Which means you're either lying to me or lying to yourself. Let's just hope you're lying to yourself, because if you are lying to me, baby, I am going to nail your ass."

Chapter 22

Robert bought the prepaid cell phone at a Wawa convenience store in Delaware, snatched it on apparent impulse off the rack and added it to a gallon of milk, a pack of Winston Lights, a loaf of Wonder bread. He didn't smoke and he didn't drink milk, so he tossed those out in a Dumpster near the state border, along with the plastic clamshell that had surrounded the phone, but the Wonder bread he kept. Growing up, Robert Spangler had lived on Wonder bread, slathered with peanut butter or surrounding a thin slice of olive loaf. He still saw himself as that kid, gripping a half-eaten white-bread sandwich in his hand as he ran out to the street to play. Wonder bread reminded him of his childhood, when he still held illusions about the bright promise of his future and the goodness of his own heart.

Both illusions had now been shattered by the way she had bent him to her will. Whatever promise his life once held had withered; whatever goodness once lay in his heart had been twisted dark. All that was left was to learn what he had become in the process. And he had the suspicion that the answer would come from that phone.

The advantage of the prepaid phone was that there were no records to tie him to the number. The only link that existed was between the anonymous number of the phone and the fake O'Malley name on the card he had given to the Byrne boy. If the phone was going to ring, it would be Liam Byrne's son calling, but no longer did he expect that to happen. It was clear the boy didn't know anything about the O'Malley file, what was in it or where it might be. Robert had sent him searching, and he had shown up at the single most obvious place, the one place Robert knew the file wouldn't be found. And then, just to scare the boy off for good, Robert had called the police and told them there was a break-in going on at the law offices of Byrne & Toth.

It had been days now, and the phone hadn't rung. His gambits had worked as perfectly as he could have hoped, there would be no need for any more violence. Robert Spangler should have been pleased. And yet.

And yet he kept staring at the phone, feeling a strange, almost erotic desire, as if he were a high-school boy waiting for a call from the one girl in school he knew would put out. It was an inexpensive black and silver thing, that phone, decidedly low-tech, but as it lay silently on his desk, lying helpless on its back, he couldn't tear his gaze from its smooth flanks and delicate keys.

He wondered if it was still working, and so, for what seemed the umpteenth time, he called the number with his other phone, his landline phone. This was a minor breach of his precautions, creating a link in a chain that could lead back to him, but he couldn't help himself, so worried and excited and fearful was he. After a moment the cheap phone shivered to life and rang with a jangling jangle, and it was as if the call were coming not from his phone but from an independent part of his soul, a frightening part, the part that had grown to like the taste of acid.

He remembered the first time he had tried hot and sour soup at a Chinatown restaurant. It was the most unpleasant thing he had ever tasted, a thick, bilious combination of vinegar and heat. After a few spoonfuls, he gagged and pushed it away. But that night he had dreamed of the soup and couldn't wait to order it again. And again. And now the vile taste of violence, a contradictory combination of power and subjugation all in service to her iron will, had left him with that same perverse craving.

Answer it, this frightening part of his soul called into his ear in a voice startlingly similar to her own craven caw. "It's just the ring from my test call," he whispered to himself. *Answer it, you never know,* came the reply. *Do it. Now. Obey me. Now.*

And in that voice was all that frightened him most. Not that the phone would ring and he might have to kill that boy; killing was merely an unnecessary task he had done before and could do again when necessity reared its fearsome head and stared at him with those ice-blue eyes. What frightened him was the part of him that wanted it to ring, wanted to be forced to confront that boy and hold the boy's head down in a pool of water as he thrashed and then panicked and then calmed. Or point the gun at the boy's chest and blast a hole in the boy's heart. Or to place a gun to the boy's head and blow his brains across the room. These first two he had done already in furtherance of her will, the third was still only a delicious possibility.

No, no, that was wrong, not what he meant at all. A horrifying possibility. Horrifying. Because this Kyle Byrne was just a boy, an orphan, missing his father, trying to recapture a little of what he had lost. Yearning for love and acceptance, that was all. And who knew better than Robert Spangler what it was like to yearn for just those things, or the price that such yearning could exact? Who could be more sympathetic to what the boy was going through? And yet, still, he couldn't help but stare at the smooth, dark skin of the phone as it lay on the television console, couldn't help but hope for the ring that would signal a problem and send him off into the night seeking the peculiar satisfactions of a bowl of hot and sour soup.

Oh, God, what had he become, what had she made of him? He didn't want to be a monster. He wanted to be the boy running out of his house with a peanut butter on Wonder bread sandwich. That boy played and laughed and dreamed sweet dreams, and yearned only for the taste of Coca-Cola in his mouth. That boy would grow up to have a family of his own, make peanut butter sandwiches on Wonder bread for his son. That boy had possibilities.

But that was before, before she made her leap and started whispering to him that maybe he could follow her path, calling him "Bobby dear," importuning him, making him an instrument of her deepest desires and her unearthly will. And in the process turning a part of him into some sort of a fiend who gloried in the taste of blood. Except he didn't feel like a fiend, which comforted him a bit. But then maybe fiends didn't ever feel like fiends, maybe that was what was so fiendish about them.

That was why the phone had become for him something of an obsession, as it reclined before him, open and easy, waiting for the ring that would force him to rise and send him into action. Its ring would be like the sweetest note of her sweet voice, reaching out to take hold and caress the monster she had created. Would he reject its blandishments and prove his utter humanity? Or would he let the monster respond to her caress, to arise and swell and march into the world to seed its darkness? Only the phone could give him that answer.

So he stayed close, sleeping with the phone resting on the empty pillow beside him, bringing it to the lavatory with him or taking it out to lunch. Or now, in the early-evening hours, sitting across from where it perched on the television, sitting in a deep easy chair, naked and alone, staring at the phone with hope and fear all at once, as if that cheap piece of disposable plastic held the very fate of his soul in its silicon chip. Hour after hour. Sitting. Staring. Waiting for the decision.

He wondered again if the phone was still operational. Maybe it needed to be recharged. Maybe something was interfering with the signal. He couldn't help himself. He lifted the handset off his landline and redialed the number.

The cell phone rang.

He hung up.

The phone kept ringing.

And ringing.

He dialed again and was sent straight to voice mail.

The phone still rang.

He stood up, stepped to the desk, picked up the cell phone, checked the number. Not his own. He pressed the talk button. "Hello," he said. "Hello."

He listened for a moment, and then, from deep inside, a voice he didn't recognize slithered like a snake from his throat. "So," it said, this other voice, sibilant and foreign. "It is you. How nice that you called, Mr. Byrne. Shall we meet once again?"

Chapter 23

Robert had picked the spot long before the call came in. Someplace remote and yet still covered with the noisome noise of traffic, someplace that seemed public but in fact could be very private, someplace where the danger was well hidden.

He arrived early, parked on the other side of the Benjamin Franklin Parkway, crossed at the light, and walked up the traffic ramp that led to the art museum. It was late enough so that the museum was closed, and an array of shadows covered the landscape. He stayed within the lines of darkness as he climbed down the broad staircase to the arcade flanked with the statues of Revolutionary War heroes and then cut to the left at the wide traffic circle. He walked through the grass and past the great columned buildings of the Fairmount

Water Works, closed now due to the hour, and headed to a grand gazebo that rested on the very edge of the Schuylkill River.

The rise where the museum now sat, which used to house the eighteenth-century reservoirs that supplied the city its water, acted as a shield to the rear of the gazebo. The Schuylkill River was at its front, with the sounds of water rushing over a low dam, and traffic on the expressway on the river's far bank, blanketing the site with a continuous muffled roar. On the left was a bend in the river, on the right a small grove of trees blocking the well-lit but deserted row of boathouses. To Robert's eye it was an almost perfect place for murder.

He cased the area for a moment more, before slipping into the shadow about a hundred feet away from the gazebo, where he could scan the parking lots and roads surrounding the area. He didn't yet know how the night would turn, he didn't yet know which part of himself would take control of the encounter with the young Byrne. He was terrified at the probability that he would be forced to use violence, and thrilled, too, and frightened at the thrill, and ashamed of the terror. The only thing he could trust was the solidity of the gun in his pocket.

He leaned against a wall and waited. And waited. He waited up to the time that had been set for the meeting, and then beyond. He let his sharp incisor bite into his tongue and draw blood as he waited.

A silhouette appeared out of the trees in the direction of the boathouses. It looked to be the right size, this silhouette, but something was wrong. It was making its way to the gazebo as if it were the shadow of a wreck of an old man, hobbled and limping. With a crack pipe and a fresh chunk of escape, no doubt. The meeting time was now long past, and Robert was beginning to doubt that Byrne would show, but Robert still needed to get rid of the old man. He pulled a ten out of his wallet, gripped his gun, and made his approach.

"You want to earn some money, old man?" he said in a hoarse whisper to the hobbling silhouette.

"I'm not that old," said the silhouette with a grunt. "O'Malley?"

Robert's hand tightened around the gun. "Byrne?"

"That's right."

"What happened to you, boy?"

"I fell into a hole," said Byrne.

"Be more careful next time."

"There won't be a next time."

"There's always a next time. Go on to the gazebo. We'll talk there."

Robert followed the boy as he limped toward the river. Byrne was taking small steps and was bent at a strange angle, as if his ribs had been savaged. Someone had done a job on him already, which was good. There wouldn't be any question of Byrne fighting back when things turned nasty. Robert gave his gun a caress as they entered the gazebo. The structure smelled furry and sickly at the same time, as if wet diabetic rodents had pissed on its walls. The din of the river hurtling over the dam grew loud enough to swallow a shot. If a body flipped over the dam, at this time of night it might not be found until it floated by the navy yard at the southern tip of the city.

"Do you have my file?" he said.

"No," said Byrne.

"But you found it, right?" said Robert as he slowly pulled the gun from his pocket.

"No."

"No?" He felt a slap of disappointment and a surge of relief all at once. He slipped the gun back into his pocket. "Then why did you call?"

"To talk to you."

"I said I'd talk only if you found my file."

"I'm not finding your damn file," said Byrne.

"But you looked."

"Yes."

"Where?"

"My father's law office. The office of his shady real-estate partner."

"What about his home? He was supposed to have taken a file cabinet to his home."

"I checked out his widow's house, although you got there before me. It wasn't there. It wasn't at any of those places. But in the process of searching, I've been arrested, insulted, beaten, and I've accomplished nothing except adding a dose of blood to my urine. I'm done."

"You're not done. We're never done."

"Maybe, but I'm not looking anymore. I'm giving up. That's what I wanted to tell you. I can't find the file."

"I'm disappointed," he said, and part of him truly was, as he fully released his grip on the gun. He pulled his hand out of his pocket and rubbed it over his mouth, catching a faint whiff of its sweet perfume, oil and cordite. "Really disappointed. But I suppose there is nothing more to be done."

"But there is. You said you knew my father."

"That's what I said."

"I want to hear about him."

"I thought I made myself clear. I would only do that in exchange for my file."

"But it's not your file," said Byrne.

Robert coolly slipped his hand back into his pocket and around the butt of the gun. "It's not?"

"And O'Malley's not your name. And I'm sick of being lied to and pushed around and kicked in the gut. I don't care who you are or what kind of money you can make with the damn file. All I care about is trying to put together the pieces of my past. You said you had something to tell me about my father. I want to hear it."

Robert Spangler felt the pimpled grip of the gun as he stared at the boy in the gazebo, and something broke in him, releasing a sweet line of emotion that dissolved the spurt of fear he had been feeling. This Byrne was just a kid, missing his father, doing whatever he could to get back a piece of him. Robert understood, Robert could feel what the boy felt, Robert empathized. Empathy. This was the one remaining gift of the child within him, the Wonder bread boy, rallying over the dark part of his soul twisted into monstrous form by her will.

"How many years has it been since your father died?" said Robert, his voice suddenly soft, even paternal.

"Fourteen," said Byrne.

"That's a long time."

"More than half my life."

"And you yearn for him."

"I guess."

"It's understandable. Family cuts deep. And what-ever comfort it actually provides for us, we want more and more and always more. But know this, young Byrne. In the end it can only lead to disappointment."

"I don't know about that."

"Take my advice, you'd be better off forgetting about your father."

"I just want to know the truth."

"Ahh, the truth. What the hell is that, boy?"

"I don't know, but you told me you have some of it."

"You don't want to hear what I have to say. You only want me to say what you want to hear. But trust me when I tell you that you won't ever get all you want. You'll just grow frustrated and bitter, and you'll end up doing things that will kill the best part of you."

"What are you talking about?"

"I'm merely giving you some friendly advice. Be careful what you yearn for, because that which you desire most will either complete you or destroy you, and you don't get to choose."

The boy stared at him for a moment, still in shadow so Robert couldn't see what emotions were playing out on the boy's face. But Robert had done his best to warn him away from a search that could only lead him back into danger. And in the process of reaching out to help a child whose uneasy place in the world was much like his own, Robert had done something good, and he felt good about it, as if he had turned some sort of corner and was freeing himself from her pernicious influence. He was wondering where else this unfamiliar impulse to do good might lead. He was imagining homeless shelters in the city, squalid villages in sub-Saharan Africa in desperate need of wells. His mind was taking flight on wings of selflessness when the boy finally spoke.

"Fuck off," said Kyle Byrne.

"What did you say?"

"I don't need your stinking advice. I'm sick to death of advice. It seems to come from every corner now. Winos I pass on the street shout it out. 'Get your life together.' I've had enough. I thought you had something to say, but it's clear you don't. All you have are your lies and your crappy advice, and I don't want either of them."

"Watch yourself, boy."

"I'm done watching," Byrne said as he started to hobble away. "Go to hell, Mr. O'Malley."

The name was spoken with an overtone of derision, and just like that the wheel turned inside Robert Spangler and the Wonder bread boy was upended. Now on top and in control was the dark part, perhaps the truer part, formed from love and devotion and obeisance to her iron will. And this part of him, Bobby dear, saw not a flailing boy searching for answers, a boy whose troubles he could relate to and empathize with, but instead opportunity to savor the taste of acid one more time, if the prodding was right.

"You want to know the truth, boy?" said Bobby Spangler to the retreating silhouette, knowing with the instinct of a brother how his words would affect the boy and hating himself all the while. "The absolute truth?"

The shadow of the boy stopped and turned and faced what Bobby had become.

"The truth is, your father was a rogue of the worst stripe. He cheated on everyone and everything. But there's more than just sexual peccadilloes to stain his name. He violated his professional responsibilities and sold out his clients and his most firmly held beliefs for a sackful of gold. Which means he was a thief as well as a rogue, leaving desolation and violence in his wake, violence that continues to this day. Laszlo Toth was killed for your father's sins, and let me promise you, the killing isn't over yet."

"You're lying."

"No I'm not, boy."

"Prove it."

"I don't have to. You'll prove it for me. And the proof of everything I say is in that file. Find the O'Malley file and you'll find your proof."

The boy didn't respond. He just stood there, as still as the shadow of a tree, and then turned again and hobbled off.

"Call me when you find it," Bobby shouted to the retreating figure. "And we'll have a celebration of the holy truth."

Chapter 24

Kyle Byrne was pissed. He was a little drunk, too, which accounted for the way the 280ZX was swerving as he punched the radio's buttons looking for something with some snap, but more than anything he was pissed.

He was pissed at that creepy fraud O'Malley for talking crap about his father, who Kyle was sure was neither thief nor scoundrel, despite the illicit circumstances of Kyle's own birth. He was pissed at Tony Sorrentino for sating his anger against Kyle's father by turning loose his goons and sheathing Kyle's body in pain. He was pissed at his best friend, Kat, and at Bubba Jr. and at Skitch and that Detective Ramirez and all the other well-meaning blowhards who thought it was their right, nay, their obligation, to tell Kyle how badly he had screwed up his life. As if Kyle weren't fully aware of exactly where his wrong turns had been taken and the prices he had paid for each. And Kyle was pissed at the radio, where all he could find were *American Idol* rejects or teenage emos or oldies that were a hit before he was born.

But most of all he was pissed at himself for caring. He had announced to the cop and that fake O'Malley that he was through, and he had been telling the truth. He'd been to enough funerals, buried enough old men. And now he had been bounced around like a soccer ball, with the promise of more to come. He was so ready to put it all behind him. His father had died long ago, his father's funeral had been a fiasco, it was time to bury him for good.

Except some questions in this life needed to be answered, some doubts needed to be quelled, and for Kyle these were the questions and these were the doubts. And so here he was, driving like an angry fool west from the city, smack into his past.

He hadn't been back to the old neighborhood since he lost the house. Which was an interesting and accurate way of putting it. Perhaps only Kyle could lose a house, like others lost their sunglasses or keys. Even though it was already dark, he recognized the landmarks as if they were great monuments in a capital city. That was the school yard where he'd first played T-ball; that was the field behind the Wawa where he'd pitched the Red Sox to their second straight Little League championship. There was Kat's street, where she and her family were right now chowing down on broiled eel. And there was his elementary school— Jesus, it looked small. He had played basketball on that outdoor court every summer of his youth, had sledded down that hill during every snowstorm with Kat, had kissed Melissa Dougherty in the trees above the playground.

And then the turn, as familiar a bend as his elbow. And then the street, her street, and then the house, her house. He stopped the red car right in front and stared for longer than he thought possible. The tour of his childhood markers had served to transform his anger into sentimental remembrance, and now, here, while remembering her, he fought against the tears.

It was a little Cape Cod, the smallest house on a crowded block. There was a For Sale sign on the unkempt front lawn that had once been lush. The paint was peeling where it had always been perfectly maintained. The flower beds were overgrown where once they'd been covered with an explosion of blossoms and swarms of white butterflies. The house's condition was sad enough in itself, but what was actually bringing tears to Kyle's eyes was the absence that lived in the house as surely as it lived in his heart.

On soft summer nights, she would sit on that front porch, rocking back and forth on her rocking chair, smoking and staring out into the night as if waiting for something brilliant to come her way.

Waiting for him.

This journey into his past was all about his father, but there was no avoiding his mother in the process. The trajectory of her entire adult life had been bent by his father's gravitational field. She had fallen in love with him at a tender age, had been impregnated by him, had set up her house and her schedule to suit his whims and inclinations, and after his death she had lived the rest of her life in some sort of bemused tribute to that early love that had altered her life so. Before Liam Byrne's death, she would sit on the porch, waiting on the possibility that he would choose this night to visit his son and then share cocktails with her on that very porch. And later, long after his funeral, she would sit on that selfsame porch, as if she still were waiting, as if that youthful love were strong enough to cheat death itself.

"He was going to leave his wife," she told Kyle one night on that porch, a few years after his father's funeral. She was smoking and staring out into the darkness, that distant smile on her face, as if her life were a cosmic joke that she was just on the cusp of understanding. "He was moving in here. We were all going to be together again."

"Did he tell you that?" said Kyle.

"In his way."

"Did he tell her?"

"I'm pretty sure."

"What makes you think so?"

"He told me once she would never let him leave. I guess she proved him right."

"Mom?"

"Isn't it your bedtime?"

"I'm fourteen."

"My big, big man. Go to bed, Kyle."

"You don't think . . ."

"You're right, Kyle. I don't."

There was something fierce in her ability to avoid his questions. She was a competent typist, a devoted mother, a fine cook and a brilliant gardener, but most of all she was a cipher. He had always believed that his mother was fooling herself about his father's moving back with them. It was the saddest memory he had of her, it made everything else in her life seem just as delusional. But suddenly, now, that very conversation seemed to harbor not delusion but maybe something akin to the truth.

The fake O'Malley had said that his father was supposed to have taken the file cabinet to his home. Yet his father's wife knew nothing about it. It didn't make sense, until the day after Kyle's strange meeting with O'Malley at the gazebo, while Kyle was sitting in front of Kat's TV, watching the baseball game and downing his traditional Father's Day case of Yuengling beer, when he remembered his mother's comment about his father telling her, in his way, that he was coming to live with them.

What would be his way? He'd bring something to the house, something to store, something most valuable. Something too heavy for him to handle alone.

"Uncle Max," Kyle had shouted over the phone after he'd thought it through but before driving out to the old neighborhood. He was shouting because he had reached his Uncle Max at the Olde Pig Snout, and the game was on and the television was blaring. "I got a question."

"What?"

"A question. I got a question for you."

"Who is this? Kyle?"

"Yeah, it's Kyle."

"Yo, Kyle, how you doing? Wait a second. Hey, Fred, turn the sound down a sec, I'm talking to my nephew."

The smooth voice of Harry Kalas dimmed. "Okay, go ahead."

"You ever help my father move anything into my mother's house?"

"When?"

"I don't know, not long before he died. I'm talking something heavy, like a file cabinet."

"Like a file cabinet?"

"No, you're right, not like a file cabinet. It would have been a file cabinet. Did you ever help him move a big brown file cabinet into my mother's house?"

There was a pause from Uncle Max's end of the line, where Kyle could still hear the game slipping away from the Phillies' bullpen. It was illegal now to smoke in Philly bars, but Kyle heard his Uncle Max light a cigarette and take a drag.

"Your mom called me," he said finally. "Asked for a favor. I had the truck then for my work with the funeral homes, and everyone was always calling me to help them move. That's why I quit and got rid of the thing, I was getting too damn helpful. But I still had it then, and she called, and what was I going to do? Say no to my little sister?"

"How come I don't remember it?"

"We did it one night when you was at that Chinese girl's house."

"She's Korean."

"You don't say? And all this time I thought she was Chinese. Funny how easy it is to—"

"Uncle Max."

"Okay, okay. Your mom, she didn't want you to know, and she made me promise never to tell. She didn't want you getting no ideas about it meaning something."

"Though she got them herself, didn't she?"

"She was my little sister, and I loved her, Kyle, I really did, but I never understood a thing about her. We even had to hide it once it was inside the house."

"From me?"

"No, that was your father's doing. He said he needed to safeguard it from someone. Toth, I assumed. But that file cabinet was so damn heavy it near gave me a hernia. You know, I never had no problem with my back until I wrestled that sucker into the basement, and since then I been no good for nothing."

From within the 280ZX now, through teary eyes, Kyle stared at his old house, gone to hell, and the top of the basement wall under the porch, behind which, he was certain, stood his father's file cabinet. Somewhere inside would be the O'Malley file, with a boatload of trouble on every page. But if you looked deep into Kyle Byrne's heart, you would see it wasn't really the O'Malley file he was after. For Kyle, the common concerns of the common world, which prized money and power over all things and was seeking mightily that selfsame file for venal ends, held little sway. But still his heart raced at the possibility of the file cabinet's being somewhere in his old basement. Because he couldn't help the feeling that inside that heavy brown cabinet, along with the useless detritus of his father's legal career, somewhere, in some mislabeled file, scrawled in his father's hand, would be the closest he'd ever come to discovering the very meaning of his life.

Chapter 25

The discussion did not go very well.

Of course, these discussions never went well anymore. In the beginning, when Robert was still the young and pliant striver, the glorious surroundings and the note of promise in their intercourse left him with a great, hopeful energy that was almost sexual in its power. He couldn't wait to see her again, the way his skin warmed as she caressed him with the gaze from her pretty eyes, the way their dreams seemed to mesh into a single glorious enterprise that would carry them both higher than individually they could ever have imagined. But as they had aged, and the mansion had deteriorated, and the promise in his life had withered, their encounters had taken on an indifferent brutality. If he did her bidding, then she merely took it as her due, with nary a word of gratitude. But if he failed to carry out her wishes to the letter, even if they hadn't been clearly communicated, then the whole inequality of their relationship was thrown into bitter relief by the vituperative nature of her rebuke.

"That's why you'll never amount to anything. You don't have an ounce of initiative. But what else could have been expected? You're a Spangler, and the Spanglers never had initiative. A clan of belching crotch scratchers, all of them. It's a wonder that any of you ever get off the toilet in the morning."

"I determined it wasn't to our benefit to kill him," he had told her.

"I'll determine what is to our benefit," she said, her voice a drip of liquid nitrogen. "You've spoiled things enough already. Once you set him on the trail, it was inevitable that he would have to be dealt with."

"I just wanted to be sure he didn't have a copy, like Laszlo."

"It didn't matter if he had it or not, he would find something. His father was greedy as a hyena, the son will be no different. Blood always tells. It's why you've been such a disappointment to me."

"If he was killed so soon after Laszlo, someone would draw the connection."

"Who, the police? That pair of fools at the funeral? Perfectly adequate for servants, maybe, but not as detectives. I hardly think those two will be swift enough to catch on. If you'll just do as I tell you, it will all work out as we hope. There are grand things afoot. I won't have the boy get in my way."

"What exactly do you want?"

"I want the boy gone. I want you to take care of him like you took care of the father. I will not have that Irish piece of trash confounding me from the grave."

"The boy's not so easy to find. He doesn't have a set place to stay anymore. He lives out of his car."

"Oh, Bobby dear, I'm sure you'll find a way."

And he had, yes he had. Bobby dear had found a way. The call had come in just a few minutes ago, from one of the spies he'd set up throughout the city. This was from one he had contacted in the boy's old neighborhood. *I'm looking for the Byrne boy. You remember him. He used to live across the street. He drives a small red sports car now, an old Datsun. I have something quite valuable to give him, but I can't seem to locate young Byrne. If you see the car, could you just give me a call? I'll make sure you're amply rewarded.* That's all it took these days to create a spy. And the spy had let him know that the boy's car was stopped right at the moment on his old street, that the boy was right at the moment in his car and staring at his old house. Now, about that reward . . .

The spy shouldn't worry, she'd have her reward: a crushing case of guilt when that curtain-twitching old biddy heard the sirens and looked out her window.

For Bobby was going to kill Kyle Byrne, yes he was. Not just because he had been ordered to kill him. And not just because part of Bobby was hungry for the taste of acid and the boy had shown him disrespect at the waterworks. But also because he sensed that she was wrong, finally, that the connection would be made and the whole enterprise would blow up in their faces and this final act would be the end of all the discussions for all time, the final revenge of the Spanglers.

And Bobby would make sure it was spectacular.

Chapter 26

In the cover of darkness, Kyle parked the 280ZX at the end of the driveway, his usual spot, and skulked around to the back, guided by the beam of his flashlight. He opened the screen door, slipped his key in the rear door's lock, gave it a twist. It wouldn't turn. No matter how hard he tried, the thing wouldn't budge. It took him longer than it should have to realize it wasn't rust.

Sons of bitches. The bank had changed the locks.

His mother's bank accounts and meager insurance had covered the cost of her funeral, with a little still left over for expenses. But after keeping his car filled and running, paying the cable bill and his phone and Internet bills, the electric bill, the water bill, his bar bills—especially his bar bills—after all that, the money from his mother and his wages from Bubba's hadn't been enough to allow him to keep paying the mortgage. He could have gotten a full-time job, sure, except then he'd have a full-time job. But even as he crumpled and tossed out the notices of delinquency as they came, first in the mail and then posted on the door, he didn't think the bastards would actually have the gumption to foreclose on an orphan.

Which only showed just how much Kyle understood about the ways of the world.

So they had booted him out and then locked him from his house. Or they had tried to, in any event. But he had lived there all his life, including the difficult years of his adolescence after his father's death, when adventure was somewhere, anywhere, beyond the walls of his mother's house and curfews were set up only to be knocked down like bowling pins. He had learned to climb into that house half a dozen ways without his mother's being the wiser, windows he unlocked before leaving, a rear door that could be jimmied open with his student ID.

He made a quick reconnoiter around the perimeter. The bankers had been pretty damn thorough for a pack of whiny money counters. All the windows had been locked tight with jamb locks added, and a dead bolt bolted onto the back door. But they had slipped up on the narrow window beside that door. The window was locked, but its sill had never been set right. Kyle's mom had often complained about the water that would sometimes leak inside, but she had never done anything about it.

He pressed hard against the top of the sill with one hand while he gave the lower right corner a quick bang with the flat of his other hand, and the bottom of the window popped loose. A little bit of prying, working the window back and forth, and it pulled out of the frame like a giant puzzle piece.

The opening wasn't big enough for any part of his body other than his arm to slip through, but that was enough to allow him to reach over and turn the knob of the newly installed dead bolt. With the bolt released, he again opened the screen door, put the butt of the flashlight in his mouth, took out his driver's license, and jimmied the door open. Quick as that, he was inside his old house.

It smelled wrong, empty and old and devoid of life. He had thought he would still be able to smell something of her, her hair spray, her soap, the lotion she rubbed on her hands, knuckles red and cracked from gardening. Nothing. And even in the darkness, he could sense the vacancy, as the sounds of his footfalls echoed without obstruction. Just a dusty emptiness. Out of habit he turned on the kitchen light and then halted at the sight of nothing.

There was no kitchen table, no freestanding cabinet for his mother's china, no table in the dining room or couch in the front parlor. Those sons of bitches had grabbed everything. A whole life, her whole life, gone, hocked to pay his debts. He had taken a few things of hers when he finally left, a scrapbook she had made, including a few photographs of her and his father, a painting she had done when she was a girl, just a scant few things that could fit in the small space beneath the hatchback of the Datsun along with his clothes and his laptop and his softball bat. He assumed he would come back for the rest, but he had never gotten around to it, and now those bastards had shipped it all off to be sold for mere pennies. While staring at the emptiness of his house and trying not to draw the connection with the emptiness of his life, he suddenly thought about the file cabinet and felt a jolt of desperation.

Damn, the bastards must have sold that, too.

He rushed for the basement stairs, flicked on the light, charged down. The basement was a dismal place beneath the old fluorescent lights that hummed and skittered to no great effect. The floor was cracked and damp, mold rising like a plague on the scuffed bare walls. Pipes and wires sagged sadly from the open ceiling rafters, the outdated circuit box dangled loosely off the wall. And it was empty. As cleaned out as a bank in the path of Bonnie and Clyde.

His mother had once envisioned a playroom for her boisterous young son and had the basement framed out with drywall. But before carpet could be laid and a ceiling hung, the remains of a hurricane had climbed up the East Coast, flooding the neighborhood and sending a slurry of water and mud through fractures in the walls and the cement floor. Soon the idea of a playroom was abandoned, and the basement instead became a storage bin for all manner of junk: old furniture from Kyle's grandmother's house, gardening paraphernalia, rolls of corroded metal fencing and stakes for the tomatoes. Kyle had figured the file cabinet would be somewhere hidden among or behind all the refuse. But the refuse now was gone—only the washer and dryer with their rusted bases remained—and the file cabinet was apparently gone with it.

He spun around in despair. They had taken it, those bastards. They didn't even know what they had, and they had taken it. He had a sudden vision of a brown file cabinet tumbling off a truck onto a pile of scrap metal, its files flipping madly as they fluttered into the wind.

But as he calmed, he considered. He'd been in this basement hundreds of times, and he had never seen the thing, had never even caught a glimpse. Had he simply not noticed it? Possibly. Or maybe it hadn't been hidden among the refuse where he could easily have spied it. Maybe it had been so well hidden that it eluded even the maniacal grasp of the money-mad bankers.

He began to pace the edge of the moldy drywall. It seemed to track quite closely the contours of the basement. From an opening for the radiator, he could see that the framer had left only a small space between the wood and the flaking stone walls to maximize the size of the playroom. But there was something about the wall on the opposite side of the radiator that bothered him.

He walked up to it. At this point on the floor above, the living room zagged a bit for an open window well with a bench seat that his mother had upholstered in purple paisley. But this part of the drywall was simply straight. And there was something about the mold. On the space right where that window well should have been, it was spottier than on the other sections, as if the paint that was used was somehow of a different quality than that on the rest of the walls and the mold couldn't get a purchase here. Or maybe the drywall was simply farther away from the damp stone.

He stepped forward and tapped the wall gently, listening for the hollow sound. The register went up and the echo died when he reached the stud, then lowered and hollowed again when he passed it.

Tap tap. Tap tap. Tap tap tap.

CRASH.

His fist ripped through the drywall. When he pulled his hand back, grabbing hold of the now-jagged edge while jerking hard with his shoulders, a piece the size of a small dog pulled off. Behind that newly formed hole, blackness. He pulled away more of the drywall, tugging and yanking as it came off in his two large hands.

When the space was big enough, he leaned in with the flashlight and turned on the beam.

His shout echoed like a shot through the empty house.

For there it stood, caught in the flashlight's stare, still as death and glowing dully in the surrounding darkness like a dimly lit sarcophagus in some long-buried crypt.

Chapter 27

It didn't take much time for Kyle to clear out the drywall from stud to stud and gain access to the damp and closed-in alcove behind the wall. The file cabinet was big and brown, with the fake wood grain and stainless-steel handles on the four drawers, just like the other three he had seen in his father's office.

And it was locked. As he assumed it would be. The locking mechanism in the top corner was pressed in, and no matter how hard he yanked, the drawers wouldn't budge.

Kyle stared at it for a moment and then took out a key.

"I swiped this sucker from one of the other file cabinets in your father's office," Skitch had said when he gave the key to Kyle.

"What the hell good is that?" Kyle had said.

"Look at it. See the way I filed it down?"

"So?"

"So? What am I good at, Kyle?"

"It's not hitting a softball, that's for sure."

"Tell me something I don't know. I pretty much suck at everything except for drinking, sex—"

"Not what I heard."

Pause. "What did you hear? Have you been talking to Allison? Because I was drinking tequila that night, and you know what happens when—"

"Skitch."

"Okay, look, the only things I know are drinking, sex when I'm somewhat sober, stealing cable, and picking locks. So when I'm talking about locks, you should be listening. This is a bump key. When you bump, all you're doing is setting the lock's pins into their proper places with a little pop."

"A pop?"

"That's it. Just a little pop. Nice and easy. Pop."

Now, in his old basement, with the flashlight in his mouth, Kyle slipped the key into the lock, pressed the key all the way in before pulling it out slightly, exactly as Skitch had shown him. Then he took a small rubber hammer out of his pocket. He twisted the key in the lock with just the slightest of pressure, popped the key lightly with the hammer, and at right that moment twisted the key a little harder.

The key turned, the lock jumped out.

"Yo, Skitch," said Kyle aloud after dropping the flashlight into his hand, "three out of four's not too shabby."

Then he yanked open the top drawer and discovered a lost world.

The cabinet was filled with the leavings of Liam Byrne's legal career, dusty old files from long-dead disputes, wills for long-dead clients, contracts no longer valid, letters referencing matters no longer mattering, useless notes on lifeless cases in handwriting barely legible. And as he quickly rifled through these files, thick with aged documents, each carefully named with a typewritten label—*Loughlin v. Ginsberg, Parvin v. United Amalgamated, In re Arco Industries, Doddson v. Fogg*—Kyle felt a wave of sadness. His father's life had been consumed by one after another of these fights between aggrieved souls over nothing more than money. These were the vital matters that kept Liam Byrne from his son's baseball games, band concerts, class shows. He had come in second to *Doddson v. Fogg*, and if his father had lived, he always would.

Among the files in the first three drawers, there was nothing that had O'Malley on the label, and in the letters he had checked in the midst of his rifling, he had seen nothing addressed to or referencing any O'Malley at all. With each failure his frustration grew.

In the bottom drawer was a group of expanding files with their flaps sealed, each labeled with a different tax year. Kyle couldn't help himself. He knelt down plucked out one, *Taxes: 1990,* opened the top, gave it a quick search. Among the receipts and canceled checks he found the 1990 Form 1040 for Liam Byrne and Cecile Byrne. It wasn't the business income he was interested in—although it was less than he would have expected—or the total income, or the adjusted gross income, or the taxes due or the taxes paid. Instead the first thing he checked was the exemptions. And smack there, in carefully typed text, was his own name, Kyle Byrne, with his own Social Security number and the word "son" under the heading "Dependent's relationship to you."

Well, then, at least he wasn't illegitimate in the eyes of the IRS, which meant something, he supposed. But it ticked him off that he was claimed as a dependent on the French wife's taxes. If Kyle's father was taking the exemption, it meant his mother wasn't able to. Screwing her again? So many mysteries in that relationship, it was impossible to unbind them all.

There were tax files going all the way to 1994, the year Liam Byrne died. Feeling a great wave of disappointment, Kyle was about to close the final drawer and start looking through the first three for anything O'Malley when he realized that the 1994 taxes wouldn't have been filed until 1995, in which case the file, along with all the receipts and canceled checks, should have been somewhere at the widow's house. So what was this file doing there?

He pulled the binder out, opened it, and there it was, as simple as that, sitting among a host of Double Eye binders. A black file with a pile of documents fastened between the two covers.

In re O'Malley.

He grunted in pain from his cracked ribs as he sat down on the cement floor and opened the file, rifling through the pages as fast as he could to get some idea of what the whole thing was about. The file was arranged in reverse chronological order, with each document fastened on top of the documents that preceded it.

The most recent documents were a series of letters dated in the fall of 1979 from Liam Byrne, Esq., to a Robert Spangler, Esq., referencing the O'Malley matter and discussing, in quite formal tones, an apparently delicate negotiation. From the careful language of the letters, Kyle sensed that the terms being exchanged involved silence and money. Kyle paged quickly through the rest of the file until he stopped at a name. Colleen O'Malley.

So she was the O'Malley of the O'Malley file. He had guessed that the creepy old man was a fraud, and now this confirmed it. If the file was to be turned over to anyone, he would find this Colleen and turn it over to her. If there was money to be made, he'd let her make it.

He kept paging back until he found, at the bottom of the document stack, an affidavit from one Colleen O'Malley. It was browned with age, and it had the caption of a lawsuit, *O'Malley v. Truscott,* with a heading claiming the case was brought in Philadelphia's Court of Common Pleas, but there was no case number on the document, or anywhere else in the file, as if the lawsuit were contemplated but never brought. The affidavit trembled a bit in Kyle's hands, and it felt to him like the key to some ancient puzzle. Kyle started reading with a hunger that surprised him.

Colleen was young, sixteen at the time, a student at a local Catholic high school. The affidavit painted a picture of innocence, a girl who entered adolescence shy and sheltered by her loving family. And then another name emerged. Francis Truscott IV, aged eighteen.

Son of a bitch.

Suddenly Kyle understood the power and danger inherent in the file, why everyone was searching for it, how much damage could be done with it and how much profit could be made. Just a boy at the time of the affidavit's telling, Francis Truscott IV was now the junior senator from Pennsylvania and one of the main Republican presidential hopefuls, with a great deal of money behind him.

Kyle slowed down and started reading more carefully. The affidavit told a classic story, as old as love itself and told with a certain panache, certainly not in the words of the sixteen-year-old who had affixed her signature to the back of the document. Kyle grew certain he was reading the words of his father, and it felt as if his father were somehow close to him now, as if he could feel Liam Byrne's breath on the back of his neck as the old man stood over his shoulder, telling him the story of these star-crossed lovers.

The shy young girl from the city, the confident older suburban boy. A chance meeting while volunteering at a homeless shelter, a flirtation, a budding romance. Love wild and on the bloom until the families catch the sweet floral scent. The O'Malleys unhappy because Francis isn't a Catholic. The Truscotts unhappy because Colleen is from a poor family with no social standing. Efforts by both families to come between them. *Romeo and Juliet* played out on a landscape of asphalt Catholic-school yards and lush suburban backyards, until the plot changes in one brutal turn and . . .

Above him Kyle heard the screen door bang shut and the creak of a floorboard. He froze, even as his heart started racing. Quietly he closed the file and clutched it to his chest as he rose from the cement floor.

Someone was in the house. How? Why? Damn it.

The why he knew already, from what he had gleaned in just a few moments with the O'Malley file. It didn't take much imagination to rustle up the scores who would kill to get their hands on the thing—Truscott himself, of course, along with Truscott's Republican rivals, Democratic operatives, tabloids looking to spike circulation. Not to mention the fake O'Malley, who was after the file for his own damn reasons, or that bastard Sorrentino, who just wanted the cash he could squeeze out in blackmail.

And the how was just as obvious. Kyle had driven here with more concern with what was on the radio than with who might be following him. He had parked right in the driveway. He had put the damn lights on in the kitchen and the basement. It was as if he had placed an announcement on the Internet. And after he had opened the door, he'd left the thing not only unlocked but also open, so that the bastards, whoever they were, could stroll right in.

How could he be so stupid? The answer to that was easy: When had he ever done anything smart?

He looked around in panic for a moment and then heard another floorboard creak, this time closer to the basement door. He lunged for the circuit box, slammed it open, started smacking closed the circuits one after the other until he plunged the basement into darkness.

With the sputtering fluorescents silenced, he could hear footsteps above him. Slow and ominous. Coming ever closer to the basement door. And then reaching the steps. And then climbing down. Deliberately and unhurriedly. One step. Then the next. One at a time. Almost leisurely, as if unconcerned about the darkness or what might be waiting for him in the basement. The way an ogre would climb down to his lair, where a captive lay in chains, waiting for evisceration.

Kyle wouldn't wait. As silently as possible, he moved toward the stairs, slinking his left side up against a wall, crouching down, flashlight at the ready. Whatever pain he was feeling from his injuries was blunted by adrenaline coursing through his body. When the bastard descended all the way into the darkness, Kyle would blind him with the flashlight and then charge, putting a shoulder into his chest and slamming him like a rag doll against the wall. It wouldn't be so easy to get up from that, unless the bastard really was an ogre, in which case it wouldn't matter.

Crouched down, the knuckles of his left hand still clutching the file, on the floor, like an offensive lineman waiting for the snap count, Kyle saw the merest shadow of a man, first his feet, then his legs, then his torso, thick and bent, then the round, bulbous head. Kyle lifted the flashlight and tensed his legs, preparing for the violent leap. Wait. Wait. Wait.

Click.

A glare of white and then that head coming clear. A mop of white hair. A gray, lined face. A tense, ironical smile with big yellow teeth.

Instead of leaping, Kyle stood up slowly and stared, slack-jawed and overcome.

"Hello, boyo," said the man, in a soft, hoarse voice smoothed by tobacco and scotch. "It's been a while, hasn't it?"

"Daddy?"

"You're looking hardy, I must say. But not for long, with what I suspect you have in there in your fist. And I don't mean the flashlight."

Chapter 28

There hadn't been enough time to make elaborate provisions, but fortunately Bobby had most of what he needed on hand. The gun, of course, and a couple of jerry cans he filled up at a self-serve gas station well out of his or the boy's neighborhood. And then, for the coup de grâce, he stopped off at One-Eyed Pete's on the way. Pete wasn't home, which was just as well. Bobby kicked open the door to the shed deep in the woods behind Pete's house, took an empty beer carton, and filled all but one of the bottle compartments with Pete's most powerful aerial shells in their mortars, scattering skyrockets and spinners around them for effect. He found an empty beer bottle from the stack in the shed, filled it from one of the jerry cans, put a rag in the top, and placed it in the final compartment.

And then it was on to the craphole house where the boy had grown up.

Robert had already searched the house a few days before, had picked the back lock and slipped in, looking for the file, so he knew the layout, a small two-story with a basement and only two exits, both on the first floor, front and back, which made things easier. The house had been cleared in anticipation of the upcoming sheriff's sale, and he'd found nothing. But there were always hiding places that a stranger might miss: a loose floorboard, a fake wall, a tile in the ceiling that could be pushed away. He wasn't surprised that the boy had gone back.

A few minutes later, Bobby was kneeling in the overgrown bushes at the rear of the house, his provisions beside him. He had parked on the opposite side of the block, across from a completely dark house, and slipped quietly through the backyard to the Byrne house. Robert would have taken far better precautions, but Bobby sensed that the time for such care was coming to an end, and he was glad of it. No longer would he skulk about as if ashamed of the darkness, he was ready to maraud like a berserker.

A dim outside light was on. The Datsun glowed with a dark bloody red at the back of the driveway. It wasn't a mystery how the boy had gotten inside, one of the small rear windows was out of its sill, leaning against the wall, and the back door was ajar. The upper windows of the house were dark, but the kitchen light was on, and, more interestingly, from the lowest windows an uneven white light shone faintly. So the Byrne boy was in the basement. It had seemed completely empty when Robert had searched it. Obviously, he had missed something, but he wouldn't miss anything now.

As quietly as he could, he moved along the edges of the bushes that lined the driveway, angling to get a view of the front door. While he assumed it was still locked, he wanted to be sure which way the boy would run.

But wait a second, what the hell was that?

A figure, at the front door, a male figure in what appeared to be a suit jacket, his face in shadow. There was something about his posture, bent at the waist and slightly hunched, by either age or caution, but something that tolled familiar. The figure tried the front door, found it locked, and then, with an almost arthritic sidestep, arms akimbo, scurried off the far side of the front porch.

Bobby hurried around the house to his spot in the rear bushes and watched as the figure darted around the back of the house, scampered up the rear steps of the porch, slipped inside the open door. Who the hell was he? What was he doing there? And why did he seem so damn familiar?

Bobby thought about it for a moment and then decided it didn't much matter. The man was obviously in cahoots with the boy, had been called in for some unknown reason. If the file was somewhere down in the basement, which only made sense, then the man would learn about it and would also have to be destroyed. Robert would have been greatly concerned about another casualty, but Bobby simply figured this made up for the one he missed out on fourteen years ago. Fine. He'd wait for the man to join Byrne down in the basement and take care of both of them together.

Then a break. The dim outdoor light went off, and the kitchen and basement lights, too. Suddenly the house was in utter darkness.

The power must have died for some reason. The other houses still were lit, so this was just the Byrne house. All the better. Rushing to take advantage of this almost magical opportunity, Bobby gathered up the two jerry cans and the box he had taken from One-Eyed Pete's. Staying low like a soldier, he quickly made his way to the rear steps, the jerry cans sloshing as he moved.

He climbed the steps, lowered the jerry cans, and placed the box to the side of the door. He peered through the screen and could spy nothing but the slight unbroken glimmer of the streetlight slipping in the front windows and bouncing unobstructed across the bare wooden floors. Perfect. There was no time to dally. Maybe the main circuit had simply snapped closed. It wouldn't be long before the boy found the circuit box and clicked it back.

Time to go.

He opened the screen door, grabbed the jerry cans and rushed inside. He took a deep breath, stuck a handkerchief into his mouth, twisted the first cap off, the second.

And then, freed from any concern about the sound he was making, Bobby took the first can and stomped like a motorcycle madman on his way to the front of the house, slopping the liquid over the walls and floor with abandon. The dark, gaseous smell almost overwhelmed him, but he forced in a breath through the handkerchief and kept going.

One can done, he went back for the second and kept stomping and pouring, stomping and pouring, concentrating now on the kitchen and the steps to the basement. He heard shouting from below, footsteps on the stairs, saw the large shadow of the Byrne boy and a beam of light. He took out the gun and fired a shot that rang down the dark stairway, followed by a howl of pain. He must have hit him. Lovely. That will slow the little bastard down, he thought as, with the dregs of the second jerry can, he traced a path out the rear door and to the box he'd taken from Pete's.

As the screen door slammed shut, he took the beer bottle from out of the box, its rag now soaked and stinking. He pulled a lighter from his pocket, flicked it to life, lit the rag.

"Ashes to ashes," said Bobby as he opened the screen door and tossed the flaming bottle into the vapor-filled house. "Like father, like son."

Next thing Bobby knew, he was flying off the porch like a batted shuttlecock.

He fell with a painful thud onto the unyielding lawn. Something cracked in his back. The handkerchief blew out of his mouth. He was blinded, his eyebrows were singed right off his skull, his face felt like he had bobbed for apples in a boiling soup pot, like the skin was peeling from his cheeks. Smoke rose from his smoldering clothes.

He struggled to sit up. His vision was a red blot, but slowly the outlines of the house emerged, and then, within the outline, the dancing, boiling flames. A wild inferno was barely contained within the house's walls. Fire shot out of broken windows, out the now-melting screen door. It wouldn't be long before it burst through the roof like a signal flare into the night sky, declaring the final victory of the Spanglers.

The bitch said she wanted initiative.

Like a wounded crab, Bobby slunk back into the bushes. He now had a view of the rear door and the boy's car. Soon the boy would come charging out the back. And if he ran out some other exit, he'd still head straight for the Datsun. Either way he'd be toast.

Bobby reached into his pocket, pulled out his gun, and waited for the fireworks.

Chapter 29

Kyle's heart jumped like a nervous rabbit flushed from hiding before taking off with a burst of terror. Something was terribly wrong. The sight of his father's face, pinned in the flashlight's beam like a moth in a lepidopterist's display, seemed to turn the ironclad rules of time and space in on themselves in a loopy, Möbius kind of way.

It was as if the flashlight were somehow allowing him to peer into the past. Cheesy science-fiction television shows were the only frame of reference he could grab hold of to understand what was happening: *Stargate* or *Star Trek* or *Lost in Space.* There was an anomaly in the universe, a rent in the time-space continuum, a wormhole. This vision of his father was either a miracle or a harbinger of doom, and either way it scared the hell out of him, as if everything in the universe, along with every certainty he held about his life, were quivering just then on the knife edge of annihilation.

He clicked the light off and then on again. The same face, the same crooked smile.

"I'll have that file if you don't mind, boyo."

"Dad? What the—"

"Watch your language, now. You know I don't abide swearing. English is a marvelously adept tongue. To use such words is nothing short of lazy."

"What the fuck?"

The old man put up a hand to block the flashlight's beam or Kyle's expletive, one or the other, Kyle couldn't be sure, and shook his head. "Ahh, boyo. As headstrong as ever. Can we do something about the light?"

"I don't understand," said Kyle.

"The light. Can you get that interrogator's beam out of my face and turn the overheads back on?"

"Who the hell are you?"

"You know who I am."

"Am I dreaming you? Have I gone crazy?"

"I know it's hard to get a grip on. Something like this doesn't happen every day, but no, you're not crazy. I've come, Kyle, to pull you out of trouble. You're in need of saving, even if you don't know it."

"You've come from where?" said Kyle. "The past?"

"No, son, not the past. That would be crazy. San Bernardino, actually."

"Dad?"

"It's rather nice. A quiet place, really, but we host the National Orange Show every spring. Juggling acts, midget racers. There's even a bean-spitting contest."

"Dad?"

"When I heard what had happened to Laszlo, that Hungarian scoundrel, I knew what it was about. It was the O'Malley file—what else could it be? I came back to make sure it didn't kill anyone else, that it didn't kill you."

"Dad?"

The old man's smile brightened. "Now be a good boyo and give over the file."

"Dad," said Kyle, the skeptical inflection leaving the word and his heart at the same time, being replaced with an impossible joy. Because he knew, suddenly, as much as he knew anything, that this indeed was his father, not a sign of incipient insanity or a culmination of all the false sightings in the last few days. Whether he came to him through the Time Tunnel or in an airplane from San Bernardino didn't matter just then. What mattered was that it was his father, and he had come.

Kyle couldn't help himself from surging forward and wrapping the old man in his arms, even as the flashlight's beam flew wildly about the room before flopping onto the stairs. Kyle pressed his head into his father's neck, breathed in the sharp reality of him, a mélange of scents that were achingly familiar, old cigarette smoke, a dab of Brylcreem, sweat and Aqua Velva, all cut with the faint tinge of gasoline.

Gasoline?

And footsteps above them. Not even quiet footsteps.

Kyle pushed away, aimed the beam again at the old face. "Who the hell is that? Did you come alone?"

"Quite," said the old man. "I made sure of it."

"Not sure enough, I suppose. We've got company."

The old man's eyes narrowed. "They've come for it, boyo, they've come for the file. You have it there, in your hand, isn't that right?"

"Yes."

"Then give it over and let's make haste out of here."

"But why the gasoline?" said Kyle as he quickly thought it through, and then he yelled, "Crap," as he began bounding up the stairs.

The crack of a shot and the whiz of something buzzing by and biting the tip of his ear came all at once. He froze, taking an instant to realize what had happened, an instant where he stayed unmoving on the stairway like a deer caught in a pair of headlights with a target painted on its chest, a red laser dot on its forehead, and a sign that read SHOOT ME BECAUSE I'M AN IDIOT. Then he dove back to the basement, rolling on the floor and howling at the pain in his bruised ribs.

The footsteps above moved away from the top of the stairs even as the smell of gasoline grew so strong it was choking. Kyle coughed as he pushed himself to standing, the flashlight and the file still gripped in his hands.

"Did he get you?" said the old man.

"I don't think so," said Kyle. "Maybe he winged me."

"Let me see."

Kyle aimed the flashlight at his ear. In the reflected light, he could see the old man wince.

"Ahh, nothing to be concerned about," said the old man. "A mere flesh wound. I can barely feel it. Now, boyo, think. How many were there?"

"I only saw a shadow," said Kyle, putting the hand with the file to his ear. He could feel a warm slickness on the back of his hand. "One, maybe."

"Is there a way out?"

"Up the stairs."

"A course of last resort, considering the thug with the gun. Anything else? The windows?"

Kyle passed his flashlight around the room. A series of narrow windows led out to cement window wells. He moved the flashlight from the windows to the old man's thick waist.

"You won't fit," said Kyle.

"Oh, I think I could make it. I've always been as wiry as a snake. But those shoulders of yours wouldn't make it through, that's for sure. I always said less time in the gym and more time in the library and maybe you'd make something of yourself. So it's up the stairs, is it?"

"Or wait for the son of a bitch to come down."

"I fear we won't have that luxury," said the old man.

Just then, as if on cue, a bomb went off.

Chapter 30

Or something that sounded much like a bomb, an explosion that blew them both off their feet and sucked the air right out of their lungs. When Kyle opened his eyes, he could see a great tongue of blue flame reaching down the stairwell and lapping at his feet. Still on his back, he scurried away, pulled the old man, lying dead flat, with him.

"Dad? Dad? Are you okay?"

The old man came groggily to consciousness. "What in the blazes?"

"He set the house on fire."

"The devil."

"He's going to burn us to cinders."

"And burn the file, too," said the old man.

"What?"

"The file. That's what he's after."

"Who?"

"Did you look in it?"

"A little."

"Then you know."

"The senator?"

"Who else?"

"The hell with it," said Kyle, tossing it aside. "He can have it."

The old man gasped, but Kyle ignored him. The heat from the flames coming down the stairs pressed upon Kyle's skin. But the heat was coming from somewhere else, too. He stood up, raised his hand, could feel it pour down from the ceiling. The floor above was burning. It wouldn't be long before the whole thing collapsed on their heads.

"We have to get out of here," said Kyle. "Now."

"All right, then. Up the stairs it is."

"But he still has the gun. He'll be lying in wait outside the house, probably in the back, hoping we'll charge up the stairs and out the open door. We'll be gasping for air as he picks us off."

"Maybe he'll get one, but it's still our only chance," said the old man. He slowly rolled onto his knees and then crawled toward the file that was now leaning up against one of the walls. "I'll follow you."

Kyle turned and looked at the old man as he scuttled across the floor. "It really is you, isn't it?"

"In the flesh." The old man grabbed the file and then, with much struggle, pushed himself to standing. "Let's go, then. Up the stairs with you. 'Half a league, half a league, half a league onward.' "

"What the hell is that?"

"Tennyson." Pause. "Alfred Lord Tennyson?"

"What was he, a ballplayer?"

"A poet. Golly God, son, have you no culture?"

"Not yours," said Kyle. "Then what's a league anyway?"

The old man thought. "I don't really know. Isn't that something?"

"That's something, all right." Kyle looked at the old man. He wasn't small, but there was something fragile about him. Kyle still wasn't sure how this miracle had happened, but he knew instinctively that this old man was his father and that he desperately needed Kyle's protection. And protect him he would, whatever the cost.

"Okay," said Kyle. "Let's do it."

Kyle made his way toward the stairway and then stopped as the flames started dropping down, catching onto the wood step by step. The idea of rushing through the fire, his feet burning all the while, only to be shot as he cleared the doorway, seemed the most futile of acts. He stopped, shook his head, turned around, saw the rusted washer and dryer by the front wall, and flashed on a memory.

It was dark in the memory, and he was scared, just like now, and he was hiding, just like now. It was when he was sixteen, and it involved the empty Simpson house, a rat, a bong, and a small fire that had been accidentally set—the less said about all of which, the better. The police had shown up with their sirens, and they had, each of them, Kat included, stormed out of there and torn off in all different directions. He had headed home but he couldn't rush in his house like a madman, he was more afraid of his mother than of the police. So instead he dove under his own front porch and stayed there, peering out, as the police cruisers slipped by, searchlights panning the doorways. And he remembered a comforting wash of warm, sodden air flowing over him as he cowered. A wash of warm, sodden air flowing from the dryer.

An explosion blasted him out of his reverie, forcing him into a crouch of fear. It was loud, but it hadn't come from the house. It had a familiar sound, as if fireworks were going off nearby. Fireworks? That made no sense, but nothing made sense just then, and there wasn't time to figure any of it out.

He pointed the flashlight at the dryer, found the exhaust pipe, followed it up to where it exited through the drywall.

"Hold this," he told his father, handing over the flashlight as he climbed atop the dryer. With a single savage jerk, he yanked out the exhaust pipe, leaving a hole in the drywall. Wildly he started ripping the drywall away until he saw, behind it, a plywood patch, larger than any of the windows, through which the dryer's exhaust had vented.

"What's that you found?" said his father.

"Our way out," said Kyle.

He banged the plywood with his fist but couldn't break through. He grabbed hold of the hole in the exhaust and pulled, but it wouldn't release. The patch had been screwed into a frame set into a large opening in the stone foundation. He reached up to an edge, worked his fingers as far into the crack as he could, pulled with all his might. Nothing.

Another explosion from outside the house, and then others closer, explosions like gunshots that seemed to come from the top of the stairs.

"I need a screwdriver, or something like a knife," shouted Kyle in frustration.

A quick *click-swish* from beside him. He looked down. His father was holding out a black-handled knife with a long, narrow blade.

"Will this do?"

Kyle stared for a moment at the incongruous sight of his father holding a switchblade, something he could never have imagined in the years before this very moment, then grabbed the thing and started working the blade beneath the plywood and around the screws. He thought it would be a tougher job, but decades of moist, warm air had weakened the wooden frame. With a shot of leverage from the knife, the plywood began pulling away from the frame. When there was enough of a gap to get a proper grip, he put the knife in his teeth, took hold, and heaved. He almost fell off the dryer as the plywood wrenched free, leaving a wide opening leading to the area beneath the front porch of his house.

"Can you make it through?" said Kyle.

"Watch me," said his father as he struggled to lumber atop the dryer.

Kyle reached out a hand and pulled him up and then dropped to his hands and knees to make a stepping stool.

A few moments later, they were lying side by side beneath the front edge of the front porch. It was a strangely delicious moment for Kyle Byrne. He was racked with fear, yes, and in pain still from the beating, yes, and the heat bearing down on the two of them from the house was excruciating, despite the cool air that was now bathing their faces. But here he was, in the same spot where he'd been lying alone ten years before, once again smack in the middle of trouble, but this time with his father.

An explosion overhead, and the street, already illuminated by the fire raging above them, lit up even brighter. In the distance, sirens could be heard.

"My car is in the driveway," said Kyle, "around the back. Stay here while I grab it."

"Don't play the fool, boyo," said his father. "The car's gone, along with the house."

"The house I don't really care about, the bank took it already, but the car's pretty much all I have left."

"Not anymore. Either it's been immobilized or he's waiting for you to jump inside before he starts shooting. It's a death trap now."

"I can't leave it." Pause. "It has your ashes in it."

"You kept them all this time?"

"Funny, isn't it?"

"Yes, actually, but not worth your life anymore, are they? I parked my rental about a block away."

"But, Dad, it's my car."

"It's our only chance. We have many things still to do. We need a clean breakaway. Trust me on this."

Kyle turned and looked at him, looked at his father, and suddenly he didn't give a damn about the rusted old

Datsun. What he wanted, what he had wanted for years, was someone he could rely on. His father, even before he supposedly died, had never been what you could call reliable, and his reappearance after fourteen years of what could only be considered desertion didn't bode well for a swift turnabout. And yet Kyle had so often dreamed over the years of just this, a chance to put his fate in his father's hands, that he couldn't refuse. There were questions that needed to be answered, and soon, but not now. Now he'd rely on the old man, because it's what he had wanted to do all his life.

"All right," said Kyle. "I'll follow you."

"Good. Are you ready?"

"I'm ready," said Kyle, and then he turned his head. "Hey, Dad."

"Yes, boyo?"

"Happy Father's Day."

A gentle smile on his father's face. "Is that what it is?"

"That's what it is," said Kyle, his voice choked, his heart so full it cracked. "Okay, let's go."

In the street a small crowd had gathered, pulled out of their parlors and off their porches by the light and the noise, watching the inferno devour the empty old Cape Cod as they waited for the arrival of the fire engines that had been summoned over and again from one cell phone after another. And every now and then, another rocket would shoot up from behind the house like a signal flare from some fiendish battle, exploding across the stars in fingers of fire emanating from a perfect blue eye hanging fierce and unblinking in the night sky. And the crowd would go "Awww" as if the display were being put on solely for their amusement.

And just as one of those rockets burst incandescent in the darkness over the flaming house, while most faces were tilted to the sky with mouths involuntarily open in delight, a young boy noticed two strange shadows rising like ghosts from the ground beneath the burning house's porch, one ghost seemingly young and strong, the other older and thicker, moving stiffly as he clutched something to his chest, both running from the house with their waists bent, as if trying not to be seen, running down the street, the young one turning back to take in the splendorous sight, and then running away, away.

"Look, Mommy," said the boy, pointing at the disappearing shadows.

"Yes," said his mother, her chin high as she stared at the sweet show in the sky, "isn't it beautiful?"

Chapter 31

Dawn was just breaking as Henderson and Ramirez toured the charred and stinking wreck with mouths shut and hands in pockets. The roof was gone, jagged shards of wall stood out from the debris, the whole site was soaked through as if it had rained nonstop for weeks on end just upon this one patch of blighted earth. The two detectives took it all in with stony expressions. This crime scene was out of their jurisdiction, and they had no inherent authority here, but they had come right out once notified of the fire by a suburban inspector named Demerit.

"I recalled the request you sent in about any information we might have on Kyle Byrne," said Demerit as he accompanied them around the scene, kicking aside any burned timbers that had fallen in their way. Demerit was short and gray and wore the cheap blue suit of a cop a bit too long on the job.

"We appreciate it," said Henderson. "It was quite a thing for you to remember that request right off."

"I knew the kid. Byrne was the best running back we ever had at Haverford High, and that wasn't even his sport."

"What was?" said Henderson.

"Baseball. I coached against him in Little League. He had a swing so beautiful it could make you cry. We didn't have a fence high enough to contain him. I could have sworn he was going places."

"A regular Babe Ruth," said Henderson. "So what happened?"

"Life, I suppose. I played drums all through high school, was going to be a rock star, right? What about you, sweetie?" he said to Ramirez. "What were you going to be when you grew up?"

"A police detective," said Ramirez.

Henderson looked at the interaction with amusement. This Demerit had been talking mostly to Henderson, which had ticked Ramirez off, considering she was the one who had put in the request for information about Kyle Byrne. And then the "sweetie" had pissed her off even more. One more strike and she'd be at his throat, which wouldn't get them anywhere but would be fun as hell to watch.

"What do you have for us, Inspector Demerit?" said Henderson.

"The fire marshal found evidence of accelerant all over the place, so it's definitely arson. The house used to belong to Byrne's mother. The son inherited it when she died."

"How'd she pass?" said Ramirez.

"Cancer. The neighbors say it came quick and with a load of pain. Nothing to be done for her. Sad. Supposed to have been a nice lady and still young. The son stayed in the house for about a year or so after, but there was a mortgage that he never paid. The bank seized it about a month ago, kicked him out, cleared it of everything, and put it up for sale. Pretty good motive for arson, don't you think?"

"You're figuring the kid for setting the fire?" said Ramirez.

"It's not so hard. We were wondering if you knew of any contact information or the boy's current address."

"You don't really have much on him, do you?" said Ramirez. "He was angry at a bank. Who the hell isn't angry at a bank? If the headquarters of my credit-card company ever exploded, they'd be looking at me. You have any evidence tying him to the accelerant?"

"Nope."

"Any fiber samples or blood?"

"Nothing that survived the fire."

"Any threatening letters to the bank, anything said to friends or relatives?"

"Nothing yet."

"Then you don't really have much tying Kyle Byrne to the fire, do you?"

"Well," said Demerit, rubbing his jaw, "there is the car."

Just then they reached the rear of the driveway, where a burned-out wreck of a sports car squatted on singed and ruined tires. The left front was still bright red, with its headlight and bumper fully intact, but the right side, closest to the house, and the whole rear end, starting with the doors and moving back, were a discolored, stinking mess of gray and black, leading to a hatchback where sheets of metal had been stripped away by fire and force.

"How long has this been there?" said Henderson.

"Wasn't there yesterday, according to the neighbors. And it's registered to Kyle Byrne, though the registration has lapsed and it's overdue for inspection, which seems par for the course in the way Byrne's life has gone lately. And then a kid on the street claimed he saw two figures running from the house. One was big enough to have been Byrne."

"I guess you might have enough cause to pull him in at that," said Henderson.

Demerit rubbed his jaw again, looked right at Ramirez. "Any idea where I could find him?"

"That's why you called us down?" said Ramirez. "To get an address?"

"That was one reason. I was also wondering why a Philadelphia police detective was so interested in the Byrne boy."

Ramirez looked at Henderson, Henderson looked at Ramirez. They could argue bitterly between themselves for hours, but throw in a third party like this Demerit, with his cheap suit and annoying jaw rubbing, like he was auditioning for the role of detective in some community-theater group, and suddenly they were a team, trying to figure out how much to hold back from this suburban stiff. Henderson gave a quick shrug to let Ramirez know it was all up to her.

Ramirez turned to Demerit. "There was a break-in at a law office. Kyle Byrne was picked up inside. Before we interrogated him, we sent a request to your office, since this was the last address he gave. But it turned out he had a valid reason to be there."

"And what was that?" said Demerit.

"It was his father's office."

Demerit looked at her for a moment, turned to Henderson and then back. "I thought his father was dead. He died . . . what?" He pulled out a pad, paged through it quickly. "Fourteen years ago. And a few days before the kid's house burns down, he has a hankering to break into his father's old office?"

"Maybe it's a coincidence. The office was in the process of being closed. No one pressed charges, and he was released."

"Did he give you guys an address?"

"This one," said Ramirez.

"What was he doing there, did he say?"

"Looking for souvenirs."

"Is that what he said? Well, maybe that's what he was doing here, too. But the bank had already cleaned the place out. So maybe he just got angry, lost control, maybe he burned the place down, and his car got caught in it. Maybe that explains everything."

"You think?" said Ramirez.

"It might," said Demerit, rubbing his jaw, "if it weren't for the fireworks."

Henderson and Ramirez looked at each other with a mutual puzzlement as a uniform came up to Inspector Demerit and motioned him away. They talked softly for a moment, and then Demerit came back over.

"Give me a minute, will you?" said Demerit. "The fire marshal just found something that might be of interest to the two of you." He left them outside and followed the uniform into the bombed-out wreck that had been the Byrne house.

"Did your boy Byrne really do this?" said Henderson.

"He strike you as a kid just welling with anger, ready to throw a bomb at anything that pissed him off?"

"Not really."

"Me neither. Best as I can tell, he doesn't care enough about anything in this world to break a sweat, better yet to set it afire. And this was his boyhood home—"

"Taken from him by the bank."

Ramirez sighed. "Do you remember the house where you grew up?"

"Sure I do. Parkside. I still pass it now and then and remember."

"You care who owns it?"

"Not really."

"Neither would he. If he wasn't paying the mortgage, he knew it was only a matter of time. And why would he burn his car in the process?"

"Maybe it just caught on fire without him trying. Maybe he's a fool."

"Of course he's a fool," she said. "We know he's a fool. But even a fool wouldn't park in his own driveway if he were going to burn down his house."

"True."

"And what was that about the fireworks?"

"Don't know. Maybe it was gunshots mistaken as fireworks."

"Or maybe," said Ramirez, "the fireworks were a cover for something else. You figure this moron will ever tell us what he knows?"

"I suppose he will when his jaw gets all itchy again."

"Yeah, what is up with that jaw rubbing anyway?"

"He's been watching *Columbo* reruns on cable."

"Next time he starts up, I'm going to smash that jaw with my fist. That would be the end of the rubbing."

"I'd pay to see that," said Henderson, laughing as Demerit came out of the burned shell.

"Why don't you two come inside and down to the basement," said Demerit. "I've got something you might want to see."

They had to climb down to the basement on an aluminum ladder placed by the firemen, since the stairs had been rendered useless. The space was a wreck of scorched framing and ruined drywall, still flooded from burst pipes and the firefighters' efforts to drown the blaze. Seared scraps and timbers floated in a few inches of dark, filthy water. The place smelled of smoke and damp cement and singed dreams. The charred overhead beams were still in place, though much of the floor above them had been eviscerated, so that slashes of sunlight gouged their way through the open roof and the two ruined floors into the basement, illuminating thick motes of drifting ash. Ramirez couldn't shake the feeling that she was entering a church.

"Over here," said Demerit as he waded through the muck to the edge of the basement. The two Philadelphia detectives followed, water seeping into their shoes. A number of fallen beams had created a blackened frame around some singed rectangular object.

"What the hell's that?" said Henderson.

"A file cabinet," said Demerit.

"I thought you said the bank had emptied the place out," said Henderson.

"I did. But if you follow the line of framing still standing, you can see that this little jog in the foundation walls was boarded up."

"So the file cabinet was hidden."

"That's what we figure."

"You check out what's inside?"

"Nothing of much interest, best as we can tell, just some outdated legal files and records, all of them at least a decade and a half old."

"You mind if we take a look?" said Ramirez, a little too eagerly.

"Not at all," said Demerit, rubbing his jaw, "once we figure some things out. So let me get this right. The boy was caught breaking into his father's old law office a few days ago. And then he's at the scene of an arson where an old file cabinet is mysteriously discovered. And there's a murder involved somewhere, because all of this is of intense interest to the Homicide Division of the Philadelphia Police Department. How am I doing?"

"Pretty damn well," said Henderson.

"For a suburban cop," said Demerit.

"I didn't say that."

"You didn't have to. So tell me, Detectives, what is this boy looking for?"

Henderson glanced at Ramirez, who shrugged.

"We don't know," he said.

"Well, that boy does," said Demerit. "And whatever the reason, it just took out a house in my township and set off a fireworks display that had the phone banks clogged for hours, so you damn well know I'm going to find that boy and get the truth. Now let me ask again, Detective Ramirez: Do you have any idea where to find Kyle Byrne so I can ask him what the hell is going on?"

Ramirez gave Inspector Demerit Kyle Byrne's cellphone number and a copy of the card of that friend of his, that Korean tax lawyer. In return, Henderson and Ramirez got to look into the file cabinet.

"It was his father's file cabinet," said Henderson as they drove east on Haverford Avenue back into the city. "And he took something from that bottom drawer, the one that was still open. And whatever it is, it is dangerous as hell."

"You figure Toth was killed for the same thing?"

"Maybe."

"By Kyle?" said Ramirez.

"Of course not. If he killed Toth in the office, he could have searched it then. Why would he go back later just so we could catch him? And you're right, why would he leave his car in the driveway so that it would go up with the house and the fireworks? No, the kid didn't do any killing, but I'd bet the killer is after him."

"The guy who put him in the hospital."

"Probably," said Henderson, "unless his problems are bigger than we can imagine."

"So who is it?"

"Don't know, but I wouldn't be surprised if it was the same person that called in the burglary."

"I'll get hold of that tape." She thought for a moment. "We need to find Byrne and warn him."

"He already knows he's in trouble, he doesn't need our warning. But this whole thing seems to be about one of his father's old files, right?"

"I suppose."

"Which means it's at least fourteen years old. And if it was dangerous now, it must have been dangerous then, too. How'd the father die?"

"No one seems to know for sure," said Ramirez.

"Well, then," said Detective Henderson, "don't you think you ought to find out?"

Chapter 32

A motel room is where romance goes to die.

The two Byrnes were in unit 207 of a cheap roadside motel in Bellmawr, New Jersey, just over the bridge from Philadelphia. The dark room was lit only by a flash of neon that slipped through a gap in the curtains. It smelled of yesterday's urine, of indifferent adulterous sex, of the smoke that had permeated their skin and clothes from the night of fire they had passed through together.

Kyle sat in the tattered upholstered chair he had dragged across the floor so that it blocked the door, and he stared at his father, who lay sleeping on his back in one of the sagging beds. His father was wearing just his pants and socks, his thick torso was bare, his sagging breasts covered with gnarly gray hair. He was snoring loudly enough to drown out the strange goings-on in room 205 next door, which was just as well. Kyle sat in that chair, watching his father sleep the sleep of the unperturbed, the sleep of the innocent, and he brooded.

The love and astonishment that had overwhelmed him upon first seeing his father's face in the beam of his flashlight had turned into something dark and sour. He thought of his years of vainly searching crowds for the father who had died. He thought of his mother sitting on the porch, staring out at the lonely darkness that had become her life. He thought of his own failures, one after the other, failures he had always secretly and comfortingly attributed to his fatherlessness. He thought of his mother lying withered and gray in the hospital, alone except for her brother and son, forcing that ironic smile onto her shivering lips one last time.

Where the hell have you been, you son of a bitch?

The ride through the city and over the bridge in his father's green rental car had been tense and yet full of the excitement of their strange reunion and exhilarating escape. But as soon as they hit the room, Kyle's emotions began to turn, and he started asking questions.

"I'm too tired to talk about it now, boyo," said his father. "I've been following you around for days. I need to sleep. In the morning we'll talk it all through, in the morning. I promise." And just a few minutes later, the snoring began, a harsh, grabbing sound, like the endless emptying of a drain partially clogged with hair and globby deposits of fat.

So Kyle waited through the night in the chair, falling asleep for brief intervals, waking each time with a start, looking around desperately until he was sure the old man was still there, in the bed. There was a television on a stand, but he didn't feel like watching. He had left his cell phone in the car at his old house, which put him out of contact with the world, but considering who was asleep in the bed, he didn't much mind. He simply sat in the chair, and between fits of sleep he stared. He felt partly as if he were watching over his father like a protector and partly like a prison guard.

Because Kyle had to know.

The next time Kyle awoke, sunlight was streaming through the gap in the curtains and his father was gone. Kyle shot to his feet, dashed to the window, spread open the curtains. Light hit his face like a fist. Then, behind him, he heard the shower in the bathroom. A moment later the water shut off, and he could hear his father whistling, oblivious to the emotional turmoil bubbling in the bedroom. Kyle closed the curtains, sat down in the chair, and waited.

"Good morning, boyo," said Liam Byrne when he came out of the bathroom, still wet from the shower.

He was naked except for a towel held around his waist with one hand while he scratched at a wildly unkempt head of hair with the other. "How'd you sleep?"

"Fitfully."

"You should have taken the other bed. I told you no one knows where we are."

"I needed to be sure."

"Well, you suited yourself as you always did, but I hope you obtained enough rest in that chair of yours, for we have much to do today, much to do."

"I thought we'd start by talking about the last fourteen years."

There was a pause as Liam Byrne drew underwear from a small, shabby suitcase. He started to collect the rest of his clothes scattered all about the room even as he collected his thoughts. When he spoke, finally, he did so without looking at his son.

"They were years in the wilderness, boyo. Fallow years. And believe it or not, I missed you more than you missed me."

"I doubt it."

"No, it's truth, believe me." He began to dress, a pair of boxers, his rumpled suit pants. "And your mother, I was so sad to hear of her passing. I loved her mightily."

"Not enough to be there when she died."

"Would it have helped? Would my presence have given her one more day?"

"She never dated, never saw another man."

"One of a kind, your mother."

"How could you leave her like that, by pretending to be dead? How could you leave me?"

Liam Byrne, still shirtless, stopped dressing and stared at his son for a moment before walking around to sit on the edge of the bed closest to Kyle. His face was drawn with seriousness. He leaned forward to put his hand on Kyle's knee.

Kyle recoiled.

"I had no choice," Liam Byrne said softly. "Believe me when I say this. They would have killed me if I stayed."

"Who?"

"The same people who came after us last night. That's why I left, that's why I ran. You've seen them at work now, so you must understand. It was the file, don't you understand? Now and then. Fourteen years ago they were killing everyone connected to it, and I was next."

And then, in the somber tones of a lawyer laying out a case for a jury, he told Kyle the sad and harrowing truth behind the O'Malley file.

Chapter 33

It began with a meeting in his office. An older couple he knew from his old church, a fine upstanding couple, the O'Malleys, childless until they were graced in their later years with a daughter, a gift from God, Colleen.

Colleen had been dating a rich boy from the suburbs, but their romance was frowned on by both the families. The O'Malleys thought he was too fast, the boy's parents thought she wasn't good enough for him. The pressure grew too much for Colleen, and she broke it off. The boy wanted it to continue. He grew crazy, calling her at all hours, holding vigils outside her house, following her home from school, home from basketball games, following. Stalking, they call it now. And then one night he seized her arm. She struggled. It turned ugly. And with a hand pressed upon her mouth and amid whispers that she was trash and no one else would have her if he couldn't, he pulled her into an alley.

"That was in 1979," said Liam Byrne. "The parents wanted protection for their daughter and some sort of justice. But in those days it wasn't the thing to testify. Reputations were easily ruined. Neither family wanted that. And the boy's family had money. We could get far more by keeping it quiet than by making it public. So instead of going to the police and bringing charges, I advised a settlement, and the parents agreed. The amount was generous, more than enough for Colleen's education, and as part of the settlement the boy was sent to counseling. I thought that was best for all, to set right two lives that had listed. I thought I was doing the correct thing. But I was wrong. Fifteen years later the boy, now working in the family's investment bank, made his first run for public office."

"Truscott," said Kyle.

"Yes, that's right," said Liam Byrne. "This was in 1994, when the Republicans took over Congress and Truscott was aiming to be part of that wave, using a scad of his money to buy the seat. I thought the republic was in danger from a reactionary cadre of the moneyed elite and thought myself obligated to do something about it. So I went to that Truscott, no longer a kid but a hard and ambitious politician, and told him if he didn't back out of the campaign, I would have no choice but to release the file. I thought I was doing the right thing for the country, but I didn't anticipate the consequences. He didn't back out of the campaign. He didn't confess and move on. What he did was to start the killing."

"Killing?"

"Colleen O'Malley, no longer a girl but a mother with two children living in Ohio. She drowned in a lake under unusual circumstances. I had kept in contact with her—both her parents had passed by then, and I felt a paternal obligation—and was horrified at the news. The funeral was a sad affair, such youth lost. But as I left the funeral, driving back to the airport, a car came from behind and rammed me off the road. My car tumbled twice before coming to rest in a ravine. I barely clambered out before it exploded. That's when I finally understood what had happened to Colleen. And I knew that the next time I wouldn't be so lucky."

"Did you go to the police?"

"And say what? What did I know? The boy wasn't doing it himself. He was all the time in Philadelphia, giving speeches. I would have been taken for a crackpot and been just as vulnerable."

"What about the press? Why not just tell the story to the press and get it over with?"

"No one would print it. His family was too powerful. And without the girl there'd be no proof. I also knew that if I went to the press, it wasn't just myself I'd be endangering but everyone close to me, including your mother and you."

"And your wife."

"Yes, well, her, too, of course. Maybe I panicked, maybe I was a fool, but I believed then that if ever I showed my face again in Philadelphia, I'd be killed right off. I found a man who could feign my death for a price, and I paid it. I paid it, and I ran, and I've been running ever since. Oh, boyo, you don't know the torture of it to be an exile from your own life. But it was the only way."

Kyle stared at his father, tried to see him fresh. For so long he had loomed huge over Kyle's life. To see him reappear was almost fitting, as if he were a superman who could accomplish anything. But this tale about his fear and his decision to run from his former life brought him down to scale. Less than scale. For a moment he looked small and tragic, and Kyle's heart reached out to him. But then Kyle thought of his mother.

"So you deserted us."

"It was the only way, boyo. Otherwise you all would have been at risk. I gave up my life here to protect you."

"How did you live?" said Kyle. "What did you do?"

"I wandered, picked up the documentation I needed to make a new life, settled down in California. I made do."

"Were you alone?"

"What is this, a cross-examination?"

"Answer the question. Were you alone?"

"Have you ever thought of law school? It's clearly in your blood. But think, boyo. Do you really want to be asking that question?"

"So you found another woman. Or maybe had one already waiting, maybe someone as insanely loyal as my mother. Maybe you even started a new family. Do you coach your new kid in Little League, Dad?"

There was a pause as father and son stared at each other and the missing years tumbled between them like clothes in a Laundromat dryer.

"He's a got a swing, he does," Liam Byrne said finally. "Almost as pretty as yours."

"You're still with her and the boy?"

"It didn't work out, it never does. I'm fated to pick women too good for me. Like your mother."

"How do you live? Are you still a lawyer?"

"Couldn't finagle myself a license. So it's real estate instead. I dabble and get by."

"With the money you stole from Sorrentino?"

Liam Byrne nodded as if Kyle's possession of the name were not a surprise. "What did that foul little monster tell you?"

"He beat the hell out of me looking for what you stole. He wants the file, too. He thinks he can make his money back with it. He says you owe it to him."

"That thief. We were in the middle of a partnership dispute when I left, that's all it was. What I took was my share only."

"You better tell him that before he comes after me again."

"I'll deal with him, don't worry."

"How, Dad? How are you going to deal with anything? You're dead, remember? And tell me, if life is so damn good in California, why did you bother to come back? And why now?"

"Because of Laszlo. I saw word of his murder on the Internet, and I knew I had to be at that funeral."

"You came to pay your respects?"

"No, you're not getting it. When I heard about his murder, I figured he had found a copy of the file and tried to weasel some money for himself. He was always a crook. He couldn't help himself. What's the opening line of every Hungarian recipe? 'First, steal a chicken.' And I remembered the cabinet I left in your house, which meant you, too, were at risk. So I came back, boyo. I came back to save you. You must believe me."

"How can I?"

"And I want to tell you, watching you hit that baseball from afar . . ."

"So it was you."

"Of course it was. I always loved watching you play ball. And now, spending this time with you, even if on the run, boyo, it fills my heart. You and me, together again, Byrne and son. We make a hell of a team, yes we do. The way we got out of that burning house, it was magical."

"It was pretty good, wasn't it?"

"So are we settled on the issue?"

"No," said Kyle.

"But someday, maybe? Someday you'll forgive the old man for doing only what he had to do?"

"I don't know."

Liam Byrne looked at his son with bright eyes, as if a jury had just come back in his favor.

"Well, that's all I can ask for," he said in a cheery voice. "It's all I deserve. I made mistakes, I know it. I've loved and lost and played the fool. But I did it all on my terms, and that made all the difference. Son, listen. I learned something in this life that has kept me on the right side of things. You need to be true to yourself, boyo. Be true to yourself and you'll be true to me, too. That's all I can ask."

He patted Kyle's knee before standing and resuming his dressing. "Come now, boyo, we have work to do."

"What are you talking about?"

"It's time to trap a senator. We're going to stomp on that rogue like a cockroach in the kitchen."

"Why are we going to do anything? Let's just go to the cops with the file and our story. There's a detective I met that I think I trust."

"We can't, boyo, don't you see? It wouldn't any longer be about him, it would be about you and about me. Your car is still at the house. They'll blame you for the fire. And then they'd pick me up, too. There was insurance involved in my leaving, with death benefits to your mother and my wife. We'd both end up in jail, and our senator would weasel his way out of trouble. You have to promise me. No one can know I'm back. I must at all times remain dead. That's rule one. Promise me."

"I don't know, Dad."

"Well, figure it out," he said angrily. "And fast. You might never forgive your poor father, and he might not deserve forgiving, but you surely wouldn't send him to jail, would you?"

Kyle looked at his father, felt some deeply held sense of misplaced loyalty well inside. "No," he said. "I wouldn't do that."

"Good boy. Now, with the file in our hands, we can go on offense. The stakes were high fourteen years ago, but they've been raised radically. It's not just a seat in Congress anymore, the assassin has his sights on the White House. He'll do anything to make sure every trace of his boyhood crime is destroyed. And that, finally, will be his undoing."

Chapter 34

For the first time in his life, Bobby Spangler's world seemed perfectly balanced, as if he were dancing on the edge of a cleaver.

There had always been a disparity between his hopes and his realities, between his vision of himself and the way she viewed him. But the fire had cleansed him, burning off not just his eyebrows, or the lank hair he combed over his skull, but also his most puerile fantasies. Through the healing power of fire, he could, for the first time, see himself and his place in the world clear. The sulfurous landscape of his inner life now matched perfectly the burned and smoking wasteland he had trudged through all his days.

And somehow, magically, this balance made him incredibly happy.

Gone were the burdens of his expectations, of the high place he saw for himself among the men who made things happen in the world. Gone was the daily humiliation as he scraped and bowed for her blessings. Gone was the incessant striving. They all belonged to Robert, and Robert had been roasted to death in the fire as surely as those poor dead bastards in the basement of the Byrne house. For the first time since he was an innocent young child in his father's meager home, he felt free of the shackles of possibility. He was no longer in the process of becoming, he simply was.

Bobby Spangler. Hunter. Fire starter. Murderer. A dangerous man and quite a nimble dancer, maintaining his balance on the cleaver's edge.

"What have you done?" she said over the phone. He was sitting in his apartment, on the easy chair, naked except for the phone covering his ear, singed and still stinking of smoke, feeling waves of burning heat flush his ravaged skin as her bitter voice surged through him. The Super 8 projector was whirling away behind him as a black-and-white female figure flickered on the makeshift screen set up behind the television. The figure was dressed only in glossy high heels, dark stockings, long white gloves. Her pale limbs writhed, her torso twisted and breasts heaved, her mouth opened with feigned passion.

"I put on a show," he said coolly. Like Clint East-
wood, like Cool Hand Luke. For the first time in their
brutally unequal relationship, Bobby felt in control,
and the feeling was as stimulating as a cattle prod.

"Don't be a garish fool," she spit out. "The fire was
a terrible mistake, coming on the heels of what happened to Laszlo. It was such a clear sign to dig deeper
that even one of those imbecile police detectives might
have picked it up."

"I told you that was a possibility. But as always," he
said, his voice turning singsong, "you ignored what I
had to say and ordered me to go forward."

"Not with fireworks. What kind of cretin would use
fireworks?"

"Once I started the fire, if they had managed to
come out of the basement, there was going to be shooting. The fireworks gave me a cover."

"But it brought out the helicopters, you idiot. It
made not only the local but the national news. Yet again
you've shown your incompetence, your unworthiness.
Spangler to the core."

He paused for a moment, recognized the line in the
sand he had never before crossed, and then, with a certain swagger, and while gazing at the gyrations on the
screen, he stepped over. "As are you," he said.

"What's that you say?"

"I'm just pointing out the obvious. Pointing out the single most important fact that has underlain all that has gone on between us over the years."

"What has gotten into you, Bobby? You sound different. Are you drunk?"

"No," he said. "It's just that some truths have been burned into my skin."

"You must be quite a sight, but you are still as ignorant as ever. *I* was *always* different."

"Not so different. I know about all the nasty little things you did in the desert before latching onto the Truscotts."

"I did what I had to do, dear."

"And with much enthusiasm," he said, as the figure on the screen shifted her position until she was facing away from him, on knees and elbows, turning her head and staring now over her shoulder and into his eyes.

"But I was always meant for better things," she said. "I once thought you were, too. Obviously, I was mistaken."

"Of course you were. That is your fate, to be mistaken about me." He glanced down at his lap. My God, it was as if he'd swallowed a bottle of those damn blue pills. Talking back to her was better than the movie. "Tell me you love me."

"Don't be a fool."

"Say it."

"You sound different, Bobby."

"I am different." He put his hand around himself, watched as the movie figure reached a white-gloved hand between her legs. As she licked her lips, he growled softly.

"You sound like the young boy I felt had so much promise," she said, her voice almost girlish.

"Say you love me."

"Maybe, yes. Maybe I do. As one loves a dog."

"I need to see you. There are issues we need to deal with."

"There is only one issue that concerns me." Pause, and then an intake of breath. "You said 'they.' What did you mean? Was there more than one at the house?"

"The boy had an accomplice."

"Who?"

"I don't know. Someone older. When can I see you? I have something for you."

"And you took care of them both?"

"Neither came out."

"Out of where? I don't understand."

"What is so confusing? Has your brain turned to mush in your senescence? They both went into the house. They both were in the basement when I burned the place down. Neither of them came out."

There was a moment of silence, but not in satisfied remembrance of two lives crushed by their common will, no. This silence was filled with the coldness of a bitter rebuke. Somehow the tide had turned; he could feel himself shrink as if he were being swallowed by the silence. The figure on the screen lowered her head and twisted her lips into a taunt.

"What's wrong?" he said.

"The most recent news reports stated that no bodies were found in the debris."

"That's impossible."

"The disappointment I feel in you at this moment is incalculable."

"They didn't come out."

"What is it like to be so wrong so often?" she said.

"I'll take care of it."

"See that you do. Find them. Find them both and kill them."

"And then what?"

"Destroy the evidence."

"I mean, what about me?"

"What about you?"

"It's time you pony up after all these years. It's time I get what I deserve."

"I like it when you whine. It reminds me of what you have become."

"You owe me."

"Oh, Bobby, Bobby, Bobby. What is one to say? I have allowed you to serve our joint ambitions at my behest. I have turned you into a malicious little pet. What more could you ever have hoped for?"

The figure on the screen rose from her elbows and, while still on her knees, turned to him, her arms outstretched, her lovely breasts shimmying. The sweet gray tongue, slipping out of her taunt of a mouth, beckoned.

"I'm going to kill them both," he said.

"See that you do."

"And then I'm coming for you."

Chapter 35

"Before we do anything," said Liam Byrne as they drove toward the city in his rental car the day after the fire, "we need to get you properly dressed."

"I'm dressed okay," said Kyle, unable to hide the irritation in his voice. After spending his whole life feeling deprived of a father, sitting in that car now, sitting beside his actual father at last, he should have felt the keen lift of elation. But instead he stared out the window, watching the scabrous landscape of New Jersey flit by, and felt nothing more than annoyance. Annoyance at having to spend all this time with an utter stranger who bore only a passing resemblance to the father he had desperately missed for so long. Annoyance that this stranger was full of crap and yet felt free to relay that crap to Kyle as if it were acknowledged truth. Annoyance that they were talking about his clothes.

"Did you look at yourself in the mirror?" said his father. "You look homeless."

"I am homeless."

"Ah, yes, I forgot. My successful son."

"Well, you know I had it tough growing up," said Kyle, still looking away. "My father died when I was twelve."

Liam Byrne gripped tightly to the steering wheel with both hands and leaned forward, an old man straining for a better view of the road. "You could use a haircut, too. And a shave. But it's the clothes we need to do something about first."

"What's wrong with my clothes?"

"Look at that T-shirt you're wearing. Besides the fact that it's really just a piece of underwear?"

"Yeah, besides that?"

"It's ripped and stained and smells like smoke. And those things on your legs—"

"Shorts."

"Yes, well. Enough said about those."

"My stuff's a bit ragged from the fire, sure. I mean, last night we were both almost killed, remember? But truthfully, Dad, their condition is not much worse than after one of my normal nights out. I need some fresh underwear and socks, is all. We can go to my friend Kat's, where I have some stuff, or buy something new. We passed a Wal-Mart just a ways back there."

"You need more than new socks, boyo. You have a suit, don't you? I saw you wearing one at Laszlo's funeral. Was the suit you were wearing there borrowed from Goodwill, or does it belong to you?"

"It's mine."

"Excellent, then let's put it on. For what we need to do today, you'll want to be wearing a suit."

"What I have on is fine. It's what I wear."

"Here's a lesson for you, boyo. You dress today for how you want to be perceived tomorrow."

"That's what I'm doing."

"If you want respect, dress like you deserve it. No one gives advancement to a sloven. Don't you want to be somebody?"

"Sure, somebody who can still get away with dressing in a T-shirt and shorts."

"Where's your pride, boyo?"

"I buried it with my father."

Liam Byrne didn't respond, he just shifted in his seat and set his jaw. This was the first time in his life Kyle had talked back to his father, and Kyle didn't like it one bit.

"My style must be too hip for you to appreciate," said Kyle, injecting a forced lightness into his voice. "It's the latest in casual bohemian."

"It's like you don't care enough to care."

"Exactly. I should start a business with that motto: 'Clothes for the indiscriminating buyer who doesn't care enough to care.' "

"That's not a style, it's a sign of resignation."

"It's comfortable."

"And that's the towering height of achievement you aspire to? Comfort?"

"Sure, why not?"

"Because comfort is for octogenarians in their nursing homes with bibs tied and diapers tight. The rest of us are here to seize what glory we can."

"Glory? Not very Zen of you, Dad. Glory's for saps."

"So you tell me now, as others leapfrog over your head."

"And what's it getting them?"

"It's getting them money and power, the corner office and the new Lexus. It's getting them laid, boyo."

"I don't have any trouble, there."

"Well, maybe not. You're a Byrne, after all. But with clothes like that, I'm sure it must be high-class stuff you're getting. Answer me this, boyo: Five years from now, where do you want to be?"

"On the couch, playing Xbox."

"That is the saddest thing I ever heard. It's all the dope you kids smoke. You smoke a boatload, I suppose."

"Not too much anymore."

"Waste your mornings with a pipe and a video game and your nights with cheap beer and wanton women."

"On good days, yeah."

"Ah, youth. I forgot how stupid it can be."

"Go to hell."

"Let me give you some advice about that marijuana. We had it in my day, too, we thought we discovered it. But stay off it, it's a curse. It kills your ambition, that stuff. It seems like nothing more than a pleasant diversion, and ten years later you're living in your mother's house and letting the mortgage lapse."

"What are you doing, Dad? Trying to jam fourteen years' worth of parental lectures into one miserable car ride?"

"Somebody needs to set you straight."

"That was my mom's job. You left it for her alone, remember? It's too late for you to get your licks in."

"You can't be blaming me for all that's gone wrong in your life, son."

"Watch me."

"What do you want from me, boyo?"

"Maybe to say you're sorry."

"I said it already."

"Funny, I didn't hear it."

"Okay, then. I'm sorry about the way it worked out."

"That's not quite it, is it?"

"Tell me what exactly it is you want to hear, and I'll spit it out like a parrot."

"Forget it."

"No, tell me."

"I said forget it."

"Okay, sure. If that's what you want. We're not here to quarrel, we're here to work together, like a real father and son, to bring some justice to the world."

"Whatever."

"Good. Now, about that suit."

Kyle was dropped off in front of Kat's apartment building. He took out a key ring from his pocket, looked it over. A key to his old house, now useless. A key to his car, just as useless at the moment. A key to Bubba's that he forgot to give back when he was fired. His key ring was an eloquent declaration of the pathetic state of his life. The only key that worked was to someone else's apartment.

Inside, scrawled on a sheet of paper was a message from Kat: *CALL ME!!!*

He did.

"Kyle, what the hell is happening?" she said. "I thought you were dead. Did you hear about your house?"

"I was there."

"Shut up. It was all over the news. And what was with the fireworks?"

"I have no idea."

"But you got out and you're okay?"

"Apparently."

"I swear I thought you were dead."

"It's not for lack of someone trying," said Kyle.

"I've been calling your cell all morning."

"I sort of left it in my car, which I sort of left at the house."

"That's a shame, right there, because that was a nice phone."

"I need to get my car back."

"Bad news, I'm afraid. Your car was totaled in the fire."

"Now you shut up."

"I saw a picture on the news, and that car was gone. It looked like the junkers you see parked on the street in Kensington, the paint all burned off, the rear end exploded."

"Kat. My car. The last thing I owned in this world was my car."

"It was insured, though, right?"

"It was. For a time. I think. Last year at least."

"Kyle, sweetie. Are you okay?"

"No, I'm not okay. I'm in the middle of something you would not believe if I told you."

"Try me."

"It's so crazy I can't even talk about it. But I'll tell you this: I'm learning a hell of a lot about my father."

"Your father?"

"Yeah, and you want to know something? The more I learn, the less I like. Best thing he ever did was disappear from my life. So why all the exclamation marks on your note?"

"Because I wanted to know if you were alive. And because some cop from Havertown has been calling. Someone named Demerit. He says he needs to talk to you about the fire. And about the fireworks. Do you want his number?"

"No."

"As your lawyer, I advise that it's better for you to get in touch with him than have him find you."

"Yeah, well, he's like ninth on my list. Listen, I need you to do me a favor."

"Okay."

"Remember that good-looking cop who was interrogating me at the Roundhouse?"

"Oh, yeah, with the lips and the hips."

"Her name's Ramirez. You've got to find her and give her something, all right?" Kyle pulled out the card O'Malley had handed him and read the phone number to Kat. "It belongs to a guy who called himself O'Malley, Thomas O'Malley, but the name is fake. Anyway, I'd bet he knows something about Laszlo Toth's murder and maybe about the fire, too. See if she can use the number to find the bastard."

"Okay. Anything else I can do?"

"Not right now. But I have a story to tell you, Kat, that will set your hair on fire."

The phone back in its cradle, he stood at the open door of the closet in Kat's spare bedroom, facing the single piece of clothing hanging on the pole. His father was insisting he wear a suit, but his father had turned out to be a blowhard, and Kyle, as a matter of principle, ignored the lowing of blowhards. Then again, maybe the old guy was right. Kyle remembered the way the secretary in his father's old office had looked at him when he came in with his shorts and T-shirt, like he was beneath even dealing with in such a place. Maybe, in this adventure, he should dress more the part of the hard-boiled detective out to solve a crime. Except he didn't want his father to have the satisfaction of successfully telling him how to dress. Then again, after all these years, maybe he ought to throw the old man a bone.

Damn, he thought, this is harder than adolescence.

Ten minutes later, showered and shaved, with his black shoes on, his gray suit buttoned, and a pair of shades covering his eyes, Kyle climbed down the stairs from Kat's apartment, slipped through the vestibule, and slowly opened the door to the outside. He looked left, nothing. He looked right, nothing. He straightened his thin black tie as he stepped out onto the sidewalk, scanning the street for his father.

"Hey."

He turned toward the voice, saw a huge figure in a purple velvet sweat suit stepping out of a recessed doorway and heading right for him. Kyle turned to tear away in the opposite direction when another figure stepped out of a second doorway. He recognized one of the lugs who'd been sitting outside Tiny Tony's place in the instant before the lug slammed him hard in the chest, spinning him around so that Vern could grab hold of him by the lapels with both hands.

"Look who it is," said Vern as he pulled Kyle close enough for Kyle to smell the espresso on his breath. "Just the Joe we was waiting on."

"Convenient, isn't it?" said the lug from behind. "The way he came right to where we was waiting."

"Mr. Sorrentino sent us over to ask about that file," said Vern. "You know, the one you said you'd find for him to make up for what your son-of-a-bitch father stole."

"I never said that I—" Before he could finish, the lug slammed a forearm into Kyle's back, denting his kidneys. Kyle's knees buckled even as he was held aloft by Vern's huge, gnarled hands.

"We don't want no story," said Vern. "Some guys, they think we're in Hollywood, all the stories they try to give. But we ain't in Hollywood, we ain't no producers, we're only a couple of leg breakers in Philadelphia, and we don't want no story. All we want is an answer. You got it yet?"

"Not yet," squeaked Kyle.

"Too bad," said Vern.

Chapter 36

Watch out for the suit," said Kyle as Vern and the second lug pulled and shoved him so quickly along the sidewalk that his feet barely touched the ground.

"Worry less about the suit and more about your skin," said Vern.

"My skin doesn't need to be pressed at the dry cleaner when it wrinkles."

"And now that you mention it," said Vern "your tie could use a little color."

"So says the heavy in the purple velvet sweat suit."

"It ain't purple, baby, it's violet. And it ain't velvet," said Vern with an extra shove, "it's velour."

They were headed toward a narrow alley that cut through Kat's block. Kyle had spent enough time with these creeps in an alley to know that was not where he wanted to go. He grabbed at Vern's wrists and struggled to get away, but Vern held on tight as he lifted him off the ground, and another blow from behind left Kyle gasping and limp.

"Don't fight so hard," said Vern. "We ain't killing you. This time. But the boss said we ought to put a bit of giddyup in your gallop."

"I've been looking."

"Mr. Sorrentino wants that you look harder."

As they approached the alley, Kyle went through his options. He couldn't go right at Vern, he was being held too close to put a shoulder in the big man's chest, and whenever he started swinging his arms, the lug clobbered him from behind. At the same time, he couldn't wipe out the lug, because Vern's grip kept his shoulders from turning. Somehow he had to switch the odds into his favor, but now it was two to one against, and the geometry was all wrong. He needed to find the correct angle.

And then, as his shoes slid over the cement, he figured it out.

Time slowed as Kyle grabbed once again at Vern's wrists. He knew that Vern would press up with his hands, as he had before, but this time Kyle wouldn't fight it. This time Kyle would wait for the upward lift and then use it to his advantage.

When it came, raising Kyle off the ground, he brought his knees forward, banging them sharply into Vern's thighs. Vern jerked back, twisting away, and Kyle twisted with him, gaining just enough room to turn his body to the side. Leveraging off Vern's bulk, he whipped his legs out behind him as savagely as he could.

He felt his heels dig into the lug's soft middle even as Vern staggered away from him, leaving him free and horizontal in the air. He stayed like that for a strange, delicious moment in the slow motion of his action time before he fell like a stone smack onto the cement.

Despite the pain, he rolled to his hands and knees and took stock of his position. The lug was writhing on the ground behind him. Vern was still on his feet and stepping toward him now, one hand reaching behind his back.

Kyle drew his legs into his chest, a sprinter readying to charge at the sound of the starter's gun, when a flash of chrome and green metal jumped the curb in front of him and slammed into Vern, sending him flying into a brick wall. Vern's head bounced off the brick like a basketball.

Kyle stood up slowly. The green car was now stopped dead and almost wholly on the sidewalk.

The passenger door swung wide. Liam Byrne, behind the wheel, leaned toward the open door. "Having some trouble, boyo?"

Kyle looked around at the two thugs sprawled on the sidewalk. "I was."

"A fine suit you have on now."

"Thanks."

"The tie could use a bit more flash, though."

"So I've heard."

"Are you okay?"

"I think."

"And the suit?"

He checked it out quickly. "Seems no more distressed than usual."

"Well, then, get in. We have much work to do yet, and time's a-wasting."

Kyle looked around at the scene one more time. The lug lay groaning on the ground, grabbing at his lower chest as if to keep shattered ribs in place. Vern was propped up against the wall, holding his cracked head with bloodied arms. Kyle himself, except for a banged hip and scraped palms, was uninjured. He had been in the middle of something dangerous, one of those intense physical moments where time had slowed down on him. These were the moments when he was always on his own, with his fate hanging by the thread of his own physical ability. But here, now, for the first time in memory, someone actually had his back. And how incredible was it that the someone turned out to be his father?

"Okay," he said as he started climbing inside. "Let's get out of here."

Before he could close the door, his father jerked the car into reverse, sending it spinning back to the road, amid the jagged sounds of brakes and horns. And then he started off again, turning sharply right and left and right again, making good their escape.

"Who were they?" said Liam Byrne. "More muscle from the senator?"

"No," said Kyle. "Muscle from your old partner, Tiny Tony Sorrentino. They were sending a message."

"And what message was that greedy little popinjay sending?"

"He wants the O'Malley file, and he wants it fast."

"Of course he does. They all want a piece. Well, we'll take care of him soon enough, but first we have a meeting to arrange. Now, you remember what I told you?"

"I remember."

"You know what to say."

"It won't do any good."

"It's all in the attitude. Don't slump in like a loser. You're now a man in control, a man bound for glory, a man in a suit. Go in like the cock of the walk."

"He's a senator. I'm a nothing. He's not going to meet with me."

"Oh, he'll meet."

"He'll come all the way up from Washington just for me?"

"He's coming up tomorrow anyway. He has a fund-raiser. He'll meet you before it. Just set it up like I told you, and he'll show like a dog chasing a bone."

"You wish."

"No wishing about it. You need to shed your doubts, boyo. Doubters end up proving themselves right by creating their failures. It takes boldness to create the world. Be bold, Kyle. It's the only way to cheat gravity. Are you ready to fly?"

"I suppose."

"We've no time for such bland equivocation. Are you with me, boyo? Are you fully on board?"

Was he? Could he ever be? Kyle knew in his bones it was daft, this whole ridiculously convoluted plot of his father's to expose the murderous machinations of a United States senator. To believe that it could possibly play out the way his father predicted, leaving a Truscott in jail, Kyle untouched, and his father returned anonymously to his second life in San Bernardino was strictly a fantasy. Not to mention the fact that he couldn't shake the feeling that his father hadn't been completely honest with him about . . . well, about anything. And yet his father had slammed Vern against the wall with the car and spirited Kyle out of there, his father had come to his rescue, and the glow of that truth illuminated his path here. The path would be trust. Despite their history, Kyle was choosing to trust his father.

"Sure, Dad," said Kyle. "I'm on board."

"No more doubts?"

"No more doubts."

"That's good. That's grand. It touches my heart, it does."

"But how will I get the senator to go along?"

"It's just like any other piece of business. You need to make him see your point of view."

"If I had a million dollars to donate, I could get him to listen, maybe. But what have I got?"

"You've got the file, boyo, which means you've got his sack in your hand. All you have to do now is squeeze."

Chapter 37

Detective Ramirez figured it wouldn't be much of a trick to get a copy of Liam Byrne's death certificate. She knew the year of death, and Kyle Byrne said it happened in New Jersey, so she assumed that after a quick drive to Trenton she'd be in and out. But of course she assumed wrong. She had forgotten she was dealing with a government agency. It took her forty-five minutes just to find the right desk.

"Name of deceased?" said the clerk.

"Liam Byrne. B-Y-R-N-E."

"Year of death?"

"Nineteen ninety-four."

"Municipality?"

"No idea. That's what I'm here to find out."

"At least you know the county, I hope."

"How many counties are there?"

"Twenty-one," said the clerk, a snappish woman with owl eyes who seemed to have already had a tough day even though it wasn't yet noon.

"That many?" said Ramirez.

"So you don't know the county either. I'm afraid this might take some time."

"I don't have much time," said Ramirez, flashing her badge. "I'm in the middle of a murder investigation."

The clerk leaned forward, looked at the badge, glanced up at Ramirez before sitting back. "That's not a New Jersey badge, is it?"

"No, ma'am. Philadelphia, actually, but I figure you guys care about homicides as much as we do."

"Only if they occur in New Jersey."

"Well, Liam Byrne's might have," said Ramirez.

The clerk looked at her flatly for a moment before saying, "Take a seat, and I'll see what I can do."

The call about the fire had sliced Ramirez's sleep in half, and now, the afternoon after, she was too tired to make a scene, too tired to insist on seeing the supervisor and banging on his desk. Instead she sat in one of the blue plastic seats and waited. TRENTON MAKES, THE WORLD TAKES, said the sign on the bridge, but as far as Ramirez could figure it, Trenton only made you wait. And wait.

She stretched her long legs out for a moment, rested her neck on the back edge of the blue chair, closed her eyes.

"Union County."

Ramirez snapped awake and looked up. The clerk, staring down at her, had a file in her hand. Ramirez glanced at her watch. She'd been asleep for an hour.

"I'm sorry," she said. "I must have dozed."

"That's okay. I suspect they keep their homicide detectives busy there in Philadelphia." The clerk opened the file, read a bit. "Your Liam Byrne died at Overlook Hospital in Summit. I made a copy of the certificate for you. But it wasn't a homicide."

"No?" said Ramirez, rubbing her eyes.

"No, dear," said the clerk, closing the file and handing it off. "It was a heart attack."

Ramirez took the file, opened it, quickly examined the certificate. Liam Byrne, born in Philadelphia, July 15, 1941, died in Summit, New Jersey, June 4, 1994. And there it was: cause of death, myocardial infarction, a simple heart attack. All of it certified by a Dr. Manzone of Overlook Hospital. That should be the end of this road, she should get back home. She had too many real crimes to investigate, too many families still raw from the pains of their loss and looking for answers that only she could give, closure that only she could provide. She didn't need to be investigating phantom crimes in a distant jurisdiction.

"Thank you so much for your help," said Ramirez. "I really appreciate it."

"Anything else I can do?"

"Just one thing," she said. "How do you get to this Summit?"

"Up," had said the clerk. Ramirez took it as a smart remark, but the woman simply meant north, Route 1 to the turnpike to the Garden State Parkway. Welcome to scenic New Jersey. Not for the first time did Detective Ramirez wonder how anyone could live here. Philadelphia had snap and life, New Jersey, other than the shore, had places to drive, and places to watch TV, and places to die. Overlook Hospital was one of the places to die. It was a large, formal brick building on the edge of one of the sprawling suburbs that seemed to make up the entire state.

It took a bit of bouncing around and waving her badge until she found the records room. This new clerk was quite busy and let her know it with a dramatic sigh at her request. When she showed him her badge, he almost sneered.

"This will take some time," he said.

"Not too much, I hope."

"It's off-site, dearie. I have to call it in and then have it delivered. It could take all day."

"I don't have all day. Do your best to speed it up, could you?" she said with a bat of her eyelashes that did nothing.

"It will take what it will take."

"Of course it will. Is there a decent place to eat around here?"

"What do you like, other than lipstick two shades too bright?"

"Right now I feel like something raw."

"Oooh," he said with a sly smile.

He directed her to a sushi joint not far from the hospital. As she banged down the number-two maki roll lunch special and a glass of tea, she wondered how much of this quixotic lurch into New Jersey was about solving the Laszlo Toth murder and how much was about solving Kyle Byrne. Somehow the kid had gotten under her skin. She couldn't tell for sure if he activated the procreating or maternal center of her brain, but she felt the intense desire to protect him. And after seeing him in the hospital and then, later, seeing the burned-out hulks of his house and car, she knew for sure that he needed protecting. He was a fool kid in over his head in waters he couldn't fathom. But he swam with such a plucky charm that he couldn't help making her smile. Who was the last man who had made her smile? Santa, maybe, when she still believed, and that was a long time ago.

Kyle Byrne was still on her mind when she returned to the hospital for the file. Except there was no file.

"I don't understand," said Ramirez. "There has to be a file."

"Well, it's not so hard to understand, is it?" said the clerk with unrestrained pique. "You were obviously mistaken. We have no record of a patient by that name that entire year."

"If he came in DOA, would there still be a record?"

"If he walks in, is wheeled in, or drops in from the sky, we don't do a thing until a file is opened. Why don't you try Summit Oaks Hospital on Prospect Street?" He leaned forward and lowered his voice as if he were confiding. "That's for psychiatric cases. You might have better luck there."

"You are a wonder, aren't you?" said Ramirez, whipping her own file out of her briefcase. "The death certificate held by the State of New Jersey has Liam Byrne being declared dead at this hospital in 1994, so I suggest you cut the cattiness and look again."

"Let me see that," said the clerk.

The clerk took the copy, examined it closely. Slowly the officious look slid off his officious little face like a gobbet of ice cream slipping off a cone and splattering on the cement.

"Ah . . . er," said the clerk. "Is your name by any chance Houston?"

"No. Why?"

"Because we have a problem."

"How delicious." She leaned forward and rested her knuckles on the desk. "Now, why don't you tell me about our little problem before I start getting curious."

"It's the doctor who signed the certificate and declared Mr. Byrne dead, the Dr. Manzone whose signature is right there."

"That's not his signature?"

"No, that at least appears to be legit."

"Then I'll need to talk to your Dr. Manzone."

"That might be difficult." The clerk winced involuntarily. "He's not with us anymore."

"No?"

"He was indeed here in 1994 when he signed the certificate, but he's gone now. Gone, gone, gone."

"I get the sense I'm being shuffled like a deck of cards, but all right, deal. Where can I find this Dr. Manzone now?"

"Rahway."

"In another hospital?"

"No, ma'am. In the state prison. There were some—how should I put it?—irregularities."

Detective Ramirez smiled a wolfish smile and sat down in one of the chairs facing the clerk, leaned forward over the desk, glanced right and left to make sure no one was in earshot. "All right, you sweet little man. Dish."

On her way to the East Jersey State Prison in Rahway, New Jersey, a quick thirty-minute drive from the hospital, she called Henderson.

"You would not believe the shit that we stepped into."

"I've been trying to get hold of you," said Henderson.

"I had to turn my phone off in the hospital. Now, listen to this. Liam Byrne's death certificate was signed by a Dr. Manzone. Manzone certified that Liam Byrne died of a heart attack at this hospital in a place called Summit, New Jersey. But the hospital doesn't have any record of Liam Byrne. It might be just a clerical error, right? Except that this Dr. Manzone isn't your normal ear, nose, and throat guy. He had something else going on the side."

"Ramirez, you need to come back."

"You're not listening. There was this place in Elizabeth that was doing embalming for a host of funeral parlors from New York, New Jersey, and even Philadelphia. I thought everyone did their own, but apparently often they outsource. But it wasn't enough to just juice these bodies with formaldehyde. These guys in Elizabeth would cut out the kidneys, the eyes, even the bones, and sell them to distribution centers, some kind of biomedical supply houses, to be used in transplants. And the guy doing the harvesting was our Dr. Manzone."

"Where's this heading?" said Henderson. "Because we got stuff going on down here you need to be a part of."

"Hang on, Pops, it's just starting to get interesting. Sometimes the corpses they got weren't in good enough shape for the transplants—too old or they died too long ago or there was some disease eating at their bones. So what did our guy Manzone do? The son of a bitch doctored the death certificates, or made new ones, so that the organs they were selling would look like A-one used parts instead of the rusted refuse of rent-a-wrecks. Are you getting me? I'd bet dollars to those doughnuts you stuff down your gut each morning that Liam Byrne didn't die of something as natural as a heart attack."

"Where are you going now?"

"Rahway. Our Dr. Manzone is in the same prison where they held Hurricane Carter. Manzone cooperated fully with the New Jersey authorities and apparently could remember the details of every doctored certificate, down to the specific parts cut out and sold. I bet he'll remember what the hell happened to Liam Byrne."

"Forget it, Ramirez."

"Forget it? Are you crazy, old man, or just lazy? We're on top of something huge here. If Byrne was murdered fourteen years ago, then Toth might have been killed by the same guy for the same reason. Which means this same bastard was probably trying to kill young Byrne last night. And the reason was in that file cabinet. I wouldn't be surprised if we have a serial killer on our hands and Kyle Byrne is next on the list."

"Forget about it. Come on back. Lieutenant's orders."

"What's going on here, Henderson? Why are you shutting this down?"

"You were right all along, Ramirez. You had it pegged from the start. We got a call from a pawnshop about the watch. We just picked up the ticket holder, with what appears to be the right gun and a box from the Toth office."

"You're killing me."

"He's waiting for us in interrogation room six. Come on back. We'll go in together and break down his ass and put the Laszlo Toth homicide to bed."

Chapter 38

Welcome to Senator Truscott's Philadelphia office," said the pretty receptionist at the desk facing the front door. "Can I help you?"

Kyle looked around at the paneled walls, the dark wood furnishings, the august seal of the United States Senate above the receptionist's desk, at the tight, smiling face of the senator himself bolted onto the wall next to the seal. Maybe this was what his father meant about glory. If so, the son of a bitch could have it. There was something forced and artificial about the whole scene, something whose only purpose was to impress. From what he could tell about the job of a senator, it was all about sucking up for money, checking your values at the door, and voting with your party. Kyle would just as soon cut out the middle stuff and head straight to the party.

He looked at the receptionist's sincere brown eyes and tilted his head. She seemed familiar. He had met her before. At a bar? At a club?

"Hi, I'm looking for that Senator Truscott," said Kyle. "Is he around?"

"No, I'm sorry."

"But he's coming to Philadelphia tomorrow, right?"

"He has an event at the convention center." She eyed his outfit. "A fund-raising event. Would you like to buy a ticket? There are still a few available."

"For a pretty stiff donation, I assume."

"Oh, it will be worth it, I assure you." Her pretty eyes widened, and she lowered her voice. "It's not definite yet, but I have it on good authority that the vice president is scheduled to attend."

"Really? The vice president?" Pause. "Do you have a fork, by any chance?"

"A fork?"

"Yeah, because I'd sooner stick a fork in my eye than go to an event that the vice president is scheduled to attend."

The receptionist leaned back and smiled a smile of sudden interest. "I know you," she said. "You're that Kyle Byrne. I didn't recognize you in that . . ." She waved her hand.

"Suit, it's called a suit. Where did we meet, again?"

"I just started at this job. Before that I worked in the lobby of the building where your father's old law firm was located."

"Ahh, of course," he said. "I remembered your lovely eyes." He waited for the blush, but she wasn't the blushing type. "It's funny how we keep running into each other. What's your name?"

"Sharon."

"So, Sharon, maybe you could help me." He sat on the edge of her desk, leaned forward. "What I'd like to do is to sort of meet with the senator before his convention center event. Could you set that up for me?"

"You're kidding, right?"

"No, actually."

"The senator's schedule is booked months in advance. There's no way they can squeeze you in. And in any event, all scheduling for the senator is done in Washington. Requests for meetings need to be faxed to his office down there. I could give you the fax number."

"How long will it take to get a response?"

"Count on weeks. And be aware that the senator's ability to meet with constituents is very limited."

"I guess that means forget about it."

She looked left, looked right. "Do you have a couple thousand to donate to his campaign?"

"No."

"Then yes, forget about it."

"How about if I just leave a message for the guy? Could you pass that along for me?"

"Again, I could give you the fax number."

Kyle stared at her for a moment and tried to think it through. Talking to her wasn't going to help, because she didn't have the power to help. But something seemed fishy. It was quite the coincidence, her being first at his father's old office and now here. But maybe it wasn't a coincidence. Maybe the cops who'd picked him up in his father's office had been waiting for him all the time. Maybe they'd been tipped by the senator himself, who'd been tipped by someone who knew that Kyle had come calling to his dad's old firm. By this Sharon? Maybe. It might be how she got this job. But girls like Sharon didn't get plum jobs by trading information, they traded something else. And he remembered his suspicion about her and that bulldog lawyer when he had seen her before. Plus, the son of a bitch had mentioned that he had already begun a new job.

"Why don't I talk to Malcolm about it," said Kyle. "Is he around?"

Sharon flinched.

"I guess that means yes."

"I think you should go, Mr. Byrne."

"I suppose you're right, I should go, but I'm not going to. Which is his office? I'll just stop in for a few minutes, chat about the weather."

"If you don't leave now, Mr. Byrne, I'll be forced to call security."

"Before you do that, Sharon, why don't you let your little buddy Malcolm know that I'm here to see him. And you can tell him that if he doesn't see me right this instant, I'm going to have to have a chat with his wife about how he swung you this sweet job and all the lip smacking and knee knocking that went with it."

Shame about your house," said Malcolm with a flickering smirk.

"Shame about your dick," said Kyle.

Puzzlement creased his pug features. "What about my . . . ? Oh. Okay, we're back in high school. State your business, Byrne. Some of us work for a living."

The little creep was sitting in suspenders and shirt-sleeves behind a desk in his private office, and Kyle could barely restrain himself from leaping over the wide desktop and throttling that thick neck. This punk was probably responsible for both his arrest and the fire, and Kyle would've liked nothing better than to batter that face bloody, while the photograph of the senator and his tight smile looked on from the wall. But then he might get some blood on the suit, and that would be a bitch to get out. Another argument for T-shirts and shorts.

"Nice digs," said Kyle.

"I like them."

"Quite a leap to go from toiling for a little troll like Laszlo Toth to becoming an aide to a United States senator."

"I got lucky."

"Oh, don't demean yourself. It was more than luck."

Malcolm's belligerent chin lifted in immodest pride. "Maybe you're right."

"Let's add thievery and betrayal and a touch of murder, too."

"Go to hell."

"Who did you call when I came looking for my father's old files?"

Malcolm twisted his head as if his collar had suddenly tightened. "No one. I didn't call anyone."

"If this is the quality of your lying, then I hope your matrimonial lawyer is a sharp little cheddar, because it means your wife already knows about you and Sharon and the whoop-de-do."

"I don't have the least idea what you are talking about."

"Funny, that's what Sharon says, too. But adultery is really a minor matter in the scheme of things. My guess is the senator asked you to keep an eye on Laszlo Toth, all the while dangling this job as bait. When Laszlo found the file, you called the senator and chirped away like a chirpy little cockatoo. But when the senator ended up having Laszlo shot to death, that made you an accomplice to murder. You're here to keep your mouth shut."

"You're way off base, Byrne."

"Maybe, but I'm getting close to something, aren't I?"

"What do you want?"

"I guess that means I'm getting damn close. The senator is coming to Philadelphia tomorrow for an event at the convention center. I need to meet with him before the fund-raiser."

"He's booked. There's a committee hearing he has to attend in the morning."

"Oh, yes, and we all know how important committee meetings are. Call him and make it happen."

"Why would I do that? Why would I do anything to help you?"

Why indeed? His father had given him the answer, now it was time to squeeze.

"Because I found it, you dork," said Kyle. "Because I have what Laszlo was killed for and what you were undoubtedly searching for even when I came knocking at my father's office. I have the O'Malley file."

Malcolm turned his head slightly. "You're bluffing."

"Maybe, but can the senator take that chance?"

"If you have it, let me look at it. If it's real, I'll see if I can do something for you."

"Oh, I have it, and it's real, don't you worry. And my bet is that you have no idea what's inside. I'm sure Senator Truscott would be thrilled to learn that his new aide has been angling to take a peek. Trying to blackmail yourself into a chief-of-staff position?"

"That's not what I was doing—"

"Save the lies for your wife and the tears for Sharon. Now, take out a pencil and a piece of paper. After three years of law school, you turned yourself into a messenger boy, so here's the message: Tell the senator that I have the file."

"He'll want proof," said Malcolm as he plucked a pen off his desk.

"Tell him I know what really happened to Colleen. That will spark his interest. We'll meet at four o'clock, which will give him plenty of time to get here from Washington, have our discussion, and still be able to stick his tongue in the vice president's ear."

"Where do you propose to meet?"

Kyle thought for a moment. "There's a bar called Bubba's in Queens Village. Your boy's a clever fellow, he'll find it. You tell him to be there at four and to be there alone. He shows up with a guard, with his mother, or even someone as weak-kneed as you, and it's over."

"And you'll have the file with you?"

"Fuck no. I'm not an idiot. The thing will be in safe hands, ready to go to the press if anything happens to me. But nothing will happen, right? Just a pleasant meeting with a constituent. I have some ideas on the immigration issue."

"Really?"

"No."

"Okay, I got it. Do you have a number where he can reach you if the plans change?"

"The plans won't change," said Kyle, standing. "We'll meet, we'll talk, we'll do a fox-trot and figure something out. Everyone will go home happy."

Malcolm stared at Kyle for a moment. "You're completely different than you were last week in the office. What the hell's gotten into you?"

"It's the suit," said Kyle.

Chapter 39

His name was Lamar, and Lamar was scared.

It was clear in the way Lamar's hands shook as he brought the can of soda to his lips, in the way the soda slopped out of his mouth as he tried to drink, the way his jaw trembled as he repeated his improbable story. Ramirez thought the fear was a pretty good indication of guilt. It wouldn't take much, she knew, to push him into abandoning his cock-and-bull story and signing a confession that would close the case. But Henderson had spent so much time in these rooms with kids who showed nothing but contempt for cops, for their crimes, for the prisons they were headed to, nothing but contempt for themselves, that in Lamar's fear he saw possibilities for some sort of redemption. Ramirez would consider Henderson's thoughts about redemption a sign of muddleheaded weakness arising from his severe case of old age. Henderson considered it his only reason for still being a cop.

"Where do you keep your drugs, Lamar?" said Henderson, who was taking the lead in the questioning and kept his voice calm and soft. Ramirez sat with her chair leaning against the wall and glowered.

"I told you, man, I don't do drugs."

"Remember that cup you peed in when they picked you up?" said Ramirez with a sneer. "Well, that says you're a liar."

"What they find?" said Lamar.

"Some sticky icky," said Ramirez.

"Hell, that ain't drugs. I just took a hit off a buddy's blunt last night. But I ain't got nothing at the house, if that's what you're asking. My moms would kill me she finds that crap. Truth is, sad as it is to admit, I don't got the money for it."

"The pawnshop said you got seventy-five for the watch," said Henderson. "What did you spend it on?"

"Food."

"Where?"

"Most I gave to my moms so she can feed my brother. But I kept enough for a rack from Ron's and some mac and cheese."

"You get it extra hot?"

"What are you, crazy? Ron's is hot enough, just regular. The extra will burn a hole through the back of your throat."

"You got that right," said Henderson. "So let's go over it again."

"I told you four times already."

"Then let's do five."

"I was out walking that night."

"What night?"

"I don't know when, a week or so ago. I was out walking."

"Looking for what?"

"Anything. Is that a crime? I was out, is all. And I saw this pack come toward me on the street that I didn't want anything to do with, account of I recognized one of them idiots, and he and me we don't get along."

"What's his name?"

"Danny something, I don't know. He's big and he's ugly, you want a description. So when I passed one of them deserted lots, I ducked into it so as to avoid his ass."

"Where exactly?"

"I don't remember. It was, like, west of Sixteenth on Montrose or something. I didn't care where it was, I just wanted to get away. He's got this nose, man, like a baked potato that exploded in the oven. You know what I mean? And so as he passed by on the street with his boys, I kind of slunk my way into one of them corners that was darker than the rest, and that's where I found it."

"Found what exactly?"

"I told you. It was a box, a white box with handles cut into the sides, and the stuff was in there."

"The box we found in your room?"

"The same."

"And what was in there again?"

"You know, the watch that I pawned. And then the stuff you found, that computer screen and the gun. There were a couple other screens that I passed out to some friends in exchange for gabbling onto their Internet, because my connection is, like, nonexistent. I thought we was supposed to be getting it free, that's what the mayor said, but I got nothing."

"We'll be sure to let him know," said Ramirez.

"Why didn't you pawn the cuff link when you pawned the watch?" said Henderson.

"Cuff link? What cuff link? I don't wear no cuff link."

"The cuff link you still had on you. There were two, but you lost the one, right?"

"What are you talking about cuff links for?"

"No cuff links?"

"Nah, man. What would I be doing with something beat like that?"

"Maybe one of your other jobs."

"I told you, I don't do no jobs. And if I did do jobs, I wouldn't be stealing no cuff link."

"So then let's talk about the gun. You use the gun?"

"Nah, man, that crap scares the piss out of me."

"So why didn't you pawn it with the watch?"

"I don't know."

"Is that your best answer, that you don't know?"

"I don't know."

"You were going to use it against that Danny character with the potato nose, weren't you?" said Ramirez, as her chair slapped down on its front legs with a crack.

"Nah, I don't know. Protection, maybe."

"Use it on him like you used it on the old man," said Ramirez, who stood and started walking toward Lamar.

"What old man?"

"Don't be cute, baby," she said. "You know just what old man I'm talking about. How are we going to help you if you don't help us?"

"I'm trying to help."

"You didn't mean to shoot him, we know that," said Ramirez, leaning forward now with her knuckles on the table so that she was peering down at Lamar with angry eyes. "The door was open, you slipped in, saw all that stuff, and started filling a box. Then the old man appeared. You panicked, you drew the gun, pointed it, the thing went off. It happens, and it was an accident, and we can help you get past it."

"That's not what happened."

"Then you better tell us what happened, and you better tell us quick, before we take a dimmer view of things."

"I found the box."

"Lamar," said Ramirez, her voice loud now, and fast. "Baby. You keep playing it like that, we're going to have no choice but to figure you did it on purpose."

"But I didn't."

"That you went in there intending to shoot that man."

"I didn't go there to shoot nobody."

"Bang you down for first degree. Twenty years. Or more. Is that what you want?"

"No."

"Help us help you."

"I don't know what to say."

"Yes, you do. We told you already. It was an accident, you didn't mean it. That's what you need to tell us. That's the only way out for you. Other than that, it's a needle in the arm, boy."

"What are you talking about?"

"Oh, come on, baby, you know what I'm talking about. It's why you're lying to us."

"I'm not."

"Another one right there. Right there, you pathetic loser."

"Take a minute, Lamar," said Henderson, who stood now and stepped between the cowering Lamar and Ramirez, whose fists were balled.

Henderson faced Ramirez and stared for a moment, before she spun on her heels and stormed out the door. Then he turned to Lamar and put a hand on Lamar's shoulder. He could feel the bones beneath his fingers shaking.

"Did it happen like that, Lamar?" said Henderson. "Did the gun go off like she said?"

"I told you. I found the box."

"That's a little hard to believe, son. And if we don't believe it, and we want to help you, how's a jury going to believe it? Stay here for a bit and think on it. We'll be back."

From the other side of the mirror, Henderson and Ramirez stood next to each other and watched the boy. Lamar wiped his eyes with his palm, his nose with the back of his hand. The shaking was worse now, the fear had clutched tight at his heart, and all pretense of faking it was gone. As Ramirez stared through the glass, she could see the ghost of her own reflection in the mirror superimposed on the boy's scared face. Her face was twisted with a strange and ugly expression that she didn't recognize and didn't like.

"Another ten minutes and it would have been done," said Ramirez. "He would have signed *Mein Kampf* if I put it in front of him."

"He just might have."

"Why'd you stop me?"

"Because I didn't want that kid saying something he'd spend the rest of his life regretting."

"That's our job, isn't it?"

"Not if we spend the rest of our lives regretting it, too."

"He already pretty much said he didn't mean to kill Toth, that it was an accident."

"He came close."

"What do you think?"

"I think he found a box."

They stood side by side and stared at Lamar as the kid tried again to drink from the soda. The stuff was flying from the can before it was halfway to his lips.

"That would mean our killer was clever enough to stage the crime scene," said Ramirez, "and then place the gun and the watch and the computer screens in a box on some deserted lot so that some chump would find them, hock something, and take the fall."

"Seems a bit far-fetched, doesn't it?"

"It would also mean that this isn't just a simple killing but probably something tied to the fire, to that file cabinet in Byrne's basement, and maybe to the questionable circumstances of Liam Byrne's death."

"It's enough to give me a damn headache," said Henderson.

"What would your boy Occam say about all that?"

"He'd say Lamar is it."

Ramirez thought about it for a moment, took a deep breath. "I owe you, old man."

"What for?"

"For pulling me out of there."

Just then there was a knock on the door, and a uniform poked her head inside. "Detective Ramirez, there's a lawyer here to see you."

"You get a name?"

"She said her name was Shin, Katie Shin. Just like that. And she said she had a message for you from some Kyle Byrne."

Chapter 40

At Ponzio's, an overblown New Jersey diner with a false stone front and overcooked peas, Kyle Byrne stared into the very face of God. Or the closest thing he had going, albeit one wiping a splotch of Hellmann's from his lower lip with his thumb.

"Now, when you meet with this walking, talking piece of corruption," said Liam Byrne, "you need come at him from an angle, keep him off balance."

Kyle listlessly swirled a french fry in a pool of ketchup and pretended to listen, more interested in the features of the face in front of him than in the plots and plans coming out of its mouth. Through the years Kyle had guarded the mental picture of his father so religiously that the image had lost its flesh and bone and become something almost holy. He was the creator, who had formed, through both his genes and his absence, almost the whole of Kyle's identity. And now, as the creator sat across from Kyle at this desultory diner, stuffing his face with a turkey club on white with extra mayonnaise, the disappointment was palpable.

"We can't let him know what we're really after, see?" said his father. "If he cottons on to the fact that we're trying to destroy him utterly, he'll disappear. So we give him something he can lunge for, something that he thinks will give him an out. We give him a feint, like a football running back. That's the position you played, wasn't it?"

"How would you know?"

"I kept track, boyo. Every week in San Bernardino, I'd gather up the Philadelphia papers and see what I was missing. There you were on the high-school sports page in living color. I couldn't have been prouder."

No matter how much Kyle mythologized it in his memory, no matter how much he exalted it in recollection, there was nothing spiritual about the face in front of him now. In the bright and unrelenting light of Ponzio's, his father looked realer than real, not to mention old as hell. And as common as the burger on Kyle's plate. Kyle wondered what question he would ask God if He were seated across from him at Ponzio's.

"How'd you meet my mother?" he said finally.

Liam Byrne looked at his son with a narrowed eye, as if he spotted the peril in the question, and then put down his sandwich.

"She came to work at the firm," he said softly. "Laszlo hired her, actually. As a secretary. There was something about her that I spotted right off."

"What exactly?"

"It's hard to say. I suppose it was that calm implacability of hers. It is impossible to overstate how attractive that is to someone like me. Of course she was a beautiful woman, but she seemed to be challenging me to try to get through her walls. And I could never resist a good challenge."

The old man's crooked smile of remembrance struck a chord of anger in Kyle. "So you charged the ramparts. How old was she then?"

"She was old enough to know better. We both were. But once it began, we couldn't help ourselves. I suppose that meant she saw something in me, too."

"Like what?"

"The same charm I passed on to you, maybe."

"So you charmed the pants off her."

"Ah, boyo, we charmed each other. Your mother was a special woman. Stronger than ever I was, that's for sure. She knew her mind and acted upon it. And

I won't be giving away any state secrets to say that I loved her mightily."

"Not enough to marry her."

"Well, of course, I was married already. To my wife, you see. An interesting woman in her own right. I saw her, actually, just a day before the fire. After you sent your friend inside."

"You saw her?"

"Yes, though she didn't see me. It was quite the emotional experience, I must admit. She's grown old. It happens, though a disappointment nevertheless. And she's married again, to an old sot too decrepit to be unfaithful. I suppose that is what she wanted all those fallow years with me."

"Did you say hello?"

"Of course not. I wouldn't disrupt her current happiness for anything. Whatever we were together in the past, and we were many things, we weren't happy."

"If you weren't happy in your marriage," said Kyle, "and if you loved my mother like you said, why didn't you leave your wife?"

"Well, we were married in the church, you see. And in those days it wasn't always so easy to—"

"Yeah, I get it."

Liam looked up sharply at the rebuke in his son's voice. "Your mother understood."

"She was a good sport, you mean."

"Here we are, in the eternal struggle, father and son battling over the affections of the mother. Oedipus redux. It would be unnatural any other way. But your mother, boyo, she doesn't need your defending. She never needed anyone. It's what attracted me to her in the first place. To be the center of her world seemed a rare thing, worth more than diamonds. But it's hard to sustain a relationship with someone so self-contained. I tried, yes. For a bit, after you were born, I even moved in, did you know that?"

"She told me."

"Yes. An interesting time. But it didn't work. She found someone else to love, someone else to stand at the center. She pushed me away for another."

"Go to hell."

"No, son, it's true."

"Who, then? Who did my mother fall in love with?"

"You don't know?"

"No. I don't."

"It was you. We don't need to battle, because you are already triumphant. She loved you so much there was no room left for me. She loved you, boyo."

"You don't need to tell me that."

"Of course I don't. That's another thing we have in common. We both loved your mother and were loved by her, in succession, I think. But you won out."

"And you went back to your wife."

"She took me back, yes. We had a difficult relationship, but we both gave each other things that we needed. So she put away her anger and took me back. But there were conditions, which made it hard for me to get away to see you."

"I missed you all the time," said Kyle, the words slipping out unbidden, as if spoken by the twelve-year-old kid still inside him.

"I know," said Liam Byrne. "It was a difficult thing for me to stay away, more difficult than you could imagine. I understand you still have issues with your old man. I deserted you, not once but twice. But I am your father, and you are in a time of dire need, and here I am. I saved you once this morning, and we'll work through the rest of it together. Some of that must matter, don't you think?"

Kyle stared at his father and wondered why all their conversations turned into him whining and his father explaining. They were caught in an eternal cycle of Kyle's longing and disappointment. But maybe it was time to stop fighting and doubting and trying to get the apology he seemed so desperately to need. Maybe it was time just to accept that his father was here, now, and to see what the future held for the two of them. Forgiveness? Atonement? Redemption? Love? It was all possible, wasn't it, as long as Kyle's father was still sitting in front of him at Ponzio's?

"I suppose," said Kyle.

"Good. Now can we get back to the matter at hand before the forces arrayed on either side lop off our heads?"

"Sure."

"We'll talk more about dealing with the senator later. I have plans. Definite plans. But I didn't like what happened this morning, didn't like it at all. I'm not willing to leave you at the mercy of Sorrentino, that Italian degenerate. The senator can wait until tomorrow. It's time we take care of my old partner now."

"Why don't we just give him the file? It's what he wants, and it will take him off my back and screw Truscott at the same time."

"Because he is a scoundrel of the worst stripe," said Liam. "Because he will care nothing about caging a criminal but instead will trade it for cash and include you in the bargain. You'll never be safe if he has the file, and that I can't allow. No, we have to take him out of the picture once and for all."

"How?"

"Ahh, that's the question. How indeed? But I know for certain we need to go right at him. There is no use waiting around for him to act. Always keep the initiative, always stay one step ahead. I learned in law that if I waited for the other side's filings, I'd get buried."

Just then Liam Byrne's features froze in startled recognition of someone in the restaurant. He quickly averted his face as an older man in a sweater, hunched and limping, shuffled by. And then the old man stopped, and then the old man turned around. His face was a haggard droop of flesh, but his eyes were curiously alert as they stared at the back of Liam Byrne's head.

"Liam?" said the old man.

"No, I'm sorry," said Liam Byrne, without turning around. "My name's Marvin."

"Did you have a brother named Liam? Or a cousin?"

"No."

"I'm sorry to bother you, but you're the spitting image of someone I used to know."

Liam Byrne twisted in the booth to stare straight at the man and give a warm, untroubled smile. "Handsome fellow, I suppose," said Liam in a broad midwestern accent.

"He would have been," said the man, "if he hadn't died many years ago. It was the strangest thing, though, because I could have sworn you were he." The old man turned to look at Kyle, blinked twice as if in recognition, looked again at Liam. "It's uncanny."

"One thing we know about the world," said Liam, turned back now and winking at Kyle, "is that coincidences happen."

"Yes, I suppose," said the old man, his face screwed up in puzzlement. "I'm sorry to disturb your dinner."

"Not a problem," said Liam, "not a problem at all. I'm often mistaken for the dead."

When the old man had walked on and sat at his table at the far end of the row, Liam let out a breath.

"That was close," he said. "We ate in New Jersey so I wouldn't be recognized, and then Johnstone has to walk into this very restaurant. I had a number of cases with him back in the day. He worked for the insurance companies. A moral failing, if you ask me. But even as he recognized me right off, I barely recognized him at all. He is ancient."

"It happens," said Kyle flatly.

"But his face did get pale, didn't it?" said Liam, starting to laugh. "I could see the blood rush away as he thought he recognized me. Like he had seen a ghost."

"He had, hadn't he?" said Kyle.

"Yes," said Liam, who reached up and scratched at his mop of gray hair, as if scratching out an idea. "Indeed he had."

Chapter 41

Skitch sat with Kyle in Liam's rental car as both stared at the empty sidewalk outside Tiny Tony's Ticket Brokerage. Kyle's father wasn't in the car with them because he insisted that no one know about his return. And Skitch was in the car because he was a crucial element of Kyle's father's plan to get Tiny Tony off Kyle's back for good. A plan that, Kyle would be the first to admit, was suicidally insane. But he was here as a matter of trust: He had decided to trust his father, and his father had said about the plan, "Trust me."

"Where is everybody?" said Skitch.

"Gone," said Kyle. "Sent home. I made that a condition of the meeting. I wasn't giving those goons another chance to rearrange my features."

"Good idea."

"Speaking of which," said Kyle, "what's with your face?"

"What's with your suit?"

"Let me give you a lesson, dude. You want respect, dress like you deserve it."

Skitch turned in his seat and gave Kyle a disbelieving stare. "What the crap's gotten into you?"

"You wouldn't believe it if I told you."

"I bet you're right," said Skitch.

"But that doesn't answer what happened to your face?"

"I cut myself shaving."

"You shave your forehead?"

"With my testosterone level, bro, I even shave my eyeballs. Maybe they're waiting to ambush you inside."

"I doubt it," said Kyle. "I have what he wants. If I give it to him, he doesn't need his goons. And if I don't, they'll have plenty of time to find me."

"Maybe he thinks he needs protection."

"Oh, Tiny Tony has enough protection for the likes of me," said Kyle, thinking of the oversize pistol that had once been pointed at his heart.

"What are you up to anyway?"

"Nothing much," said Kyle. "Just a little séance. It's time for Tiny Tony to get a warning from the dead."

"Bro?"

"Forget it. If we punk him right, I'm off the hook."

"And if not, will I be scraping you off the street like I did last time we were here?"

"Most likely. You sure you can do what we need you to do?"

"A piece of cake. Two locks, both so old I could blow into them and align the pins. The only hard thing will be finding the right circuit breaker, so screw it, I'll just use the master and shut everything down."

"Ninety seconds, that's it. Off and on."

"I got a watch and a flashlight. I'm set."

"Just be as quiet as a cat and keep the back door open so you can get the hell out of there."

"No one's as worried about getting the hell out of there as I am."

"And you'll get home on your own?"

"As soon as I hit the back door, I won't stop running till I reach Bubba's."

"Good. So what's really with the gash on your forehead?"

"Nothing."

"Are you in trouble?"

"Forget about it."

"What kind of trouble?"

"I don't know, maybe I'm in the middle of something I just want to get out of, but it's not proving to be so easy."

"Dude," said Kyle, shaking his head.

"Skip it, all right?" said Skitch. "I know you told me so, and I know I'm a screwup."

"I did tell you so, but you're not a screwup, Skitch. I've been thinking about you."

"Me?"

"Yeah, you. You're bold as hell, and I don't think I ever told you how much I admire that."

"Kyle?"

"I could use a little boldness in my life."

"That tie must be cutting off your oxygen."

"Maybe," said Kyle. He picked up the loose end of his tie and stared at it. "How is it possible to wear this every day? You want to know why the world is so messed up? Too many ties." Pause. "You think I should get something with a little more color?"

"Cyan," said Skitch.

"Cyan?"

"It's a tropical blue. Quite festive."

"You're watching way too much cable. Look, whatever you're into, as soon as this is over, we'll get you out of it."

"Oh, yeah? How?"

"I'll talk to your guys."

"Really?"

"Sure, why not?"

"Because you're a lazy fuck. And what would you say anyway?"

"I'll make them see your point of view."

"How?"

"Easy. First I'll wear the suit. Then I'll find something to squeeze." Kyle checked his watch. "How long will you need to pick the locks?"

"A minute or two, tops."

"Okay, get in position. In five minutes exactly, I'll start making a racket. That's when you start."

"Good luck, bro."

"Thanks, I'll need it." As Skitch quietly opened the door and started slipping out of the car, Kyle put a hand on his shoulder. "Dude, I owe you."

"You take care of my problem, we'll owe each other," said Skitch, and then he was gone, the door still open.

Kyle flashed his headlights twice and waited one minute, two minutes, four minutes. Then he slid across the front of the car and out Skitch's open door, slamming it shut so only one closing would sound. With a hop in his step and a swivel in his neck, he loped toward the beat old storefront.

At exactly five minutes after Skitch had slid out of the car, Kyle started banging at the edge of the door with the flat of his fist. A polite knock-knock would have been enough, but Kyle banged like a herald from some dark, hungry place.

"Stop all that hullabaloo," shouted Tiny Tony Sorrentino as he unlocked the door from the inside and opened it a crack. "What are you trying to do, wake the dead?"

"If I have to," said Kyle.

"You got it?"

"I can get it."

"What the hell does that mean? I'm not here for my health. It was just supposed to be a handoff."

"I have the file, but not on me," said Kyle. "You don't get it until we decide how it's going to work out between us in the future."

"How it's going to work out between us? I'm already married."

"Are we going to talk, or am I going to walk?"

Tiny Tony opened the door a little wider and stuck his head out, looked left, looked right. "Get the hell in here," said Tiny as he pulled Kyle inside. Sorrentino took a final scan outside before slamming the door shut behind them.

Chapter 42

Did you see his face, boyo?" said Liam Byrne, peering into the car after Kyle had sped from the meeting to pick him up. "It was like someone had taken hold of his heart and squeezed the squirmy little frog until it leaped. Jumping Jehosaphat, I don't remember whenever I've had so much fun."

"Neither do I," said Kyle, both astonished and delighted that it was true. "It was freaking bold."

"Indeed it was, boyo. Truly it was."

"Get in," said Kyle, and when his father did, they sat there, side by side, not moving for a moment, thinking, both of them, about the appearance of Liam Byrne's ghostly apparition in the corner of Sorrentino's mysteriously darkened office during negotiations over the file. And then, in that car, starting with restrained, almost amazed, chuckles and ending with belly-jostling guffaws, they laughed together, father and son.

"Did he buy it all the way?" said Liam when they had caught again their breaths and Kyle started driving. "Was he as scared as he looked?"

"I think so," said Kyle. "Calling him a 'marinated piece of malfeasance' from the grave and promising to 'crush his skull like a dung beetle' seemed to do it."

"It was more the tone than the words," said Liam. "I put the ringing tone of righteous retribution in my voice."

"It even scared me, and I knew what was going on," said Kyle. And then, in imitation of Tiny Tony's deathly rasp, he said, " 'Lamb? Burnt lamb?' "

And the words set off another round of laughter. Before the appearance of Liam Byrne's ghost, there had been a strange phone call with abysmal reception, as if the call had come from some nether region. "What the hell?" had said Sorrentino. "Lamb? Burnt lamb? Who the hell is talking about burnt lamb? This ain't no Greek restaurant." It had taken every ounce of his self-control for Kyle not to burst out laughing right there in the office.

"But did he keep threatening you?" said Liam after the second bout of laughter had subsided. "Did he insist on still getting the file?"

"No," said Kyle. "Not after. He looked up at that painting of his first wife, let a shiver roll through him, and told me to get the hell out of there."

"Ah, Eleanor." In his mock ghost voice, Liam said, " *'Should I summon Eleanor to convince you? She's here. She says your new wife is a bigger whore than the last one.'* That was the final touch that put it over, I believe."

"How did you think to bring her in?"

"It was the painting. When he lit his lighter and backed away from my ghost, I saw it in the glow of the flame. I knew Eleanor. No one in life had ever frightened that scoundrel more. It's good to know that some things survive the scythe. So you're off the hook?"

"It appears I am. Thanks."

"Ah, think nothing of it, boyo. What else could a father do? But we put it over together. You and me, father and son. And we still have that Truscott in our crosshairs. It's a grand night for the Byrnes, yes it is. We need commemorate the event with a celebration worthy of the achievement. Pull over there."

"Where?"

"There. Right there. The state store. It still seems to be open. Pull over, and I'll grab us some libations, and we'll toast to the budding partnership of Byrne & Son."

Kyle sat in the car, suffused with an exuberant joy. He did feel good, great, free. Part of it was getting out from under the thumb of Tiny Tony Sorrentino, but it was more than just that, far more. These last two nights and a day with his father, first coming through the fire, and then the altercation outside Kat's place, and now this supernatural trick played on the bookie bastard who had beat the hell out of him a few days before, all of it had been the realization of the secret dream of his life. His father was back, and it wasn't working out horribly, it was working out well—hell, it was working out great. He almost liked the old guy, and the old guy almost liked him, and they actually seemed like a pretty good team. What could be better? He had a father again.

Yes, a celebration was in order. His father would come out with a bright bottle of champagne. They'd go back to their motel room and fill a couple of glasses with the bubbly. They'd make a toast to their successes in the past twenty-four hours, to their blinding boldness. And as they sipped and celebrated, they'd talk to each other about all the hours of each other's lives they'd missed and all the hours together still to come. Kyle's eyes grew unaccountably misty as he thought about it.

When Liam Byrne danced out of the state store, there was a gleam in his eye and a large paper bag in his hand. He smiled his broadest smile yet and winked as he stood in the headlights of the car and pulled out a gallon of something, its amber color swallowing the light.

And later . . .

"It is what I miss so much about the law," said Liam Byrne, as he paced around the motel room, waving his arm in emphasis, the cheap scotch sloshing wildly in his water glass. The rumpled bedspread had a brown and red checkerboard pattern that failed to hide the stains. The place smelled of ammonia and piss. Liam Byrne was walking around in his socks, and there was no champagne.

"The drama of it all, the oratory," said Liam Byrne. "To be armed only with your words and your wits, but all the while keeping the audience rapt as you push it to do your will. That's what it is to be a lawyer. And that's what we did tonight, boyo. It was an audience of one, true, but we had him believing in the impossible, and he did as we bade. It was my one great talent, to be a trial lawyer, and I miss it. But you have it in you, all of it. You should find a place for yourself in the law."

"You're kidding me, right?" said Kyle, holding his own glass of scotch as he sat in the chair. Kyle was still on his first, his father had poured three times. Kyle could drink to distraction, but he didn't like the taste of the cheap scotch, and he didn't like drinking in a motel room. There was something about it that gave him the skives. These rooms were made for bad sex and hard, hopeless drinking, and though he preferred the first to the second, he didn't really want any part of either. So mostly he nursed his drink and watched as his father poured from the rapidly emptying bottle.

"I'm serious as the devil," said Kyle's father. "You have it in you."

"I don't want to be a lawyer," said Kyle. "I can't get churned up about other people's money."

"Oh, it's not just money, my boy. Money's only the marker. It's right and wrong, it's passion and anger and love, it's the world with all its dramas playing out in a single confined space: the courtroom. It is a grand profession, a noble profession. Losing the law is my greatest regret about leaving like I did."

"I know how much it meant to you."

"Ah, do I detect a pout in your voice?" Liam shook his head and took a long swallow. His eyes fluttered as he smacked his lips. "I thought we were beyond that."

"It's hard."

"I know, but it's time to move through the resentment to something better." A fist pump, a quick swallow. "Something together."

"Okay," said Kyle. "You're right. Cheers."

"Cheers back to you, boyo. Cheers back to you."

And later . . .

"Don't doubt that you were marvelous in there, boyo," said Liam Byrne after a few more drinks. The old man's breathing was heavier now, his anxious gait slowed as he shuffled about the room. "You had that popinjay believing in your evident sincerity all the while you were playing your part in our little joke. It is a talent, yes it is. Don't turn your back on it. The law is a possibility. And if not the law, then something else. You could be an actor. A politician. My God, man, you could even be a mortgage broker."

"You're sending me lower and lower," said Kyle.

"Now, when you meet the senator, you have to play the same kind of role. You can't come right at him, he's far too dangerous. Remember what I said about giving a feint?"

"Yes, I remember," said Kyle. "But I wasn't sure what you meant."

"You have to let him think we're after the commonest thing, the one thing he'll be sure to believe. The one thing men like that think everyone is after."

"Sex?" said Kyle.

"Well, it is always that or money, isn't it? But for this it makes more sense to go with money. And lots of it."

"How much?"

"Half a million, I think."

"You're cracked."

"No, it's enough for him to know we're serious, but not too much to get his hands on."

"I don't want his money."

Liam looked at his son for a moment, then sat on the stained bedspread right across from Kyle and put his free hand on Kyle's knee.

"I know you don't. We don't, I mean. It's just a feint, remember. But he'll be sure to believe it, and that's the point. What other motive could he hope to find other than sheer venality? We have to let him think he can buy the file and buy your silence. It's the way to keep him interested, the way to keep his violence at bay. And then, when he comes to make the payment, that's when we have him."

"How?"

"With a wire."

"You're really cracked."

"We need more than your word about what he tells you. With a wire we can hoist the mealymouthed fish on his own petard. I'll tape it onto your chest myself. He's got more crimes to cover up now than what he perpetrated upon poor Colleen O'Malley. There's what he did to Laszlo, too. And your mother's house, don't forget that. When he hands over the money, he'll admit it—that kind always does—and we'll record it all. And then we'll turn everything over to the police. It's the only way. And only you can do it."

"I don't know, Dad."

"Oh, boyo, don't underestimate yourself." He took a drink, patted Kyle's knee, struggled a bit to stand again, lurched to the left as he tried to catch his balance. "You told me how you pushed that Malcolm into arranging the meeting. I saw what you did to Sorrentino. There is no limit to what you can achieve, if only you believe in yourself. Believe in yourself, boyo. You're a Byrne, never forget it."

"I never do," said Kyle, taking a sip of his whiskey.

"Good boy," said Liam as he moved to refill his glass. "So how about a toast? To a successful partnership and one burned senator. More for you, boyo?"

"I'm good."

"Yes, I know you are." He poured. "To the partnership of Byrne & Son."

"Here, here," said Kyle.

And later . . .

"It's quite a town, San Bernardino," said Liam. He had grown weary enough from the sound of his own voice to find respite atop the checkerboard bedcover, his head propped on a pile of pillows, his legs straight out, the tips of his socks flopping over his toes. His voice was soft with reminiscence, and his drink, still in his hand, rested upon his belt buckle. "Nice, friendly, sunny. I've lived a fine life there after I was forced to flee. And yes, it's been hit hard by the real-estate slump, but that only means it's ripe for easy picking. Have you ever thought of coming out to California?"

"I guess everybody does," said Kyle.

"You ought to, boyo. The sun. The girls. The girls lying in the sun. It's a land of opportunity. Especially now. Why, there are banks so laden with bad loans they are practically giving away houses just to get the losses off their books. A bit of money, a bit of shrewdness, the ability to close a sale, that's all it would take for a partnership to make a fortune."

"I don't know much about real estate."

"But I do, boyo. I do. After this you could come out, take a vacation, look around. And if the place captures your fancy, maybe we could go into business together for real. Byrne & Son. You know, my father was in real estate. Tenements and the like. He came over from the old country and made a roaring success of himself. Not such an easy thing. A hard man he was, and many was the time I was on the wrong end of his belt. But I was his boyo, his only one. He tried to bring me into the business, I opted for the law instead. But I understand him now in ways I never did before. The human desire for a legacy. There is nothing I'd like better than to work with you, side by side, to build our empire."

"That's nice, Dad."

"So you'll come on out?"

"I'll think about it."

"Byrne & Son. Our signs will be all over that town, like a plague, striking fear in every timid heart playing at the real-estate game. Byrne & Son."

"Sounds good."

"That it does, boyo. That it does."

And still later . . .

As Liam Byrne lay sleeping noisily on the bed, the garbage disposal cycling on erratically, Kyle stepped out of the room and stood in front of the door, leaning on the railing that overlooked the parking lot. The traffic on the highway was intermittent, the sky was gray, the cement under his feet was stained with all manner of foul fluid. A car pulled into the lot, and a mismatched couple fell out, laughing as they collapsed on each other. Kyle watched as they struggled to their feet and made their way, in fits and starts, to their door, the thin old man staggering, the heavy young woman holding him up, a brown paper bag clutched in her hand.

Just as the night was being burned away by the encroaching dawn, Kyle felt the exuberant joy he had experienced earlier in the evening being burned away, too. Maybe he was just tired, or maybe deeper truths were roosting in his psyche. There was something his father had said in his nightlong soliloquy that had stayed with him. *To be armed only with your words and your wits, but all the while keeping the audience rapt as you push it to do your will. That's what it is to be a lawyer.* And tonight, Kyle knew, he was the audience.

But his father need not have bothered with the shimmering oratory. Earlier Kyle had decided to trust his father, and the wild success with Sorrentino hadn't done anything to change his mind. He would trust him tonight and tomorrow and again; he would give himself wholeheartedly over to the relationship. Byrne & Son.

He was getting a sense of where this partnership might lead. To motels much like this one, with different names, perhaps, and in different states, but with the same bedsheets, the same drinking glasses for the same cheap scotch, the same drunken neighbors with their strident attempts to rut. To other bold schemes devised by his father to grab opportunity by the horns and wrestle it to the ground so that Byrne & Son could have its way with it. To a life where his role was laid out for him and the decisions were made for him and his ambitions set for him by the father he had decided to trust.

Even as the sun peeked over the desolate New Jersey landscape with a terrible brightness, Kyle Byrne peered into his future with eyes as wide as Speed Racer's. He saw it all unfold, a life determined by the schemes and fancies of the old man sleeping now his dreamless, drunken sleep. And he reached for it, greedily, like a man dying of thirst reaching for a bottle of malt liquor.

Chapter 43

B obby hated blood.
Not the spilling of it, that he had learned he liked fine. It was the stains that it left. The whole right sleeve of his shirt was spattered with it. He had gone a bit too far, maybe, in learning what he needed to learn. He was sure she would think so. But this was no longer the sober and careful Robert Spangler running her errands. This was Bobby Spangler, the new man, born of fire, and for Bobby Spangler too far was barely far enough.

"Bobby dear, we have a problem."

"You, maybe. I'm doing just fine."

"Be nice."

"I'm done being nice."

"I like it when you talk fresh. It means there's still a spine buried in all that mush. There was a young man in Laszlo's firm named Malcolm. In exchange for keeping an eye on the old goat, I promised him a job with the senator. And I always deliver on my promises."

"Not always."

"Don't be bitter, it's unbecoming. You haven't held up your end of the bargain the way I had hoped. But there is still time. Now, this Malcolm received his new job as promised. Quite a step up for the young man. But since he started, he hasn't been taking my calls."

"Perfectly understandable. He doesn't need you anymore."

"It is simply rude, Bobby. And I don't tolerate rudeness, of any form. I have it on solid information that this young man had some sort of conference with our Kyle Byrne. But now Malcolm is avoiding me. I can't get in touch with him, which means I haven't been able to learn what the conference was about."

"It's obvious, isn't it? It means the kid found the file, or at least is pretending to have found the file. He wants to trade it for money. He's trying to set up a meeting to lay out his terms."

"But where, Bobby? Where?"

"Ask Francis."

"No, dear, no need to trouble him with such trifling matters. I want you to ask Malcolm."

"He might not like the question."

"I don't care what he likes, as long as he gives an answer."

It was an assignment to his taste. Bobby Spangler had waited outside the senator's office until this Malcolm left for the day. The cleaners and then home and then out for a run along a secluded path in Wissahickon Park. A perfect place for Bobby to ask his questions. And he had gotten his answers, too. Quickly, actually. Malcolm caved at the first sight of the blade. That should have been satisfactory, but Bobby was rarely satisfied these days.

So now he stood over the kitchen sink, in his white Jockey shorts and T-shirt, trying to scrub out the blood. But no matter how much he rubbed the detergent into the cloth, filling the sink with bubbles, the dark blotches wouldn't disappear. Gouts of blood staining his shirt for all eternity. And his soul, too. Which he didn't mind so much. There was no turning back from what he had become. But the stains on his shirt were a different matter entirely. It was European cut and almost new. And it would be Kyle Byrne who paid.

Byrne was meeting the senator at a dive in Queens Village at four o'clock. When Bobby had told her the location and time, she had given him orders not to interfere. All she wanted to know was when the senator went into the bar and when he left. The rest she preferred to take care of on her own. She was pushing him aside. But these days he cared little for her preferences. He had given Kyle Byrne his best and heartfelt advice, and Byrne had shown him only the back of his hand. *Go to hell, Mr. O'Malley,* the boy had said. And, in his way, Bobby had. And now he'd take the Byrne boy with him.

After the near miss at the house, Bobby decided this was no time for the subtlety of his .38 automatic. His aim wasn't what it once was. So he had bought himself a Remington 870 Express HD twelve-gauge pump-action shotgun from the Wal-Mart with a tube-type magazine and a dozen boxes of high-velocity loads.

Pump and squeeze. As simple as that. At the distance he expected to fire, the shot pattern would be as wide as a small dog. Pump and squeeze.

The Remington and his automatic were in a bag on his bed, cleaned and loaded, ready for Byrne. Along with the knife he'd used in the park. He glanced at his watch. Plenty of time. Enough time to keep working at the stain before he took the bag to the car and headed to the bar.

Bubba's. What a dump. He had cased the place after he had hidden Malcolm's body with brush and leaves in the park. He hadn't gone inside the bar—he would be recognized, of course, from his previous visit. Yes, the fire had singed his skin and burned off his hair, but Bobby had made some additions and didn't now look much different than he had before. As soon as they saw him inside, they'd know what was up.

So he had checked the streets and alleyways front and back to figure out the best place to wait. And he had found his spot, where he'd be facing the entrance almost head-on. He'd sit in his car, and when the senator left, he'd call her and let her know, and then, against her firm instructions, he'd follow the Byrne boy. If he followed him long enough, the boy would take him to the accomplice Bobby had seen go into the house before he burned it down. It was the accomplice who would be holding the file. Then he could take them both out and have the file for himself.

Pump and squeeze and pump and squeeze.

And that would be just the start. Because Bobby was in charge now, no longer sitting back and waiting for her orders. Whatever she thought about Robert—how she could exert her control over him, how she could offer him everything and deliver nothing and he'd still kneel at her feet panting for more—was now obsolete. Robert was gone, and Bobby was in his place, and Bobby had every intention to run free like an arctic wolf, to rut like a goat, to dance along the knife's edge, to rampage. He would kill the Byrne bastard and his accomplice, he would grab the file for his own, and then the rampage would begin. And it would start at her doorstep.

He was still scrubbing the shirt, scrubbing as his hands turned raw and scaly, when he heard the footsteps in the hallway and then—

Knock, knock.

His head turned so fast his neck cramped.

Who the fuck is there?

Chapter 44

Knock, knock.

Ramirez heard some sort of snarl inside, like a ferocious cat protecting its food. And then the creak of the floorboards as something approached. As she took out her badge, she placed her free hand on the grip of her revolver, knocking off the leather holster strap with her thumb.

"Mr. Spangler," she called out through the door.

She saw the light from the peephole disappear. "Yes?" came the voice through the door.

"My name is Detective Ramirez, from the Philadelphia Police Department. I have a few questions to ask you."

"You do?"

"Do you mind if I come in?"

"A police officer? Really?"

She stepped back and put her badge up to the peephole. "Just a few questions. Can you open the door, please?"

"Of course. Just wait one moment, will you? It would be a scandal if I open the door now. I need to dress for guests."

Ramirez didn't like the sound of that. This Spangler's voice was strangely familiar, soft and almost effeminate. There was nothing threatening in it, but still he was going off to find either a pair of pants or something a bit more deadly. She backed to the side of the doorway, took out her gun, and wished she had waited for Henderson to come along. It had seemed like a wild-goose chase, not worth wasting two detectives' time on, but that didn't mean the chase didn't have its dangers or the wild goose a .44.

The building, a run-down old place wedged between two taller and wider buildings off South Broad, didn't give her much comfort. Above the outside door was a stone lintel with the word APARTMENTS carved into it, as if to announce that the structure had never aspired to be anything grander than a cheap place to hang your hat. It now held a combination of longtime tenants lacking the wherewithal or the desire to find something better and transients struggling to slow the slide of their fortunes. By the yellowed state of the slip of paper with his name typed on it, she assumed that this Spangler was the former. The vestibule door was unlocked, the stairs were worn, the walls dark with decades of shoulders rubbing the paint on their way down, down.

When the door opened, Ramirez stood by the side of the doorway with her gun drawn, waiting for something lethal to come through. It turned out to be an old man, slight and harmless. He wore a wavy dark toupee on his large, round head and had red, blotchy skin on his face and his slightly palsied hands. The man stuck his head out the door, looked right and then left. When he found Ramirez, his gaze drifted down to the gun, and then he smiled thinly.

"There you are," he said in a drawly, affected voice. "And you're holding a gun. Oh, my. What terrible things must I have done."

Gay? she wondered. With that mop of fake hair, probably yes. And definitely not frightening. If they got into a dustup, one elbow to that outsize head and he'd be on the floor in a heap.

"I'm sorry," she said as she put the gun back into the holster. "In my business they train us to be careful."

"As they should, Detective, because one never knows. One never does know. You said you had some questions?"

"Yes. Can I come in?"

"Of course. How rude of me." He opened the door wider and beckoned her inside. "I wouldn't want to be rude."

She entered a dark old apartment, its walls papered in faded yellowed paisley, dusty red tassels hanging from its lampshades. There was a creepy, anachronistic feel to the place, as if by stepping through the doorway she had spiraled through time into some spinster's house in the nineteen fifties. Black-and-white family photographs on the walls, an old-style console television, a loaded Super 8 projector set up behind the couch and pointed toward a stained white sheet tacked up on the wall above the television. A skirted couch and chair, upholstered in a greasy plaid fabric, was undoubtedly inherited from a grandmother and untouched out of sheer sentimentality. Ramirez wouldn't have been surprised to find the grandmother herself in a closet, untouched just as long for the selfsame reason.

"Sit, please, make yourself at home," said the man.

She did as he asked, sitting on the edge of the couch. The man was standing before her, in suit pants and a cardigan over a very nice shirt, with the soft folds of his cuffs just peeking out from the wool. He was younger than she had thought at first, maybe late fifties, early sixties. He leaned toward her, hands clasped together like an insect. He was a strange sight, with his gray pallor beneath the red and blistered skin, his bad toupee, his dark and arched eyebrows. She took a closer look and realized with a start that the eyebrows were drawn on, crudely, as if with a Sharpie. Her holstered gun began to dig into her hip.

"The face of the police department certainly has gotten prettier over the years," said Spangler. "It's a welcome change, I must say. Very welcome."

Was he flirting? Ramirez fought against her instinct to cut him down with flippancy, even as she began to feel sorry for the man: stuck in this tomb of an apartment, desperately holding on to a self-image that was as sadly off base as it was ridiculous. She shook her head at the emotion, as if trying to shake Henderson out of her consciousness.

"That's very nice of you to say," she said. "I understand you're a lawyer, Mr. Spangler."

"That's right," he said as he backed away from her and sat down in the easy chair catty-corner to the couch. He settled in, tilted his head down, and put his hands on the armrests like Lincoln in his memorial. In that moment Ramirez had the sense that she had seen this man before.

She took another scan of the apartment. There was a kitchenette, its sink filled with pinkish soap bubbles, and at the end of a short hallway a bedroom. A black bag was sitting atop the bed. Spangler was about to take a trip. Interesting.

"Are you still practicing?" she said.

"Until I get it right." His chuckle sputtered to life for a moment, like a sick outboard motor, and then ran out of gas. "But only odds and ends now. Just a little family business."

"Do you have an office?"

He waved his hand around his entombed apartment. "I do most of my work here. I have a few friends remaining in the profession who let me use their clerical staffs if the need arises."

"I'm wondering if you have a client named O'Malley."

"O'Malley?" he said. "No, I'm sorry."

"Do you know a Mr. O'Malley? Thomas O'Malley, I believe it is."

"O'Malley? O'Malley?" He exaggerated the name as if the query were one of the great mysteries of the universe. "No, I don't believe I do. Why are you asking me these questions about a Mr. O'Malley?"

"There is a man named O'Malley that we are looking for in connection with a homicide."

"A homicide. Oh, my. Who died? Someone I know?"

"Laszlo Toth," said Ramirez. "Also an attorney."

"Ahh, yes. I heard of his murder. I thought it was a robbery."

"We're still looking into it."

"I didn't know him personally," said Spangler, "but by reputation, of course."

"All we have to locate this O'Malley is a name and a phone number. From the phone records, the only calls he's been getting have come from your phone."

"My phone?"

"I'm afraid so."

"And only mine?"

"The only ones we can't account for."

"Ah, I see. When did I make these calls to Mr. O'Malley?" said Spangler.

Ramirez took a sheet of paper from her pocket, unfolded it. "Last Friday, at 6:02 P.M., 6:49 P.M., 7:12 P.M. . . . I could go on. But you called that number repeatedly, Mr. Spangler, almost obsessively, one could say, over the course of two or three days."

"Obsessively, hmm? That doesn't sound like me. And those calls were to an O'Malley?"

"They were to a number that we have connected to a Thomas O'Malley, yes."

"Because I was trying to call my brother."

"Your brother?"

"Yes, my twin brother. He lives in Des Moines. Lovely town. Have you been?"

"No."

"You mustn't miss the cow made of butter at the state fair. My brother recently was given a new cell phone, and I've been trying to reach him but have gotten no answer."

"Did he give you the number?"

"Yes, or my aunt did. Someone. I must say, I didn't recognize the area code. Do you suppose there was a mix-up of sorts?"

"I'm sure that's it. Could you tell me your aunt's name?"

"My aunt?"

"Just for our information."

"Gloria," he said. "Gloria Spangler."

"Do you have a phone number for her?"

"Not offhand, but I could get it for you, I suppose."

"Thank you."

Spangler stared at her for just a moment, as if waiting for her to say it was not necessary. She stared back flatly at him until he finally stood and walked to a little table by the television console. He flipped the pages of an address book and read out a number for Ramirez.

"Is my brother in trouble?" he said, still standing by the television.

"No, Mr. Spangler. I'm sure it is just a mix-up. But why were you calling so frequently? Over and over?"

"He's been sick lately, and I've been quite worried."

"Nothing serious, I hope."

"But it is, I'm afraid. Quite fatal. And as a twin, I can sense his emotions and well-being. Those things you've heard about us? All true. And more. What I sensed was a shift taking place. So you can see the reason for my distress. But if the number is wrong, then I am quite relieved. That explains why he wasn't answering."

"I'm sure that's it. I notice some blisters on your hands and face. Were you in a fire recently?"

"Fire?" He stared at his hands, turning them over as if they were fascinating artifacts that he had never in his life seen before. "No, these are not burns, Detective. The condition of my hands comes from a disease I have. Chronic psoriasis. Heartbreaking, actually."

"So they say. Are you going on a trip?"

"Why would I . . ." He stopped, swiveled his head toward the direction of the bedroom. "Ahh, so you've seen my bag. You are a detective, aren't you?"

"It's part of the job to be observant."

"And someone's been training you well. I'll have to write my councilman about the improvements in the force. Yes, I am going away, actually." He took a watch fob out of his cardigan, gave it a quick look. "In fact, I need to be going. Off to Des Moines to visit my brother."

"Flying?"

"No. I can't afford such luxuries. And being in an airless tube hurtling through the heavens makes me nervous. I'm a bit of a scaredy-cat, I'm afraid. So I'm driving."

"Long drive."

"Not as long as if he lived in Omaha."

"I suppose not," she said, forcing out an appreciative laugh. There was something very strange going on here. She'd like to look in that bag, she'd like to look in that sink or see what the movie was in the projector. But he had the right to refuse to allow a search, and if she pushed, he might sense her suspicions. It was better not to kick this sleeping dog while she tried to figure out what the hell was going on.

"Thank you, Mr. Spangler," she said, standing. "I so appreciate your help."

"It is no problem," he said, standing himself. "Especially being interrogated by someone as pretty as you." He dipped his chin, gave a strange, devilish grin, smoothed a fake eyebrow with the flat of his finger. "You wouldn't perhaps want to have coffee sometime, would you, Detective?"

He was . . . oh, my gosh, he was preening like a movie star and asking her on a date as if he were a genuine lothario. There was something unnerving, and terribly sad, in the disconnect between his self-image and his reality. But it could be useful, too. "I'm not sure I'm allowed, Mr. Spangler," she said, putting a girlish note in her voice.

"Call me Bobby."

"I don't know, Bobby. We're prohibited from fraternizing with witnesses we meet on the job."

"Is that what I am? A witness?"

"Yes."

"How exciting."

"And there are rules."

"Oh, rules," he said with a dismissive wave of his blistered hand. "It's only coffee. And we can discuss your Mr. O'Malley a bit further."

"Well," she said with a smile of her own. "Maybe you're right. Coffee does sound nice." She reached into her pocket and pulled out a card.

As he reached for the card, the sleeve of his white shirt extended from the cardigan. A French cuff. She held on to the card a few seconds to take a better look. A round silver cuff link. And was that a spot on the cuff link? Dark. Like a drop of something. Something like blood. She looked up at his face, at the deranged eyebrows and the lidded eyes that were hiding everything but their dementia. In a strange way, she wanted to hug him like a lost child even as she wondered where he was in such a hurry to get to.

Still holding on to the card, she stared into his eyes and said, "What's your brother's name, Bobby?"

He licked his lips. "Eugene."

"Eugene Spangler of Des Moines, Iowa."

"He's in a home now, a hospice, preparing for his death. They overcook the green beans."

"Please give Eugene my best wishes," she said before letting go of the card.

"I'll do that . . ." He glanced at the card, looked back up at her. "Lucia."

"Give me a call when you get back," she said in a voice as breathless as Marilyn Monroe's. "I'll be waiting."

Chapter 45

A Senator walks into a bar.

The amazing sight of Senator Francis Truscott IV walking into a joint like Bubba's seemed so surreal to Kyle that it could only be the setup of a joke.

A senator walks into a bar. He orders ten martinis lined up in a row. "What's the occasion?" says the bartender. "I'm celebrating," says the senator. "I just raised a million dollars for my reelection campaign."

Truscott, a tall man in his late forties, wore a pair of jeans, a leather jacket, and a baseball cap, trying hard to hide his senatoricity. But the jeans were pressed, and the leather of the jacket was butter soft, and it was a Phillies cap he was wearing, which was like a sign saying NOT FROM HERE. And of course there was the gaunt and severe face, chiseled by the gads of press coverage he had garnered over the years into something like a monument.

"*Congratulations,*" *says the bartender as he lines up eleven martinis side by side.* "*Have another on the house.*" "*No thanks,*" *says the senator.* "*If ten don't wipe out the taste of all the dick I've been sucking, I don't think eleven will either.*"

Or something like that.

Kyle was waiting for the senator in a booth, alone. But not entirely alone. There was Skitch at the bar, throwing dice with Old Tommy Trapp while keeping an eye on things. And Kat was parked in a car across the street, ready to call the police if something looked fishy. And there was Bubba Jr. himself, unhappy as hell that Kyle had volunteered his place for the meeting, but behind the bar all the same, with his shotgun oiled and loaded. They were all there just in case the senator had ideas of being a bit too clever.

And of course when did a senator ever not think himself a bit too clever?

The senator walked into the bar with a hesitant step, like a tenderfoot walking into a Wild West saloon, ready to duck if a spittoon were hurled at his head. While he looked around, Bubba and Skitch made an effort not to stare, but Old Tommy Trapp couldn't help himself.

"Pussy," said Old Tommy, in a whisper loud enough to have been heard in Cleveland.

Kyle raised a hand and nodded Truscott over to his booth. The senator swiveled his head guiltily, before slipping into the bench seat across from Kyle.

"Are you Kyle?"

Kyle nodded.

"Pleased to meet you, Kyle," said the senator, smiling and holding out his hand as if the bar were a campaign stop. "I knew your father."

Kyle looked at the proffered hand for a moment. It was the hand that had burned down his mother's house. It was the hand that had tried to kill his father, sending him into exile and Kyle's life into a tailspin. That it had also raped Colleen O'Malley and killed both her and Laszlo Toth were other, less personal reasons to let the hand hang there, its offer of reciprocal respect unreciprocated.

"Can we get to it?" said Kyle.

"A man of purpose, is that it? Not unlike your father in that. Though not as I expected. Malcolm said you were—how did he put it?—'a slacker dude.'"

"I slack with purpose, too," said Kyle. "You know that my mother's house was burned down just two nights ago."

"No, I didn't. I'm sorry." Pause, the fake political concern in his eyes replaced quickly with real concern, maybe even a touch of fear. "Wait, not that thing in Havertown with the fireworks?"

"That's the one."

"My gosh, I didn't know it was yours."

"Tell me about it," said Kyle. "Before it burned down around me—"

"You were inside?"

"Can we not play our little games?" said Kyle. "The 'My gosh' and the 'I didn't know'? Before you set the fire—"

"You have it wrong," said the senator, interrupting him calmly. "I didn't set any fire, or have any fire set. I wasn't involved, and I'm sorry about what happened. Was it arson? Are you sure? The papers said it might have been an accident. That maybe there was a cache of fireworks hidden in the property."

"It wasn't an accident. Check it out if you want to be sure. But what I'm trying to say is that before the fire I found an old file cabinet of my father's hidden behind some drywall in the basement. And in the cabinet I found the file. The one you've been running from most of your life."

"You mentioned the O'Malley file to Malcolm. Is that what you're referring to?"

"That's right. The one that shows conclusively that you raped the O'Malley girl when you were eighteen."

Truscott winced.

"The one with her notarized affidavit inside," said Kyle. "That's why you're here, isn't it? To make the file disappear?"

"No, actually."

Kyle tilted his head. "It's not?"

"I'm sorry to disappoint you, Kyle, but you can keep the file. Do whatever you want with it."

Kyle examined the senator carefully, trying to find the trick. Because there had to be a trick. All the uproar and death over the file had to be coming from this one powerful man. So his nonchalance had to be a trick. But there was something in the senator's face, a sort of rueful weariness that seemed to belie the possibility that any confidence game was going on. It was as if he really didn't care.

"You don't want the O'Malley file?"

"No."

"But if I turn it over to the press . . ."

"Then I probably will be seen by the world as a rapist unless I challenge the affidavit. Which I won't."

"So it's true."

"No, it's not true."

Kyle just stared at the man. Nothing was making sense. "If it's not true, I don't understand why you wouldn't contest it."

"Let me ask you something, Kyle. Was your life ever planned out for you? Did you have dreams that you were supposed to fulfill, even though they weren't your dreams?"

"My mom wasn't the type to plan anyone's life, even her own, and my father wasn't around."

"Then you were lucky."

"Screw you. I didn't have a father because of you."

"Because of me?"

"That's what I said."

"I think you're gravely mistaken. But what you did have, Kyle, was a clean slate. A chance to invent yourself. I never had that. You know what I always had? A future. Italicized and with a capital *F*. My *Future*. It was a beast that consumed everything. Every school I went to, every course I took, every girl I dated and job I accepted was only fodder to be fed to the beast. No youthful folly allowed, no mistakes. 'Think of your *Future*,' I was told over and again. 'Consider your *Future*.' And now I'm in the middle of it all, with the brightest part yet to come, and it doesn't seem so damn capital anymore."

"You want me to be sympathetic, is that it? You want me to feel pity for the poor rich senator?"

"No. I want you to be a little grateful for what you did have. And I want you to show at least a little respect."

"Go to hell."

"Yeah, well, it's happening sooner rather than later. You asked for this meeting, and now here I am. Tell me, Kyle, what were you going to ask for?"

Kyle looked carefully at the man across from him and saw something in his eyes. Concern? For Kyle? Son of a bitch must be a hell of a politician, because Kyle almost believed it.

"I was going to . . . you know . . . I was going to trade it for . . ."

"Money?"

Kyle nodded, and at that moment—even sitting across from this man who he was certain only a few moments before was a rapist and a murderer, and even believing that it was all just a ruse on his part—at that moment he felt ashamed. All the more so when the senator laughed. But it wasn't a mocking laugh. It was gentle, and almost appreciative.

"You can't even spit the word out of your mouth," he said. "Money's not what you want, son. And you have no idea of the price you'd end up paying. Though the affidavit isn't true, I paid to keep it quiet twice already, paid to stop it from infecting my glorious future. And I've regretted both acts ever since. I'm sorry, but I'm not paying again."

"No money?"

"Nope. Sorry."

"If it wasn't true, why did you pay before?"

"Because I had my future to think about. Lies always stick around longer than the truth. But I'm sick of my future, sick of the price I've paid for it, so I'm going to think about yours. What do you want to do with your life?"

"I don't know."

"Isn't it time to figure it out?"

"God, I'm getting it now from an asshole like you."

"If I let you turn yourself into a blackmailer, that's exactly what I would be," said the senator. "I did that once, I won't do it again. I'm going to tell you a story, Kyle. About an arrogant little prick and a sweet girl who loved him and that file of yours. I'm going to tell you because I've been wanting to tell someone for years. And I'm going to tell you because it involves your father, and I think you have the right to know."

Chapter 46

"O ne of my great-grandfathers was a crony of Morgan's," said Francis Truscott IV. "Another played golf with Rockefeller."

"Bully for you," said Kyle.

"I'm not bragging here, Kyle, I'm explaining. The Truscotts were a family of grand ambitions. My father could never live up to them, and eventually they broke him. He had once had the grandest of Truscott dreams. He was going to be a titan of industry, a poker champion, a pilot, the president, something big, something great, maybe even a race-car driver. While still a young man, he disappeared into the West to make his own way. But in his forties he returned to his dour family, with nothing to show for his time away except for a raging alcoholism and a pregnant wife. But his megalomania wasn't completely burned out of him by his failures, he transferred all his thwarted hopes onto his only child. Me.

"How did you handle the pressure?"

"With a purposeful nonchalance. I was always the star of my sports teams, I was the class president. My grades were only adequate, but I had a confident manner and the Truscott name. By my senior year at Haverford Prep, I was already accepted into Yale. Let me tell you something, Kyle, no one feels more atop the world than a high-school kid on his way to Yale. There were girls, parties, trips to Cabo. Life was brilliant, and my future, the one that had been lined up for me since birth, was well on track.

"But this is a love story, first and foremost, and I found it at a homeless shelter, on Christmas Eve, where, at my mother's shrewd request, I was helping serve dinner to the city's least fortunate. It was something for the résumé, something to polish my image and show I could give as good as I got. I had started it two years before I applied to Yale, had featured the experience in my application essay, and I continued after my acceptance only because my mother convinced me that to stop would appear churlish. It was as I was dishing out the mashed potatoes that I noticed the girl beside me pouring the gravy.

"Blond hair, blue eyes, a slim figure, all standard enough as far as I was concerned. But there was a sweetness there, too, and an innocence, two traits sorely lacking in the girls I dated. I almost believed that she was at the shelter because she wanted to do good for others, not for herself. The idea was so foreign to a Truscott as to be revolutionary.

"That was Colleen O'Malley.

"I didn't think she would be much of a challenge, and truthfully, she wasn't. She was swept away by my charm, my ease, maybe even my money, as I arrogantly expected she would be. But it wasn't long before I was swept away, too. It was her unaffected goodness, her purity of intention, the way she stared at me with so much love. Looking into Colleen O'Malley's eyes was like peering out of a tunnel and catching a glimpse of transcendent sunlight in an otherwise dark, monochromatic world.

"We dated in secret—neither of our sets of parents would have approved, she was poor, and I wasn't Catholic—and we fell in love in secret, and we made love in secret. But sex with Colleen wasn't about getting something, a piece or an advantage or a prestigious date for Saturday night, it was about giving, not just pleasure but the whole of ourselves, one to the other, together. One heart, one breath, our souls twining together like the braided candles stuck in the silver holders in the dining room at our estate, the ones that burn down so prettily until they are mere sputtering heaps of blackened wax. Like the pair that was lit one evening when I was summoned to that very dining room by my mother.

" 'Francis,' said my mother, sitting at the head of the table, her mouth pursed like the painting of my father's mother on the wall above her. She was eating her dinner alone. A bowl of consommé. My father was away at the club, where he would spend the night after another evening of hard drinking, as had become his custom. 'We need to talk about this nonsense with the O'Malley girl.'

" 'How do you know about her?'

" 'Francis, dear, we are your parents. It is our job to know.' She lifted the spoon to her lips, lapped up the broth like one of her prized Burmese. 'Now it is time for you to prepare for Yale. You need to concentrate on getting ready, not on dillydallying in the sun. And it is not fair to string that young girl along through the summer. It is time to end it.'

" 'I'm not stringing her along.'

" 'Francis, please. She goes to a Catholic school in Darby.'

" 'She's different from the other girls I've dated.'

" 'I know she is, dear. The exotic young Catholic-school girl with her plaid skirt and saddle shoes. It is a ready-made fantasy for a young boy. Trust me, I know.' She lifted the spoon to her lips. Lap, lap. 'Which is why we didn't stop it when it first broke out. But it has grown beyond what is tolerable. Now we've already spoken to the O'Malleys, and they are fully in agreement.'

" 'What did you do? What the hell did you do, Mother?'

" 'Watch your tone.' Lap, lap. 'Francis, they have plans for their daughter, just as we have plans for you. And she is rather young.'

" 'You had no right.'

" 'You didn't say that when we promised a wing for that science building at the university. And you'll happily accept our tuition payments and the money you'll need to live in New Haven in the style you've grown accustomed to here. So, dear, I think we have every right to ask that you respect our wishes when it comes to this one minor matter.'

" 'It is not a minor matter.'

" 'But that's exactly what she is. Have you read the penal code lately? Do you know what you are risking?'

" 'I love her, Mother.'

" 'Yes, yes. And I love chocolate. But I have learned to do without to maintain my figure. As you must learn to do without to maintain your future.' Lap, lap. 'Now, think of the right way to break it to her. Young hearts are often so fragile, and we wouldn't want to see such a precious flower unduly bruised.'

"It was the first real test of my life, Kyle, my first chance to stake out my own path. No one should be surprised that I failed. Along with the ambition that had been instilled in me from birth, there was a tendency toward acquiescence, too, which allows ambition to find the simplest way to rise. It does no good to fight the man when being the man is your deepest aspiration. So I broke it off, ignored the wailing of my heart as I delivered the news over the phone, and found some solace in the long-legged, straight-haired girls in the groves behind my classmates' pools.

"I was already at Yale when I heard the news. A lawyer named Liam Byrne had contacted my family before going to the police. Colleen had accused me of rape.

"It wasn't true, of course. But Colleen had discovered she was pregnant after I'd broken it off. She didn't know what to do. She was alone and scared, and abortion was out of the question. When she told her parents, they were so hurt and angry, both, that the word 'rape' just slipped out. It was perfectly understandable; it was a direct result of my cowardice. But once it was out, her parents seized upon the accusation, and it snowballed.

And soon the charge had taken on a life of its own, and she was unable to take it back. I called her from Yale, and the conversation didn't go well. We were both hurt and angry and scared, and I said some things I should never have said. It was going to get ugly, I could feel it. But your father gave everybody a way out.

"He went to my family before going to the police. Once the police had it, it would be part of the public record forever. But your father promised to make it disappear, for a price. There would be money exchanged, of course. But also custody of the child was to be considered. In light of the accusation, and the phone call, I had to agree to counseling and to never try to contact Colleen or the child, ever. Under the circumstances it was a price my parents were only too happy to pay. One of my mother's relatives handled negotiations on our side, to make sure it all stayed quiet, and the agreement was signed and the money transferred.

"'Let that be a lesson to you, Francis,' my mother told me. 'Always be careful with whom you associate. And never underestimate the brutal dishonesty a woman is capable of, despite her gleaming surface. I know, dear, believe me, I know.'

"And it was a lesson I took to heart. Seeing my future suddenly imperiled and then revived, I began to cultivate it avidly, as if it were a rare orchid that needed constant care. I excelled at Yale, was inducted into Skull and Bones, married into an old-line Boston family, went home to Philadelphia and claimed my place in the family business. It was only a matter of time before I would take the next step. And so, in 1994, with the Republicans poised to gain control of Congress, and with the financial backing of both my wife's family and my own, I declared my candidacy for the United States Congress.

"I won the nomination in a hotly contested battle, determined by an onslaught of hard-hitting television ads, and looked to be a lock in the general election, when I was approached by a figure from my distant past."

"My father," said Kyle.

"It felt like a ghost had come back to haunt me," said the senator. "The ghost of my own desertion of Colleen. He told me that he couldn't, in good conscience, allow a rapist to waltz into Congress without the public becoming aware of what had happened. He told me it was a matter of national interest. Despite the nondisclosure clause in the agreement, despite the injury it would cause to his client, Colleen, who had started life anew in Ohio with her son and a husband, despite its being a violation of his code of professional responsibility, he said as a patriot he had no choice. He was going to give the file to the press if I didn't pull out of the race."

"So what did you do?"

"I panicked," said the senator. "It wasn't just my future I was trying to protect, it was Colleen's, too. And my son's, the son whom I had never met but still thought about frequently. My father had drunk himself to death by then, so I went to my mother. She told me to offer him money. I told her that Liam Byrne wasn't interested in money, and she gave me one of her smiles, like I was nothing more than an innocent fool. I didn't think it would matter, but I gave it a shot. I was ashamed to broach the subject, just as you were today, but I did it. And to my surprise, that's when the negotiation started."

"Negotiation?"

"Yes. We bought off your father. We bought the file."

"How much did you pay him?"

"A lot. Enough for him not to have to worry about money for a long time. Half a million dollars."

"Are you kidding me?"

"No. The transfer took place in a deserted lot by the river. A suitcase full of cash. And he took it, and that was the end of it. But it felt wrong, it felt rotten. I was disgusted with the whole thing, and I was thinking of quitting the race. But then your father died. And later I learned about Colleen. It was too much. My mother told me to forget it all, that it was over. 'Think of your future, dear,' she told me. 'All that remains is your future.' And so I stepped into it."

"Half a million dollars?" said Kyle.

"Yes. But it always rankled, not the money, but the denial. And I was disappointed in your father, too. Maybe because I secretly hoped he would release it, and then my future would go down the tubes and I'd be free in a way I never had been before. Things would have changed, that's for sure. I would have had to deal with Colleen and my son. Who knows what would have happened? But I always regretted that I never found out. And I won't do it again. Colleen's gone, my son is a now a doctor in Cleveland; he can take the truth. Do what you want with that file, Kyle, and do it with my blessing."

"But if you didn't want the file, then why did you come?"

"I came because of something Malcolm said. By the way, have you been in touch with him today?"

"No."

"He seems to have disappeared. Strange. Anyway, he told me you knew what really happened to Colleen."

"And you don't?"

"No. But I'd like to know."

"She died."

"I know that. She drowned accidentally in a lake."

"No, she was murdered."

His eyes widened. "By whom?"

"I thought by you."

The senator shook his head. "I loved her," he said. "Even after everything that happened, I still do. She was the love of my life. I could never have hurt her. How do you know she was murdered?"

"Because after she drowned, somebody tried to kill my father."

"When was this?"

"Nineteen ninety-four."

"How do you know that someone tried to kill your father?"

"I just do."

"Okay," he said. "I'll believe you."

"But whoever killed her and tried to kill my dad, it didn't end there. I believe that the same person killed Laszlo Toth and then burned down my old house."

"Because of the file?"

"Why else?"

Francis Truscott IV sat there and thought for a bit, and then he closed his eyes, put his hands over his face. "My God," he said softly.

"What?"

"No matter how sharp we think we are, Kyle, the only ones we're able to fool all the time are ourselves."

Chapter 47

As Kyle watched Truscott drag himself out of Bubba's, looking as if something had broken inside him, Kyle felt as if he himself had been punched in the gut. It could have been an act, the senator's sorry tale, a ruse, a pack of lies told by a merciless killer. And that the teller was a politician made such a possibility seem all the more plausible. But there was something about the story, and the telling of it, that rang so true. As did the tolling of that half a million dollars.

His father had never mentioned the payoff when he told Kyle of why he left. Kyle bet the half a mil made the exile a hell of a lot easier. And the fact that he had told Kyle to ask for the same amount put his father's present motives in serious doubt. Was he really trying to catch a killer, or was he merely using Kyle to set up another half-million-dollar score? Kyle had never realized before how difficult it was to be a son.

"Did the son of a bitch confess?" said Skitch, slipping into the senator's seat after a suitable interval.

"Not really," said Kyle.

"Bastard. But did you get what you needed?"

"I don't know what I need," said Kyle. "That's the problem."

"Bro, what's going on?"

"I have no idea," said Kyle, "but I don't have long to find out. And let me tell you something, Skitch. Once I do, somebody is going to pay."

"You got the look, man."

"What look?"

"Remember that game with Chaucer's when that creep tackled Bubba Jr. with a takeout slide into second? And you slammed the ball into the outfield and then jogged around the bases slow enough to ensure a play at the plate, and then you laid out the catcher so brutally they had to cart his ass off to the hospital?"

"I broke his jaw."

"That look," said Skitch.

"Hey, Kyle," said Bubba Jr. from behind the bar. "You got a call."

Kyle scooted out of the booth and reached for the phone, but Bubba pulled it away before he could get his hands on it. "Everything go okay?"

"I suppose. No gunplay at least."

"I got to tell you, Kyle, seeing a United States senator walk through my door scared the hell out of me. Do you have any idea what you're doing?"

"Do I ever?"

"Be careful. You're in deep water now, where the sharks swim. And thanks a hell of a lot for pulling me in with you."

"I was wondering who I could rely on in the middle of a god-awful mess, and I realized it was pretty much only Skitch and Kat and you."

"That's plain sad. But I got to tell you, you look damn good in a suit."

"Now you're scaring me, Junior," said Kyle as he took the handset.

Kyle figured it was Kat calling from her perch outside, letting him know where the senator headed after he left. He was hoping it was Kat, because if it wasn't, it was probably his father, and he had no idea what the hell he'd say to him, at least not yet. But he was wrong, it was neither.

"Is this Kyle Byrne?" came the voice, a female voice, old and tremulous, but with a brutal self-possession.

"Yes, this is Kyle Byrne."

"You just had a meeting with Senator Truscott, and the senator just left, isn't that correct?"

"That's right. Who is this?"

"And in that meeting you discussed with the senator a certain file that you found in your old house, even as it was burning down around you."

"Maybe," said Kyle slowly.

"Dear, don't try to play games with me. You don't have the testicles for it."

Kyle couldn't keep himself from laughing.

"What was decided in your meeting?" said the voice.

"None of your business."

"But it is, you see. Nothing could be more my business. You wanted to sell the file to him, isn't that right?"

"Yes, actually."

"And is he buying?"

"No. He refused. He told me to do with it as I wished."

"The truculent fool. So then the file is still for sale, I presume."

Kyle thought for a moment and laughed again. This time he laughed because, even though he had never heard the voice before, he realized exactly whom he was talking to. "Yes, it's still for sale."

"Do you have a price in mind?"

"Half a mil."

"You are an ambitious guttersnipe, aren't you?"

"Aren't we all?"

"Yes, I suppose. But it's important we each remember our respective stations. That's something your father frequently forgot." She gave him an address in Chestnut Hill, among the toniest old-line neighborhoods in the city. "Can you find it?"

"Probably."

"You will come tonight, you will bring the file, we will discuss your price."

"There won't be any discussion," said Kyle. "And no checks. Cash."

"I wouldn't have it any other way. And of course you will come alone."

"Don't worry about that, I'm not into sharing."

"Just like your father."

"You'll have the money when I show?"

"Of course I will, dear. I'll keep up my end, I always do. Nine o'clock. Don't be late. Ciao."

Kyle shook his head for a bit, listened some more to make sure the line was actually dead, and then tossed the handset back to Bubba Jr.

"Who was that?" said Bubba Jr.

"That," said Kyle, with a smile both broad and dangerous, "was a cold-blooded killer. And I am next on her list."

Chapter 48

Even with his black bag on the passenger seat beside him, Bobby Spangler felt under-armed.

Parked in the alley he'd found that faced Bubba's almost head-on, he had the uncontrollable urge to ram his car straight through the bar's front door. And he was ready to do it, too, because just then he had that potent combination of aggrieved self-righteousness and sexual frustration that was detonating murderous explosions all over the globe. If only he had a swill of fertilizer and nitromethane in his trunk, or a huge sack of hand grenades. If only he had something devastatingly powerful that would crater that bar and obliterate everyone inside, including Kyle Byrne, who had dismissed his help, and Senator Francis Truscott IV, who had been the bane of Robert's existence for pretty much his entire life.

He wondered what they were talking about in there, Kyle and Francis. Of course there was the file to discuss. Kyle had found it, that clever boy, and Francis wanted it, and an agreement would be made, because that was the way Francis worked: give them everything they wanted so long as Francis got more. It was what the O'Malley file was all about in the first place: take a girl against her will and buy off the rape charge, the whole time maintaining the loving support of the mother who provided him everything.

But they were taking too long a time. This had gone beyond "How much do you want?" and "We have a deal." Maybe they were laughing together, telling jokes. Maybe they were laughing about him.

He wanted a bomb, he needed a bomb. Bobby slapped the steering wheel in frustration. One bomb and he'd destroy the Truscotts' fondest hopes once and for all, obliterate Kyle Byrne, and end his own torment at the same time. A bundle of dynamite, tied tight like a fasces, or an empty fifth of vodka filled with nitroglycerin, or a half ton of Semtex sculpted into a ten-foot phallus. He closed his eyes and imagined the sensation of the car engine coming to life, revving higher and higher until he punched it into gear and plunged it into the bar's cheap doorway, shattering brick and wood as he rammed through.

And then being lifted by the fire and force, by the sheer power of his unleashed anger, rising ecstatically through the flame and blood as his will consumed everything about him until he felt himself all-powerful, all-knowing, the creator.

But he had no bomb, no grand instrument of destruction. He wondered what would happen if he set his car on fire and then, with flames shooting out the rear, barreled into the heart of that bar. Would they all be exploded into the sky, or would only he flame out, screaming horribly as he burned, while they laughed at him once again? No, he couldn't allow that. He had to stick with his plan.

The door of the bar opened, and he spied once more the chief antagonist of his life, Francis Truscott IV. Francis was dressed down, jeans and leather and a silly ball cap, but it was still the same old prig who looked around guiltily and then made his way down the street. Bobby fought the urge to pick up the shotgun right then and there. Francis had gotten everything from her, while Robert had gotten nothing. Francis had been groomed for greatness by her, while Robert had been forced lower and lower until there was nothing left of him but the lowing beast inside. And what was the difference between the two in her eyes? Simple. Francis was half a Truscott, while Robert was all Spangler. But she underestimated her birth family. She thought she could outrun it and create something new, but there was no running from blood. He would prove that soon enough. First, though, there was business.

"He just left," said Bobby into his cell.

"Thank you, dear. I might need you tonight."

"I'm busy."

"Not too busy for this."

"What kind of job is it this time?"

"Your specialty, you naughty boy. If things in that bar went as I expected, and go as I expect, young Byrne will be coming to the house tonight at nine. I want him to come but not leave, do you understand?"

"Perfectly."

"You don't sound enthused."

"I'm tired of taking your orders."

"It's not an order, it's an offer. Anything he has on him is yours. And there will be plenty, trust me. One more job, Bobby, and then it's over and my promises will finally be fulfilled."

"Liar."

"We'll see, won't we?"

Yes, we will see, thought Bobby as he hung up his phone. They'd both see when he showed up at nine with the file and a gun and had his sweet way with her. And then, when it was all over, he'd give that young thing from the police department a call. She seemed interested enough in a Spangler. Maybe all along his problem was shooting too high. She was just low enough to be in his range. He'd wow her with his charm like he wowed her before. She wouldn't know what hit her as he took her from behind. Yee-haw. But now it was just a matter of waiting until Kyle Byrne slipped out from the bar like the insect he was and then, shotgun at the ready, following the son of a bitch to his death.

The door opened, and there he was, Kyle Byrne, in a suit, with some fat little tattooed spark plug by his side. Bobby turned on the car engine and prepared to follow when something stopped him.

Who was that approaching Byrne? With that walk. It was her, the pretty detective, that Ramirez. She was grabbing Kyle Byrne's arm, hard, like she knew him. She was grabbing his arm, like she knew him, like they were great friends, and she was looking around, and she was pulling him back into the bar.

What the hell? What was her connection with Byrne? Bobby thought it through, quickly, let the possibilities fall like dominoes one after the other in his consciousness. Maybe she was in on it all. Maybe they were a team. Maybe they were lovers. That two-timing bitch. Or wait. Something else, something far more disturbing.

Maybe he hadn't played the scene in his apartment as well as he had thought. Maybe her suspicions hadn't been quelled but instead ratcheted higher. Maybe her romantic interest was feigned. Maybe she had followed Bobby to the bar. Maybe she herself was waiting to see who came out. Which meant she saw Truscott. And then saw Byrne. And now was escorting that Kyle Byrne to safety. As if something were about to happen on the street. Which meant she wasn't alone. Which meant—

He didn't wait to figure out the rest. He grabbed the black bag, leaped out of the car, ran as fast as he could down the alley and away from the bar. He tripped as he heard the police cars slam to a halt in front of the alley, rose back to his feet amid shouts from behind him and sirens in the distance.

He cut through one alleyway and another, stopped, searched for refuge like a hunted animal, spied a Dumpster out behind a restaurant. He dashed to it, threw the bag in, pulled himself up and over, buried himself in a week's worth of garbage—pizza boxes, newspapers, rotted vegetables, maggoty knuckles of meat, excrement leaking from those little blue doggie bags—buried himself until he was completely covered.

He waited for the police to arrive, which they did. He waited as they searched, waited as they left. He waited as the sirens in the distance died. He waited, and waited some more, he waited for hours, just to be sure, he waited, and every breath through the fetid garbage was a reminder of exactly what he had become.

And it was sweet as honey cake.

Chapter 49

After Detective Ramirez yanked Kyle Byrne back into Bubba's, she twisted the lock in the door and pushed him into a booth halfway down the bar. Then she stood with her back to him, facing the rest of the bar, and pulled out her badge and her revolver.

"Police," shouted Ramirez.

"Hello there, Detective," said Kyle. "Thirsty?"

"Just shut up, you. Now, I want everyone to get down. Something might be coming through that door, and if it does, it won't be pretty."

As the bar's patrons scattered to the floor and started crawling behind the bar, the bartender, still standing, reached down and pulled out a shotgun. With a quick pump, he slid a cartridge into the chamber.

"What the hell are you doing?" said Ramirez.

"This was my father's bar," said the bartender. "You think I'm not going to defend it?"

She looked at him, a skinny black kid with raw hands and a mouth set like granite. The gun sat solid in his hands. "What's your name?"

"Bubba."

"Bubba? You're kidding, right?"

"Bubba Jr."

"Well, listen, Bubba Jr.," said Ramirez. "You point the muzzle at the floor and don't raise it an inch until I give the word. Understand?"

"I understand," said the bartender.

"Something's going down outside right about now, so it's probably safer for all of you in here. But don't be surprised if what comes through that door next is a car."

Ramirez squatted down and faced the door with her gun, held in both hands, pointing right at it. She spoke softly enough so that only Kyle could hear. "Remember that number your girlfriend gave me?"

"She's just a friend."

"Really?"

"You sound pleased to hear it."

"Shut the hell up." Ramirez was angry at the lift she felt. She shook her head to bring herself back to business. "There was only one person other than you who called it. I traced the guy down and asked him some questions, and I got to tell you, he creeped me the hell out. Then I realized that his voice matched the voice on the 911 call that reported your break-in at your father's old office. So as I called for backup and a warrant to search his place, I stayed outside his building to make sure he didn't run. Next thing I knew, he was lugging a black satchel to his car. And I have to tell you, I don't think the satchel was filled with underwear. I followed him to here, though I wasn't sure exactly what he was doing until I saw you step out of the bar."

"You think he's here to kill me?"

"He's here to something you, baby. Didn't I tell you to stop stirring the pot?"

"The pot kept stirring me. So we're just waiting here like sitting ducks for him to come and get me?"

"I called in the cavalry," said Ramirez. She glanced at her watch. "They'll be here about—"

The squeal of brakes slipped through the door, and then shouting, and then sirens.

The short, fat kid who had left the bar with Kyle popped his head above the bar.

"Get down, you fool," said Ramirez.

The kid's head dropped below the bar again.

There was a knock. Ramirez put a finger to her lips and gestured at Bubba Jr., who pointed his shotgun at the door.

"It's Henderson," came the voice from the other side of the door.

"Henderson who?" said Ramirez.

"Henderson your mama. Open the hell up."

Ramirez smiled as she stood and holstered her gun. "Put it away," she said to Bubba Jr. while she twisted open the lock. "It's one of the good guys. Or at least a reasonable facsimile."

Detective Henderson stepped into the bar with wariness, looked around, spotted the shotgun still in Bubba's hand, and raised an eyebrow. Then he spotted Kyle Byrne, sprawled in the booth where Ramirez had pushed him, and he growled.

"You get him?" said Ramirez.

"Not yet," said Henderson. "You talk to the kid, find out what the hell is happening?"

"Haven't had the chance."

"Want to take him down to the box?"

"We can do it here."

"And if he clams up?"

"Then we'll box him nice and tight for a week," said Ramirez. "Let's see what's going on outside first." As they both walked to the door, Ramirez turned and pointed at Kyle. "Don't you dare move," she said. Then she turned to Bubba Jr. "If he stands up, shoot him."

"With pleasure," said Junior.

Ten minutes later Ramirez and Henderson were sitting in Kyle's booth, Henderson beside Kyle, blocking his exit, and Ramirez across from him. The two cops had mugs of soda before them, Kyle a half-finished bottle of Rolling Rock.

"What was in the file cabinet, Kyle?" said Ramirez.

"What file cabinet?"

"Stop being cute."

"I can't help it," said Kyle, smiling. "I was born this way."

Ramirez stared for a bit and couldn't stop herself from laughing. He was cute, and he knew it, which didn't obviate the fact that he was playing it way too cute for his own good.

"Did I see who I thought I saw coming out of the bar a few minutes before you?" said Ramirez.

"Who did you think you saw?"

"Who do you think I saw?"

"Who do you think I think you—"

"Can we get on with this?" said Henderson. "The two of you are giving me a headache."

"We've got a United States senator involved in our murder case," said Ramirez. "How do you like them apples, Henderson?"

"I don't," said Henderson. "It means this peckerhead's got us mixed up in something explosive enough to put my pension at risk."

"You wouldn't want to risk Henderson's pension, would you, Kyle?" said Ramirez.

"No, ma'am."

"So let me do some guessing here, just off the top of my head. Your father had something going on with Truscott before he was a senator. Your father died in 1994, right? That was when the senator was running for Congress the first time, if I'm not mistaken."

"I don't follow politics."

"You follow it enough to know that there was something of interest to a United States senator in the file cabinet your father hid in the basement of your old house. It was probably of interest enough to get your house and your car torched. And whatever was in that cabinet was of interest enough to said U.S. senator for His Eminence to show up at a dive like this. How am I doing?"

"Not bad for a cop."

She didn't like that comment, and she let him know it with a glare. "A shame about the Datsun. Was it insured?"

"At some point it was, I suppose."

"The breadth of your stupidity is astounding. Ever hear of a guy named Spangler?"

"No. I don't think . . . Wait. Spangler?"

"That's right."

"A lawyer?"

"That's the one. How do you know him?"

"I don't," said Kyle. "But I think my father might have known him."

"Pretty damn well, I'd bet. You see, we think this Spangler might have killed Laszlo Toth. And his face and hands were covered with something that might have been burns, maybe from your house. And he was waiting outside this bar with what appeared to be a bagful of firepower, looking, we guess, for you."

"Where is he now?"

"We thought we had him, but he disappeared."

"Nice work."

"It would have been easier," said Henderson, "if we knew even a little of what the hell was going on. And the reason we don't is because you've been telling us squat."

Kyle looked at Henderson and then at Ramirez. "Why do you say he knew my father pretty damn well?"

"Kyle, we want to impress upon you how dangerous your situation has become," said Henderson. "We think whatever you found in that file cabinet might have gotten Toth killed, and maybe your father, too."

"He died of a heart attack," said Kyle.

"That's what the death certificate reads," said Ramirez. "But it was signed by a New Jersey doctor who was convicted of falsifying death records for an embalming factory that processed bodies for a load of funeral parlors in the tristate area. The embalming house was selling body parts and made them more attractive by altering the death certificates. Your father was cremated, right?"

"Yes," said Kyle, looking distracted.

"So maybe it wasn't a heart attack. Maybe he was murdered by this Spangler character and then shipped up there for his death certificate to be faked and his parts sold. Anyone in the funeral business could have set it up. What you found in that file cabinet would put you next on this guy's list."

"If you want our help," said Henderson, "it's time to come clean. What did you find, son?"

"Nothing."

"You know that blackmail is against the law."

"That's not what I'm doing."

"Then what the hell are you doing?"

"I'm not so sure anymore," said Kyle.

He clasped his hands tightly in front of him, closed his eyes, leaned his mouth on his thumbs. As Ramirez stared, she could see him thinking something through. Then the blood seemed to drain from his face. So they'd finally scared the little bastard, thought Ramirez. She was a bit saddened, actually. She had liked his unflappability, had liked that his wide and wicked smile seemed impervious to fear. It hadn't seemed so much foolish as foolhardy, which was a different thing entirely. But now he was just another scared little rat in over his head. Why were men always such disappointments?

"Am I under arrest?" said Kyle finally.

"No," said Ramirez. "But we'll protect you, if that's what you're asking. We promise. Tell us what you know, and we'll take care of you."

"No, I mean am I free to leave?"

"You want to go? Even with that murderer out there hunting for you?"

"I have something I need to do."

"Your laundry?" said Ramirez.

"Family business."

"Don't be a fool, son," said Henderson. "Let us protect you."

"Thank you for your concern. It touches my heart, truly. But there is something I need to do right now. Am I free to go?"

Ramirez looked at Henderson. Henderson shrugged.

"Yes, you're free to go," said Ramirez wearily.

"Then that's what I'm going to do," said Kyle.

Henderson shook his head as he rose from the booth, making way for Kyle to leave. "It's your funeral."

"At least he's dressed for it," said Ramirez.

"Thank you, both," said Kyle, sliding out and standing. "Yo, Skitch."

"Bro?" said Kyle's squat friend who'd been hiding behind the bar.

"I need your bike."

"But I'm using it tonight. I'm hooking up with that girl from Jersey, and we got—"

"Give him the bike," said the bartender.

"When will I get it back?"

"Hell only knows," said Kyle.

"Bro?"

"Dude."

"Crap," said the kid as he reached into his pocket and threw a set of keys that Kyle snatched out of the air. "Take care of my baby."

"Don't worry, I'll treat it like it was my own."

"After what happened to your 280ZX, why don't I find that comforting?"

Kyle turned again to Ramirez. "You got a phone number, Detective?"

She leaned back, narrowed her eyes. "Yeah, I have a phone number."

"You want to give it to me?"

"I'm not sure," said Ramirez. She looked up at Kyle and saw the smile and felt it slice into her with its sweetness. He scratched his cheek as if to signal that she had something on her own, and she couldn't help but wipe at it with the edge of her thumb.

"Let him have it," said Henderson. And as Ramirez took out a card and handed it to Kyle, Henderson added, "You call us if you need us, son. We'll be waiting."

"Thank you," said Kyle as he put the card into his jacket pocket.

After Kyle left, Ramirez looked at the closed door and said, "What do you think?"

"I think we'll be on duty tonight," said Henderson. "And poor little me, I was planning on going bowling."

"He has no idea what he's gotten himself into."

"I'm not so sure about that," said Henderson. "He strikes me as someone who has every idea of what he's gotten himself into."

"I'm worried about him."

"I know you are," said Henderson. "It's why you followed the lead he gave you and traced that number and found that Spangler and kept your eye on him all the while we were putting this operation in place. Because you were worried about him. This Byrne kid is not just a piece of a puzzle, is he?"

"No."

"See there, Ramirez, now you're making me cranky."

"Why? Because partnering with me, you actually have to do some work?"

"No. I just get cranky when my expectations are confounded. And here all along I thought you'd never make it as a detective."

Chapter 50

Uncle Max was sitting at the bar of the Olde Pig Snout, smoking a cigarette, nursing a beer, watching the local news on the television as his life ticked away swallow by swallow. When the door opened, he palmed his cigarette and turned his head to get a look at who was walking in. He instinctively smiled when he saw it was Kyle. And then the smile froze on his face, as if something in his nephew's eyes made it clear that this was not simply a sweet familial visit.

"Kyle, what a surprise," said Max. "And in a suit, no less. Who died?"

"No one," said Kyle. "Yet."

"Want a drink?"

"We need to talk."

"What, you dress like that just to break up with me?"

"Over there," said Kyle, pointing to a booth.

"Sure thing, Kyle. No problem. Let me get us a round, first."

Max waved Fred the bartender over. Fred smiled crookedly. "How you doing there, Kyle?"

"Not so good," said Kyle.

"What happened?" said Fred.

"I've been betrayed," said Kyle.

Max's head swung toward Kyle as if his ear had been yanked, but Fred just kept on nodding and smiling. "Good, good. You still playing ball?"

"Not anymore."

"Just keep swinging. Anything I can get you?"

"A beer."

"Two," said Max. "With a couple shooters." Max glanced back at Kyle's stone face. "On my tab."

"Good," said Fred. "So everything's good, Kyle?"

"Yeah," said Kyle. "Everything's just swell."

"Good," said Fred. "That's good."

"Have you ever noticed," said Kyle when they were in a booth with their drinks, "that no matter how terrible the news, Fred always tells you how good everything is?"

"That's about the extent of his charm," said Max, "but somehow I find it comforting. Everything's always good at the Olde Pig Snout, except the food, the beer and the company. So what climbed up your butt?"

Kyle looked away, let his eyes harden, and then turned back to stare at his Uncle Max. "I want to know," he said, his teeth clenched, his voice suddenly low and hard, "how you could do it to my mother. Forget about me, a twelve-year-old kid forced to go to his father's fake funeral, forget about how your little trick twisted my life into knots. I want to know how you could do it to my mother, your sister, how you could do it to her."

Max stared at Kyle for a long moment, lit a cigarette, took a draw, downed his shot while smoke leaked out his nose, and then promptly burst into tears. It was not a tidy little cry, it was red and wet and full of sob and self-fury. Max's cheeks burned, his bulbous nose turned red and ran, his beady little eyes squeezed out bucketfuls, and in the middle of it he slammed his forehead on the table once and then again, before grabbing Kyle's shot, downing that, too, and sobbing some more.

Kyle was unmoved.

"I thought," said Max, his broken voice coming in gasps as the sobs stole his breath, "I thought . . . I was doing the . . . right thing."

"How could a betrayal like that ever be the right thing?"

"Because . . . because . . . because he was no damn good for her," said Max, catching his breath now between words. "Because he seduced her and impregnated her and then just left her there in that crappy little house. And she wouldn't move on, she wouldn't date, she wouldn't do anything but wait for him. It broke my heart."

"So you faked his death."

"I helped him do it. Yeah, I admit it. But she was still pretty, still young. I thought with him out of the way, she'd find someone new. I thought you'd end up with a real father. I thought—"

"You thought wrong."

"I know. God, I know. But she deserved better. And so did you. You don't know how many times I tried to set her up. She wasn't interested. She did nothing but mourn the bastard. And you did nothing but mourn him, too. And every time I saw you both after that, it broke my heart."

"Fuck you and your broken heart," said Kyle.

"You're right."

"Just go to hell."

"Okay, I will."

"Good."

Max pulled his cigarette to his lips with shaking hands, took a drag, and then wiped his eyes with his other palm. Kyle drank from his beer and looked away.

"Is that it?" said Max.

"No."

"There's more?"

"Yeah."

"Christ. Okay, whatever you want, Kyle. I'll do anything. Anything to make it up to you."

"You can't."

"I know."

"Damn right you know."

"I was afraid you might find out when you started nosing around into what happened to your dad."

"Then why'd you tell me to look?"

"Because I wanted you to know what he was really like, to take your blinders off."

"You put them there when you fake-killed him."

"You think I don't know that? You think I don't know?" Pause. "How'd you find out anyway?"

Kyle searched for some suspicion in Max's eyes, found nothing but Max's own tortured memories. "A cop," Kyle said.

"Jesus. Are they coming after me?"

"No, they just think my father was murdered and the certificate was forged to hide the fact. But I figure if you were involved, there was no murder. You're a jerk, but you're not a killer."

"You got that right. Of everything I am, I'm not that."

"I still have some questions, though."

"Okay. Sure. Whatever you want to know."

"How did it happen? When exactly did you guys start planning this thing?"

"Can I get another beer before I tell you?"

"No."

"Please?"

"Talk."

"Okay," said Max. "It started when I still had my truck and was working for the funeral home. They had me delivering these bodies up to some place in Jersey for embalming. I could tell that something was wrong, there was too many bodies going up, and it was too hush-hush. So I did some asking and found out they was stealing body parts and faking death certificates. The whole thing scared the hell out of me. So I decided to talk it out with a lawyer."

"My dad."

"Yeah, well, he was available, and he wouldn't charge me, you know. I told him everything, and he told me to quit, but I ignored him and kept driving, because . . . hell, the money was good. I thought that was the end of it. But then, later, he came back to me with some questions."

"When was this?"

"A week or so before the funeral. Over the phone. And then he mentioned the possibility of him getting one of them fake death certificates."

"Did he tell you why?"

"He said he was in this real-estate thing, with a partner who was going to dissolve the partnership with a gun. And he had fallen into something that might be real money, but he didn't know if he'd be alive to keep it. And there was other stuff. He just wanted to get away. I asked about you, and his Frenchie wife. He said he had taken out insurance, that everyone would be better off. I told him he was crazy. I told him to forget about it. But then . . ."

"He offered you money."

"Yeah."

"How much?"

"Does it matter? I didn't do it for the money. I did it to get him the hell out of her life. Kyle, he was no damn good, I'm telling you. Anyone who would run like he did . . . well, I thought you was both better off without him."

"So when you put the file cabinet in the house, you already knew he was going to fake his death and run away."

"Yeah, he just wanted some stuff kept safe for after. Just in case."

"How much did he pay you for the whole thing?"

"Fifteen."

"In cash?"

"Yeah."

"You sold yourself cheap, Max. Did he pay you up front?"

"Nah. I wanted it that way, but he said he was working on a couple things and could only make the payment right at the time. So he gave me the envelope on the ride up. My share and the twenty the doctor demanded. Thickest envelope I ever got in my life. I had some dead alky's body in the back of the truck, someone who I was supposed to take to get dumped in some pauper's grave. I just did the switcheroo and had them burn it. Simple as that."

"Did my mother ever know?"

"Nah. I tried telling her once, after I realized there wasn't going to be anyone else, but I chickened out. And then she got sick. And then what was the point?"

"You sold her out, Max."

"Kyle, I didn't do it for the money. I ended up giving her the fifteen anyway, and more. Plenty more."

"Why?"

"For you. She had too much pride to ever ask for anything for herself, but she'd swallow it to ask for you. And the insurance money she got was less than she needed to keep going. Those braces you got, when you busted your arm, the money you needed for school after the scholarship went kablooey."

"She would rather have had my father than the money."

"Kyle, it wasn't my idea. I just helped. He'd deserted her before, he was deserting her again. I thought finally getting rid of the creep would be good for her, is all. I'm sorry."

"Yeah."

"You don't know how sorry."

"You're right, I don't." Kyle felt his anger subside and fought to keep it boiling. "You said there was other stuff that made him want to leave. What kind of other stuff?"

"I don't know. Women stuff."

"What are you talking about, Max?"

"Well, you know, there was his wife and your mom and—"

"Someone else?"

"Yeah."

"Who?"

"I don't know. Does it matter? There was always someone else, that's just the way he was. And he said it was getting too complicated. He'd said he do them all a favor with the insurance and start over."

"Is that what he said?"

"Yeah."

"He was a son of a bitch, wasn't he?"

"That's what I been telling you. I thought it would work out for the best." Pause. "So we still good?"

"No."

"Okay. We're still not good," said Max. "We'll never be good."

Kyle took a peek at his uncle. "Maybe not never."

"Not never, maybe, but not for a while," said Max. "I know. I got it coming."

"Damn right."

"Damn right is right." Another drag. "How you doing, Kyle? Really."

"I don't know. Good, I guess."

"That's good."

"Yeah."

"It's good that you're doing good."

"Yeah."

"Good that everything's good."

Kyle stared at his uncle for a moment, then turned his head to look at Fred, smiling like an idiot behind the bar. "You want to know something, Uncle Max? I hate this fucking place."

Chapter 51

Kyle Byrne was drunk with whine.

It might also have been the beers he had consumed at Bubba's and at the Olde Pig Snout that intoxicated him, or the growl of the engine between his legs, or the bugs caught in his teeth, or the way his tie snapped behind him as he sped recklessly on Skitch's motorcycle through the wilds of West Philadelphia. But more than anything else, it was the whine.

Yet who the hell had more of a reason to whine than Kyle Byrne? Everyone blames his parents for purposely screwing up his life, but Kyle now had absolute proof. His father had deserted him not out of fear for his own safety or for the safety of his only son, as he had claimed, but out of greed and lust. The truth of it filled Kyle with anger and resentment, with a sour consolation at being proved right all along, and with a feral sadness that tore through him like choked sobs. Betrayal to the left of him, betrayal to the right, and here he was stuck in the middle, stuck in this nightmare, stuck in this life.

For a time he pretended not to know where he was headed, imagined he was just accelerating into the setting sun, feeling the wind in his face and the pumping of the pistons through his bones. Speed was what he was after, raw speed, as if he could outrun the emotions that were overwhelming him. But he wasn't running away from the source of his pain, he was running to it, inexorably. He was like the noble salmon jumping up the falls as it returned to its childhood home. Except he wasn't a fish. And he wasn't going to spawn. And he didn't go well with a beurre blanc and a risotto, though being poached that very night was a real possibility.

It wasn't long before he was back in the old neighborhood, back on the old street, sitting on the bike and surveying the charred ruins of house and car. And at the sight of it, the sadness nearly overwhelmed him, until he transmuted it into raw bitterness. Aimed at his father.

Liam Byrne was responsible for this, for everything about this. The fire, yes, of course, because of his ruthless pursuit of the O'Malley file for his own damn profit. But even before the fire. The loss of the house, because of the way he had left Kyle and his mother practically destitute. And the loss of his mother, as if the sadness of Liam's fake death had metastasized into the cancer that failed to respond to any treatment and overwhelmed her body. And the ruinous choices in Kyle's own life that had led him to where he was at this moment, without anything to claim as his own but the suit on his back and the target on his forehead.

He was wondering how to play the next few hours, but the sight of the burned wreckage made everything clear. He was going to do whatever he needed to betray his father the way his father had betrayed him. Ashes to ashes, baby.

He looked up and saw a police car slip onto the street, and suddenly he remembered all the trouble he was in. With his toe he tapped the gearshift into first as he popped the clutch, lurching off down the street, speeding away, a left, a right, losing the cops when he made another left. He didn't think it mattered where he was headed, but it did. Because he was traversing a course that had become familiar in the past year. Up City Line, down Lansdale Avenue, up State Road, along the low stone fence to the cemetery. The same cemetery where his father's fake funeral had happened fourteen years before and where his mother's real burial had taken place just about a year ago.

He parked the bike on the narrow road that wound its way through the burial ground and walked over to her grave. He read her name, the dates, the words on the stone: LOVING MOTHER AND SISTER. Not wife, though. You couldn't say wife. He had betrayed her there, too.

Kyle leaned over to brush some leaves away from the grass atop her plot. He rubbed his hand across the carving of her name. He dropped to one knee.

"The old bastard's come back," he said to the stone.

He knelt there for a moment, as if waiting for a response. He lifted his chin and saw a woman in the distance who appeared to be walking toward him, and his heart clutched with an insane hope. But why the hell shouldn't she come back from the grave just as his father had? It only fit everything else that had happened to him the past few days. And he'd trade a hundred of him for one of her. But it wasn't her, it was just some older woman who stopped and turned and bowed before a patch of grass far away. And like a stone falling in a dark, cold pond, his heart fell.

No, his mother wasn't coming back, and yet he could hear her voice, soft but insistent, the way she spoke to him whenever his father made those rare visits to the house. *Go to him,* she would say as they sat on the porch and saw his car pull up. *Go to your father.*

He closed his eyes, and he remembered a shard from his boyhood, when he'd asked his mother about the father who had always been a mystery to him. They were sitting on the porch, and his mother was in the rocking chair, smoking, staring off with those impassive eyes of hers. "He's a complicated man," she had said to Kyle. "He's difficult to understand."

"And do you understand him?" Kyle said.

"No. But I love him, and you should, too."

"Why?"

"Because he's your father, Kyle. That's just the way it is. And without him I wouldn't have you."

"Does he love us?" Kyle asked.

"In his way."

"And what way is that, Mom?"

"The only way he can. And, Kyle, that's all you'll ever get from anyone."

Kyle didn't understand then what she had meant, didn't understand it still, but he remembered how he felt when his father's car would pull up to the front of the house and his mother would tell him, "Go to him. Go to your father," and off he'd run, down the steps to the car. And when the stranger stepped out, Kyle would hug his legs and the old man would pat him on the head and Kyle would smell the braided scents of old cigarette smoke, of Brylcreem and Aqua Velva, and the fear and the love both would overwhelm him.

But things were different now. Kyle was no longer a child with all a child's pathetic needs, and his mother was dead, and all kinds of truths about his father had been branded into his soul. The way his father had used privileged information to extort money from a congressional candidate. The way his father had returned from the dead only to extort more money from the same candidate, and to rope his son into the scheme. The way his father had lied to and betrayed him all the years of his life. It would be different now, absolutely. He wouldn't run to him and hug his legs, absolutely. All he felt now was anger, a seething anger that strained for release.

"So, boyo," said the old man in the doorway of that New Jersey motel after Kyle had made his way back. The old man's eyes were lit with greed, his smile yellow, his hands reached out with expectation. "How did it go? Are we in business?"

Kyle stared at his father for a long moment and felt the tectonic plates shift within him, before he lunged. And grabbed his father close. And buried his face in his father's grizzled neck.

"I love you, Dad," he said as his tears rubbed off on his father's skin.

Fourteen years after Liam Byrne's funeral, Kyle was finally crying for his father. And Kyle wasn't lying. He did, truly, love his father. Despite all he knew, despite the anger that remained inside, despite the past and despite himself, he loved his father. Unqualifiedly. As had Kyle's mother before him. Kyle didn't trust his father, or admire him, or particularly like him. But a part of Kyle lived forever beyond the realm of reason, and that part had taken control. "I love you," he said again.

"I know you do, boyo," said Liam Byrne, patting his son's head as he had all those years before, drawing out thick tears. "I know you do. Now, come inside. You have much to tell, and we have much to plan."

Chapter 52

B obby dragged the black satchel through the rhododendron, bony stalks tearing at his flesh and filthy clothes, grabbing at the bag, which more than once he had to yank free. It was almost nine, he was almost late. He needed to be in position for when the boy showed up.

It had been no simple task getting here, with his car being watched and his whole body covered in filth. When he climbed out of the Dumpster, he knew he had to hurry, but he couldn't just hail a cab. That Puerto Rican slut had probably called in his description to all the taxis in the area, hoping he'd turn up in the street with his hand raised as if volunteering for the electric chair. So instead he decided to move. Out of the area. North would send him through Center City, east was the waterfront, so he chose south, into South Philadelphia, stepping through the narrow streets with cars lined on either side. It would have been easy just to break open a window and steal one, except he didn't know how to steal a car.

So he kept moving, ignoring the reactions to his filth-streaked clothes and the way he smelled, always moving, slipping into doorways and alleys when police cars cruised by and then moving again, ever south. He figured if he could just keep moving, he would come up with a plan. And then he spied the instrument of his salvation, under one of the spans of the highway, a sweet little angel with a baby and a Buick. As she leaned into the backseat to pull her baby from the car seat, Bobby pulled his pistol from the black bag.

He had parked the Buick behind a hedge beneath a wide sycamore about half a mile from the Truscott estate. He hadn't killed the mother and child—some remnant of Robert had stilled his hand—and by now the police would have the model and license plate in their computer. But he needed the car to start off his journey after he took care of business here, so he had made sure it was well hidden before he walked the rest of the way to the mansion. At the black iron fence, he had thrown his bag over and then climbed after it. Now he was batting fat-fingered rhododendron leaves away from his face as he maneuvered himself into position to have a view of the mansion's front door.

His plan was simple. He'd stay out here until the Byrne boy came and went. Bobby imagined that Byrne would have a file in his hand on the way in and a briefcase full of money on his way out. It was this briefcase that she had promised to Bobby as payment for all his services, as if he were a mere handyman who'd been patiently waiting all this time for a cash payment. Well, he'd take the payment all right, killing the boy in the process, but that wouldn't be the end of it, that would be just the start. And irony of ironies, it would be her hush money that would finance all the rest. He'd trade in the Buick for a Maserati, he'd slip hundred-dollar tips to strippers, he'd tour the country killing Truscotts, starting with a broken-down old whore. Just the thought of it sent a shiver through his veins.

A final yank of the bag and he was through, to the wide front lawn that led to the great house with its majestic pillars, the house that had been the repository of all his fondest hopes for decades now. He knew its lines and curves, the texture of its skin, knew it as intimately as a lover. Every perfect piece of stone, every lovely blemish in its mortar. He adored the house, its shape, its scent, the movement through its rooms. Maybe when this was all over, he'd come back and blow it into splinters.

The driveway itself was flanked with gardens framed by low walls of boxwood. Bobby looked left, looked right, and then, like an infantryman advancing on Omaha Beach, ran toward the garden in a zigzag pattern, bent low at the waist with the bag clutched to his chest. When he reached the closest of the gardens, he jumped over the boxwood and rolled toward the house, knocking down pink-tipped Cleome like he was a scythe.

He peeked over the evergreen hedge just in time to see the great gate at the front of the property open. A car slowly made its way up the drive, its tires grinding at the gravel, its headlights painting the stone white before the car entered the circle and the headlights suddenly veered to the left, pointing straight at his garden. He ducked down and listened. A door opening and closing, a few words from a voice he recognized. The headlights washed by him as the car turned out of the circle and back up the drive.

He raised his head again to see the tall, lanky figure of Senator Francis Truscott IV entering the house.

Bobby dropped to the ground, spun around, took a deep breath. What the hell was Francis doing here? He was supposed to be at some sort of fund-raiser. Bobby panicked for a moment at the unexpected development before he pulled himself together. This was good. This was great. This made everything easier. Of course the senator would be here at the exchange. It was his crime they were covering up, after all. And now Bobby wouldn't have to go hunting for Francis. He'd be right here, in Bobby's sights. Perfect.

Bobby checked his watch. It was after nine. He turned around and lifted his head over the hedge and looked down the drive. It was just a matter now of waiting, waiting like a hyena for his prey, fighting not to laugh out loud.

Chapter 53

I feel like there are ants crawling across my chest," said Kyle as he drove along a dark, private street.

"It's just the tape," said his father. "You'll get used to it. I put it on tight so the thing won't come loose in the middle of it all and give away the game."

"I think they'll figure out I'm wearing a transmitter when they see me scratching like an idiot."

"Then don't scratch. Show some control."

"We should just tell the cops everything and let them deal with it."

"That won't do it. They'll get away with what they've done, the two of them, if it's only your words against theirs. In this world theirs count more. I should have known that the mother was involved. She might have been responsible for the killings without her son knowing. That would be quite politic of the old crone. Plausible deniability. Nixon still haunts the sordid edge of politics, I suppose. Will we never be free of that ghost?"

"What was so bad about Nixon anyway?"

"Ah, the sad ignorance of youth. But you're a swift one, you'll get her to admit everything, and I'll have it right here on tape. Except don't you dare forget, boyo, it only works if you bring out the money."

"Are you sure about that?"

"I told you, yes. That's the key to everything. Tapes can be disputed, but the money is proof of their guilt. You bring back the money, and we'll take it, along with the tape, to that police detective you go on about so much. That will jolt her career. She'll be grateful, you can bet, and she'll show it, too."

"You sound like a pimp."

Liam Byrne laughed. "Life is sweet, boyo, and you shouldn't be denying yourself all of its pleasures. But reward or no, it's a grand thing we're doing here. Father and son, working together to right ancient wrongs. In all my days, I never thought I'd see it. I have to tell you, I don't think I've ever been more excited."

Kyle turned and looked at his father in the glow from the dashboard. His face was ruddy and beaming. One hand was shaking with excitement, the other was clutching the file on his lap. This was a moment Kyle would always remember, father and son on a bold mission of justice, bonded at last. No matter how it ended.

"And after?" said Kyle.

"Then it's time for me to lie low. That's why I already packed my bag. Just get me to a bus station, and I'll be on my way."

"You don't want to maybe stay around a bit?"

"Too dangerous. They'll be hunting me for sure."

"Who?"

"The senator, his mother, that little killer the cops told you about." He glanced to the side as if suddenly scared and lowered his voice. "Not to mention the first Mrs. Byrne, if she ever got an inkling of the truth. Trust me on this, that would be a frightening thing indeed."

"Tell me about it."

"No, boyo, I've been too long here already. Remember the scare at Ponzio's? It's time I get back on the road."

"Dad?"

"Kyle, son, I've got no choice. But you can come along if you choose. I've enough for two tickets. Have you ever seen the way the country unfurls on a slow trip west?"

"No."

"It's a grand sight, boyo, something to share and build on. But those considerations are for after. We need to focus on the here and the now. It will be dangerous in there. You need to keep your wits about you. And we're agreed on the plan?"

"Sure," said Kyle, "we're agreed."

"And everything's clear?"

"Absolutely."

"Good. Now, that must be the gate. I'll duck down so the cameras don't catch me."

Kyle pulled up to the gate, leaned over and pushed the button to the squawk box. There was no response, so he pushed it again. And again. He waited, figuring that a fourth time might be rude, but after a few moments he thought what the hell and pushed it once more. He looked around for the camera, saw it turning like a robot's head above the gate. He gave it a wave, and at that very moment the gate slowly swung open. Kyle drove through.

The lawn was wide and open as it rose toward a cold stone monstrosity of a mansion with huge gray pillars and wings wrapped around it like a great Gothic bat. Lights dimly illuminated the circular gravel drive, leaving dark blobs of shadow across the pillars and the front door. The windows in front were all dark. Kyle drove into the circular drive, stopped in a gulf of shadows between two weak patches of light, killed the engine. He tapped his father's knee, and his father sat back up in the front seat.

"I guess this is it," said Kyle. He looked into his father's eyes once more before he opened the door. The car beeped, and he pulled out the key to silence it. He pocketed the key as he climbed out of the car and slammed shut the door. He leaned into the open window.

"Whatever happens in there, I'm really glad you came back."

"As am I, son."

"Whatever happens, know that I love you."

"Nothing but good will happen, don't you worry."

"Okay," said Kyle. "I won't." Pause. "I suppose I'll need the file now."

"Of course, yes," said his father as he raised his hand and offered the black folder. When Kyle took hold, it was the first time he had touched the file since he had given it to his father in his old house. He had to tug twice till the old man released it.

"Good luck, boyo," said Liam Byrne. "And remember the plan."

"I'll remember," said Kyle before straightening up, looking at the creepy old place. He heard something rustling to the left of the house. His breath caught, and his head turned quickly. He could just make out a small garden there, but nothing else. A squirrel, most likely. Or a chipmunk, a frightening little chipmunk. He took a deep breath to settle his nerves. This was delicate work, he couldn't be so jumpy. Calm down, boy, he told himself.

Inside the car his father put on a set of headphones connected to the receiver. Kyle tapped his chest, his father raised a thumb. It was time. He took another deep breath, and then, with file in hand, he headed across the drive, up the stairs to the portico, past the pillars and to the front door. He knocked a couple of times, heard nothing, reached to the handle, pressed down the latch.

The lock released, the door opened. Kyle Byrne stepped inside, into the darkness.

Chapter 54

Bobby peeked over the hedge and saw the Byrne boy get out of the car.

He could pop the little bastard now, one pump, one shot, and he'd be free to take care of the two Truscotts inside. Ram the shotgun up their throats and fire away and away and away, spattering their flesh and blood on the walls and columns until it was only the spatters that were getting ecstatically spattered. His breath quickened as he imagined it.

But taking out the Byrne boy now would be sloppy. They might hear the gunfire from outside and call the police. They might hide the money before he made his grand entrance. Even as Bobby lay in the mud, his clothes stained with rotted vegetables and his hair stinking of garbage, even as the flies buzzed around him as if he were a pile of feces, he prided himself on not being sloppy.

But wait a second, there was someone else in the car. How could he have missed it at first? Because the second man had been ducking down to avoid the camera at the gate, that's how. Bobby watched as Byrne leaned toward the car window, reached in, and pulled out something. A file. The file. So this was the other man, the accomplice. And what was the accomplice putting on now? Earmuffs?

No, headphones.

Which meant that Byrne would be wearing a wire. How delicious was that? A wire. The only disappointment was that Bobby hadn't thought of it first. The whole enterprise would be recorded for posterity.

The Byrne boy straightened up with the file in his hand, hesitated for a moment before heading for the front door of the mansion. Bobby would wait until he got inside, then scuttle over to the car and kill the accomplice. He'd do it quietly, silent as a ninja, just a quick slice of the neck so as not to alert the primary players inside. When Byrne entered the house and closed the door behind him, Bobby rose to his knees, opened the bag, pulled out a knife the size of a squirrel's tail, a knife still stained with Malcolm's blood. With blade in hand, he slithered through an opening between two of the boxwood plants and crawled toward the car.

Halfway there he stopped and stared. It was the man in the car, there was something familiar about him. Round face, a mop of gray hair, something knowing in the tilt of the head. At the house, before the fire, Bobby had seen only the outline of the figure, and yet even that had seemed familiar. But now he knew he had seen this face before. Where? Where?

When the answer came to him, his body tensed with such excitement that he almost stabbed his own chest with the knife.

It was impossible. He was dead. Robert had even gone to his funeral. But Robert hadn't killed him, he knew that, despite what he had led his aunt to believe, so the impossible was indeed a possibility. And in its own perverse way, it made so much sense. How else could the boy have gotten his hands on the file? How else could the boy have known exactly what to do with it? Because he had been guided all the time by the venal hand of his father.

Liam Byrne had known he was targeted after the O'Malley girl drowned and his car was run off the road. He must have taken the half million paid out by the senator, faked his death, and run away with the cash. Amazing. And for his long run to end at Bobby's hand fourteen years after he had first escaped Robert's grasp . . . well, the irony was too perfect to ignore.

With renewed purpose Bobby crawled closer to the car. He would come around to the passenger side, rise onto his haunches, jerk open the door, and grab the old bastard by his forehead with one hand as he slid the knife across the neck with the other. It was so simple, so tasty.

He looked up again, could see the old man's head through the windshield, his eyes closed as he tapped one of the headphones, trying to hear. He was the one listening, the one charged with making the tape. Bobby could just imagine it all as it imprinted itself on the magnetic ribbon. Her sweet and deceitful mewings, the senator's fraudulent oratory, the Byrne boy's demands for money, the whole story of the rape and its cover-up spilled to the waiting tape. And then Bobby Spangler arriving heroically to punish all for their sins, to save a grateful nation, to raise again the banner of the Spanglers. The tape would be played nationwide, all day long, over and over again on cable television. Even as he ran off with the money, first to wreak havoc on the Truscotts and then maybe to Mexico, maybe to Peru, his legend would rise.

But if he killed Liam Byrne now, who would take care of the tape? If he killed Liam Byrne, who would make sure the truth was known? And wouldn't the pain he inflicted be all the sweeter if Liam Byrne were forced to hear the death of his son through the headphones?

Bobby took a deep breath and then backed away, backed away, slithered through the grass and back between the boxwoods, where his black bag awaited.

Chapter 55

The house Kyle Byrne found himself inside smelled ancient, dank, and strangely like licorice. There were no lights burning in the hall, but a sliver of light slipped out around a door frame back through the house to the right, so he made his way toward it. He banged a knee into some hunchbacked piece of furniture placed smack in the middle of the hall, felt his way around the piece, and kept going.

When he reached the wide door, he heard the low hum of conversation coming from the other side. There was no handle, but he placed his hand into the gap and slid the door open.

"Ah, there you are," said an old woman in a voice Kyle recognized. She was sitting regally on a high-backed chair, her bony body twisted and shivery, arms and neck jerking hither and yon as she sat there. She looked vaguely familiar, with her tall gray hair and twitching limbs, and he stared a bit before realizing he'd seen her before, sitting next to the widow at Laszlo Toth's funeral.

"No need to be shy," she said. "Come in, come in. We've been discussing you. Would you like a drink?"

"Not really," said Kyle. "I only drink with friends, or at least with people who haven't been trying to kill me."

"Oh, you must be exaggerating, Mr. Byrne. Why would anyone want to kill you? Now, your father always loved a stiff drink. I admired that in him. But come in, come in, dear, and let us get our business out of the way."

The room was a large parlor, with blue walls, twin crystal chandeliers, fancy French furnishings perched on dark, delicate legs. There were grand landscape paintings on the walls, thick rugs on the floors, vases the size of ponies. In its day that room had been quite the fancy place, but its day was not this day. The paintings were browned with grime and age, the rugs in some spots were worn through. And the smell of licorice was overpowering.

When he stepped into the room, he looked to his left and then did a double take. Standing by a fireplace, his arm on the mantel, was Francis Truscott IV. Above the senator was a painting of a blustery man in hunting clothes and with a bully's lip leaning on that very same mantel.

"I'm surprised to see you here, Senator," said Kyle. "I thought you would be on your knees in front of a pack of fat cats, working for your money."

"I ducked out of the fund-raiser," said Senator Truscott. "Our discussion raised a number of questions that I needed to ask my mother."

"Did you get your answers?"

"Yes."

Kyle looked back at the old woman. The phone call had convinced him that the murder of Colleen O'Malley, the attempted murder of his father, the murder of Laszlo Toth, all of it had been at her insistence. "I wouldn't rely too much on what she told you, if I were you."

"Is that it?" she snapped. "Is that the O'Malley file?"

"This is it," said Kyle. "The whole caboodle."

"Any copies?"

"Not that I made."

"How about your . . . accomplice?"

"Accomplice?"

"The man you were with. Your partner in crime. Oh, one needn't be a genius to know you've not been alone. It would take more than the likes of you to get this far."

"There are no copies," said Kyle.

"Good," she said. "I'll trust you, because you are young and I am idealistic. But be forewarned, Mr. Byrne, you'd be wise not to trifle with me."

"No chance of that," said Kyle with a wink. Then he turned from her and walked over to the senator. "I thought you weren't buying."

"I'm not," said Truscott.

"But she is. Isn't it the same thing?"

"I don't have control over what she does."

"But she apparently has control over you."

"Don't be impertinent," said the woman, interjecting herself forcefully into the conversation. "He is a United States senator, and I am nothing but an old lady."

"Don't sell yourself short for my benefit," said Kyle, still looking at the senator, whose chiseled face turned even more stony under Kyle's gaze. "You might be as old as dust, but you're no lady."

"Feisty for a messenger boy, aren't you?"

"This is all her doing," said the senator. "I didn't even know about it until you showed up. But I admit I've had second thoughts since we spoke. I believe I can do more good in the Senate than out on the street."

"Oh, I get it," said Kyle. "You wouldn't want to deprive the republic of your irreplaceable value. Your patriotism warms my heart."

"I simply began to see that maybe it is not the worst thing for everyone if the file disappears once and for all."

"She's persuasive, isn't she? I suppose she keeps your balls quite safe in her pocketbook."

"That's enough," she hissed from her side of the room.

Kyle turned his head toward her. "What, now you're going to tell me you don't like feisty?"

"Let's get this done and you on your pathetic way."

"Fine by me," said Kyle. "But I must say, I'm disappointed in you, Senator. You impressed the hell out of me this afternoon. I thought I had actually met a politician with sincerity, but I suppose that's like a vampire with sincerity—does it really matter if he sincerely wants to suck your blood?"

"I meant what I said this afternoon."

"That means you were against buying the file before you were for it. Those questions you had for your mother. Were they about what happened to Colleen O'Malley?"

"My mother assured me that she wasn't involved."

"How about Laszlo Toth? What did she say about him?"

"My mother is not a murderer."

"She didn't pull the trigger, if that's what you mean. I guess she's in no condition to do her own wet work. But I've watched enough TV to know that you don't have to pull the trigger to be guilty of murder."

"Can we end these mad ravings and make our deal?" said Mrs. Truscott. "And then, dear, I have a psychiatrist I can recommend. He is quite fashionable—all the best loons see him."

"What are you getting at, Byrne?" said the senator.

"You know a Spangler?"

"Spangler?" He looked at his mother. "What about it?"

"There's a Spangler wanted in the killing of Laszlo Toth. And I'd bet he was involved in Colleen O'Malley's strange drowning death, too. And the funny thing is, if you look in this file, the lawyer opposing my father, the one representing your interests in the O'Malley matter, was a Spangler, too. Want to look?"

"What's he talking about?"

"I don't know, dear."

"Mother?"

"I have no idea what this maniac is talking about."

"Well, there you go, Senator. Another mystery for you to solve, or to sweep under the family carpet, though I imagine it's getting pretty lumpy by now. Here's another lump."

Kyle spun the file in the air toward the senator. Truscott didn't move to catch it. The file hit the floor with a plunk, and he just stared at it while a briefcase appeared, as if magically, in the old lady's twitchy hands.

"Take your money and get the hell out of my house," she said.

Kyle gazed at the briefcase for a moment, thought of all the dreams contained within its flat gray walls, the new car, the trip to Aruba, a real start in life. And he also thought of his father outside, listening intently to the headphones as the scene audibly played out for him.

"Keep it," said Kyle finally. He could almost see the wince on his father's face, as if he'd been slapped. "Spruce the place up. Buy another pillar for outside, you can never have too many. I don't want your damn money."

The senator looked up, his face creased in bewilderment.

"Don't look so puzzled, Senator," said Kyle. "You're the one who convinced me. You told me you weren't going to turn me into a blackmailer. After talking to you, I decided I wasn't going to let anyone else do it either." Another shot across his father's jaw. "So take the file. For free. This story belonged to Colleen O'Malley, not my father. He didn't have the right to use it for his own gain, and neither do I. My father was wrong to bring it out fourteen years ago, and I'm trying to right the wrong by giving it back to you." Slap, slap, slap.

"If you don't want the money," said the senator, "why did you come?"

"To put Colleen's ghost to rest," said Kyle. "And to see what I could learn about Spangler." And to tell Liam Byrne over the wire what Kyle couldn't tell him face-to-face: that he loved him, yes, but he wasn't going to be him.

"My mother's maiden name is Spangler," said the senator. "And the lawyer whose name you saw in the file is my cousin Robert, my mother's nephew. But he's hardly a murderer. If you could meet him, you'd know that. He's a harmless old man, I'm sure."

"Don't be, because he's now on the run and considered armed and dangerous."

"Mother?"

"I don't know what he is talking about," said the old lady, her chin jerking spasmodically upward. And now, strangely, beneath the licorice scent floated a line of something fetid, as if the rot at the heart of this old woman's ambitions for her son were finally being exposed.

"Mother?" said the senator.

"Look at me, dear. I am telling you the truth. I don't know what he is talking about. But whatever Robert might have done under an excess of zeal, he did it without my knowledge. You must believe me, dear. You must."

"Oh, yes, you must," said a voice from the doorway to the room. Kyle turned quickly, and there, with a bulky black bag in his hand, was O'Malley. His clothes were streaked with stains, an obviously false hairpiece was comically out of place, his face was filthy, and he smelled god-awful.

"Robert?" said the senator.

"O'Malley?" said Kyle.

The man sneered and gave the bag a quick hoist as if it were quite heavy. The bag's zipper was open, and something shifted so that the thick black barrel of a shotgun poked out of the end.

"I wondered when you'd show up," said Mrs. Truscott, even as she curled into herself and away from the stench. "Unfortunately, Bobby, we have ourselves a problem."

Chapter 56

There was a time, during his youth in Iowa, when Robert Spangler became intoxicated with Scripture. As he followed along with the preachers in their crowded tents, the words glowed on the pages of his Bible and spoke to the deepest yearnings of his immature heart: faith, love, redemption, sacrifice. And even in this new incarnation that owed more to Nietzsche than to Luke, the old stories lived as counterpoint to the dreams he had finally found courage enough to summon into reality. Now, as Bobby stood in the dark hallway, staring in at the scene playing out before him, it was as if one of those stories had sprung fully to life.

"Look at me, dear," said the wellspring of Robert's love and his cursed ambition, her fierce attention pressed wholly and urgently on the son, Francis, passing

entirely over Bobby's presence in the doorway just as
it had passed over Robert lo these many years. "I am
telling you the truth. I don't know what he is talking
about. But whatever Robert might have done under an
excess of zeal, he did it without my knowledge."

And somewhere a cock crowed.

"You must believe me, dear," she said, her voice
trembling with her delicious insincerity. "You must."

"Oh, yes, you must," said Bobby as he stepped forward and took his rightful place in this elegant room,
the very room of power where she had made her promises about Robert's future over and again and where, in
the next few moments, that future would finally come
to its blood-spangled fruition. They all turned toward
him with a start—the son who had stolen all her love
and all his glory, the interloping Byrne boy, and she,
too, the object of all their fantasies, fixing him with a
blue-eyed stare both malevolent and full of desire. A
stare that brought him instantly hard.

"Robert?" said Cousin Francis.

"O'Malley?" said the Byrne boy.

Bobby shifted the bag to cover his erection, and in
his so doing, the barrel of his shotgun slipped out of the
bag's open edge. He looked down at the gun and back
up at the two men, who had become transfixed by the
sight as an understanding dawned of exactly whom they

now were facing. No longer would they see him as little Robert Spangler. He was new and newly powerful.

"I wondered when you'd show up," she said, as if she were happy to see him, even as that magnificent tortured body involuntarily pulled away at the same time. "Unfortunately, Bobby, we have ourselves a problem."

"You maybe," said Bobby, "but I've never been better. Isn't this cozy? A family reunion. But where was my invitation? Oh, that's right, no Spanglers need apply. I haven't seen you, Francis, in . . . oh, ages and ages. No time for your cousin?"

"What is going on, Robert?" said Francis. "What have you done?"

"Only what I needed to do to protect the future you almost threw away on some Catholic-school skank. Isn't that what family does? Though while I was out paving the way for your sparkling career, what was being done for me? Tell me, Francis, how have you shown your appreciation to the poor side of the family, you ungrateful snot?"

"Careful," she said, as if she still had any hold on him.

"Why should I be careful, Aunt Gloria? I'm sure we can speak freely. There are no secrets here. We're all family. Except for Byrne, who has secrets of his own—like the one waiting for him outside."

Bobby liked how Byrne's face froze. It was the way you looked when your deepest secrets spilled out onto the floor like steaming intestines from a split gut.

"What are you talking about?" she said.

"Call me Bobby, my one true love, and I'll slip you a treat when this is all over."

"Robert, did you kill Colleen?" said Francis.

"That little whore?" said Bobby.

Francis's face twisted into a politician's pretend look of righteous anger, and he took a step forward toward Bobby, as if the mama's boy had the wherewithal to do anything in support of his false emotions. Even so, just to freeze him in place, Bobby pulled the shotgun out of the bag. He dropped the bag and gave the gun a pump, loading a cartridge.

"Save your annoying Truscott self-righteousness for *Meet the Press*," he spit out. "It's amazing how ungrateful you can be when everything is handed to you on a silver serving dish. I did what I had to do to protect your career. I did what you would have wanted me to do if only you had the courage to see inside your blighted soul. And let me tell you something, Francis. Nothing cuts right to the core of your soul more than blood."

"So who are you going to kill today?" said Byrne, stepping into a conversation in which he had no business. "Me?"

"Yes, for starters, you foolish tool. But I won't stop there."

"Don't be ridiculous," she said.

"Oh, I was, sweet Gloria, but I'm not anymore. The blood has changed me. Before, I wouldn't have dared to walk into this house and take my rightful place by your side. But now I have the courage of a cougar, now I dance naked in the moonlight."

"Stop talking like a cretin," she said, her voice arrogant and dismissive even in its shaking. "And what happened to you? You look and smell like you rolled around in a garbage heap." She waved at the air in front of her nose. "I think I'm going to be nauseous."

"I would think you'd be proud of me, Auntie dear," he said, "finally standing up for what's mine, taking initiative, like you've always told me to do. But the truth is, right now I don't give a damn what you think," and he realized that, for the first time in his adulthood, he truly didn't. He didn't care about her or her disappointment or the favors she could grant. It was complete, the transformation, he was finally free of her power and his own failed expectations.

"Bobby dear—"

"Shut up," he shouted as he waved the gun and watched them all pull away in fear. "I'm in control now, and I like it." His head swam through the emotion that swelled over him in a glorious wave as he reached, he realized, the absolute pinnacle of his life. Everything before had been leading here, to this magnificent moment of freedom and retribution. "A Spangler is in control, and all of you, even you, sweet Aunt Gloria, will bow down in obeisance."

"Mr. Spangler?"

He spun his head quickly toward the sound, and the sight was so out of place that it took him a while to process it. Two characters of dubious race, standing on either side of the wide doorway to the room. One was the woman who had come for him earlier, the policewoman, Ramirez, with her long neck and pretty face and something sticking out of her ear. He hadn't noticed before that she was deaf. The other was a much older black man. Another police officer? Yes, of course, Bobby had seen him at the Toth funeral. And both of them, shockingly, had guns in their hands, and the guns were pointing at him.

"Mr. Spangler," said Detective Ramirez, "we need you to put the shotgun down."

This was not in his plan. Everything had been going so well, but this was not in the plan. "Excuse me, Detective Ramirez," he said, trying to keep the edge of hysteria that was now slicing through him out of his voice, "but I'm talking here. Can you give me a moment? Or will I have to start shooting?"

"You can have your moment, Mr. Spangler—Bobby," said Ramirez. "You can take as long as you want to have your say. I guarantee it. But first you need to put down the gun."

"Don't worry, Detectives," said Francis. "He won't hurt me."

"Oh, yes I will, Francis, you little prick," said Bobby with a jerk of the gun that aimed it right at Francis's chest. "With relish. And mustard."

He turned his head to Ramirez and saw the fear crease her features, and that brought a calm. She hadn't been afraid for herself, or for Byrne, or for the Qing vase in the corner. No, all she cared about, like everyone else, was the smarmy politician standing before him. It was funny how training a gun on a U.S. senator brought a flush of power. Life would be grand if he could only pull a shotgun on a senator every day. The truth of it caused him to smile.

"You don't want to do this, Bobby," said Ramirez.

"But I do, Detective, trust me on that. And what about our date? Are we still on?"

"Of course, Bobby," she said with a false, nervous smile. Bobby liked that finally it was a woman who had the nervous smile instead of him. "Coffee, just as you said."

"And more?" said Bobby.

"And more. Yes. So much more. But please, first, you need to put down the gun."

"See, Aunt Gloria, and all this time you were worried that I didn't get out enough. I guess all I needed was a twelve-gauge."

"What is it that you want?" said Aunt Gloria.

"All I ever wanted was for you to honor me like you honored him."

"Well, dear," she said, her chin dropping, "he is my son. But you, Bobby, have come so much further."

"Then why is everything always him, him, him?"

"Because he is our shared enterprise, darling. Yours and mine, the entire family's. Everything he achieves, it's as if we've achieved it, too. And don't forget, dear, he's half Spangler."

"Bobby, listen to me," said Ramirez. "We want to help you, we really do. Talk to us."

Aunt Gloria turned to the police and spoke in a tight, angry voice. "If you detectives will . . . calm yourselves for a moment. I'll take care of this."

"Bobby, we can't help you until you put down the gun," said Ramirez. "I'm afraid of how things might turn out if you don't put down the gun."

"Threats won't be necessary," said Aunt Gloria. "Come here, dear, come by my side."

Bobby felt himself pulled in two directions, by Detective Ramirez with her lips and her tawny skin, with her promises of more, much more, even as her gun pointed at his chest. And Aunt Gloria, who had once been his guiding light. And who was finally acknowledging how far he had risen.

"Come, dear," she said. "I have something to tell you. A secret."

He hesitated, looked at the detective once more, and then, with the gun still pointing at Francis's atrophied heart, he took a step toward his aunt. He felt warmer suddenly, comforted, as if the twisted old woman in that chair were the hearth and home he had pined for over the years. He took another step, felt the heat of her as if she were a toasty fire of aromatic love.

"Come closer still," she said. "The secret I have is for you alone."

He couldn't help himself. No matter how far he had risen, she could always pull him to her with a sweet purr from her lovely throat. He went to her, squatted beside her, all the time keeping his gun steady on Francis and his gaze steady on the pretty detective.

His aunt leaned over to him and put her twitching lips close to his ear. With the palsy, she couldn't help but brush his flesh with her own.

"You're going to ruin everything," she whispered so softly that no one else could hear.

"That's the point," he said just as softly.

"No, dear. Don't forget all we owe each other."

He pulled back as he exclaimed loudly, "Each other?"

"Bobby," said Detective Ramirez, "Bobby. This isn't going to end well. Please, I'm asking, I'm begging. Please put down the gun."

"Listen to her, son," said the older, black detective. "She only wants to help you."

"Oh, why are you two bothering me?" he spit out. "Shouldn't you be outside arresting the man in the car? Do you know who it is? Do you have any idea?"

"The car in front?" said Ramirez.

"Yes, of course, the car Byrne came in," he said as he let the gun jerk toward the boy standing stock-still in his stupid gray suit before it rested again in the direction of Cousin Francis. "Do you know who is inside that car, listening to our conversation?"

"Listening?" said Aunt Gloria.

"Don't be dim-witted, any of you. Byrne is wearing a wire, and the accomplice in the car is listening to every word. And here's the joke of it all: It's his father. It's that lying Irish blackmailer Liam Byrne."

"Don't be ridiculous," said his aunt.

"Oh, it's him. Check it out. Back from the grave. He's the one you should be after. And the son there, who has caused nothing but trouble by following in his father's footsteps." Somehow strengthened by his outburst, Bobby turned back to his aunt. "And what the hell do I owe you?"

"You'd still be in Des Moines without me. You'd still be driving a milk truck."

"You made promises."

"I know, dear," she said, again in a soft whisper so that no one else could hear. There was a briefcase beside her chair. She tapped it. "And they are about to come to fruition."

"It was never about money," he whispered back.

"I know."

"Why can't it be me?"

"It can."

"Why him?"

"Why not both?"

"I'm tired of waiting."

"You won't be waiting anymore."

"All the promises."

"Yes, dear."

He dropped his head as he further dropped his voice. "It's hard to admit this."

"Go ahead, dear."

"I can barely say it."

"Try."

"I love you."

"I know you do."

"No, it's not just like . . ."

"I know, dear. I love you, too."

"No, I love you in the other way."

"You're my special boy. Remember I used to tell you that?"

"I watch your movie. I found a copy and watch it in my room. You, with your gloves, your special white gloves."

"Aren't you naughty, my special boy?"

"I watch it over and over."

"I was something when I was younger, wasn't I? I could turn men to slaves with just a look, a gesture. I was special in every way." She pulled his head closer and patted the front of his neck. "And you're my special boy. We are linked, Bobby dear. Forever. You and me. We're Spanglers."

"Yes."

"And with Spanglers the family always comes first."

"Yes."

He turned his face to hers, so that their eyes were staring directly each into the other's and their lips were a hairsbreadth apart.

"Do you love me?" she said in a voice below a whisper, in a voice more breath than anything else.

"More than you know," he replied in a voice just as soft.

"Then there is one more thing you need to do."

"I'm tired."

"I know, dear. But just one thing more, and then you can rest."

"I want to stay here, close to you."

"And you know what it is. To protect the Spangler line. You know what you need to do."

"I don't think I want to."

"And I don't want you to, but we have no choice."

"Must I?"

"Yes, dear."

"I love you."

"I know you do, Bobby. Do it for us. Do it for our love."

Bobby leaned forward and closed his eyes, saw a thin, nubile figure twisting in his mind's eye in Super 8 black-and-white, felt his lips brush hers and then press harder. The joy, the sweet joy, rose through him like a wave, flushing out everything before it, leaving just his raw emotions and her desire.

"I love you," he murmured into her mouth.

"Show it."

He kissed her again, felt her lips and something else, sweet and slippery. He sucked on it as if it were a life-line, sucked on it until it pulled away.

"Now," she whispered.

"Yes."

"For our love."

"Yes," he said, pulling back and nodding, knowing exactly what he must do, how it would end, why it was necessary. Seeing the whole of his life unspool in that perfect kiss.

Slowly he stood, nodding all the while. Slowly he caressed her withered cheek with the back of his hand. Slowly he turned and aimed the shotgun straight at the Byrne boy standing there with his mouth agape. Slowly he squeezed the trigger.

Chapter 57

Later Detective Ramirez would squat beside the bloodied body and feel the emotions rise to choke her throat. She'd seen scores of dead, it was the currency of her new post, but this one bit into her in a way that none had before. The sight of the blood, his blood, the sickly sweet smell of the iron and rot released by a body split open by the gunfire, the sick, dead eyes that were full of intense life just a moment before. She was dry-eyed, and her chest wasn't racked by sobs, but in the storm that raged beneath her brow, she was weeping nonetheless.

A hand fell onto her shoulder, solid and warm. She didn't need to look up to know to whom it belonged.

"You okay?" said Henderson.

"No."

"Good," he said. "When you ever get okay with any of this, then it's time to hang up your hat."

"Is that why you're retiring, old man?"

"Oh, I don't know," he said. "I been thinking about sticking around a little longer."

"I thought you wanted to get yourself a puppy."

"Maybe I already found myself one."

Ramirez shrugged his hand off her shoulder, took a final look at the corpse, her corpse, and then rubbed her face with her hands, hard, as if rubbing out her very features, before standing and turning away. Henderson was looking at her, not the dead body, but his eyes were staring at a casualty.

"They find him yet?" she said.

"Not yet," said Henderson.

"They won't."

"No," he said, "I don't expect they will."

The car outside the house was empty when they checked it right after the shooting, but someone had been there all right. There was a set of headphones, a receiver, and a tape deck, just as Spangler had said. But the tape was gone, and so was the person who had been listening in with the headphones. A host of uniforms were now going door-to-door, and four black-and-whites were cruising the neighborhood, trying to grab whoever had been in that car.

"You think it was him?" she said. "You think it was Liam Byrne?"

"Seems a bit far-fetched. But after what you learned about the guy who signed the death certificate, I'd certainly want to go up to Rahway and ask him what he knows. And we'll see if this Liam Byrne had any fingerprints on file to match what they already peeled off the car."

She turned and gave the corpse a quick glance. "You want to know something that makes me believe it, Henderson? Spangler had a bizarre integrity about him. I don't think he would have lied about it."

"He was certifiable. Who the hell knows what he was thinking?"

"And we'll never know now."

"He had taken at least two lives already, and he would have taken two more if things worked out tonight the way he wanted. Maybe even three. You did the right thing."

"Okay."

"And even with all that he was, you tried to save him. I heard you trying."

"Yeah, well, I've tried and failed before," she said, "but never like this."

She had been trying, pleading with Bobby Spangler to put down his gun. She had made no threatening moves, beyond, of course, keeping her gun aimed at his heart, and had promised whatever she could think of promising to avoid having happen what actually happened. But whatever she was saying was obviously counteracted by the witch, who was whispering incessantly in his ear and who gave him that nauseating kiss of death.

"What did you say to him?" she screamed at the old lady when it was over. "What did you say?"

"I told him to stop all this nonsense," said Mrs. Truscott with her hands suddenly becalmed and her lips tight. "I told him to put down the gun and surrender to the nice police officers. I told him that was the only way."

She was lying, Ramirez knew she was lying, but all she had to go on was what actually happened. Spangler slowly rising, Spangler gently caressing the old woman's cheek, Spangler slowly turning as the gun swiveled from the senator to Kyle Byrne, Spangler slowly squeezing the trigger.

Ramirez shot him three times in the chest. Henderson fired at the same time, hitting his shoulder and spinning him around, but it was Ramirez's shots that killed him. Spangler, already dead, fell back as his shotgun spurted upward along with the blood from his chest. When the shotgun fired, finally, the blast took out not Kyle Byrne or Senator Truscott but the imposing portrait above the fireplace.

It played out as quickly as that, so quickly that Kyle and the senator didn't have time to throw themselves onto the floor until all the danger had passed. And when it was over, Lucia Ramirez, God forgive her, had her first kill.

"Why did you try so hard to help him?" said Henderson. "Most cops, seeing a killer with a weapon pointed at a politician, would have shot first chance they had. And there were chances, moments when his attention wandered, when the gun was pointed nowhere specific. Why didn't you take him out when you could?"

"I don't know, Henderson. What are you, my therapist? What do I get, forty-five minutes to pour out my soul before you tell me my time's up?"

"I'm just asking."

"I felt sorry for him, all right? I saw his apartment, I saw his desperation. He was living a twisted little life, and I know the witch who was doing the twisting. I had my choice, I'd have shot her."

"You'll be thinking about this man next year, and ten years from now, and ten years after that when you're in my position, standing on the lip of things, looking over the edge. And when you do, knowing that you cared, even a little bit, and did your best to save him . . . well, knowing that is the only thing that's going to keep you from tearing out your heart, or drowning it in alcohol. Trust me, I know."

"What do you know?"

"I know what it feels like when you do it on the other side of caring, and let me tell you, it leaves you haunted."

"Old man."

"You got that right, but my hair turned gray a long time ago."

Ramirez looked at Henderson and for the first time saw the hurt in his eyes. Something had happened to him, something had damaged him badly. And all this time he'd been trying to protect her from the same fate. Someday she'd get the story, she was a detective, after all, someday she'd wring it out from him, but not this day. This day she was just glad he was by her side.

"Detectives," came a voice from the hallway, "can I get the hell out of here? I've been here way too long already, and this shirt is getting ripe."

It was Byrne. Ramirez offered a quick and uneasy smile to Henderson in thanks, and then she stepped away from the man she had killed and out of the room where she had killed him.

"Didn't we tell all of you just to stay put?" said Ramirez as she and Henderson approached Byrne. Byrne's jacket was off, his tie loose, but he looked calm, as if he'd already gotten over the violence that had burst about him just an hour ago.

"Yes, you did," said Kyle Byrne. "But the senator was whisked out with his lawyer before the news trucks showed up, and Mrs. Truscott did that little fainting thing that got her a quick trip to the hospital, which leaves just me."

"And you're lonely, is that it?"

Kyle smiled. "Actually, yes. So I wanted to know if I can get out of here, too."

"Do we have anything we can hold this boy on?" she said to Henderson.

"Extortion?" said Henderson.

"I don't know," said Ramirez, staring at Kyle with a critical eye, as if he were a painting, or a horse. "From what we heard over the radio frequency he gave us, he wasn't trying to trade the file for money."

"Arson?"

"Based on the burns on Spangler's skin, I'd put the arson on him."

"How about theft of a valuable file?"

"Taking his dead father's file from his own former home? That won't stick."

"Obstruction of justice?"

"Maybe," said Ramirez. "But we wouldn't have found Spangler without him."

"Abject stupidity?"

"Well, there you go," said Ramirez. "We're just going to have to hold him over on the grounds of abject stupidity. Because who else but an idiot would put himself in the middle of this craziness for no apparent purpose?"

"If stupidity was a crime," said Kyle, "I'd have been locked up long ago."

"Answer one question and we'll let you go," said Ramirez. "Who was in the car?"

"What car? The rental thing?"

"Yeah, the rental thing."

"Nobody."

"Did you hear that, Henderson?"

"I heard," said Henderson. "Now we got him for lying to a police officer."

"It's a shame," said Ramirez. "He was almost in the clear. Have you seen your father lately, Byrne?"

"My father?" said Kyle. "Are you kidding me? You didn't believe that maniac, did you?"

"He seemed to know what he was talking about."

"He also drew his eyebrows in with a Sharpie."

"Someone was taping the whole scene," said Henderson. "That someone took the tape. To clean things up, we'll need it back."

"Let me get out of here and I'll see what I can do about getting you that tape."

Ramirez looked at Henderson, Henderson blew out a cheek and then shrugged.

"Okay," said Ramirez. "If the techs are done with your car, you can get the hell out of here. But tomorrow you're going to have to go on up and talk to an inspector named Demerit with the Haverford Police Department about the fire at your house."

"Deal," said Kyle. He stepped toward Ramirez and lowered his voice. "Now that this is over, can you see me?"

"I can see you fine."

He glanced at Henderson and then gently took hold of her arm and pulled her into a corner. Henderson turned his back and pretended to read something.

"You know what I mean," said Byrne. "Look, let's say tomorrow night at eight, at the same bar where you found me this afternoon. We'll have a few beers, have some laughs, talk about something that has nothing to do with any of this."

"I might be busy."

He leaned forward, scratched his lower lip. Instinctively she licked her own lip with her tongue. He leaned farther forward, and she was surprised that this soon after the death and the blood something inside her was able to open up so quickly and urgently. She was surprised even more at the disappointment she felt when he pulled away without kissing her.

"Tomorrow," he said with a smile before he turned and headed out of the house.

"And tomorrow and tomorrow," said Henderson.

"What the hell is that?"

"Shakespeare," said Henderson.

"Don't give me that Shakespeare crap, like you're some student of fine literature. We got reports to write, a case to close, an IAD shooting investigation to deal with. We've got ourselves a mess to clean up."

"Yes, we do," said Henderson.

"So let's keep our eyes on the ball," she said.

"Absolutely. But he's a pretty interesting kid, isn't he?"

"Don't even," said Ramirez.

"Pretty damn interesting," said Henderson, laughing.

And Ramirez couldn't help but laugh with him.

Chapter 58

In the middle of the night, lying awake in the sagging bed in that fetid motel room, still waiting for his father to reappear, Kyle Byrne gradually grew more and more certain that his father had never returned, that his father's body had fully and truly been rendered unto ash fourteen years ago, that the whole renewed relationship was a piece of wishful thinking hatched in the fevered recesses of Kyle's own deranged brain.

The evidence of Liam Byrne's phoenix-like rise was less than scant. When Kyle quickly searched the rental car outside the Truscott mansion, his father's luggage was gone, along with the cassette tape that he was recording off Kyle's wire. When Kyle drove rings around the Truscott neighborhood shortly thereafter, he saw nothing on the dark streets but police cars. When he returned to the New Jersey motel room, there was no hard evidence that his father had ever been there, no toothbrush or strange pair of socks or discarded bottle of aftershave, only a few empty bottles of scotch and the light, lingering scent of cigarettes and Aqua Velva. But maybe he had drunk the scotch himself, and maybe the scents emanated from the guy in the room next door.

Oh, things had happened in the last few nights, he knew that. His house had burned down, his car had burned with it, he had recovered one of his father's old files, and that file had led him to the bloody events at the Truscott house. And that it had all turned out pretty well for him in the end maybe meant that the spirit of his father had been looking out for him, just as it might have been the spirit of his father that had frightened Tiny Tony Sorrentino off his case. In a way it was a comforting thought, because it was considerably less crazy than what had passed for reality the last few days.

Kyle sat up in bed and took a deep breath. He wanted proof, he needed proof, and he knew where he might get it. The door to the motel's office was locked, the lights off, but that didn't stop Kyle from banging on the door like an escaped lunatic.

A pimply-faced kid, whose hair was sticking out wildly, as if he'd just been dosed with static electricity, straggled out of the back room and flicked on the light. He scratched the top of his head, scrunched up his face, opened the door.

"Yeah?" he said, eyes bleary and drool slipping down his slack mouth.

"Did an old man come by and leave a message for room 207?" said Kyle.

The kid looked at Kyle with an uncomprehending stare, as if he weren't sure which of the two of them was the idiot here. "No," he said, having finally decided it was Kyle before starting to close the door.

Kyle stuck his foot in the gap and pushed the door open, shoving the kid back into the office at the same time.

"Do me a favor," said Kyle, "and let me see the registration card for room 207."

"I'm not really allowed," said the clerk with a yawn.

"Dude, it's my room. I've got the key, and I'm staying the night. Let me see the damn card."

"There are rules."

"But if I happened to slip you a twenty?"

The clerk's eyes brightened. "Well, you know, there are always exceptions."

"Good, so here's the way it's going to work. I'm not going to slip you a twenty. But if you show me the card,

I also won't grab your nose in my fist and kick you in the head either."

"Just a second, sir," the clerk said as he made his way behind the desk with surprising alacrity.

The room was registered to a Byrne, all right, but to a Kyle Byrne, with the signature suspiciously like Kyle's own, and paid for in cash. The son of a bitch hadn't used his real name. If indeed the son of a bitch had signed the card, as opposed to Kyle himself in a fit of psychotic self-identity theft.

Back in the room, Kyle grabbed the little chair from the desk, put it on the cement walkway outside the door, and sat down facing the parking lot and the Target beyond that and the McDonald's beyond that. He leaned back, propped his feet on the railing, tried to make sense of things.

Maybe he had made the whole thing up. Maybe his dead-father mania had grown like a spider to spread its hairy legs into his brain and drive him, finally, insane. Other than that lawyer at Ponzio's, whom Kyle would never be able to find, or Robert Spangler, who now was dead, no one besides Kyle had seen him clearly. And without any physical evidence, to even broach the story to someone, anyone, even that Detective Ramirez, would be a no-win proposition. If he was telling the truth, she would mistakenly think him crazy; if he was relaying the cracked fantasies of a schizophrenic personality, she would correctly think him crazy. No, he'd keep it to himself, tell no one, except maybe Kat, only because he told everything to Kat.

But he wondered if the truth or falsity of his father's reappearance even mattered. As he sat there, in the cool of the early dawn, watching the horizon lighten above the hard landscape of the asphalt parking lot and the cornucopia of crap beyond, waiting for his father to return and prove him sane, the years suddenly contracted like a clap of hands. And here he was, sitting on the porch of his mother's house, waiting for his father. Or on the mound, waiting for his father. Or in a bar or at a softball game or in the heat of the night, waiting for his father. A lifetime spent waiting for his father.

Sitting there now, facing the coming of a new day, Kyle realized, whether the old man was a figment of Kyle's own feverish imagination or a brutal and disappointing reality, that Liam Byrne wasn't coming back. Not tonight, not tomorrow, not ever. And Kyle was okay with that. Surprisingly. Astonishingly. Okay.

Whatever had happened in these past few days had burned the need right out of him. It was as if the filial relationship he had craved for so long had happened in a matter of hours, moving swiftly from childish love to adolescent rebellion to a sort of blind adult mimicry to a declaration of independence. And he no longer felt deprived, he no longer felt gypped out of some grand paternal presence, he no longer harbored any illusions about how terrific his life might have turned out if his father had only been a father and not some detached presence that died way too soon for Kyle to cope. No, as the bright top of the sun rose above the cement boxes of New Jersey, he felt lucky. Lucky to have had his mother to himself for as long as he had. Lucky to be young and strong, with opportunities to seize and a future to mold. Lucky to be free.

He was certain that would be the end of the father sightings that had plagued him since the funeral fourteen years before, but he was wrong.

Chapter 59

She wasn't Detective Ramirez on this night, she was Lucia, her badge and gun worn not on the hip but stashed inside her bag, her hair up, her lips freshly glossed. She was wearing a silk blouse, a pleated skirt, spiky red high heels, and she didn't need any leering Neanderthal to tell her she looked damn good, she knew it already.

Even as she had passed through the administrative and media whirlwind that accompanied the closing of the Laszlo Toth murder case, she couldn't stop herself from thinking of this night with a visceral anticipation. She had imagined something romantic and intimate, something candlelit and soft, something leading to something, leading most definitely to something. And so she was keenly disappointed to find herself vastly overdressed while sitting at a Formica table at Bubba's with Kyle and his motley crew, drinking from pitchers of Rolling Rock and just hanging.

"So is it heavy?" said Kyle's squat friend with all the tattoos, who was named Skitch.

"I'm used to it," said Ramirez.

"Can I see it?"

"No."

"Dude, lighten up," said Kyle.

"I'm just asking to see it. It's not like I want to take out a window or anything."

It was a laid-back gabfest, going nowhere quite slowly, and she was frankly bored. Add to that the way Kyle was back to dressing in his black Chuck Taylors, cargo shorts, and a ringer T-shirt, looking very young and very aimless and very much without the dangerous edge she had found so attractive during the Toth affair, and the whole thing left her wondering what she'd been so hopped up about in the first place. She began checking her watch, wondering when would be a polite time simply to leave.

"Don't mind Skitch," said the bar's owner, that skinny Bubba Jr. "It's not often we have a celebrity with us," he said, hoisting a beer in Ramirez's honor.

Ramirez forced a smile and raised her beer in return. She and Henderson had become briefly famous on the local and national news shows for neutralizing the now-infamous Toth murderer as he'd tried to add a U.S. senator to his list of victims.

"You seemed to like being in front of the camera," said Kyle.

"Just part of the job," she said. But she had liked it, and was good at it, and realized during her fourth television interview that the center of attention was exactly where she wanted to be. But hanging at a bar with these losers wasn't helping her get there, that was for sure.

"You know where they make this now?" said the old toothless man, staring sadly at his beer. "New Jersey. It makes me want to puke."

"I feel the same way," said another older man, with a bulbous nose, whom Kyle had introduced as his Uncle Max. "But it's from them pills I take for my back. So what's going to happen to that senator?"

"My guess is not a damn thing," said Ramirez.

Senator Truscott had held a press conference to announce his horror at what his cousin had done. Truscott had promised full cooperation with the ongoing police investigation even as he vowed to continue to vigorously represent the interests of Pennsylvanians in the United States Senate.

"But it's the end of his presidential ambitions at least," said Bubba Jr.

"Don't bet on that," said Ramirez. "He's getting coverage in the national press, he's gaining a celebrity beyond politics. That stuff can be intoxicating."

"And it's not really his decision to run or not, is it?" said Kyle. "His mother has been calling all the shots for him since he was a baby. That's a hard habit to kick."

"It's going to be tough for her to keep doing it from where she is now," said Ramirez. "They put her in an asylum in North Carolina. We've been trying to speak to her, but they claim she's suffering from shock and dementia."

"The only dementia she's suffering from is her own overblown sense of entitlement," said Kyle. "She married a Truscott, her offspring is entitled to the presidency, and there's nothing she won't do to make it happen."

"What a fun gal," said Kat.

"Maybe sometime I'll show the movie we found in Spangler's apartment," said Ramirez. "Puts the old lady in a whole new light."

Kyle raised his beer. "Dudes, I have, like, a toast."

Cutlery clanked against beer mugs.

"It's been an insane couple of weeks, starting with my wig-out at the ball game—"

"We had that game won, bro," said Skitch.

"Yeah, maybe, though it wasn't exactly Willie Mays in the on-deck circle. But from the ball game through the violence of last night, I have to say, the whole experience for me wasn't altogether horrible. You might have heard I lost my dad when I was twelve—"

"No, we hadn't," said Bubba Jr. "You ever hear that, Kat?"

"Not in, like"—she checked her watch—"the last ten minutes or so."

"And my mom died last year," continued Kyle, ignoring the sarcasm, "and I've been feeling sorry for myself, abandoned and alone, the poor little orphan boy."

"You're making me cry," said Tommy. "Stop it. No, really, stop it."

"But in the middle of the insanity," said Kyle, "each of you guys came through for me when I needed it. Junior letting me use his bar for the meeting even after giving me the heave-ho, which I fully deserved. Kat getting me out of jail, staying in touch with the police, and keeping me grounded. My Uncle Max, who's like family to me—"

"I am family to you, you putz."

"For giving me his sage advice and his unflinching honesty."

"Does that mean we're good again?"

"No," said Kyle.

"You let me know."

"I also need to thank Lucia, who saved my life not once but twice from a homicidal maniac. And finally Skitch, who stood with me during the entire time and helped out in ways we won't talk about with a cop present."

"He's just talking hypothetically," said Skitch to Ramirez. "What I would have done if it wasn't, you know, against the law."

"You all helped, each of you, except for Tommy, actually, who didn't do a thing except call a United States senator a pussy to his face."

"I was right about him, wasn't I?" said Tommy.

"Yes you were," said Kyle. "So I just wanted to thank you. We all want to know we're not alone in the world, and right now I feel less alone than I've ever felt in my entire life. Which is good, since after Kat kicks me out, I'm going to need a place to stay. So here's to all of you, even to Old Tommy Trapp. Thanks for taking up the slack in my life."

They were clinking glasses, and Ramirez was ready to take her cue to up and leave, when she saw it, above the neon hanging in the window, a quick bob of gray hair passing to the left. And even as she saw it, she noticed that Kyle saw it, too, and reacted to it like a slap in the face. He stared for a moment, dropping his jaw like a ventriloquist's dummy, and then he was on his feet and heading out of the bar without so much as a word to anyone else at the table.

"What the hell?" said Ramirez, as she stood to go after him.

"Leave him be," said the pretty lawyer, smiling kindly at her as she put her hand on Ramirez's arm. "Welcome to Kyle World."

Ramirez sat down again, and Skitch leaned over to her. "Just a peek?"

"Forget about it."

"There any other hotties like you on the force?"

"You mean," she said, "hotties who'd be interested in someone like you?"

"Yeah."

"No."

Kyle knew it wasn't his father. It didn't even look right, and after his morning watching the new day dawn he would have been ready to bet that the sight wouldn't affect him like it had in the past. But then the emotion rose in him, pure and full of its lovely pain, and he was up, and out of his chair, and out of the bar. He couldn't help himself. He would never be able to help himself. Despite everything he had learned, he'd never be totally free of him, because it was his father, and as someone told him long ago, that's just the way of it with sons and their fathers.

He looked left, nothing. He looked right, nothing. He ran to the other side of the street, climbed onto the roof of a car, scanned as far as he was able, and from there he saw it, the head of gray hair bobbing atop a bent figure that had just turned the corner.

He jumped down, chased the man around the corner, saw him, gained on him, grabbed his shoulder as he called out, "Dad?"

The man spun around, old, decrepit, his pocked face marked with fear. The man raised his gnarled hands to ward off Kyle's attack.

"I'm sorry," said Kyle, backing away. "I didn't mean. . . . I'm sorry."

He felt deflated as he walked back to the bar, when he saw it, resting against the wall of Bubba's, right by the door. An envelope. He stared at it for a moment before picking it up. No address, no postage, just his name scrawled across its surface. Kyle Byrne. With shaking hands he opened it, reached inside, pulled out a piece of paper wrapped around something flat and rectangular, bound with a rubber band.

A few moments later, he opened the door, leaned into the bar, and motioned for Ramirez to come out. She glanced around, puzzled, as if he were surely looking for someone else, but then grabbed her pocketbook.

"What happened?" said Ramirez, outside now. "Your jaw dropped as if you saw a ghost."

Kyle laughed. "I have something I need to give you."

"Flowers?"

"Better," he said as he handed her the tape that he had found in the envelope.

Ramirez stared at it for a moment before glancing up at Kyle, who beamed at her, like a hunting dog who had just retrieved a dead quail. She gave him a questioning look, he nodded. She took a tissue from her bag, wrapped the cassette carefully.

"Where'd you get it?" she said.

"I found it right there on the street."

"Just sitting there, outside, just like that."

"Strangest thing," said Kyle.

But he didn't tell her who the tape was from, he didn't tell her that there was no reason to dust the cassette for fingerprints because he had wiped them off on his T-shirt, he didn't tell her anything. He just stood there for a moment, smiling and letting the emotions that blossomed from the envelope, all good and all surprising, rise through him.

"My father once told me," he said finally, "that life was about seizing glory. I didn't know what he meant then, but I think I know now."

"And what's that?" said Ramirez.

Without any preamble or his usual grab bag of feints or tricks, he leaned forward and kissed her.

He leaned forward and kissed her, and she kissed back, closing her eyes and letting her body fall into his, and they each felt something happen that was both startling and new.

Ramirez felt the cold hardness at the core of her ambition, a hardness that lived like a tumor in her gut, soften and slowly begin to melt. And Kyle felt something stiffen—not just that which was always stiffening from a kiss or a look or a stray thought, but something else, some resolve that had for most of his life been airy as a fog. And her hurry, her worry, her innate brutal competitiveness, it all seemed to float from her. While he wanted to shout, to dance, to do something, anything, to grab hold of life in a way that was far beyond his usual meander to nowhere. She suddenly didn't have anyplace more important to be, and he suddenly was in a rush to get there. She had no priority other than to feel his lips on hers, his large body pressed against hers, and he wanted to take her to the moon.

"I feel like I'm on a tropical island," said Ramirez after they slowly pulled apart to catch their breaths.

"You make me want to put on a suit," said Kyle.

"I liked you in a suit."

"Except for the tie. Nobody likes the tie."

"It is a little grim. What would you do in a suit?"

"I don't know. Something bold."

"I like the sound of that. You want to go back in with your friends?"

"No. Let's go someplace."

"Where?"

"Anyplace. Let's just get in a car and drive."

"Okay." She laughed. "I guess that means my car."

"I guess it does."

"Can we kiss again first?"

They kissed again, and then she took his hand and led him down the street to where her car was parked. She led, and he let her lead him, and all the time he felt as if his heart were imprinted with the words of the note he found wrapped around the tape.

"I couldn't be prouder, boyo. I could be richer, sure, and wouldn't that be a pretty thing, but I couldn't be prouder. Partners on the tape? I'll be waiting."

He would never fully understand their power, the first five words of the note, never understand why they mattered so, coming from a man who hadn't said an honest word to him in decades, but they did, beyond measure, and as he held tight to her hand while she pulled him down the street, he felt his feet skip across the cement as if he were flying.